DEIR
AL
LAUZ

DEIR AL LAUZ

Breaks Its Shackles and Embraces the Dream

LAMA SAKHNINI

iUniverse

DEIR AL LAUZ
BREAKS ITS SHACKLES AND EMBRACES THE DREAM

iUniverse books may be ordered through booksellers or by contacting:

iUniverse
1663 Liberty Drive
Bloomington, IN 47403
www.iuniverse.com
1-800-Authors (1-800-288-4677)

ISBN: 978-1-5320-2724-6 (sc)
ISBN: 978-1-5320-2725-3 (e)

Library of Congress Control Number: 2017912869

Print information available on the last page.

iUniverse rev. date: 10/24/2017

To you, who taught me the magic of speech.

And to you, who released flocks of pigeons in my heart.

And a call.

Do not search for the village of Deir Al Lauz in an atlas. Instead, search for it in your memories and the memories of those who passed through it, as well as the memories of those who may reach it. There you will certainly find it.

I call on you to release it from its shackles of waiting and anticipation.

—Lama

Breathe in Sunlight and Exhale the Darkness of the Previous Night

He lay on his bed with frozen limbs, keeping a thin layer of air between himself and the mattress. He tried to relax. He loosened his limbs and sunk into the soft cotton. But his heart could not be relieved. It was beating loudly.

The night before, she'd been shivering, trembling, and pleading, "Hold me in your arms. Don't kiss me. I just want to hear your heart beating and feel your breath on my face."

He hesitated. He heard his heart pounding in his ears. He pulled her to himself. He hugged her head to his chest. There she stayed like a bird with broken wings.

"Basheer, I love you," she whispered. "I saw you in my sleep. I saw you as if in a nightmare."

He did not believe in dreams, but that time, he'd been scared by the terror in her eyes.

After his flashback of the previous night, he tried to relax, but he was cold. He got under the warm sheets and closed his tired eyes. Instead of sleeping, he saw her shadow haunting him. The night laughed at him. It was his tenth sleepless night.

He recited an evening prayer again. "We reached this evening, and the kingdom belongs to God. Thank God there is no God but Allah, alone with no partner. To Him be praise—and He over all things. I ask You for the good of this night and the good of what follows it, and I seek refuge in You from the evil of this night and the evil of what follows. Oh, Lord, I seek refuge in You from laziness, aging, and senility. I seek refuge in You from the punishment in the fire and the torment in the grave."

Before he ended his prayer, her shadow died away, leaving him worried and wanting what he once thought was gone. He opened his eyes to the loneliness of the dark night with only the sound of his steel bed moaning under his weight. He kept still to not wake his mother, who was in the next room. He held his breath and tried to continue his prayer, but he lost the words and dozed a little.

When he awoke, her shadow was floating in his head again, and the taste of the discontinued prayer was still on his lips. He shut his eyes and went into a slumber. Then the voice of his dad awakened him. *It won't be as you want!*

He looked around, but no one was there. He wondered whether that was a prediction of what was to come. He was saved by the call to the Morning Prayer and the chant of two nightingales on the windowsill. He jumped out of bed and prayed and prayed and prayed. It was the longest prayer he had prayed in years, the only cure for a hopeless, wounded heart.

Dim light snuck in from the bare window, casting shadows behind the furniture. He opened the window and let the cold, humid autumn breeze in. The two nightingales were standing on a bare branch of the almond tree in the garden. The female looked at him and then at her mate. They exchanged chants and flew off toward the rising sun.

He inhaled the fresh morning air and exhaled the darkness of the last night. His head cleared, but his heart was still wounded. His chest was tight, burning. If only he had believed his intuition, his brother would still have been alive. He had to live with remorse for the rest of his short life, the remorse of having been able to prevent Omar's murder.

I Came to Harvest Olives

Basheer stumbled down the stairs that morning and saw his mother, his father, and Omar sitting around the pallet. Glasses of hot tea were lined up on a plastic tray. Out of happiness, he stammered and choked on his tears and words. Some happiness crept into his heart and healed some of its wounds.

"Omar! When did you come? How? Your wife, Saniya. She knows?" he whispered.

Omar smiled. "I didn't want to wake her and scare her. She will wake up soon and find out on her own."

He smothered his brother with hugs and kissed his cheeks. Omar laughed till his eyes teared up. He released himself from his brother's embrace.

"I came to harvest olives with you, Basheer."

Basheer looked at him with sadness in his eyes and saw a halo around his brother's head that left a trail of sparks behind him as he moved. Again, he ignored his instincts. They had not seen him for three months after his escape to the East Bank following his military operation. He had been sentenced to life for killing three Israeli officers. He had escaped to an aunt's house in Wehdat Camp, where he had stayed for three long months eaten with hatred and a yearning for his fatherland.

Then one harsh night filled with the pain of departure, a night of no reason, he decided to return to Deir Al Lauz. His uncle tried to talk him out of it, but he had set his mind to it. He looked for someone to smuggle him across the Jordan River and to his surprise found someone to take him on this dangerous journey for little money—half in advance and half upon arrival.

He reached home a bit before the Morning Prayer and saw his mother weighing flour on her scales, preparing to make bread. A teakettle was simmering quietly on the fire, releasing a waft of mint into the air. He snuck to her quietly and whispered, "Good morning, Mom."

She trembled and mumbled the name of God. She turned around with eyes full of tears and hugged him. She made his face wet with her joyful tears. She wiped them off with her white shawl and hugged him once more. She smelled his neck and felt his ribs and whispered, "You got so thin!" He chuckled at her words. She put her hand on his mouth. "Shhh! I don't want anybody to hear you." She grabbed his shoulders, pushed him back, and gazed into his face. "Oh thanks, God … Thanks, God," she muttered with tears and a gentle smile.

She gazed into his eyes and laughed at her reflection. She felt a rush. Her chest closed as if she were about to fall off a cliff. She saw her image in his eyes fading away to be replaced with the gray ashes of an extinguished fire. She said the name of God. He hugged her, and she rested her head on his shoulder.

Soon after that, his father entered the kitchen and froze with surprise when he saw his son. The Morning Prayer calling and the chanting of birds lent a perfect beginning to the day.

Omar let go of his mother and hugged his father, who was still in shock and surprise. No words came from his lips. His brain shut down. He hugged his son stiffly.

Omar's mother felt a fraction of a second of happiness. For that instant, she forgot all they had gone through while he was away. She forgot all the times the house had been broken into by the Israeli army. Saniya used to be forced to take out all of Omar's belongings to the garden, where she had to wait for hours beside them on the ground. Once, a soldier pointed his rifle at her head with a blank look on his face. He released her when his arms became weary. Saniya had to drag all her belongings back to her room. This same scenario was repeated so frequently. She wanted to find Omar or at least learn his whereabouts.

Omar's wife, Saniya—his cousin on his mother's side—had been raised in their home; that was the dying wish of her mother. Saniya was a pretty girl with sharp Bedouin features. She had Omar's mother's eyes, and her hair was black as the night. But she did not have the kindness or brains of her aunt; she hid her ignorance behind an empty smile. Omar's mother, on the other hand, had smiles that hid a wealth of stories and secrets.

She tried to teach Saniya needlepoint and sewing but to no use. Saniya used to sit for hours listening to the radio or leafing through magazines she got from Abu Rebhi's grocery. When his mother told Omar of her plan for him to marry Saniya, he did not accept or object to it.

Omar and Basheer were twins; they shared the same features but little else. Omar was educated and worked as a physics and mathematics teacher; Basheer had not succeeded in high school and preferred to work with his father in the mill grinding wheat throughout the year and pressing olives in October. As Omar was the firstborn, his father was called Abu Omar according to Arab tradition. It was also his nickname, which had been given to him long before Omar had been born, in honor of his own father.

Omar Utters a Letter, a Number, and a Rifle— Basheer Gathers Rain

Omar and Basheer loved their land but each in his own way. Omar swore revenge on whoever defiled the land, while Basheer tilled the soil with his plough, sowed seeds, and brought it to life.

Year after year, he gathered the tears shed by the clouds and collected them in vials of nostalgia. He watered his seeds and waited patiently. He supplicated to God and waited. He prayed and waited. He sang and waited. When the first sprigs appeared, he thanked God with fervor, cared for his plants, and waited for them to grow.

He waited for spring to pass and turn into summer with its golden wheat combs. In autumn, he pressed the green olives of the holy land of Jerusalem for the beautiful, golden lava of pure olive oil that brought tears of joy and contentment to his eyes.

Poetry and prayer were the languages of Basheer, but Omar had his own language of a letter, a number, and a rifle. When Omar spoke, his students listened intently. What he wrote on the board, his students wrote in their books. He taught them arithmetic and algebra. He performed his rituals of mathematics and algebra on the altar of Einstein.

Omar waited patiently for his enemies to pass and shoot them in their chests. He was a mixture of Che Guevara and Saint Augustine, an eternal searcher for the meaning of time. He tied the past, present, and future with letters of doubt, for there are three facts in the mind: the present from the past is the memory, the present from the present is listening and attention, and the present from the future is anticipation. The mind predicts, listens, and remembers; that is how time is measured.

The impressions we make on ourselves during daily events stay with us even after those events pass. Therefore, either time is that impression or what is measured is not time.

Omar learned from Einstein that time was relative. He said, "The people of my nation are like the twin paradox. One of the twins stayed in Palestine and lived a boring life of routine, and the other moved into isolation with the speed of light and longed for change. He started a revolution wherever he set foot and forgot his own brother, who suffered from the occupation that led to hunger, despair, and feeling of strangeness in his own land. He gave up his children to serve the enemy."

Basheer is a Sufi, a Sufi drunk with his faith. That made him seem crazy to some people. As he was the son of time who had no tomorrow on his agenda, he lived his day ready for eternity.

A Sufi does not remember what was because his life is a permanent advance or retreat. Always asking and desiring afterlife, dreaming of it and of an existence that liberates him from the illusion of time. A place of no waiting or anticipation, a place with only one truth, a place that promises eternal happiness for whoever seeks His company as there is no tampering with His existence.

Despite their differences. Omar and Basheer completed each other. Omar was clean-shaven; his hair was trimmed. Basheer's beard was uncared for, and his hair was frizzy. Omar had eyes glowing with the fire of revolution while Basheer's eyes were as calm as the eyes of a monk. Omar adored a holy land, and Basheer lived in the heavens.

Bidwen Baheya
Plants a Rose

Time for me is measured by the number or tears and laughs, the number of people who passed through my life, the number of words said and those that will be said. My life started at the age of fourteen the day Abu Omar married me. That day, we came in a parade of cars from Beersheba. When we arrived at the entrance of Deir Al Lauz, my dad was determined that I be celebrated on a camel's back with a saddle that my mother had decorated with beads and wool tassels dyed red.

I was dressed in a black silk dress embroidered with red. A veil adorned with golden coins covered my face. Though my clothes were heavy, I felt light in body and soul. I was floating on a cloud of the fragrances of wheat from the fields, musk from my skin, and henna enveloping my hair. I was surrounded by the color red. I felt my blood glowing. I was a princess who had come out of the stories of 1,001 nights.

I entered Deir Al Lauz in the afternoon. The freshly harvested golden wheat was shining under the June sun. My belongings reached Deir Al Lauz before me in chests on the backs of three camels. All people young and old came to watch and celebrate me. My wedding was like a fairy tale—three nights of dancing and singing. Many sheep and calves were slaughtered. I was filled with joy and happiness. I was safe in the loving presence of my mother and father, and I waited eagerly to meet my husband.

I had seen my husband only once for a few minutes when he came to ask for my hand from the *jaha*, a group of elders and the educated who solved problems or listened to requests for the hands of girls in the Arab tradition. My heart fell for him. He was a young man with flames of desire and compassion alike in his eyes. I had heard a lot about him before I had met him. My father and his father had been partners in their carpet trade before 1948.

On our wedding night, when he saw me trembling with fear and excitement in my dress and veil, he kissed my head over the thick shawl and said, "You are my guest for the next three nights. I'll sleep in the hall."

In the morning, he entered my room and found me sitting on the edge of the bed wearing my white lace nightgown with hair down and face uncovered.

"Glory to God! Who created such beauty!" he said. "I don't want you to ever wear your veil in front of anyone. It's a shame for anyone to be denied the vision of your beautiful face!"

He came close to me, released my braids, and broke his word about staying in the hall. And oh how glad I was that he did! Since that morning, he has called me only "My Baheya."

Our home was in the middle of an olive grove at the western foot of Deir Al Lauz. The house had two bedrooms, a hall, a kitchen, and a bathroom.

Abu Omar built a stonewall around the garden and planted two almond trees and one apricot tree. I loved the view of green trees around us especially after my life in the desert and its yellow sand. Our house in Beersheba was made of baked bricks; my new house was built of white stones. The whiteness of the houses around brought peace to my heart.

Then on a rainy day of February, Abu Omar came home wet. He held my hand and said, "Come with me. I have a surprise for you." I followed him out to find two dry stems planted in rusty tins. My tongue was tied up. I stared at him in total ignorance.

He smiled at me patiently. "These are two rose saplings. Let's plant them together. I dig and you plant."

I released the saplings from their containers, and we planted two dry stems, or so they appeared to me, in the rain.

When March came, they sprouted and became green. And in April, little rosebuds appeared.

One day, Abu Omar woke me up and put a red rose in my hand. That was the first time I had smelled a rose. I touched its fragile leaves. I was enchanted with its pure redness. He put my hands in his and from over these delicate petals, he kissed the tips of my fingers and whispered, "I love you." Even the rose smiled with delight. He recited a prayer in his heart, and the rose came to life and played a heavenly tune on a violin. He returned my hands to my lap and gazed quietly in my eyes. At that moment, my heart sang and surrendered to its master.

Oh, God, please protect the man who makes the land turn green with just his touch, a man with great love and compassion, a man whose eyes are my shelter, who supports me after every fall and forgives me with no question. My desire is to spend my life in his shadow.

I Mature at Full Moon and Flow at Moonset

After the first year of our marriage, my mother-in-law—or as I call her, my aunt—covertly asked me if I had gotten pregnant. Months had passed, but I had not conceived. Um Fathi, the midwife, used to come and examine me before every menstrual cycle in hopes to find what I did not feel.

At first, she used to say to my aunt, "Let her be. She is still young. She will soon grow up and conceive." Two years later, she started saying, "The girl is weak. Feed her and care for her. God is generous."

Another year passed, and still I was not pregnant. Her tone changed. She started meeting Abu Omar on her way out and hinting to him that there was no use for me, but Abu Omar tried to avoid her. When he could not, he would say, "God is mighty, Um Fathi. God is great and is capable of everything."

After that, Um Fathi became more courageous. She told him that if he wanted a son to carry his name, he had to marry another. She told him she was ready to find him a suitable and fertile bride. She said that God should forgive whoever had cursed him with me. She said his mother should have chosen a girl from the area, not a foreigner like me.

All that happened in front of me; she meant for me to hear it so I would convince my husband to marry another, but Abu Omar ignored her.

"Allah is mighty, Um Fathi," he told her. "Allah is mighty. He is capable of anything."

She answered, "All this wealth and no heir."

For six years, I suffered the burning looks of the women around me. Six years of monthly painful blood drops. The women thought I had a dry womb. I told them I matured at full moon and flowed at moonset. But they did not believe that. They thought I was barren. The cruelty of those women was bitter; their jealousy was painful. As soon as one of them opened her mouth, she would say, "May God give you, sister, may God give you," or, "You haven't tried it yet."

One winked at her friends and said, "God damn kids. Why do we have them?"

All that was said so I would not envy the blessing of children God had given her. They did not want me near their kids for fear I might harm them, not because I hated them but because of my inexperience with children.

That whole time, Abu Omar—God keep him for me—waited with me. In the cold winter evenings, we sat together in the hall in front of our wood stove roasting chestnuts and toasting oiled bread. He never asked me to join the big family gatherings. It was as if he wanted to spare me the humiliation. Each time he saw me down, he told me, "Smile, my beloved! Your beautiful black eyes light up my night." I would smile at that and laugh sometimes; I knew his happiness was linked forever to mine.

On special occasions such as holidays, my parents and siblings would visit me. They would fill my little house with happiness and joy. At times like that, I would almost forget my problems, but unfortunately, my neighbors never did. They spoke hurtful words to my mother intentionally and unintentionally.

My aunt, who heard all their hurtful words, never interfered as if what they said did not concern her. Maybe they said what she had not had the guts to say. But my mother told me to be patient. She said that my husband—God protect him—was a treasure and that my aunt did not mean what she said as she did that for her love and fear for me. I was patient, but alas, patience was a stranger.

The Thorny Road
of Anticipation

In the middle of October 1948, thirty-one years after its fall to General Allenby, Beersheba fell once more into the hands of the Israelis, who took it over from the Egyptian army with no shots fired.

Many rebel fighters from Negev were imprisoned in the Rafah and Braige prisons. That time, the Zionist criminals desecrated the city's houses and killed all who were breathing. Baheya did not know the facts and details about that massacre till she met her family after the setback of 1967.

It had been a thorny road of waiting and anticipation. Contradicting news came from the people who had fled the massacre, but no one knew for sure of the number or the identities of the casualties.

Some witnesses said that bodies were piled up over one another on the streets of Beersheba and that the few who remained had been transported by truck to Gaza or the Egyptian border. The few who refused death or deportation found themselves in concentration camps where they were left and forbidden to leave for around sixteen years for so-called security reasons.

This cleansing of all that was Palestine happened quickly, before it was decided how the law of the transfer of ownership declared in 1950 was to be implemented. The Development Organization was about to pass on April 1, 1952. The devilish idea was to empty the Negev area of most of the Arab tribes there and confiscate their lands with the excuse that it was absentee property.

Sometimes, convoys of fugitives—so-called refugees—passed Deir Al Lauz. Zahra used to ask of her family's fate, but she heard no news about that. Where were they? Were they still in their homes? Were they dead? Alive? No one knew.

The rebels were barricaded in the mountains and were under siege from all sides. They had sworn allegiance to their leader, Abdul Qader Al-Husseini. They believed in him as if he were a prophet. He led them through many battles and won the battle of Soraif. They had seized many weapons and much ammunition.

That night, Abu Omar returned to his Baheya and told her all the horrific details of the war. He was especially happy about possessing bullets for his rifle and a few Bern cannon. He said they could fight with the same capabilities as their enemies. But the ammunition did not last long. Without bullets, rifles died. Al-Husseini pleaded with anyone with ears. But how can dead people hear? He wrote pleading letters to whoever had a conscience: "I am going to Castell. I will conquer and occupy it even if it leads to my death. By the name of God, I am fed up with this life. Death has become more desirable to me than this inaction of the Arab League and the way they treat our cause. I desire death before my eyes see Israel occupying Palestine."

He entered the war with only half a bag of bullets. He was granted his wish; he was martyred on April 8, 1948, as he defended the homes of Castell. On the occasion of his funeral, the Zionists rewarded him with the massacre at Deir Yassin in retaliation for his men's courage at Castell.

On May 4, 1948, the establishment of the state of Israel was declared after all the massacres and displacement of all the people there. Palestine was cut into three districts: the West Bank controlled by Jordan, the occupied land of 1948 controlled by Israel, and Gaza strip controlled by Egypt.

The people of Deir Al Lauz were granted Jordanian nationality, those who remained in Beersheba received Israeli nationality, and those who stayed in the Israeli district were called Arab Israelis or Palestinians of the inside. Those in these three worlds were isolated from the rest of the world. It became impossible for them to move between these three districts.

There was no hope for Baheya to get any news about the well-being of her family.

Abu Omar Buried His Rifle

The remaining rebels came home. Everything ended quickly. One day, Abu Omar came back home carrying his rifle wrapped up in his *kufiyah*, an Arab men's headdress. His eyes were lost in grief. He dug a hole beneath a tile at the kitchen door and buried his rifle in its shroud. (For years after that, I could not step on that tile—I was afraid to harm what was buried under it.) He sat on the doorstep, held his head in his hands, and cried. I sat beside him and hugged his head. That was the first time I had seen him cry.

We were united with Jordan, but my family was trapped in Israeli-occupied land. Though I could see the coast from the roof of my house, it was impossible to reach it as it was part of what is called Israel. Visiting my family or having visits from them was absolutely out of the question at that time.

I became an orphan. My sense of loneliness grew. My man was broken and defeated. War breaks men. He had lost his smile that made his eyes glow like two stars in a moonless night. He left his trades and planted the land. He inherited an olive press as well as a wheat mill from his father.

I stopped counting my menstrual cycles and accepted my fate. Then in 1950, the first full moon of March passed. And then another in April. I did not see any nasty blood drops. But I did not tell anyone. I was not sure of my speculations, so I hid my happiness in my heart. My morning sickness revealed the secret I tried to hide. Um Fathi came, and after checking me, she let out an ululation, a sound Arab women used to express their jubilation. Happiness came back to Abu Omar's eyes. He hugged me tightly and whispered, "No more work for you! Relax, my Baheya."

I loved every moment of my pregnancy. I even loved morning sickness. Every morning, Abu Omar would bring me bread, cheese, and a glass of tea to start my day. He sat beside me on my bed, and we shared our meal.

A few years later, I had three children—Omar, Basheer, and Zahra.

Following my usual habit of asking anyone passing through our town about the whereabouts of my family, I made the acquaintance of a woman from Amman who was visiting her refugee relatives. I asked her about my family, and to my surprise, she told me my sister was residing in the Wehdat refugee camp near Amman. I was so happy about that piece of news that my heart burst with excitement. But I could not travel because Omar and Basheer were too little and Zahra was still nursing in the cradle.

Abu Omar traveled and returned with Saniya, my niece, with news that my sister was very ill and had bequeathed me the care of her daughter.

I asked him about the rest of my family. He told me they had not left their homes but their land had been confiscated with the excuse that it had not been registered in the legal records. It was considered unused government land.

A few days later, I got the news of my sister's death. Saniya stayed with me. Her father remarried and did not want her in his new life.

Zahra, the Forever Child

Unlike my pregnancies with Omar and Basheer, my pregnancy with Zahra was hard. But even with the constant morning sickness, Abu Omar complimented me and said I was becoming more beautiful. His words always healed my heart.

But my feet did swell to twice their size. I saw horror in Um Fathi's eyes each visit she made. In my last month of pregnancy, she advised me to stay in bed and elevate my feet on cushions.

My aunt took Omar and Basheer, so I had to care only for myself. The birth was hard. The labor was long and painful. But as soon as I saw her little, round, brown face with a reddish tinge, I forgot all my pain and long wait.

Um Fathi put her on my chest and set her on my breast. But unlike all other babies, she refused. She was tired; life was undesirable for her. She did not cry, and she never asked for food. I always had to remember her eating schedule and persuade her to eat.

The little child became spoiled. She rarely played with girls her own age or even with her siblings or Saniya. She was attached to me. She never left my side except to sleep, and she did most of her sleeping on my lap or next to me.

She uttered her first word on her third birthday; we had thought she was mute, God forbid. Even when she grew older, she spoke little. When her father would speak to her, she would stare into his eyes with a blurry look as though she did not see what was seen but rather what was unseen inside or behind him.

Many times, I caught her talking to someone invisible—listening and then talking. I told my aunt about that, but she told me that children played with angels. But this playing with angels kept going on till I suspected she was possessed.

Her happiest moments were when I took her to the ruins on the eastern foot of Deir Al Lauz to pick thyme and sage. There she ran around the Roman columns laying on the ground and stuffing colored mosaic stones in her pockets. She let her spirit loose there with no rush to regain it. Once, I found her looking into one of the many wells in the area and listening intently. When I came near her, she raised her head and said, "Mom! He says what's coming is frightening."

I trembled at her words. "Who said that?"

As usual, she smiled, looked behind me, and embraced me. I took her home.

That night, she was totally delusional. She repeated what she had told me at the well. I read some of the Qur'an to her and cooled her forehead with vinegar compresses. When she awakened in the morning, she was totally out of her mind. I let her rest her head on my chest, and little by little, her scattered soul returned to her body. Her spirit, however, was like a child lost in the wilderness.

Two days later, I returned to the ruins searching for the well but could not find it; it was as if the ground had swallowed it up. I sat on one of the columns and listened. I had to hear what my daughter heard, but I could hear nothing except the wind blowing through the few bushes nearby. I started weeping. I thought, *Oh, God, I fear that girl, and I fear for her.*

She was only thirteen when her aunt, who lived in Zarqa in the East Bank, asked for her hand for her son. To my surprise, Abu Omar approved the marriage. He said, "I won't let down my elder sister. Isn't it enough that her homeland is out of her reach?"

I screamed and cried. "I won't send my daughter away! She is still too young. Please, Abu Omar, the girl still needs me. She is not in her full capacity."

But all that was in vain. Abu Omar did not like to anger his sister. He said, "Maybe if the girl felt the happiness of marriage, her soul would find its way back to earth."

He got what he wanted. I bought my daughter clothes with what I could afford to spend. But the girl did not feel the usual joy a bride feels; she locked herself up in her own world.

I gave her my braided bracelet so a part of me would always stay with her, and we traveled to Jordan to increase the number of refugees by just one more.

I will never forget the look in Zahra's eyes as she whispered, "Mom! Keep me in my country! Why do I have to immigrate, Mommy?" The simple words of a child touched the heart that should have protected her.

Haleem, her groom, was a young man with little spirit or principle. During her first night in his house, he did not approach or even talk to her. The house was a disgusting mess. I wanted to take Zahra home with me, but for the second time, Abu Omar refused. *Oh, my beloved Zahra! Why didn't you refuse? Why didn't you scream?*

On her wedding day, I had to fill her bra with cotton because my little girl had not matured yet. I delivered her to her husband with a broken heart and returned home.

The next time I visited her, she was expecting her first child. She was as pale as the sheets she lay on. The bleeding and morning sickness left her powerless and weak. With her absent eyes, she was forever a child. The doctor said she was too young for childbearing.

What pained me the most was her refusal to talk to me or even look me in the eye. She just lay there in her bed facing the wall and refusing to eat or talk. I became so frustrated. I tried to scream. But what was the use? She was at that point a member of another family.

Her aunt was continuously complaining. She complained about their poverty and their estrangement, and about Zahra's weakness and silence. A mother-in-law is not a mother. I should have taken her home with me, but I did not.

On the day I was to leave, Zahra looked into my eyes. All I saw in them was rage, blame, and pain. It was terrifying. I knew I had done a terrible thing to her. I should have been more determined to keep her. Only God could grant my heart some peace.

Awaiting Another
Passing of the Carnival

On a Sunday evening in April 1971, Omar arrived in Beirut on a Middle Eastern plane. Sabry stood waiting for him on a porch viewing the runway. He took him in his red Beetle to his apartment they would share. It was in one of the colored Rustum buildings in the Harat Huraik neighborhood. The airport street was crawling with people. Sabry pointed out to them and said, "Your people!"

The air was filled with the residue of joy much as the air is after a carnival comes and goes. People were reserving their leftover happiness. They sat in groups around little trees that lined the road. Street vendors selling julep juice and corn grilled over hot coals advertised their offerings intermittently. Girls were walking around in their best clothes and distributing charitable smiles to the young men. If the girls were more generously inclined, they would give certain boys a longer look.

Groups of men and women seated on straw chairs were waiting for the carnival to pass by again. Children were running between the chairs wondering how many lifetimes would pass till they actually shared in the dance of happiness.

The pink-walled apartment was on the ninth floor of a group of look-alike buildings. As Omar looked out from the balcony, he felt dizzy and sick; it was the first time he had been higher than the second floor. The neighbor's voices came through the thin apartment walls; that at least made it feel more like home.

Omar was a student in the physics department at the college of science. His new world enchanted him. The books, the lectures, and the discussions were like magic to him. He walked confidently in the paths of scientists. During his four years there, he never missed a class. He engaged himself in new mathematics and physics theories. But he never missed a day of weapons training in the Fateh training camps either.

The world of numbers called out to him. He roamed through its mazes trying to comprehend mathematical facts as easily as he could comprehend a sight or a smell. He was always seated in a front seat in the lecture halls, and like a sponge, he absorbed the knowledge. He was always quiet; he never grabbed anyone's attention till after midterm exams. His grades were perfect.

He could be silent for hours and totally content in that silence. Even with Saniya, he was never in a hurry to say anything mentionable. He never wanted to share his feelings or emotions with Saniya or his mother. But it was a different story with Professor Ellie Haddad, a visiting professor from New York University. Omar dropped all his restrictions when it came to talking with him, not about his personal life but about research or a theory whose mysteries he wanted to unravel.

He did not like to talk about his village or its people. He separated his two worlds. For four years, he lived a double life; his heart and memories in Deir Al Lauz and his brain and logic in his life of science. That strange logic that accepted light turning into material and material into light carried a destructive energy. He was juggling his life between two different worlds in every respect.

His college mates mocked him and made him the butt of their jokes. His hair was always neat. He shaved even on exam days. His clothes had been in fashion the previous decade. His tight-legged khaki pants and thin-collared shirt did not match the fashion of the time in Beirut, where Charleston pants were all the craze. They were tight at the waist showing all they could but then widened below the knees like the sails of a boat.

One morning, Professor Haddad told him, "I nominated you for higher studies at New York University with a full scholarship funded by NASA."

Omar asked with little concern, "What am I to research?"

The professor replied hesitantly as he had expected Omar to be more enthusiastic about the offer. "The curvature in space-time in outer space. Proving Einstein's general relativity theory. You know that this subject is one of the hottest topics in science these days."

Omar was silent as though he was suffocating on words that could not be spoken.

"If I were not committed to Deir Al Lauz, I would have accepted. I'll continue studying for my bachelor's degree and earn a PhD as would any other overachieving student. But my commitment is firm. I am committed to duty. I'll seek freedom."

"You will be killed."

"Why don't you say I'll live free?"

"You're insane!" the professor said. "How can you refuse such an offer?"

"What would I do with a PhD in theoretical physics and no country?"

Omar's days in Beirut were regimented at the university and at the training camp. He started early in the morning. He took a taxi to the College of Science in Al Hadath. At the end of any month, he would walk to the university to save the taxi money and buy a simple lunch.

When Sabry graduated and left Beirut to Hebron, Omar bought his red Beetle even though it had a hole in the exhaust. He drove it every day to the university, making sounds like little explosions; that made his classmates mock him even more.

1971

Omar was hanging out with Sabry in Al Hamra Street when they were caught by surprise by the first December rain. They entered a café frequented by students at the American University. As they did not have enough money for two cups of coffee, they ordered just one and a glass of water to share.

The atmosphere in the café was smoky from all the cigarettes and the steam from the mouths and noses of the young people seated around steel tables with pink Formica tops.

A girl in a leather miniskirt that was even shorter than the fashion grabbed Omar's attention. She was slurping coffee and smoking a long cigarette she held between her dainty fingers. She blew the smoke out of her mouth and nose in a way that triggered feelings in him he could not explain.

A young blond man who was handsome but in a sickly way was hugging her shoulder. She put her head on his shoulder sometimes, and other times, she released herself and let out laughs that rang throughout the room. Something about her expression was artificial; she was like a bad actress.

Omar's friend noticed he was staring at her. "Omar, do you know her?" Omar shook his head. But he was not sure; something about her was familiar. Omar sensed something relaxing in her, an old desire for what could not be touched.

He stared at her for some time till someone called her by her name. "Khawla!" She flirted with a few words in the slang of Deir Al Lauz. That was when he remembered her and whispered, "Khawla, the daughter of Abu Amjad."

His friend asked, "What did you say?"

He simply mumbled, so his friend let him be and turned his attention to others in the café.

Omar had heard from his mother that Khawla was studying in Beirut, but he had never seen her before that moment except for a few minutes in Abu Rebhi's grocery. Oh, how much she had changed. Her black, frizzy hair had been transformed into straight blonde hair done up on the sides of her face like curtains.

Omar had to wait three years after high school before he could leave Deir Al Lauz to study in Beirut. In those three years, he worked many jobs to save money for school. But she had left straight after high school to study in the most prestigious university in Beirut.

He could not take his eyes off her. He was on the verge of going to her, pulling her by her arm, and confronting her with, "This is not acceptable!" But he refrained. He just waited and observed.

It was 1971, and freedom was in the air. There was no clear border between right and wrong. By using a symbol, you could wipe out the line that separates light from darkness. You could invent your own words and sentences that had no meaning or substance but nonetheless earn the title of intellectual.

Perhaps what he saw as inappropriate was viewed by others seated with her as the most natural thing; she was extroverted, educated, and always ready to start a new relationship. Her duty was to please all who was around her. He was not satisfied with his thoughts. He felt bitterness in seeing her in that condition. He told himself repeatedly, *It's 1971.*

That was the first year Arabs faced the world without Gamal Abdel Nasser. The first year the Palestinian Liberation Organization actually existed in Beirut. The first year John Lennon took his music to America. The first year the *Palestinian Affairs Journal* of the Palestinian Research Center was published. It was the first year Omar was in Beirut after such a long wait.

Hippies dropped their protest signs and positioned themselves in chairs and at desks in banks. Love phrases were smothered, and the daisy petals drawn on the cheeks of girls dropped from sight. Arab poets adopted that symbolist poetry that widened the gap between them and those who could read.

Vietnam was still resisting. The people of the Lebanese camps were living on the banks of rivers full of sewage and infested by mosquitoes. The resistance could not grant its people much pride though their voices were heard around the world in the cultural institutions they established. They did not care much about their day-to-day lives. They stayed where they were and worked at low-paying jobs; they were forbidden any government positions.

Omar thought, *A new contradictory life.* Khawla's laughter brought him back to reality. He turned from her, got up, and walked toward the door. He stopped for a minute. He wondered if he should approach her, remove the arm that was around her shoulder, crush her cigarette out, and take her to her parents. *But who am I to her? She might be the one in the right. Maybe the life she's chosen for herself is the one right for the new era. How would I know?*

She Charged Her Weapon, and the Steel Joints Clicked

Omar found out from a friend that Karmel elementary school of the United Nations Relief and Works Agency needed a math teacher; the previous one had gone to Moscow to study medicine. He thought the position would be a great opportunity to break his boring routine. He went to the headmaster of the school and was hired on the spot as a substitute mathematics teacher.

Omar entered the schoolyard with the headmaster. The ground was of uneven gray cement full of holes; the water in them mirrored the dim noon sunlight. The wall surrounding the yard was worn out. A silver lizard sunbathing on the wall noticed them and fled to one of the many cracks in the battered wall. The purslane and mallow growing between the wall and the dull concrete floor were a meager sign of life. The smell of coffee came from the janitor's room near the main building.

A child in blue pants and khaki vest was running across the yard toward the school campus. An old teacher stood at the steel gate staring into space. The child's passing caught his attention, but he soon went back to staring. A white cloud covered the sun's face for a few minutes, making shadows that disappeared when the sun returned. A sick lemon tree stood in one corner of the schoolyard. A gray-winged sparrow was moving between its branches making adorable swishing sounds.

Omar stood there staring at his surroundings and ignoring the headmaster beside him. A small but new world opened itself up to him. A group of sixth graders surrounded a boy wearing green clothes of the revolutionaries with a white and black kufiyah around his neck. He saw a girl with ginger hair bound in the back with a rubber band. Her fingers were as slender as a spider's legs. She was carrying a Kalashnikov. She took it apart with the sure confidence of a fighter, and she polished the pieces with an oily rag. She greased it and then with swift fingers put it together again. She readied her weapon and made sure its joints clicked as they should.

At whose chest will she aim her weapon? Does this child know her enemy? What does she know of her country? Does she know what her father lost?

The child stood and grasped her weapon to her chest in military fashion. A boy saluted her like a real fighter, and her classmates applauded her. She did not smile; her face was stern. Her eyebrows were tensed.

Another boy with an eagle's eyes took a Kalashnikov from his teacher and started disassembling it as though he wanted to teach those around him how to do that. The children's eyes were focused on his; he was teaching what he had known from birth.

How do these children leave this place?

The principal whispered, "Teacher!"

The phrase was not familiar to Omar's ears, so he did not respond.

The principal said a bit louder, "Mr. Omar, we have to go to class."

How Would You Know
What's in the Sky?

In the sixth-grade classroom were two rows of seats beside each other, a blackboard, a table, and a chair. Omar put his bag on the table and waited.

His students followed their mentor into the room. They sat three to a seat. The girl with spider fingers was one of his students. They shouted and talked as though Omar did not exist. He grabbed the chalk and wrote on the blackboard, "Mr. Omar Abdul Rahman." His students were still shouting. He wrote on the top of the blackboard, "Subject: Mathematics; Lesson: Decimal Fractions." He faced his students and in a shaky but loud voice said, "Good morning!"

The students stood and said in one voice, "Good morning, teacher!"

He smiled to himself and admired his courage. He asked his students to introduce themselves. Each stood and shouted his or her name in a way that made their classmates laugh. But Omar kept his calm and swallowed his laughs.

A redheaded boy with gray sad eyes introduced himself in a whisper. "Ali Tea Kittle."

The other students laughed hysterically. Omar thought they laughed because his surname was funny; so he let himself laugh too. He raised his voice and asked for silence. But the class was in an uproar. Omar was confused and agitated. He decided to put an end to the farce. He turned to the board and started writing the terms of the lesson.

The children quieted a little, but Ali was sobbing quietly. Omar finished his lesson, called the crying child forward, and asked him why he was shedding tears.

"My stepfather made me sleep on the road last night, and all the kids know about it. That's why they laughed."

"What did you do to get such a punishment?"

"I was hungry and ate his dinner."

"What about your dinner?"

"My mother forbad me to eat it."

"Why did she do that?"

"Because I had come home late."

"Where were you?"

"I was with Faten in Sahet Al Burj."

"Who is Faten?"

Ali opened his eyes wide and whispered, "You don't know Faten?"

Omar laughed and took a breath. "No, I don't know who Faten is."

"Faten is the most beautiful girl in the fifth grade. No, the most beautiful girl on earth and in the sky."

"How do you know what's in the sky?"

"Because my dreams can reach that high."

"What were you doing with her in the Sahet Al Burj?"

"I took her to buy her some notebooks."

"You?"

"Yes. I work, and I have enough money. I promised to spend on her till we are old enough to marry. My stepfather wants me to give him all the money I earn, but I want to take care of Faten."

"Your Faten, does she have parents?"

"She does, but her father is very poor. He works only during the orange-picking season."

"What about you? What work do you do?"

"I am a tailor's apprentice in Sahet Al Burj. Teacher, come to our shop. I'll give you a special discount. My mentor is a good tailor."

Omar was lost in thought for some time. He could not remember ever being with a girl anywhere. Not even with his fiancée, Saniya. His mother took her everywhere she wanted. He saw her only at home.

Saniya would bring him a tray of food, put it on the pallet, and sit quietly opposite him. He tried to recall the color of her eyes but could not. His memory awakened a yearning for his village and a taste of the thyme *za'tar* between his teeth.

The young man with dreams brought Omar back to reality. "Teacher!" He was waiting for a reply.

Omar looked at him with gentle eyes and whispered as if he were coming out of a coma, "Divide your earnings between your stepfather and your Faten. Do you have anything to eat?"

Ali shook his head.

"Sit. Let's share this roll of fava beans."

Ali sat with the confidence of a grown man but the teary eyes of a child whose lack of food had made his skin yellow. He took half the roll. He was hungry, but his pride forbad him to show his hunger. He chewed slowly to hide his weakness. Hunger weakens and breaks the strongest of men.

Omar did not touch his roll. He waited till Ali finished and handed it to him. Ali did not refuse; he took the other half and nibbled at it.

An old nostalgia swept Omar away. He loved the boy and wished he could know more about him.

A bell declared the end of the school day. Pure affection replaced the fake harshness in Ali's eyes. He ran to the door and said, "Faten is waiting for me."

That was how the first day ended. Omar left school, a cascade of emotions digging deep tunnels in his existence. He got in his car. A fly followed him in and swarmed around his head before resting on his arm. He opened the window to let the fly go. A cold, humid autumn breeze entered the car and refreshed him. He took a deep breath. He felt cold, so he closed the window and forgot about the fly.

He started his car. A driver behind him blew his horn. He moved his right foot from the brake and stepped on the accelerator. His left foot rested on the clutch, and the car roared a little. The driver behind him drove around him with a long wail of his horn.

Omar was alert. He sped away. The fly was still hovering around his head. Thoughts of Basheer raced through his mind and left behind a refreshing, friendly feeling like that after the first rain of October.

The fly's humming prompted Omar to open the window, and the fly escaped. A rush of fresh, icy air brought back that refreshing, friendly feeling. He closed the window and tried to visualize Ali and Faten.

The Bitter Taste of Hope

He did not sleep that night. He got up in the morning with a bitter taste in his throat. He smoked a cigarette and had a few sips of coffee while standing on the balcony leaning over the railing.

He watched pretty Linda staggering toward the school bus. He went back in, shaved, put on cologne, and dressed in the clothes he had worn the previous day as he was not in the mood to iron a fresh shirt. He went out the door.

He pushed the elevator button and listened, but there was no sound. He pressed the button once more. Still no sound. He yelled, "Abu Ghaleb! The lift!"

He heard Abu Ghaleb downstairs answering him in laconic brevity, "It's out of order."

Omar sighed. He stumbled down nine floors. At that time in the morning, all Omar's neighbors were on the stairs. Um Fadi, who lived on the sixth floor, smiled at him and asked about his health, his university, and his family all in one question. When he answered her briefly that everything was fine, she sulked. He smiled because he knew that the next day, she would smile at him and ask the same questions.

On the fourth floor, he met Abu Mohammad. He was sitting on a straw chair in the corridor wearing a white cotton undershirt as well as white, faded blue pajama pants. His potbelly was resting on his thighs. His wife, Um Mohammad, was standing next to him holding a tray of coffee. In her eyes was a constant expectation that something was about to happen.

Omar greeted them and asked about their son, Mohammad,

who was in school. Um Mohammad looked at Omar with waiting eyes as though she was on the verge of starting a long conversation, but she said nothing. Omar did not wait for an answer; he hurried downstairs. He reached the school after the end of little traffic skirmishes on Burj Al Barajenah Street.

He parked his car in the alley parallel to the western wall surrounding the school. He saw a boy carrying a bucket and an old rag running toward him. "Shall I wipe your car, teacher?"

Omar nodded and hurried to the gate. He tripped on a rock and almost fell.

The boy yelled, "God protect you, teacher!"

He looked at the boy, who had black, naughty eyes that lit up his dark face.

"Is it your first day at school?" the boy asked.

Omar answered without thinking, "No. The second."

"Strange. I didn't see you yesterday," the boy said.

Omar thought the boy was about thirteen. "Why aren't you in school?"

The boy was busy cleaning Omar's Beetle. "School is not for people like me."

Omar left the boy. He reached the school gate and pushed it open; the gate moaned disturbingly. He saw students standing in rows around the flag. Mr. Sobhi was standing in front of them and shouting in an orderly manner, "Ready, relax, ready, relax." The students were ready, and they were relaxed. The Palestinian flag was raised on Lebanese land, and the children sang the Palestinian national anthem by the poet Sa'ed Al Mzayan.

feda'e [guerillas] feda'e
fedaa'e
Oh my country, oh my land, oh the land of my ancestors
fedaa'e, fedaa'e
fedaa'e, oh my people, people of perpetuity
with my determination, my fire, and the volcano of my revenge
with the longing in my blood for my land
and my home
I have climbed the mountains and fought the wars
I have conquered the impossible, and crossed the frontiers

With the resolve of the winds and the fire of the guns
The determination of my nation in the land of struggle
Palestine is my home, Palestine is my fire
Palestine is my revenge and the land of resistance

A Palestinian crises oasis in exile. A beautiful image made his heart beat wildly. An overflow of love washed his soul. He wished to embrace these kids. The promise of a return soon was fake. *Alas! What would they return to? Conquered homes? Dug-up graves?* But it was the idea that was important, a painful hope. Bitter-tasting hope coated with a thin layer of revolutionary sugar.

Sabri had once told him when they were in the Fateh training camp, "Stay in Beirut and fight from here."

Omar had shaken his head and chosen just a few words. "The struggle must be from within."

That afternoon, he returned to his car expecting it to be clean, but it was as if the boy had bathed it in muddy water. He still gave the boy one lira in Lebanese money with a clear conscience that turned to remorse. He gave the boy money to make peace with himself, not for the boy's work but so he could feel superior. He wished he could get back what he had paid, as the boy did not deserve it. But how could he, especially after seeing the boy taking it happily with frozen fingers?

That boy needs to learn how to do his work professionally. But it's only a small car. Does it require professionalism? Yes, it requires professionalism. The boy must learn, but maybe next time.

How Many Hearts Must Burn Till My Nation Accepts Guidance?

The death of the three martyrs in what the newspapers called the massacre of Firdan bowed Omar's back. *What revolution is this that cannot protect its intellectuals and fighters?* They were martyred in their home in front of their children.

What caused Omar even more misery were sad stories that were told after the tenth of April. The disappearance of the son of Abu Yousif Alnajjar and the psychological shock it gave his daughter. The demise of Kamal Naser, whose body lay sprawled like a cross after his death, glory to God, all because he was a Christian. He had asked in his will to be buried next to his dear friend Ghassan Kanfany in the Islamic martyrs' graveyard. Or the divine intervention that forbad Abu Iyad from being with his friend Kamal Odwan that night that ended his life.

The Israeli army shot us down day and night, and all we did was count bullets in the chests of our comrades. We flirted with death on the lips of our loved ones. We had to get them the same way they got us.

On one of those numerous mornings when the elevator was out of service, Omar was stumbling down the stairs as usual when he noticed Um Mohammad lovingly carrying some clothes in her hands and weeping. She did not need him to ask what was the matter. She just told her story.

"The day before yesterday, a volunteer came from Hebron. He was only twenty. He dressed in his commando suit and gave me his old clothes to wash. They took him and went south. I asked him, and he told me that he had never in his life even seen a rifle. How could that be, teacher? Can they take him to fight without even training him?"

She was silent. She stopped sobbing for a few seconds. She went on without waiting for Omar's answer. "Today at dawn, the news reached me that he had been martyred. These are his clothes. I didn't even wash them yet." She started sobbing again.

"He was supposed to come back for them. What shall I do with them? I'll wait. Perhaps his mother will come for them." She hugged his clothes as though she were hugging her own child. "His mother must be heartbroken. Why did she send him here? Why?"

Omar whispered, "How many hearts have to burn until my nation accepts guidance?"

Um Mohammad stared at him. "What did you say?"

"God bless his soul, and give strength to his mother."

Saniya! Did You Know?

I surrendered Omar to another woman, but she did not receive him. She kept him for me, and that did not please me. In a way, I wanted him to be hers; she wanted them to be mine together.

When he returned from Beirut, I saw that he had changed. I felt I did not know him anymore. Every morning, I searched his eyes looking for happiness and contentment, but I never found that. He always had a craving for the unknown. Was he in love? Secrets were hidden! I thought it was his estrangement in his own home. I thought he missed his days in Beirut and his friends there. I thought that his mood would pass in a few days, that he would adjust to his new life. I once asked him in a joking manner about it, and he said, "Bahia, you always exaggerate things."

My heart was right. A mother's heart never lies. I did not know his secret until two soldiers with their officer and an Israeli recruiter with ruffled hair broke into our home looking for him. I yelled, "Saniya! Did you know?"

She denied it. What wife does not feel her husband and does not know the absence of his eyes from her and his heart busy with another? I had felt his absence but had misinterpreted it.

The questions that burned my heart were, *Should I stop him? Can Saniya stop him?* I knew he never loved Saniya the way a man should love his wife, but surely, he liked her. *Could she deter him from his plan? What about Abu Omar?* He blamed me for keeping from him what I knew would happen. But all I knew was that his mind and heart were preoccupied with some other yearning.

He loved Palestine more than anything else. He loved her children, her land. He loved her farms. He loved everything in her in his own way and awarded her the dearest thing to me—himself.

When Love Is Misled

I am his mother. I know him as I know my own heart. He is Basheer, a hermit in his sanctum. He never leaves his room that is next to the mill except to go to his fields, his trees, or the monastery of Sheikh Abdul Hadi Al Kaderi on the top of the mountain.

"You can find clarity of the heart only in seclusion," he always said. That was Basheer—a stranger in his own world. You thought he was with you, but you'd find out he was with himself. That was because "The person is the religion of his mate," and he never found a mate he could trust.

He had no interest in the girls who passed his mill. He talked to them with his eyes on the ground, or he looked at them without seeing them. I became worried. I thought there might be a problem, God forbid.

I told Abu Omar what was in my heart. He assured me and said his time had not come yet, but my heart was not at ease. I wanted to marry him off, so I sent Nahla, the daughter of Abu Sami, to him with a sack of wheat.

I winked at her; I wanted her to grab his attention, but it was no use even though she was a very beautiful girl. I thought she could win his heart with her coquetry and fair skin. She returned to me saying, "Your son is either an angel or crazy. In either case, he's not for me."

I used to tease him by saying, "Your books and the sheikh ruined your mind."

He always answered me in his divine calmness, "My sheikh and my books made me who I am. I prevented myself from looking at whatever is forbidden and kept my other senses away from it. I ask God, the Almighty, to keep it in its pristine state until the hereafter. Traveling without guidance is a rocky road full of temptation, fear, and danger. You should not walk alone on that road. You should not be distracted from reaching your ultimate goal."

I did not understand most of what he said, but I always loved talking to him and listening to his wisdom.

Then Khawla, the daughter of Abu Amjad, came along. She studied at the American University in Beirut and spoke their language. She enthralled him; he dedicated all his hours to her.

He came to me one day. "Mom, I want you to ask for her hand for me." He took me by surprise. I did not know what to say.

After a long silence filled with confusion, I told him, "Son, she is out of your league."

That was the first time I saw him like that. The smile that always brightened his face disappeared. He said, "She is the one I want."

"But her father is an—" I could not say it, but he was silent. His eyes focused on my lips encouraging me to talk. Then I said these damned words. "—an infiltrator! And her brother is Amjad!"

I expected him to revolt or at least say something, but he kept quiet. I did not want him to be quiet. He knelt, held my hands in his, and shed tears. I stroked his thick hair. He bowed and rested his head on my lap. Oh, how my heart ached for him. I wished love for him, but when he came to love, it was cursed.

The Riddle Awaits Solving

Basheer dropped off a bag of flour at the house of Um Basel. He rarely did that, because he disliked mixing with people, but Um Basel did not have anyone. All her kids were in different places around the world. That moment changed his life. The moment he first laid eyes on Khawla, she was visiting Um Basel. She was on her way out while he was coming in.

She was a full woman wearing a black miniskirt and platform sandals. Her hair was as black as night and loose; it framed her beautiful face. She looked beautiful and desirable. She noticed him staring at her and smiled at him fondly. That was the first time Basheer had noticed any woman's clothing. Something in the way she moved attracted him. Their eyes met for just a fraction of a second. He saw a riddle in her eyes.

He saw her once more at the grocer's. She was joking with the grocer spontaneously; she was at ease. He greeted them hesitantly. She answered with a simple smile and "Hey, Basheer!"

She knows my name? He dared to gaze in her eyes. The puzzle was waiting to be solved. Curiosity overcame him, but he looked away. He looked at her once more, convinced it would be the last time. But that time, his heart skipped a beat. Before he could comprehend what had just happened, she got ready to leave.

"See you later, Uncle Abu Rebhi. Bye, Basheer."

She left him hanging between two looks and two skipped beats of his heart. He watched her from afar stumbling in her high heels. Then he noticed he was covered in flour. He was as embarrassed as Adam had been when he realized he was naked and asked for a cover.

His roaming the alleys of Deir Al Lauz increased. He was looking for her. He regularly passed her house in hopes of meeting her.

Then, after he had lost hope of seeing her, he met her by chance at Abu Rebhi's grocery. She was leaning over a tomato box to select tomatoes she put in a paper bag. He watched her and waited till she finished. He approached her and whispered, "I will wait for you at the door."

It did not appear as if she had heard him. She started a conversation with Abu Rebhi. Basheer did not catch what they were saying; he was too busy wondering if she had heard him. After some time, measured by thousands of heartbeats, he heard the words he had been waiting for.

"See you later, Uncle Abu Rebhi."

She approached him with a puzzled look in her eyes. They walked together like any two friends walking on a road together.

She told him that she had finished her studies in English literature at the American University in Beirut and that she was teaching at a private school in Ramallah. She said she was returning to Beirut for a PhD. He did not know exactly what she meant, but he did understand that she would be leaving.

They walked together until they reached her house. At the gate, she looked at him. "I'll see you tomorrow at the same time and place."

His heart trembled with fear when he saw an invisible creature accompanying her.

The Grief Hidden
behind Her Smile

He left his house after the Afternoon Prayer and walked to her house with hesitant steps. He wished he would meet anyone on the road to distract him from meeting her. But at that time of day, in the steamy, hot weather of July, no man dared walk outside. And most of the younger men working in Israel had not returned for the day. He had showered and had trimmed his beard; he felt fresh in a way he had never felt before.

He reached a crossroad. The road to the left went up the mountain toward the shrine of Sheikh Abdul Hadi Al Kaderi. The road to the right went down a small slope toward the house of Khawla. He pleaded for mercy for the soul of the sheikh. He missed him and his reciting sessions. He promised himself to spend the night at his shrine on his way back to rest his conscience. A question kept repeating in his head: *What is drawing me to her?*

Perhaps it was impossible to solve the riddle. Perhaps it was the grief hidden behind her laugh and smile. Perhaps it was the urge to know who she really was. *I'll help her.* He walked confidently. *But who am I to help her? Can I actually help her? What if my guess is wrong?* He slowed down. *Support me, my master, my sheikh, my father. Keep me safe in the name of God. Help me, my beloved master Jilany. Support me, my master Abdul Hadi Al Kaderi. Support me!*

He would tell her to wear more-conservative clothes. He sped up; his shadow could not keep up with him and was gasping for air. He tried to count the thoughts that went through his head. Then he laughed at himself about the idea of counting his thoughts. That thought had added one more, and he lost count.

What if she forgot our date? Or pretends to have forgotten it? That would be insulting. No, she would not forget this. That would be impossible. If she doesn't come, there would have been an urgent reason for that. I'll help her! And that will be the last time I see her. Then he caught up with his thoughts. *Why would it be the last time? She may need me longer than that.*

Allah, I ask You the best of this day. I ask You by the glory of the prophet to rest my heart. There is no God but You. In You I trust. You are the God of the exalted throne. What Allah willed, happens, and what he willed not, happens not. There is neither might nor power except with Allah. His heart slowed down. His legs regained strength back. He walked with strength and determination.

He reached her house. The window on the second floor was open; the breeze was pulling on a pink curtain. *Is that her window?* His heart was beating fast. He searched for his breath but could not catch it.

She was suddenly standing right in front of him. It was as though she had blown in on the breeze. "Come. Let's walk to the spring," she said.

As though he were enchanted, he followed her, and so did her mate. From that moment on, a love story began with all that love means.

Love stories are like time. They have no beginning as they are prior to time. And they have no end as they are close to eternity. Love is like water in color and shape. It can form itself to anything while not having any substance itself.

Adoration is a denial of the mind and existence. Adoration is absolute madness.

Didn't Your Heart Tell You
I Was Waiting for You?

He met her on his road to the spring again. She had left the main road that connected Ramallah to Deir Al Lauz and was walking toward the spring. She did not notice him till he shouted, "Khawla!"

She looked at him. That was the first time he had seen such a beautiful smile, the most beautiful smile in the world. She was wearing the same skirt he liked and detested. She noticed his stare and turned around half a turn. "Do you like it?"

"Yes, but it's too short."

She laughed.

"I waited for you yesterday evening," Basheer said.

"Did we agree on a date?" she asked with a mixture of surprise and flirtation.

"No, but didn't your heart tell you I was waiting for you?"

She noticed his seriousness. She whispered, "My dad was home. I could not leave."

They walked side by side to the spring. The dusty road descended and curved west. The afternoon November sun created a lovely pattern of almond tree shadows and spots of golden light. A butterfly was seeking a flower amid lifeless autumn thistles that glistened in the dim sunlight. Khawla was stumbling a bit over the pebbles on the dirt road. Her soft, long black hair flew and covered one side of her face but exposed her fair skin on the other. Their shadows followed them, sometimes meeting and other times separating. He tried to hold her hand, but she pulled it away and folded her hands at her back.

At the bottom of the slope near the pond, he felt an urge to hug her. His feeling was not a desire. *What is this urge? A need for food is hunger, a need for water is thirst, but what is this? What is this feeling called?*

He came closer to her and put his arms around her shoulders. She did not resist. She lay her head on his shoulder and buried her nose in his neck. She lost balance and tripped, but he held her up.

"Basheer! I was married before."

"I know."

She looked shocked "Who told you?"

He wanted to say, *Your invisible friend told me, trying to keep me away from you.* But he stopped himself so she would not accuse him of being insane. His eyes filled with tears. "I am sorry for you. Your suffering hurts me."

"How did you know, Basheer? How? And how do you know of my suffering? I wanted to pray, but I forgot how. I wanted to supplicate myself, but my soul was silent and far from the altar of forgiveness. Please show me the way, Basheer. I am tired and lost. Take my hand and show me the way. My sins are hurting me. My heart and soul are void."

"Ask forgiveness from the almighty God! God is the All Forgiving and the Most Merciful. Keep offering this prayer. 'For truly my Lord is He, the Hearer of Prayers.' He is near and will answer your prayer. Hold the holy Qur'an in your right hand and the teachings of His prophet in your left hand, and follow the guidance of the Lord. All paths are open to those who follow the lead of God's prophet. You may rescue your soul by going against its wishes. That is when you cleanse your heart utterly from all but our mighty God. Pray, Khawla. Keep praying. Drown your heart completely with thoughts of God."

"Oh, Basheer, will my salvation be at your hands?"

"Your salvation is in His hands if you keep Him in your thoughts. Pray to God. Oh, Khawla, pray to Him. He is with me if I pray to Him. I keep Him always in my thoughts, hungry for forgiveness and His great reward. If I keep Him in my thoughts, He thinks of me. I come closer to Him with love and passion, so He comes closer to me with forgiveness and wellness. You who does not need us for a thing, You are the One who can relieve us every moment from any obstacle."

"I want your guidance. Please guide me!"

"I am nothing but a shadow of God on earth. Do not look at me. Look at the source of all this infinite light. Get rid of all your confusion and be the guide of yourself. There are a thousand shades in this lightness. You have to choose your own path. Oh, Khawla, when God opened my eyes, I saw a thousand other worlds. This world is a prison for my free spirit, but my faith drives me to a vast, liberated place far from all emotions and materialism."

She whispered as if she had not heard what he had said. "I killed the one who was living inside me."

"Ask God for forgiveness. Keep begging for it. You won't see the light without that. Look at the world around you. A thousand worlds were created by a single puff of God's breath, but the angels prostrated themselves in front of Adam. The earth, our thoughts, and our comprehension are illusions. If you stay intoxicated in the material world, you will be blind to the prize of the soul."

She looked at him with questions in her eyes. "You are drunk in His love! How can I come closer to Him?"

A few days later, she came wearing a dress that covered her knees and a scarf that covered her hair. He said to her with a smile, "Now you are more beautiful."

She said, "This is my gift to you."

"No one but the deplorable will get God's grace."

He did not believe the purity of her soul because her invisible companion was still with her. His heart shuddered. *I will help her.* "Renew your faith with your heart, not by your words."

I Take a Turn around the Crescent to Make a Full Moon

Oh, my love, Basheer! I stare and stare at everything and nothing. You always visit me in my mind, a fantasy that takes me away from my existence and creates a world with you and in you. A world between the petals of a flower on the verge of falling, on the wing of a bee dancing her last dance before losing her way to the hive.

I am a new existence pledged to yours. You dictate its words. You structure its sentences. But I cannot find myself in it though I try to learn some of your skills. I repeat in my head all your words and all our conversations, afraid to find in them what could make you upset as you are flawless.

In the night's darkness, I turn into a column of white smoke that dances a little to the melody of eternal music, music heard by no one except those whose hearts are smoke. It takes me for a turn around the crescent to make it a full moon. I carry in my hands a fallen star and put it back to light the sky. I stretch myself to my limits till I reach the sky and let the rain of love and passion give sustenance to old wishes and hopes.

In the old age of the first creation, only humankind could declare the end of a long drought. Hidden happiness was planted and grew blossoms and bore fruit during the night. I spread their seeds and send them to each heart that knew no love. When the oldest god sent rays of its light, I return to my old hiding place and regain my former state to recover my breath and heartbeats. I relive the memories I kept in your heart and the whispers you entrusted to mine. I perform my prayer as passionately as the thirst in the desert. I close my eyes and pray with every breath I take in the hope of finding peace for you and me.

In the morning, I look in my mirror and do not recognize myself. I am not me. I put eyeliner on eyes that are not mine. I comb hair that does not belong to me. *Who am I?* I ask myself. With a touch of my hand, I give life to all that is around me. I let them speak and beg them for answers to my questions.

They whisper among themselves and sometimes even giggle, "Today, we do not know you; you are not who you were yesterday or who you will be tomorrow." Then I say, "He will know me." Their whispers become screams in harsh words, and their giggles turn into loud, bitter, tortured laughs. "No! He will not recognize you, and we will not let him do so."

I am the one who made you in my imagination. I gave you life. Damn you! I gather the sparks of my soul and leave them as lifeless bodies with their words frozen on their lifeless lips. Their harsh laughs were sprinkled like ashes throughout my room. I say, "I'll see you tomorrow, or maybe it won't be me who sees you."

Her Mother Sewed It for Her and Sent It to Ramallah to Be Embroidered

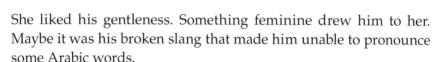

She liked his gentleness. Something feminine drew him to her. Maybe it was his broken slang that made him unable to pronounce some Arabic words.

She was in the college cafeteria leafing through a book and trying to hide her embarrassment from a world she knew nothing about. He came close to her, and as simple as could be, he pulled out a chair, put it beside her, sat, and relaxed his elbows on the table. "You want some tea?" She nodded. She had never seen him before. Her soul was still troubled. He got up and left her sight. He soon returned with tea and slices of lemon.

She was enchanted by him. She forgot what she was; she wanted to become someone who suited him. Someone to suit his infinite gentleness and his overwhelming elegance. She looked around her. *Why did he choose me?* She was not the prettiest girl in the cafeteria. She was not the most elegant either. But she was sure she was the smartest; her grades proved that.

She wore a short red dress her mother had sewn and had sent to Ramallah to be embroidered with black threads. It was a nice dress, but not for the morning.

She promised herself she would go to Al Hamra Street and buy Charleston pants and a tight shirt just like all the other girls were wearing.

His voice brought her back to reality. He did not ask her name. He just started a long talk with her. She tried to remember where she could have met him before but failed at that. *Who am I to him?*

Why has he chosen me? Does he love me? He may have loved her, but not enough to introduce her to his family.

Tony was his name. He was a teaching assistant in linguistics in the English department. He was waiting for paperwork before going to the United States to work on a PhD.

Day after day, they became inseparable except for sleeping. He would stand at the doors of her lecture halls waiting for her. He would wait for hours in the cafeteria for her. They would have casual conversations, but he never told her he loved her, and they never spoke about their different religious backgrounds.

Khawla started to wear the latest Lebanese art that showed creativity and vivid imagination. Like all the residents in her neighborhood, she had her morning coffee on the balcony of her apartment in Firdan. It had become her habit. She learned to smile at all her neighbors. She learned how to engage in small talk and how to end it anytime she wanted. Every morning, she would jump over a few steps that were between her building and the street. And every morning, Tony would be there in his red Renault.

One night after he had dropped her off at her building, he walked her to the door of her apartment and pulled her to him. He tried to kiss her. She resisted fiercely. She pushed him away. "No!" He turned, jumped over the steps, and drove off. She did not sleep that night.

The next morning, he was there as usual. "Let's get married."

She went out of her mind with that thought. Everything in her screamed no, but she said yes. *A Christian man with a Muslim girl?* That was an impossible marriage. In what court would they marry? He said they would have a civil marriage in Larnaca. She accepted that but asked, "What about your family?"

"We'll tell them later."

A marriage without a mother-in-law was every bride's dream. There was nothing to lose, she thought. Her father and brother would not know, and her mother had passed away the previous summer. *I won't lose anything.*

Tony lived in Khawla's apartment in Firdan. She was surprised when he told her they had to share the house. She convinced herself it was the modern lifestyle.

Then one day, she found out she was pregnant. Tony kept silent when he heard the news.

A Mechanical Atmosphere in the Room

That evening, Tony took her to a clinic on the third floor of a fancy building in Firdan. The ceiling and floors of the entrance were clad in white marble. The names of the doctors who had offices there were engraved in black letters on sheets of copper. She did not have enough time to read her doctor's name, and she could not ask Tony either.

A notice stuck to the elevator door said it was out of order. She climbed the steps with much difficulty. Every time she stopped to catch her breath, Tony urged her to speed up. She was tired. Because of morning sickness, she had not eaten much the past few days. She felt degraded; her other emotions weakened her even more.

A rosy-cheeked nurse with a big smile met them at the door of the clinic. Though Tony tried to hide it, Khawla thought she must have known Tony very well; she asked him about his mother and sister. He did not answer directly. He mumbled something as if he were embarrassed to know her.

Khawla's legs were shaking; they could not carry her anymore. She sat on the first seat she found in the waiting room. She heard rain hitting the window. The room was illuminated by a billboard across the street that shone orange and green. The moving colored light was tempered by the shadows in the room; it created orange and green headless ghosts. The figures merged to create creatures with multiple legs, separated, and merged again.

Khawla hid her head in her hands and tried to remember any verse from the Qur'an, but she could not. She felt as if there were demons all over the room who were trying to keep her from remembering. She stared at Tony, but he was not present. The nurse came over and told him, "You have no place here. Come back in an hour. The doctor will check her and set a date for her operation."

Tony left without saying a word. Without even a look, he left her all alone. From that moment on, she hated him.

The constant nausea she felt in her stomach turned into chronic pain that spread throughout her body to her chest. The nurse took her by the hand to a small room to take her blood pressure and record her weight and height. The nurse drew her lips together. "Your blood pressure is quite low! Why don't you eat well?"

Khawla just shut her eyes. The nurse led her back to the haunted room to a chair and went back inside. *Do I need Tony now? No!* But she wanted her mother. *Where is she? What if he doesn't come back for me?*

A cold breeze sneaking in from the window prompted her to pull her jacket tightly around her. She tucked her feet under herself; the edges of her boots pained her thighs. She enjoyed that sharp, piercing pain, and she pressed harder. She put her arms around her legs and rested her head on her knees. She closed her eyes waiting for what was to come.

The pain inside her was still there. The nausea and acidity in her stomach pushed up into her, toward her mouth and nose. *Where is he?* She was scared.

Colorful ghosts were still jumping around the room. *How could he just leave me alone?* The door of the clinic was opened allowing a demon hiding in a black cat to pass by. She tried to mention the name of God, but her soul did not utter a word. She did not find Him in her.

Khawla did not know how much time passed till the nurse came back out holding a pale-looking girl by her hand whose head was lowered in shame. When she lifted her head, her face was blue, her skin was dry, and her lips were cracked. The residue of freshly removed makeup was showing on her sad face. Her top was outrageously open showing most of her breasts.

The eyes of the two girls met. Without speaking a word, the girl said, *Do not enter! Go back where you came from!*

A woman appeared. She was sitting two seats from Khawla. It was as though she had come in with the ghosts. Khawla had not noticed her before. The woman held the girl and led her out of the clinic as though she were protecting her property. The view of the girl and the way she was treated by the woman made Khawla think she might have been a prostitute. She was frightened by the thought. Her humiliation increased. It turned into bitter colocynth.

The nurse came to the window and closed the steel blades of the blinds, which gave off a mechanical sound. The ghosts left the room. Dim light came from a fluorescent bulb on the ceiling. She watched what seemed to be a movie in her mind.

She had been living a nightmare since the day she had discovered she was pregnant. For many days after that, Khawla stayed in bed weeping quietly and feeling very depressed. Tony would come home and treat her as if she didn't exist. The first two nights, she watched him gathering his things to sleep in the living room. She pretended to be asleep when he came in to use the bathroom. After that, her quiet crying became loud sobbing.

After a few such nights, Tony came into the room with erratic eyes. He sat beside her. She expected him to say words that would calm her down. If he had done that, she would have forgotten the past and given herself to him. She would have gotten up and walked with him on the corniche just as they had done after each fight. He raised his hand, which Khawla thought would land gently on her head. Instead, he hit her shoulder hard. He squeezed her bones tightly and said, "Enough crying!" His tone expressed his anger. "Enough! Have you lost your mind?"

She shook her head and pressed it to the pillow. Oxygen was not reaching her lungs. She felt a headache coming on like the music of a horror movie. *The scary scene will come soon! Shut your eyes, Khawla.* And that is what she did. She covered her nose with the blanket and breathed in the air she had just exhaled. She whined in intermitted breaths from behind closed eyes.

He was cold. "We have to end this!"

She no longer had the strength to argue with him.

"I'll take you to the doctor to take care of this."

In a weak voice, she said, "That's Haram!" It was unacceptable according to her religion.

"Well, it's your body. You're free to do what you wish."

"But I'll kill a soul! I can't do that."

He left the room. She soon heard the apartment door slam. That night was very hard on Khawla. The morning was even worse. She endured hours of blackouts between hours of insomnia and dizziness. The nausea haunted her, but she could not throw up anymore; her stomach was empty except for burning, sour acid.

Just two days before that, she had been yearning for who was living in her. *Will it be a girl like me with black hair? Or will it be a boy with her father's absent eyes?* But then, she felt a weight pulling her insides down. She wanted to get over this and get back to the university and her classes.

Her endless nightmares in her head ended when the nurse came in the room with a smile duller than the dim bulb. She led her by her hand into the doctor's room. It was so white that even the ghosts did not dare enter. It had a bed with white, pristine sheets.

The doctor looked at her blankly. "Lie on the bed." Khawla did. The doctor listened to her heart and lifted her legs into the stirrups on the edge of the bed. He gave her an internal examination and said to the nurse, "Six weeks, not more."

Khawla felt dizzy. *Hold on, Khawla! But where am I?* She felt fear. The doctor stood wordlessly next to her.

Tony came in. "She is too weak," the doctor told him. "We will keep her here overnight and give her intravenous nourishment. We will operate on her first thing in the morning."

Tony opened his mouth as if to speak, but he changed his mind. The doctor stared at Tony waiting for any reaction from him.

"Then I'll come back in the morning," was all he said.

The nurse came close to Khawla and said in a voice she tried to make affectionate, "Don't be afraid. I'll be beside you all the way."

The morning came after an endless night. The nurse prepared her for surgery. The doctor put a mask on Khawla's face. She suddenly remembered she still did not know the doctor's name. *And why is he giving me anesthesia? Why isn't there an anesthesiolo—*

She became unconscious.

When she regained consciousness, she found herself lying on her left side holding her knees to her chest. She tried to move, but the nurse's voice ordered her to stay in the position she was in.

She still worried about not knowing the doctor's name. Tony was seated on a chair next to the bed. She felt numb and dizzy. Tony came over and stroked her hair. She tried to lift her hand to push his away but did not have the strength.

Khawla lifted her head to see what was around her. She saw the nurse busying herself with some tools on the table in the corner of the room. She saw her wrist still attached to a pipe that dripped a fluid into her veins.

"It's finished. You're free now!" Tony whispered.

The colors around her were bright and vibrant. She relaxed. She felt relieved.

The unnamed doctor came in the room. "Thank God for your safety. You are in good health today. I just want you to relax a little bit. We will keep you here till the evening, then you'll be free to go home."

Two Separate Roads
with No End

I lived a morning, an evening, and then a divorce. I had a wedding in Larnaka and a divorce in Beirut. I have my own rainbow now, a rainbow that has all the shades of black in it with a white hole in my womb and remorse that bites into my soul.

My companion left me; he became bored with my sadness. He left in the night lit only by a full moon. I was always scared of nights with full moons. One of the invisible creatures I had met told me, *You have two separate roads with no end to them, with two men waiting at each source. You will have to travel and wait. There are two roads that do not meet. Treason with the first and death with the second.*

Will meeting the other be inevitable? Why isn't it meant for me to leave before meeting the second? Will his death be my punishment?

My loneliness became my friend. Long hours passed with me just staring into darkness and calling on the demons. At my call, they came out of the cracks in the ground and walls. I could distinguish them all by their thin, colored halos and the colors of their long fingers. I gave them all names. Their voices were like bells each ringing alone, and they were dancing to the tones of the bells. They were sneaking into my thoughts with the same ease with which they had come out of their hiding places. Their movements in my head made it buzz. A terrible ache crept into my head. I felt as if sledgehammers were banging my scalp. With all that pain, I felt tears flowing down my cheeks. I begged the creatures to let me be.

Then after all that, an answer came like an echo in my head. *You called us! You brought this pain on yourself. You asked us to dance in your space. We will stick to the lashes of your thoughts and swing in your dreams. We will feed on your blood. You have to endure us.*

My screams became as loud as their giggles that rang like bells in my head. The stomping of their little feet pained my skull. Their burning fingers charred what was left of my heart and left it in ashes. When I realized there was no escape from this, I surrendered. I called their names and cursed them. It sounded as though I were reciting a prayer to the unknown.

I looked for the Most Merciful in my heart, but He was not there. I could not find Him. How could I ask God for forgiveness if I could not find Him?

Someone slipped into my soul and sprayed his poison into my heart. He said, *I'll be your companion till you lose the one who loved you. When you don't need me anymore, I'll leave you to your fate. Only then will you be on your own.*

You Will Receive Orders in the Next Two Days

Omar was sitting and waiting on the western wall of an olive grove. He was looking out as Amjad gave him an M16 machine gun. He lifted the gun to his nose and smelled steel, oil, and burned gunpowder.

Omar put the gun on his knees and passed his fingers over its cold steel, which sent the chill of death running down his spine. He shivered.

"What do you think?" Amjad asked.

"It's a little longer and lighter than the Kalashnikov."

"It's bullets are faster and lighter than those in a Kalashnikov, and its aim is wonderful."

"Where did you get this from?" Omar asked.

"Do not ask me that!"

Omar held the weapon as if to weigh it.

"You will receive orders in the next two days," Amjad said.

Omar simply stared at his weapon.

The orders came a few days later. Five fighters were to attack an Israeli patrol on the road going toward Deir Al Lauz.

At dawn, four fighters met and introduced themselves. Amjad was not among them. They waited for him for some time, but he did not come. They wondered whether they should proceed with their operation. They had planned for Amjad to be the lookout; he was supposed to give the signal to go.

After some time in silence, Omar decided to execute. The four fighters knelt hugging their weapons to their chests. They were behind rocks that hid them from the eyes of those who feared them. One of them read the Fateha, the first verse of the Qur'an, and another traced a cross on his chest. His comrades looked at him and laughed. He exposed a little cross-shaped tattoo on his wrist. He touched the cross and smiled. "This was my mother's vow."

It did not cross their minds that they could die as martyrs. In their minds, life would go on. But even so, Omar started reciting the Fateha. His Christian friend joined him, as did another of their comrades.

The fourth one shouted, "Stop that! A cross and the Holy Qur'an? All that's missing is a sheikh to read on our souls. We will not die here today. I will leave you to your prayers and supplications and go up the hill to watch the road as Amjad isn't coming. I'll whistle to you when I see the jeep at the top of the road. You count to five before facing our enemy as we had agreed with Amjad."

The Christian guy started mumbling prayers again and retraced the cross on his chest. The forth guy shouted, "For God's sake stop that! A cross and Fateha? Are you a Muslim or a Christian?"

"A Christian! A Christian! But my friend was a Muslim, and I used to read the Qur'an with him."

"Oh my God! I don't want to hear the story of your life. Concentrate. After I whistle, count to five. Do you understand?"

"Yes, I do."

He hung the machine gun on his shoulder and started climbing the rocky hill.

Where is Amjad? Omar wondered. *Why didn't he come? It may be best to call off our operation. Only three guys to confront the patrol? That won't be enough.* Omar grabbed the Christian's shoulder and noticed he was shivering as though he had a fever.

They heard the whistle. They stood up with machine guns in hand, counted to five, and jumped to the road. Omar shot the wheels of the car, and the others shot the passengers. The operation ended in success. The look in their Christian mate's eyes was one of pride, not fear. Instead of chills, their bones felt the warmth of victory. The four retreated through the mountains each to his own place.

In the evening, the following news was broadcast by the Voice of Israel from Orshaleem in Jerusalem: "A patrol of Israeli border guards was gunned down at dawn. Three soldiers were assassinated.

And as per our reporter, a great number of forces rushed to the scene and combed the area surrounding Deir Al Lauz in search of the saboteurs."

Security forces had indeed gone to Deir Al Lauz in search of certain people. Omar crossed the river and escaped toward the East Bank.

The radio broadcast a second piece of news: "The security forces captured three members of a destructive cell made up of four members of the Fateh party. This cell had killed the border patrol at dawn today. One fighter had a stolen machine gun."

That evening, the house of Abu Omar was broken into and all who were in the house were taken out to the garden. Omar's room was ransacked, and all that was in the cupboards was scattered on the floor.

Um Omar did not know what was happening. Absent Saniya was in a state of bewilderment. Basheer was in his eternal isolation. Abu Omar was moving through the house hurting from the security ring that strangled his manhood.

With the soldiers going back and forth in his house, Abu Omar was muffled in sound as well as in pride. He walked fast to Omar's room and stood at the door watching the soldiers searching for something. He did not know what. He tried to scream but was suffocated by his words.

Who gave information about this cell? Was Amjad the only one who was not arrested? It must have been him! And what makes it even worse is what was said about his father. It was terrifying and shaming! As it was said, Abu Amjad had sold the Be'r Mountain to the Israelis.

No Thoughts, No Memories—Just Emptiness

Khawla climbed the Be'r Mountain—the haunted mountain, the cursed mountain. The moon was full; it was similar to the night she had killed the one who had lived in her. The white hole came back to her womb. The emptiness in her soul and heart returned. At that moment, she had no thoughts, no memories—just emptiness.

In all the months of summer, they had met there, seeing off the moon in the hopes of meeting again. She turned once around the well. She took another turn, and then another. She put her hands on the wall around the well. She lowered her head into its mouth. She listened carefully to the humming of the sleeping ghosts shackled at the bottom.

She had always feared that place but at the same time had always been drawn to it. She asked Basheer once to build their house there if they ever married. She said, "We will share our residence with them and quench their sorrows with our love. Perhaps their troubled spirits would get relief, and they could rest eternally."

The rotten smell wafting up from the still water filled her nose; it was similar to the smell of vomit. The sun set, and he did not come. She let out a scream; her voice echoed in a distorted and ugly sound.

I will jump and be their sacrifice. Perhaps they will be cleansed from their sins, and perhaps I can pass over to what is purer and shake off those shackles of waiting and anticipation.

Remorse is like a mouse nibbling on the soul leaving it full of holes. The memories were in contrast to the reality she lived in. The past, present, and future became the same, entwined. She had only one choice, and that was to suffer. She did not jump. She dared not. She felt insulted.

It was impossible for her to jump, so she squatted with her back to the well's stones, which pricked her. She enjoyed the pain. She pressed harder against the stones. She dug her elbows into her thighs. She grabbed her face and covered her eyes. *I'll wait here till he comes. He will come. I know he will.*

She felt his presence but did not lift her head. Basheer was standing looking at what was behind her. His legs were apart with his hands in his pockets unconcerned with his tears that were moistening his beard.

The shackled demons at the bottom of the well woke up after a sleep of a thousand years. They shook their fiery chains; the rattling deafened the ears of all who could hear. Thunder roared through the clear sky. Khawla shook and shivered in fear. At that moment, all that lived on the mountain fled.

"Basheer, I am scared! Please take me to your chest. Don't let the prophecy of the invisible people come true. Basheer! A part of you and a part of me can still go on together. Don't say what you are about to say. Please, don't let the demons loose. Love me! Take me to you!"

"I'll kill him!"

"A hermit does not kill."

"And a lover does not die. How can you kill a lover? What kind of being is capable of killing a lover? Omar was a lover. He loved her till infatuation. He loved her till he reunited with her. And till he entered her in his own unique way."

"Basheer! I loved you, and I still do. Oh, please take me to you."

"How can I when your brother is Amjad and your father is Abu Amjad? Tell me how?"

"Please forgive me for a sin I did not commit. We'll start over new, you and me."

"Omar will be between us. And I see Amjad in your eyes each time I look at you. They shot him, Khawla! They killed him with twenty bullets. Was not Amjad capable of killing him?"

The shackles broke. The demons were freed and were wandering the old mountain. The moon exploded over their heads and rained ashes on them.

"I did not free the demons! Your father and brother did. How much did they get for his blood?"

She leaned her head back. The stone at the edge of the well hurt her. He knelt next to her and grabbed her wrists firmly. She lifted her head, and their eyes met. He called her name and pushed her backward. She felt the stone pushing into her back; sticky blood was flowing on her skin.

He whispered, "Khawla! You knew Omar was here. You told Amjad about him!"

"No!" she said with a suffocating rasp in her voice.

"Your house was under surveillance. You know! Did you know your father sold the Be'r Mountain? Our mountain, Khawla! Didn't we agree on building our house here beside the demons' well?"

"Yes! I know."

He was still holding her wrists. Her head was searching for refuge.

"Where is Amjad?"

"I don't know. He left this morning. I stayed back to be with you."

"What is between you and me is a killer, a killed one, and vengeance."

He pushed her back and let her wrists go. Her arms fell lifeless next to her body like two creatures that had lost their lives.

"I changed for you!"

"You changed because you wanted to be the best. You wanted to be closer to Him."

"I became what you wanted me to become!"

"You became simply what you should have become!"

"How can I live without you?"

"You will live. Don't worry! You don't need me!"

"Don't kill him. Amjad is too small and low to have his death on your hands. He is not worth it. Don't leave your land. It'll turn into desert."

"I swore to end his miserable life!"

He walked away, dragging his broken shadow behind him and went on tripping on the shards of the pain caused by the departure of half his soul. She kept curled up in the light of a cursed moon, surrounded by graves of all the brokenhearted of the world.

"Basheer! Don't leave me!" she screamed. "Don't read the letters I wrote you. It's sinful for me what I wrote, and a sin for you to lay eyes on what is written! Remember me when you read Sourat Al

Najem, the star verse from the Holy Qur'an. I'll remember you in every thought and every word I utter."

The earth became tight with all its width. Their breaths became tight. There was no shelter but God, the Almighty. The fire shackles were broken, and the demons were loosed. All the images built up by their words were shattered. She shouted once more, but her screams did not echo. Her invisible companion united with her and led her back to the village, saying, *Don't come back here! You are free now. You are the boss of yourself with your own choices. Didn't we promise you that? The mountain belongs to us now!*

A voice of fire and flames was audible. He broke up with her and left her alone. She felt a loneliness that carried the chill of eternity. It was as though the universe had not been created yet. A desert of emptiness was created. Time was free of itself.

Khawla Leaves, and
She Looks Behind

Khawla was sitting on a wooden bench in an Israeli lounge waiting to be called by an Israeli officer. A three-year-old boy was rolling a cucumber on the floor just to amuse himself. He threw it, ran behind it laughing, and picked it up to take a bite. He rolled it across the floor again. She watched him and thought she could have had a child that age if things had been different.

She swallowed her pain and smiled at the little one. He giggled, toddled over to her, and offered her his cucumber. Khawla took his hand and kissed it. When his mother noticed what he was doing, she snapped at him. "Don't disturb auntie." The little boy walked away with his eyes on Khawla that displayed only love and kindness.

She was still waiting. Khawla felt all eyes were on her as though all heads knew what had happened to her. She looked three times in a row at her watch but could not read the time. She took off her watch and dropped it into her purse.

A dry breeze blew yellow dust in. The child rubbed his eyes and sneezed. The dead yellow mist covered the whole place. She felt dryness in her throat, and fossilized tears in the corners of her eyes. Memories of him came to her but in fragments. The tips of her fingers became numb. Everything she touched held the coldness of death. She noticed a hair stuck on her clothes. She took it and turned it around her finger and pulled the edge of it till the tip of her finger turned red. She pulled some more till the hair broke into pieces and dropped to her lap. *London, with all its trees, rain, and fog, as well as its strangeness, awaits.* Its estrangement was the memory she held.

Now, as me and myself are in exile, why do you still come to me with all that strength and all that depth? No, I am not alone. You are embracing me with your arms and warm breath. Oh, my Basheer, you still fill all the voids in my soul.

Today, there is no gravity, no air to breathe. Everything around me is floating, lifeless. My birth was in autumn, my death in autumn, and between those two autumns, I had a life with a thousand autumns planted in it. It was as though all the lovers of this world had been resurrected.

I wish I had not gone up the haunted mountain that night. I wish your words had died before they had left your lips. I wish they would have been killed before they reached my ears. I sit here all alone, forgotten just like the leaves of this autumn. Did we not agree that my time with you was over? Why were you watching my steps while I was leaving? I saw you. You were sitting and watching. I did not lift my head to see you with my eyes, but the sound of your supplications was in my ears. Your prayers were transparent though surreptitious. They were coated in a tenuous layer of lust.

What path could I take now? How can I go down a path where I can see everything but can't be seen? Someone is watching my thoughts. When a woman loves and gives her all but is not answered with gratitude, she feels contempt for herself. She feels filthy in her clothes. How could you leave me all alone? What can I do to face all that emptiness on my own? You should have taught me how to live before you left me. All the time I spent without you! I forget all that I had to face and remember only the smell of olives on your neck.

I dreamed of a tomorrow with you. I dreamed of being your bride. I thought you would compensate me for the early death of my mother and my father's departure as well as my brother's betrayal. But instead, you blamed me for all their wrongdoings. I have become bereaved twice—once when I killed who lived inside of me, and the other time when I killed the one who brought my heart to life. You killed me, did not revive me, and killed me again. Do I think of having my revenge on you? The word *revenge* is a horrific, scary word. But what about you? Are you satisfied with your revenge on me?

I will take you with me in bags of oranges of the sunsets. I will squeeze them and smell their scent in times of despair. I am the bride of the demons in memory as well as in imagination. All who come near me are cursed and forbidden. I am bound by chains of desire for you, and I have a long road ahead of me to freedom. I am living an eternal life of illusion. From my pain grew separation. And that separation created eternal nights, nights that make us sleep with open eyes and ruled by our torn memories. I ask mercy from You, the Most Exalted. I am hallucinating.

I am not going to be who you want me to be.

She removed her head scarf and tied it on the bench she was sitting on. The child watched her intently. The Israeli officer finally called her name. She stood and walked toward the window with heavy steps. She grasped her passport. She stopped, turned, and went back to the child. She found him holding her scarf. She grabbed his hand and kissed it and asked his name.

"Basheer." He gave her scarf to her. "Don't leave this. You will lose it."

She took it and crossed the Israeli border. She boarded the bus that would take her to another exile.

The Hermit Sheikh Climbed the Mountain Once More and Did Not Come Down

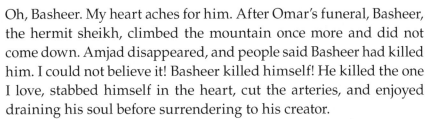

Oh, Basheer. My heart aches for him. After Omar's funeral, Basheer, the hermit sheikh, climbed the mountain once more and did not come down. Amjad disappeared, and people said Basheer had killed him. I could not believe it! Basheer killed himself! He killed the one I love, stabbed himself in the heart, cut the arteries, and enjoyed draining his soul before surrendering to his creator.

He vowed to fast long days with no sunsets. Every day, I carried food to him and washed the dishes of untouched food from the day before. I saw the angel of death coming nearer and nearer to him day after day, but Basheer did not resist him; he just surrendered himself. He coughed and gasped for each breath and refused any remedy.

On his face, I saw signs of surrender and longing for death to take him. All that and Abu Omar was drowning in himself trying to comfort me by saying, "He'll come back. Let him be. He'll come back." But he did not. Basheer was ending his life just as he had ended his relation with Khawla.

I thought maybe Khawla was the only way of salvation for Basheer, so I got over my pride and went to her home. I knocked, but no one answered. I saw Abu Rebhi, and he told me she had left the village alone after the disappearance of her brother and father.

What about us? Aren't his father and I worth living for? What about his fields that were green and were now drying off and dying out, weren't they worth living for?

Then the day my heart had dreaded came. I carried the basket on my head and went toward the tomb, but before I reached my destination, an Israeli officer stopped me and shouted, "It's forbidden to come nearer. This is a military area. Go back!"

He had not been there the previous day. I was stunned. I was not scared; I was worried about the one who was staying in the shrine. I asked him, "Where is the sheikh?"

"I don't know! I didn't enter the house."

I walked toward him staring straight into his eyes. He retreated in fear. Like a lioness, I smelled his fear and dared to come even closer. As if he were enchanted, he put down his weapon and whispered, "Come in."

"This is the shrine of sheikh Abdul Hadi Al Kaderi and his grandfather before him and probably his great-grandfather before him," I said. "How dare you! Damned is the day we saw you in this land."

I entered the monastery and saw my son kneeling on the mat near the door. What remained of my heart tumbled to my feet. I touched his palms. They were stiff and frozen. I dug my fingers into his hair and tried to scream, but there were no screams or cries left in me after the martyrdom of Omar and the absence of Zahra. The last of my tears had been shed when Basheer moved to the mountain.

I knelt next to him and gently lifted his head. The mat had left crosshatched lines on his forehead. I tried to wipe them off with my hand. While doing so, my knees touched his knees. I rested his head on my knees and knelt over him. I was as still as he was with only one difference; I had blood flowing through my veins. His were lifeless. His heart had lost the ability to beat.

I did not know how much time passed till I heard the soldier's footsteps behind me. I did not lift my head. I asked the soldier if he could be buried next to his spiritual father, Sheikh Al Kaderi.

"That's not allowed!" he shouted, but then he whispered, "Okay, but in secret."

I nodded.

His father washed his lifeless body and covered it in shrouds. He prayed over his body and buried him, but we could not visit his grave and read the Fateha on him.

I Will Call Him Omar

I was not even fifty when I sent my kids to their fates. Abu Omar and I came back to the way we had started—alone together. But the difference was that that time, a yearning for the afterlife was what kept us going, not hope for the future.

I simply turned from beautiful Baheya to old Um Omar. Abu Omar started to spend all his days on the veranda smoking and drinking cup after cup of sweet tea. And slowly, slowly, day after day, he stopped eating and talking.

Slowly, slowly, I lost the taste of life. I looked around me and saw all the stuff that I had gathered throughout the years, all my presents and belongings. I hated them all. *I don't own these things. They own me.* Those wooden boxes decorated with seashells and copper that had carried my wedding belongings. The rugs that had been a present from my father. The sheets embroidered with silk. My dresses that had been sewn by the best tailors. I told Saniya, "Get rid of them all. Feed them to the fire. Just keep what I need to live." She looked at me and apparently did not understand. I said, "I want to return to Him just as I came, clean of all vows." She nodded. I did not think she understood, but in the evening, I saw a fire in the garden.

I know she did not burn them. I know she hid them. She maybe did so out of pity for me or to keep some of me after I left. Saniya was a loving girl even though she had not been able to get close to Omar. But it was okay; she had freed me from my slavery to my possessions, and that was exactly what I wanted.

Almost a month after Basheer's death, I was sitting in the corner of my room. It contained nothing but the mattress I was sitting on and a few dresses hanging on nails on the door. Saniya came close and squatted next to me. I made space for her and invited her to sit beside me. She sat and put her arms around me. I rested my tired head on her chest, and she pressed her head gently on mine. She was all I had left after Omar. We stayed in that same position for a long time, she inhaling quietly and I choking on my bitter tears.

After some time, she put her hand on her slightly round belly and whispered, "Don't cry, Mom! Omar is coming back God willing."

I saw a smile behind her tears. For the first time in months, lightness snuck into my heart.

I decided to name him Omar. He would have the revolutionary spirit of his grandfather, the love of his father, the holiness of his uncle, and a heart as pure as the hearts of all the women of Deir Al Lauz.

From behind My Hidden Tears and Suffocation, I Said Omar Did Not Die

They carried Omar's body out of the house on their shoulders. I bade him farewell with an ululation and hidden tears. It was a farewell suitable for a martyr. I celebrated him in his death just as I had celebrated his marriage to Saniya. Our land is a holy land that cannot be satisfied. My son was a legendary hero. He was a groom wrapped in a flag.

I overheard an Israeli soldier saying, "Her son died, and she ululates." From behind my hidden tears and suffocation, I said, "Omar did not die. Omar was martyred." The women around me said, "She is lucky. The mother of a martyr will have intercession by her martyred son on Judgment Day." What would they know of the bitterness of departure! A piece of my heart was under the soil. How would they know? He took his last breath and surrendered his soul to his creator in my arms while his father was trying to close his numerous wounds.

One bullet was enough to kill him. Why did they mutilate his body with twenty? He had lived in silence and had surrendered his soul in the same peaceful silence. All through his life, he was a man of few words. He was always surrounding himself with silence mixed with adoration. Oh, one bullet had been enough! The ghost of a smile remained drawn on his dry, lifeless lips till he was buried.

How would they know? I miss him and pray to God to be reunited with him soon. But I am afraid of meeting God, afraid of meeting Him with all my sins, the biggest of them being to have married Zahra off. Oh, please, God, forgive me! And oh, my little Zahra! Why didn't you come? I want you by my side. I want you to be a mother to me for once. I want to cry on someone's shoulder.

DREXEL UNIVERSITY
College of
Arts and Sciences

This book is dedicated to the memory of Kathleen (Kathy) McNamee, beloved teacher, colleague, and friend in the Department of English and Philosophy.

Managing Editor	Gail D. Rosen
Director Drexel Publishing Group	Kathleen Volk Miller
Layout Editor	William Rees
Graphic Design	Miles Waldron
Editorial Co-op	Sharee DeVose Sara Aykit
Digital Communications Co-op	Sharee DeVose Karnik Hajjar
Student Interns	Linda Croskey Victoria Daughen Sharee DeVose Heather Heim Daniel Holl Jaycie Jaskolka Jasmine Jones Alexander Konyk Julie McGlynn Johanna Oberto Nicholas Oberto Cindy Phan Miranda Reinberg Isabella Schnoering Benjamin Teperov Angel Vergez

Sponsors:

Drexel University
The College of Arts and Sciences at Drexel University
The Department of English and Philosophy at Drexel University

Dr. Donna M. Murasko, Dean, College of Arts and Sciences,
     Drexel University

Dr. Ira M. Taffer, Interim Department Head, English and Philosophy,
     Drexel University

The 33rd Volume 10
Drexel University
Department of English and Philosophy
3141 Chestnut Street
Philadelphia, PA 19104
www.5027mac.org

Cover photo by Michaela Michener.

The 33rd is published once a year.

Submissions are open via contests each academic year.
See www.5027mac.org for submission guidelines.

ISBN 978-0-9820717-8-6

Deepest thanks to: Dr. Donna M. Murasko; Dr. Ira M. Taffer: all the judges from the Drexel Publishing Group Essay Contest, the Drexel Publishing Group Creative Writing Contest, Literature Essay Contest, and the First-Year Writing Contest (Jan Armon, Joshua Benjamin, Ken Bingham, Valerie Booth, Ingrid Daemrich, Anne Erickson, Valerie Fox, Casey Hirsch, Jacqueline Landau, Deirdre Mcmahon, Karen Nulton, Gail D. Rosen, Sheila Sandapen, Fred Siegel, Errol Sull, and Maria Volnosky); Department of English and Philosophy, especially Mary Beth Beyer, Eileen Brennen, and Nicole Kline; contest participants; and Drexel Publishing Group staff.

The fonts used within this publication are Archer and Avenir.

Credits:

Ackert, Lloyd. "Origin of Life" was originally published as "History of Origins of Life," in *Encyclopedia of Evolutionary Biology*, 1st Edition, Ed. Richard Kliman. Elsevier, Academic Press, 2016.

Ake, Stacey. "Scientists in the Cosmos: An Existential Approach to the Debate between Science and Religion" was originally published in the *Journal of Science and Religion*, 51:4, 1011-1022, December 2016.

carrington, andré. "Spectacular Intimacies: Texture, Ethnicity, and a Touch of Black Cultural Politics" was originally published in *Souls*, 19:2, 177-195, 2017.

Daeschler, Ted. "Invited Remarks at the Public Rally for the March for Science PHL" was delivered at The Great Plaza at Penn's Landing in Philadelphia, April 22, 2017.

Fitts, Timothy. "Does Anything Beautiful Emerge?" was originally published in *The Bible Belt Almanac*, and appears in *Hypothermia*, MadHat Press, 2017.

Fox, Valerie. "November Nightmare" was published in *Cleaver 18* (Summer 2017).

Israeli, Henry. "Our Age of Anxiety" was originally published in *The Literary Review*, 2017.

Kotzin, Miriam. "Bluff Note: Desdemona's Handkerchief," "Emily," "Tiger Lilies," "To a Man From Last Season," and "Upstream" were originally published in *Debris Field*, 2017.

Levin, Lynn. "Baby and Gorilla" was originally published in *The Monarch Review*, September 2017.

McCourt, Richard. "Life Finds a Way: Novel Algae in Reactor Cooling Pads" was originally published in *The Journal of Phycology*, 52: 687–688, October 2016.

O'Donnell, Sean. "Bushwhacked" was originally published in *Natural History*, February 2016. "Keep Your Distance" was originally published in *Natural History*, June 2017.

Riggs, Don. "Building Epic Anticipation: Peter Jackson's Hobbit Videoblogs" was originally presented at the 38th International Conference on the Fantastic in the Arts in Orlando, Florida, March 24, 2017.

Seltzer, David. "The Meno Paradox in Augustine and Kierkegaard" was originally presented at the Kierkegaard, Augustine, and the Catholic Tradition conference at Villanova University, on October 27, 2016.

Siegel, Fred. "Magic Class" was published in *The Smart Set*, November 7, 2016.

Volk Miller, Kathleen. "Let's Not Stay Inside" was originally published in *O, The Oprah Magazine*, May 2016.

Warnock, Scott. "Writing, Technology, and Class Mannequin Challenges" was published in *When Falls the Coliseum*, November 28, 2016.

Watts, Robert. "Breaking Baccalaureate" was published in *The Smart Set*, July 26, 2016.

Welcome

The 33rd anthology is a visible expression of the College of Arts and Sciences' commitment to interdisciplinary scholarship and writing excellence. Within its pages is an eclectic mix of short stories, essays and scientific articles written by students and faculty from fields across the University. This volume demonstrates the incredible diversity of Drexel scholarship: we are one institution composed of diverse perspectives. These unique perspectives enhance our community and have the power to inspire others to pursue new insights and innovations, whether that's writing the next best-selling novel or discovering a new molecule. But powerful stories and miraculous discoveries are nothing without the skills of communication. These skills allow us to share our ideas, our research, and our vision, with the world.

Whether you dream of being an author, an architect, or an environmental scientist, your training starts here with the tools of communication.

Donna M. Murasko, Ph.D.
Dean
College of Arts and Sciences

Preface

On behalf of the Department of English and Philosophy welcome to the tenth annual edition of The 33rd. This anthology of student and faculty writing has become a mainstay of the department and a critical component of our First-Year Writing Program. The works published in this edition showcase a variety of writing genres and highlights the interdisciplinarity so important to a Drexel education.

Our department plays an important role in the education of all Drexel students. One of the most important skills to master regardless of intended occupation is the ability to express oneself clearly, whether it is through verbal or written communication. The literary pieces published in this edition allows us to highlight the excellent writing of many students and faculty from across the university. In the true sense of peer learning, when we use this as a compendium to our First-Year Writing Program, current students can find good examples to emulate as they hone their writing skills. We hope you enjoy this anthology, and we look forward to seeing your submissions in future editions.

Ira M Taffer, Ph.D.
Interim Head, Department of English & Philosophy
Associate Dean, College of Arts and Sciences

Table of Contents

First-Year Writing Contest
Erika Guenther and Gertrud Daemmrich Memorial Prizes

Merit Winners		2
Introduction		3

Winner
Hunter Heidenreich   The Negative Effects of School Choice on Charleston County   5

First Runner-up
Hannah Pepper   Can Homosexuality be "Cured"?   9

Honorable Mentions

Eunhye Grace Cho	My Synonyms and Antonyms	13
Tamyka George	Memory and Doorways	15
Angelina Gomez	Urban Decay: When Lives are Cut Too Short	19
Joshua Jager	The Tinker	23
Shelby Jain	A Competitive Life	30
Kate Medrano	Is It Used and Abused, or Abused and Used?	33
Julian Zemach-Lawler	Villains of Our Own Story	41

Drexel Publishing Group Essays
Introduction   49

Humanities

First Place
Samantha Stein   Closet Voters, Junk Food and the American Dream: Education's Invisible Ties   51

Second Place (tie)
Caitlin McLaughlin   Beyond Catherine Barkley: Analyzing the Writings of WWI Nurses   148
Zachary Stott   "London": A Comparative Analysis   133

Both essays won in the Literature Essay Contest and appear in that section.

Honorable Mention
Sharee DeVose   African American Literature & Urban Life: *A Raisin in the Sun* by Lorraine Hansberry   57

Social Sciences

First Place
Yih-Chia Lam   Reflection: Halden Prison   62

Second Place
Sharee DeVose   The Painful Irony   66

Zelda Provenzano Endowed STEM Writing Award

First Place
Samantha Stein   Interdisciplinality: The Solution to Integrating the Populace into the Ever-Deviating Scientific Disciplines Commandeered by Executives, Reinforced by Journalists, And Fed by Researchers   69

Second Place
Kimtee Dahari Ramsagur   The Voiceless   75

Graduate First Place
Sarah Julius   The Lobotomy: Surgical Procedure or Surgical Oppression?   79

Drexel Publishing Group Creative Writing

Introduction   91

Poetry

First Place
Nicholas Yurcaba   Cranes on a River Bank   93

Second Place
Jesse Antonoff   Overture   94

Fiction

First Place
James P. Haes   Smirk   95

Second Place
Cindy Phan   Watchmaker   98

Honorable Mention
Samantha Stein   The Dying Game: An Allegory in the Chronicles of Stephen and Nick   104

Creative Non-Fiction

First Place
Neida Mbuia Joao   Telling College Stories   106

Second Place
Sarah DrePaul   Shared Language   110

Honorable Mention
Benjamin Folk III   Nine Thirty-Nine Post Meridian   113

Humor

First Place
Pauline "Daisy" Good   Feed Him Once a Day   116

Second Place
Heather Heim   The Tomatometer   119

Op-Ed

First Place
Stephanie Heim   The Necessity of Zoos   122

Second Place
Samantha Stein   Against the Adoption of Aramark; For the
                          Upholding of Our Values   125

Literature Essays

Introduction   131

First Place
Zachary Stott   "London": A Comparative Analysis   133

Second Place (tie)
Chandni Lotwala   The Full Circle of Shakespeare's Rosalind 141
Caitlin McLaughlin   Beyond Catherine Barkley: Analyzing the
                          Writings Of WWI Nurses   148

Third Place
Heather Heim   Literary Devices in Gray's "Elegy Written in a
                          Country Churchyard"   152

Honorable Mention
Davina Lee   Contextual Analysis in Poetry   156

Faculty Writing
Introduction 163

Lloyd Ackert — Origin of Life — 165

Stacey Ake — Scientists in the Cosmos: An Existential Approach to The Debate between Science and Religion — 178

andré m. carrington — Spectacular Intimacies: Texture, Ethnicity, and a Touch Of Black Cultural Politics — 191

Ted Daeschler — Invited Remarks at the Public Rally for the March for Science PHL — 213

Timothy Fitts — Does Anything Beautiful Emerge? — 216

Valerie Fox — November Nightmare — 226

Henry Israeli — Our Age of Anxiety — 227

Miriam N. Kotzin — Bluff Note: Desdemona's Handkerchief — 228
Emily — 229
Tiger Lilies — 230
To a Man From Last Season — 231
Upstream — 232

Lynn Levin — Baby and Gorilla — 236

Richard McCourt — Life Finds a Way: Novel Algae in Reactor Cooling Pad — 238

Sean O'Donnell — Bushwhacked — 241
Keep Your Distance — 243

Donald Riggs — Building Epic Anticipation: Peter Jackson's Hobbit Videoblogs — 245

David Seltzer — The Meno Paradox in Augustine and Kierkegaard — 251

Fred Siegel — Magic Class — 258

Kathleen Volk Miller — Let's Not Stay Inside — 262

Scott Warnock — Writing, Technology, and Class Mannequin Challenges — 264

Robert Watts — Breaking Baccalaureate: Why non-academic skills are as important as the traditional academic stuff — 266

Contributors
271

Writings Arranged by Context

Argument

Stacey Ake   Scientists in the Cosmos: An Existential Approach to the Debate between Science and Religion   178

Hunter Heidenreich   The Negative Effects of School Choice on Charleston County   5

Sarah Julius   The Lobotomy: Surgical Procedure or Surgical Oppression?   79

Samantha Stein   Closet Voters, Junk Food and the American Dream: Education's Invisible Ties   51

Scott Warnock   Writing, Technology, and Class Mannequin Challenges   264

Commentary/Editorial

Ted Daeschler   Invited Remarks at the Public Rally for the March for Science PHL   213

Stephanie Heim   The Necessity of Zoos   122

Samantha Stein   Against the Adoption of Aramark; For the Upholding of Our Values   125

Creative Non-Fiction

Eunhye Grace Cho   My Synonyms and Antonyms   13

Sarah DrePaul   Shared Language   110

Benjamin Folk III   Nine Thirty-Nine Post Meridian   113

Angelina Gomez   Urban Decay: When Lives are Cut Too Short   19

Pauline "Daisy" Good   Feed Him Once a Day   116

Neida Mbuia Joao   Telling College Stories   106

Kate Medrano   Is It Used and Abused, or Abused and Used?   33

Sean O'Donnell   Bushwhacked   241
    Keep Your Distance   243

Fred Siegel   Magic Class   258

Kathleen Volk Miller   Let's Not Stay Inside   262

Robert Watts   Breaking Baccalaureate: Why non-academic skills are as important as the traditional academic stuff   266

Education/Teaching

Fred Siegel   Magic Class   258

Scott Warnock   Writing, Technology, and Class Mannequin Challenges   264

Robert Watts   Breaking Baccalaureate: Why non-academic skills are as important as the traditional academic stuff   266

Environmental

Benjamin Folk III   Nine Thirty-Nine Post Meridian   113

Stephanie Heim   The Necessity of Zoos   122

Richard McCourt   Life Finds a Way: Novel Algae in Reactor Cooling Pads   238

Sean O'Donnell   Bushwhacked   241
    Keep Your Distance   243

Ethics

Stephanie Heim   The Necessity of Zoos   122

Yih-Chia Lam   Reflection: Halden Prison   62

Sarah Julius   The Lobotomy: Surgical Procedure or Surgical Oppression?   79

Kimtee Dahari Ramsagur   The Voiceless   75

Samantha Stein   Interdisciplinality: The Solution to Integrating the Populace into the Ever-Deviating Scientific Disciplines Commandeered by Executives, Reinforced by Journalists, and Fed by Researchers   69

Explanatory Writing

Lloyd Ackert   Origin of Life   165

Stacey Ake   Scientists in the Cosmos: An Existential Approach to the Debate between Science and Religion   178

andré m. carrington   Spectacular Intimacies: Texture, Ethnicity, and a Touch of Black Cultural Politics   191

Richard McCourt   Life Finds a Way: Novel Algae in Reactor Cooling Pads   238

Caitlin McLaughlin   Beyond Catherine Barkley: Analyzing the Writings of WWI Nurses   148

Donald Riggs   Building Epic Anticipation: Peter Jackson's
        Hobbit Videoblogs   245

David Seltzer   The Meno Paradox in Augustine and
        Kierkegaard   251

Samantha Stein   Interdisciplinality: The Solution to Integrating
        the Populace into the Ever-Deviating
        Scientific Disciplines Commandeered by
        Executives, Reinforced by Journalists,
        and Fed by Researchers   69

Exploratory Writing

Sharee DeVose   The Painful Irony   66

Tamyka George   Memory and Doorways   15

Angelina Gomez   Urban Decay: When Lives are Cut Too Short   19

Shelby Jain   A Competitive Life   30

Kate Medrano   Is It Used and Abused, or Abused and Used?   33

Hannah Pepper   Can Homosexuality be "Cured"?   9

Robert Watts   Breaking Baccalaureate: Why non-academic
        skills are as important as the traditional
        academic stuff   266

Scott Warnock   Writing, Technology, and Class Mannequin
        Challenges   264

Julian Zemach-Lawler   Villains of Our Own Story   41

Fiction

Timothy Fitts   Does Anything Beautiful Emerge?   216

James P. Haes   Smirk   95

Joshua Jager   The Tinker   23

Miriam Kotzin   Upstream   232

Lynn Levin   Baby and Gorilla   236

Cindy Phan   Watchmaker   98

Samantha Stein   The Dying Game: An Allegory in the
        Chronicles of Stephen and Nick   104

Gender, Race and Sex

andré m. carrington   Spectacular Intimacies: Texture, Ethnicity, and
        a Touch of Black Cultural Politics   191

Sharee DeVose	The Painful Irony	66
Miriam Kotzin	Upstream	232
Chandni Lotwala	The Full Circle of Shakespeare's Rosalind	141
Caitlin McLaughlin	Beyond Catherine Barkley: Analyzing the Writings of WWI Nurses	148
Hannah Pepper	Can Homosexuality be "Cured"?	9

Humor

| Pauline "Daisy" Good | Feed Him Once a Day | 116 |
| Heather Heim | The Tomatometer | 119 |

Literary Criticism

Sharee DeVose	African American Literature & Urban Life: *A Raisin in the Sun* by Lorraine Hansberry	57
Heather Heim	Literary Devices in Gray's "Elegy Written in a Country Churchyard"	152
Davina Lee	Contextual Analysis in Poetry	156
Chandni Lotwala	The Full Circle of Shakespeare's Rosalind	141
Zachary Stott	"London": A Comparative Analysis	133

Memoir/Personal Essay

Eunhye Grace Cho	My Synonyms and Antonyms	13
Sharee DeVose	The Painful Irony	66
Sarah DrePaul	Shared Language	110
Angelina Gomez	Urban Decay: When Lives are Cut Too Short	19
Pauline "Daisy" Good	Feed Him Once a Day	116
Neida Mbuia Joao	Telling College Stories	106
Kate Medrano	Is It Used and Abused, or Abused and Used?	33
Kathleen Volk Miller	Let's Not Stay Inside	262

Persuasion

Yih-Chia Lam	Reflection: Halden Prison	62
Kimtee Dahari Ramsagur	The Voiceless	75
Samantha Stein	Against the Adoption of Aramark; For the Upholding of Our Values	125

Poetry

Jesse Antonoff	Overture	94
Valerie Fox	November Nightmare	226
Henry Israeli	Our Age of Anxiety	227
Miriam Kotzin	Bluff Note: Desdemona's Handkerchief	228
	Emily	229
	Tiger Lilies	230
	To a Man From Last Season	231
Nicholas Yurcaba	Cranes on a River Bank	93

Popular Culture

andré m. carrington	Spectacular Intimacies: Texture, Ethnicity, and a Touch of Black Cultural Politics	191
Heather Heim	The Tomatometer	119
Donald Riggs	Building Epic Anticipation: Peter Jackson's Hobbit Videoblogs	245
Scott Warnock	Writing, Technology, and Class Mannequin Challenges	264
Julian Zemach-Lawler	Villains of Our Own Story	41

Profile

Yih-Chia Lam	Reflection: Halden Prison	62
Julian Zemach-Lawler	Villains of Our Own Story	41

First-Year
Writing

First-Year Writing Merit Winners

The following students were nominated for the First-Year Writing Contest.
Congratulations to all!

Colleen Ahern
Benjamin Ahrens
Maria (Joey) Antohi-Craciun
Alyssa Balzano
Tyler Banas
Evelyn Baran
Alaina Barca
James Bradbeer
Ethan Chang
Sara Corson
Bela Delvadia
Will DiNola
Kevin Doughery
Devon Drexel
Carmelo D'Angelo
Jeffrey Forbes
Nancy Gaillard
Anjali Ganguly
Pauline Good
Kaya Gravesande
Christopher Haely
Zayed Haq
Milan Harris
Haley Herron
Jessica Hoban
Madelyn Jacobs
Naseem Jamal
Samantha Johnson
Kristina Jones
Nicholas Kennis
Vriti Khurana
Vriti Khurana
Jerome Kiesewetter III
Sarah Kilborn
Emily Kosten
Jason Kusmierz
Sabah Lala

Marta Lawler
Zoe Levy-Dyer
Alexander Tomasz Ligier
Jacob Manera
Brian McGarry
Sara Meixner
Mariah Menanno
Bianca Mitchell
Daniel Patrick Moton
Jacob Nanzz
Danielle Nester
Jason Ngo
Myranda Oettel
Shikha Patel
Theerea Pearce
Camille Prairie
Corrine Mastrella Presti
Tanner Richardett
Chloe Richardson
Gabriel Sable
Elizabeth Sinclair
Shashwat Singh
Kristin Snodgrass
Mark Sorrentino
Cody Stephen
Patrick Stewart
Luanyue Sun
Fatima Talebi
Amy Tieu
Craig Van Remoortel
Shantal Perez Vasquez
Katy Vieira
Casey Warfel
Ari Weiss
Anna Zachwieja
Anastasia Zafiris

Introduction

As the Director of the First-Year Writing Program, I work with over 60 dedicated instructors who coach, cajole, and mentor some 3,000 incoming students who produce tens of thousands of pages of writing. One of the best parts of my job is working with Sheila Sandapen, our Assistant Director, on the First-Year Writing Contest.

This section of *The 33rd* includes essays written by the winners, runners-up, and honorable mentions from the contest that ran in the academic year 2016-2017. Here is how the essays get from the classroom into this book:

• Students work very hard in their classes to produce lively, engaging writing about themselves and the world around them. Their instructors work hard, too, giving advice and encouragement throughout the writing process.

• Towards the end of the fall term and again in the middle of the spring term, we ask instructors to invite no more than two students from each of their sections to submit their best work to the First-Year Writing Contest. Last year, we got 80 excellent entries.

• With the help of 15-20 faculty members, we go through a two-step judging process. The first group narrowed the 80 essays to 20. Then, a second group ranked the 20 and came up with a winner, a first runner-up, a second runner-up, and seven honorable mentions.

• During the spring term, the winners, runners-up, and honorable mentions are announced at the English Awards Ceremony, along with the winners of various other contests. This ceremony is the "big event" of the yearly Drexel Festival of Writing. And if that were not enough, our winners receive prizes supported by a very generous endowment from the Erika Guenther and Gertrud Daemmrich Memorial Prizes.

• Then, the staff of *The 33rd* steps in to get permissions, to edit, and to create the book you are holding.

So, here is *The 33rd*. Your instructors in the First-Year Writing Program will ask you to read essays that won prizes last year so you can discuss them, debate them, and learn from them.

Are you interested in writing? Will you be in this book next year? On behalf of the First-Year Writing Program, we look forward to reading your work.

Fred Siegel, Ph.D.
Director of the First-Year Writing Program

Evaluating and Solving a Problem - For this assignment, you will research a problematic issue, propose one or more solutions to the problem, and present an argument supporting your solution. One effective way to approach this assignment is to identify a problem in a profession or discipline of interest to you. Another is to deal with a problem local to Drexel, Philadelphia or your hometown, and relevant to your experience there.

- Professor Bob Finegan

Hunter Heidenreich

The Negative Effects of School Choice on Charleston County

Since the 1990s, school choice has played a significant role in reshaping public schools throughout America. The idea is simple; allow families to choose any public school in their district and schools will be encouraged to perform better. The idea is very American. It embodies freedom and echoes the ideas of a free market. Competition leads to better products. However, what school choice lacks is the element of social context. Instead of creating a better system, it mirrors a modern-day form of segregation, particularly in the South where segregation was the worst. As Julian Heilig, an education policy expert at California State University, says, "in a market approach, the market approves winners and losers" (Hawes). And in states like South Carolina, where I attended middle and high school, the losers tended to be those who were nonwhite and poor.

When I moved to Charleston, South Carolina in the 6th grade, I was confronted with a new education system. Previously, I had lived in a district where there was no choice in public schools. Charleston County is not that simple. There are magnet schools, charter schools and public schools. There are schools that focus on the arts and schools that emphasize STEM education. I was zoned for St. Johns High School which was a failing school. When my parents would ask advice on what to do from neighbors, they were always told to seek other options, for even if I did go, I would "be the only white kid there."

Herein lies the problem. In 1954, *Brown v. Board of Education* determined that segregation in schools was not only inherently unequal, it was also unconstitutional. But South Carolina was reluctant to listen, refusing to completely desegregate their schools until 1963 ("Desegregation at Last"). Less than thirty years after that, the idea of school choice came about.

It increased in popularity through the nineties, until the No Child Left Behind Act was passed in 2003, giving Charleston County schools more freedom (Hawes). The law "supports the growth of more independent charter schools" and encourages parents to seek different schools if their student "attends a school that needs improvement" or "is unsafe" ("Choices for Parents"). When that law was passed, parents began seeking new options like Academic Magnet, a high school currently ranked number 8 nationally by US News and World Report ("National Rankings: Best High Schools"). Yet, not all parents can seek other schools. The South Carolina Department of Education states that when seeking a different school, "parents assume the responsibility of providing transportation" ("District School Choice"). With no widespread, public transportation in the county, those who cannot afford the cost find themselves stuck.

All of this results in two major effects. The first is educational stratification. Each year, Charleston releases report cards as a measurement of school performance. The reports from 2016 illustrated that Charleston County has some of the most extreme discrepancies in the education of the rich and the poor within the state. In the tri-county area of Charleston, Dorchester and Berkeley counties, Charleston is home to the 11 wealthiest schools as well as the 20 poorest schools, 15 of which are predominantly black (Pan). This highlights the second issue: white flight. White flight is means that white families decide to relocate based on the influx of minority populations; in reference to education, it refers to the abandonment of a school when the population has more minority than white students (Zhang). Factor in that many studies of school choice have shown that students "were no more likely to graduate, have higher gains in test scores, or have higher credit-accumulation rates" when they used school choice, and these issues start to paint a more sinister picture (Lauen).

I will admit, I opted to attend Academic Magnet, instead of my zoned high school. After two years, I transferred out. The lack of diversity at the school was evident in the ways that students talked. It was not unusual for me to encounter students arguing about who had a bigger house, a better car, or a more expensive vacation planned for break. It was also not uncommon for me to encounter only white students as well. In fact, in 2016 reports showed that the school was "2 percent black in a school district that is 42 percent black" (Kerr). When Academic Magnet's 100% graduation rate is contrasted with North Charleston High, a school with 95% minority students and a 54% graduation rate, the problem begins to stand out ("North Charleston High").

Over the past few years, students in the district have begun to speak out against the educational inequities. Some argue for a lottery system as a fair way of accepting students into charter and magnet schools, as opposed to

private applications (Kerr). I agree that this will solve some selection issues, but it does not address issues like the transportation challenges of low-income district residents. Recently, groups of parents in the district have advocated for a plan that would create a magnet, art, traditional and STEM school in each zone. This would be effective, but is the most expensive option. Similar plans opt for partitioning schools to allow choice within a zone without the drastic effects of changing zones.

I believe that an effective way to fix the current system is to phase out school choice. Diversity educates students in ways that cannot be taught solely through academics. During the time I spent at Academic Magnet, I encountered statements of ignorant bias towards people who were poor, nonwhite, and non-Christian. The environment promoted a belief within the student body that students there were superior to those who were not, and because those who were not were poor or minorities, it promoted a very dangerous thought. I am not saying all the students were like this, but the attitude was widespread, and because of that, I chose to leave. By phasing out choice within the county, schools are created that represent the diverse bodies within each zone. Parents whose children attend schools operating at sub-par levels will devote time and resources to improving those schools, instead of seeing themselves as removed from their communities and different from those who lack the mobility to pursue choice. As in the 60's when South Carolinians opposed desegregation, I anticipate there would be major pushback against decreasing school choice. However, such a policy is critical to achieving a system that is diversified and fair for all, not a system in which education resembles a market where some lose based solely on socioeconomic status or race.

Works Cited

"Choices for Parents." U.S. Department of Education. US Department of Education (ED), 2 Aug. 2013. Web. 25 Jan. 2017.

"Desegregation at Last." South Carolina's Equalization Schools 1951-1960. Rebekah Dobrasko, 2009. Web. 25 Jan. 2017.

"District School Choice." South Carolina Department of Education. South Carolina Department of Education, n.d. Web. 25 Jan. 2017.

Hawes, Jennifer Berry. "Left Behind: The Unintended Consequences of School Choice." The Post and Courier. The Post and Courier, 18 Aug. 2015. Web. 24 Jan. 2017.

Kerr, Amanda. "Academic Magnet Students Want More Diverse School, Urge Board to Take Action." The Post and Courier. The Post and Courier, 22 Feb. 2015. Web. 25 Jan. 2017.

Lauen, Lee Lauen. "Contextual Explanations of School Choice." Sociology of Education 80.3 (2007): 179-209. Web.

"National Rankings: Best High Schools." U.S. News & World Report. U.S. News & World Report, n.d. Web. 25 Jan. 2017.

"North Charleston High." U.S. News & World Report. U.S. News & World Report, 2014. Web. 25 Jan. 2017.

Pan, Deanna. "Education Report Card Data: Charleston County Schools Have Highest and Lowest Rates of Poverty." The Post and Courier. The Post and Courier, 20 Nov. 2016. Web. 25 Jan. 2017.

Zhang, Haifeng (Charlie). "White Flight in the Context of Education: Evidence from South Carolina." Journal of Geography 107.6 (2009): 236-45. Web.

The prompt for the assignment: For Essay #2, you will write an exploratory research paper based on a complex research question of your choice. We will do various exercises to help you narrow your topic and research it effectively. Exploratory research aims to teach you something you don't already know, and it begins with a question to which you do not know the answer. You will start with this type of question, and end with conclusions based on your research. The purpose of the overall essay should be to inform and explore, rather than to persuade. Your essay should make use of significant research, which should be incorporated smoothly and effectively, but it can be creative and should be engaging.

- Professor Elizabeth Thorpe

Hannah Pepper

Can Homosexuality be "Cured"?

Imagine waking up one morning and your parents telling you they hate how your nose looks. Your nose makes them sick, and so they want you to get surgery to make it look more normal. While this may sound insane, in a nutshell, this is what conversion therapy is: taking a trait people are born with and changing it to something more "normal." Conversion therapy is attempting to change a person's sexual orientation in some sort of therapeutic method. In America it is becoming less prominent, but its history can show a lot about what we should and shouldn't do for today's LGBT people. By looking at conversion therapy's history, it can be seen what parts could be helpful for LGBT people, and what parts can cause damage.

Until 1973, the American Psychiatric Association (APA) listed homosexuality on the list of mental disorders. That means that until 1973, only 43 years ago, people could be committed to mental asylums for simply being gay. And sadly, they were. Homosexuals in the 1940s were committed into psychiatric facilities by their families (Scot). These people who were committed told they would be "fixed" and then allowed to go home, but for most of them, that time never came. Many were kept indefinitely and put through daily treatments. These included castration, torture drugs, shock therapy, and lobotomies (Scot). In the 50s and 60s, homosexuals began to receive court-orders that made them receive these treatments (Gunsallas). By the 70s, these practices became less common, but there was still a push to cure homosexuals through "aversion" therapeutic methods, which still included electric shock therapy (Vider).

How effective were these methods? Some claimed to have positive results. In 1962, Dr. Irving Bieber conducted a study of homosexual men over a nine-year period. The resulting data was biased and skewed towards positive outcomes, but ultimately stated that 27% of the men were heterosexual after long-term therapy (Haldeman). It was also reported, however, that only 18% of these men were fully homosexual in the first place (Haldeman). Another study done around the same time period showed that there was basically no change in the behavior of homosexual men after treatment (Haldeman). Other studies done in this time period showed varied results, making determining the effectiveness of these treatments difficult at best. However, most studies seemed to lean towards no effectiveness or very low levels of effectiveness.

Since the removal of homosexuality from the APA's list of mental disorders, licensed therapists have taken a step back in treating homosexuality. In fact, there are more than 20 states that have or are trying to ban conversion therapy for minors. However, this ban only applies to licensed health professionals. In their place, religious organizations, mainly Christian organizations, have come up with their own programs to treat LGBT people. In 1976, right after the removal of homosexuality from the APA's list, Exodus International was founded. This group combined religious counseling, psychotherapy, and aversion therapy and promised a complete cure for homosexuality (Vider). However, in 2013 it shut down, saying their methods were ineffective (Haldeman). The co-founders of Exodus stated that the program was "ineffective... not one person was healed" and that it promoted feelings of guilt and failure that often led to suicidal thoughts in patients (Haldeman). Furthermore, in 1998 the APA acknowledged the risks of conversion therapy as "depression, anxiety, and self-destructive behavior" (Vider). However, there are still many organizations that claim conversion therapy can be highly effective. Brothers Road, previously known as People Can Change, is a group that "supports adult men who voluntarily choose to address their same-sex attractions." On their website they have success stories of men that have gone through their program and report having no more homosexual attractions. This program is also completely voluntary, meaning that no one is enrolled without their consent (Brothers Road).

Unfortunately, not all people who go through conversion therapy have happy success stories. Many lead to tragic endings, leaving damaged people who are insecure and lost. When I was 15, I came out as gay. Well I should say, I was dragged out of the closet. A friend of a friend decided that everyone needed to know my secret, including my religious and conservative parents. They were displeased to say the least when they found out, and immediately tried everything they could to change my mind. It started with them banning me from seeing my girlfriend, then escalated to banning me from seeing anyone who wasn't a part of our church, all the way to mild conversion therapy.

I was sent to my church to meet with "a very nice lady," as they put it. My first meeting was an hour and a half of pure hell. She tried to convince me that my emotions were lying to me, and that I was acting out for attention that I didn't get as a child. And the worst part is, it worked. Immediately after that meeting, I tried to convince myself of all the things she put into my head, and for a short time, it worked. Although I may have believed what she put into my head, it came at a cost. I became depressed and suicidal. For years, I struggled with finding who I really was, and ended up hating myself for not knowing. It wasn't until I fully accepted that I was gay and nothing was going to change that I finally felt like myself again.

Sadly, my story is mild in comparison to some stories of people, adolescents in particular, who go through conversion therapy, willingly or not. Luckily, in recent years, alternative methods have been developed. There are many therapists that are referred to as "ethical therapists" who provide unbiased help for those struggling with gender or sexual identity. These therapists intend to help people through difficult times, and lead them on a path of healthy personal growth. They do not intend to change or influence any type of identity.

So what can we learn from all of this? By looking further into the past of conversion therapy, it seems to be clear that forcing people into conversion therapy showed little or no change in sexual orientation. However, still today there are claims that conversion therapy is effective in willing individuals. But there are also cases, like my own, that lead to depression, suicidal thoughts, and irreversible emotional damage. There may never be an exact correct answer to whether or not conversion therapy is ethically correct or effective. But what has been right about conversion therapy all along is that LGBT people need their own form of therapy, something that will help them specifically. Maybe the past methods of conversion therapy weren't what they needed, but therapists have been make advances to soon hopefully find the perfect therapy for the LGBT community.

References

Brothers Road. Brothers on a Road Less Traveled, 2016, www.brothersroad.org.

"Conversion Therapy." *GoodTherapy.Org*, GoodTherapy, 23 Sept. 2016, www. goodtherapy.org/blog/psychpedia/conversion-therapy.

Gunsallas, Rick L. *Historical Review of Conversion Therapy & Aesthetic Realism.* American Academy of Clinical Sexology, Nov. 2013, www.esextherapy.com/ dissertations/RickGunsallas0HistoricalReview0ConversionTherapyand EstheticRealism.pdf

Haldeman, Douglas C. "The Practice and Ethics of Sexual Orientation Conversion Therapy." *Journal of Consulting and Clinical Psychology*, vol. 62, 2, The American Psychological Association, 1994, pp. 221-227.

Myers, Steven Lee. "Irving Bieber, 80, a Psychoanalyst Who Studied Homosexuality, Dies." *The New York Times*, 28 Aug. 1991. www.nytimes.com/1991/08/28/nyregion/ irving-bieber-80-a-psychoanalyst-who-studied-homosexuality-dies.html.

Scot, Jamie. "Shock the Gay Away: Secrets of Early Gay Aversion Therapy Revealed." *The Huffington Post*, 2 Feb. 2016. www.huffingtonpost.com/jamie-scot/shock-the-gay-away-secrets-of-early-gay-aversion-therapy-revealed_b_3497435.html.

Vider, Stephen. "A Half-Century of Conflict Over Attempts to 'Cure' Gay People." Time, 12 Feb. 2015, http://time.com/3705745/history-therapy-hadden

Our course theme of inference touches many people's' lives in a variety of ways. In this essay, consider the ways in which inference has or may have an impact upon your personal life, your academic life, or your professional future. By way of preparation, review Chapter 22, "Writing as Inquiry" and Chapter 18, "Reflections." Think of this essay not as an end in itself, but as preliminary thinking about your research throughout this term. Your personal reflection should be no longer than 1000 words.

- Professor Donald Riggs

Eunhye Grace Cho

My Synonyms and Antonyms

When I typed the word "bicker" into Google's online thesaurus, I saw synonyms including "argue," "brawl," "quarrel" and antonyms including "agree," "concede," and "concur." The word "cloudy" has the synonyms "opaque," "dull," and "murky" and the antonyms "clear," "bright," and "luminous." Just as each of the thousands of words in the thesaurus has its own set of synonyms and antonyms, as a child I felt as though I had my own set as well. I identified simply as "Asian female" with synonyms including "quiet," "dull," "traditional," and "submissive." My antonyms consisted of "unique," "funny," "interesting," "athletic," "strong," "powerful," "rebellious," "care-free," and many, many more.

Another word: infer. Synonyms include assume, deduce, presume, and guess. These synonyms were the seedlings that brought about the term "Asian female" in my mental thesaurus and its specific set of synonyms and antonyms. My teachers assumed that I would be the quiet, well-behaved student in class that they would never have to worry about. My coaches deduced that I would be the runt of the team. My parents presumed that I would be the perfect, docile daughter they planned on having. And everyone else guessed that I was no different from the next girl with yellow skin.

The small string of inferences people in my life made twisted into a thicker rope of synonyms and Asian stereotypes that tethered and suffocated me throughout my childhood, and I did everything in my power to break free.

As a rebellious third-grader, rather than learning the clarinet at home just as my parents originally planned, I insisted on learning tennis. Somehow, they reluctantly agreed, and once I started playing, I instantly fell in love with the sport. Over the years, I became an increasingly better player, and as my

parents saw my improvement and joy, their reluctance became enthusiasm and support. They sent me to me to camps, private clubs, and hired me private coaches in order for me to continue practicing. Breaking the rope of an Asian female not being athletic was the first of many stereotypes I planned to cut.

At one particular tennis club I practiced at, I was given a new coach. I knew he was notably very tough on his students, but being me and naturally enjoying a good challenge, I was more than excited to learn from him and push my own limits. During our first practice, he tirelessly drilled me with workouts and exercises, and I thought he was pushing me because I was good and he believed I could be even better. But once I made a mistake on my serve, he began to scream furiously about how "chinks can't play." The feeling of suffocation of being tied down by the stereotypes resurfaced. Without saying a word, I picked up a ball, angrily served, and got it perfectly in. I looked at him and walked out.

For quite some time, the root of all my rebellious behavior was simply the desire to rebel against the stereotypes of the "Asian female." However, over time, the rebellion actually helped me to discover my identity; it helped me figure out who I am as an individual, and what I wanted my personal synonyms and antonyms to be. Especially through tennis, I learned to not only defy stereotypes, but become confident in my abilities and character. Over the years, the term "Asian female" has changed into my name, and with that new transformation, the synonyms and antonyms switched. My antonyms are "quiet," "dull," "traditional," and "submissive," and my synonyms include "unique," "funny," "interesting," "athletic," "strong," "powerful," "rebellious," "care-free," and many, many more.

Work Cited

"Bicker thesaurus" Google search. Google. Web. 25 January 2017.

"Cloudy thesaurus" Google search. Google. Web. 25 January 2017.

"Infer thesaurus" Google search. Google. Web. 25 January 2017.

Honorable Mention — First-Year Writing Contest

Your goal is to explore a *specific* area of memory research and present your findings. Ideally, you can make connections between your sources. Don't be afraid to think outside the box. This essay is short so you can investigate one thing very thoroughly.

- Professor Matthew R. Smith

Tamyka George

Memory and Doorways

So why am I in here again? Every day people ask themselves this simple question after entering a room to perform a task, and they have turned up empty handed on the answer. I cannot count the amount of times I have forgotten my purpose after entering a room, and I also cannot count how many times I have gotten frustrated with myself for forgetting said purpose. However, recent studies have found that these memory lapses may not be a sign of a compromised memory but may be linked to the presence of a doorway between your thought and actions. The simple act of entering or exiting through a doorway is to blame for our temporary memory loss.

Psychologists have found that the brain tends to link memory with the rooms in which they occurred, and because of this it is very troublesome to remember things that occurred in different rooms. Statements like these seemed to intrigue psychology professors Daniel Peterson and Zachary Lawrence to further investigate this phenomenon and write their journal entitled "Mentally Walking through Doorways Causes Forgetting: The Location Updating Effect and Imagination." During this investigation Peterson and Lawrence used The Event Horizon model, a theory used to explain these types of data, to show that our forgetfulness is not reliant upon a physical presence of doors. They had participants take part in two experiments, one being that they familiarised themselves with real rooms and then were given pictures to memorize. Peterson and Lawrence instructed them to imagine themselves walking between rooms. Experiment 2 had the participants familiarise themselves with virtual rooms, were given more images to remember and, like before, were instructed to move between these rooms. Results showed that if participants had to leave or enter a room, they were more likely to forget their images than those who were instructed to only move within one specific room. They concluded what is now called the 'location updating effect" which shows that our memory is linked to perceptual information and the simple act of moving from one location to the next causes our brains and the things we record and retrieve to "update" to this new location (Peterson and Lawrence).

Peterson's and Lawrence's theory of location updating effect was one of the basis used for similar research studies done at Notre Dame university by a team of Psychology` professors including Gabriel Radvansky and David Copeland. In their Journal article "Walking through doorways causes forgetting: Situation models and experienced spaces," Radvansky and Copeland investigated people's ability to retrieve information about objects as they moved through virtual spaces. A group of 55 participants were probed with objects that were either associated, (they carried them) or dissociated, (set down in front of them) and instructed to move within virtual regions. Results showed that it was more difficult to remember objects that were dissociated with individuals and furthermore, information about objects were even less accessible when their virtual movements included walking through doorways. In their second study entitled "Walking through Doorways Causes Forgetting: Further Explorations," they went a step further and had their participants re-enact these movements in real spaces. Results show that even though the same distance was placed between the activities that some had to do in the same room and different rooms, people who had to walk through doorways were hugely affected by memory lapses. Radvansky calls this an "event boundary." He explains that "Entering or exiting through a doorway serves as an 'event boundary' in the mind, which separates episodes of activity and files them away." To further test this, they added a third experiment. Radvansky and Copeland had participants return to their original rooms in hopes of retrieving their memories in the setting in which they were formed but found that reinstalling the context did nothing for memory improvement. Recalling the decision or activity that was made in a different room is difficult because it has been compartmentalized. "Once put in the memory's archive, they cannot be called up so easily" (Radvansky). What Radvansky found to be so interesting about these experiments were how little information these subjects had to remember, yet they were totally wiped out by walking through a doorway (Radvansky and Copeland).

An article entitled "Danger lurking in doorways" written by Jim Coyle in the *Toronto Star* helps break down these scientific studies into layman terms. He summaries Radvansky's and Copeland's findings to say that when someone crosses a doorway they forget more than if they had not. He states that our brains at boundaries start to record information to the new location, and compares it to that of a file on a file card on a computer. Because of this when people try to retrieve the old information, the "two storage units compete with one another for retrieval and results in slower and less accurate information." This explains why when people picked up an object from one room to move to another in these experiments their brains linked the objects with two locations making retrieving memory about its whereabouts difficult (Coyle).

The new sights and sounds that come with a new environment also to our memory lapses at these event boundaries. An academic study done at the Cardiff University by Professors Simon Barbury and William Macken found that sounds tend to break through selective attention and impair cognitive performance. They show that although we may try to focus on engaging in mental activities our brains naturally get side-tracked by extraneous noises. The functional character of hearing is that; it has the ability to receive information at all times and the capacity to respond to changes. This capacity to capture attention even when someone is otherwise engaged, may contribute to forgetfulness as when someone crosses an event boundary, their brain is side-tracked by the auditory distractions that this new environment is bombarding them with. This is the same for moving from a quiet room to a loud room and vice versa. They also speak of how irrelevant sounds causes a breakdown in attentional selectivity which means that despite how hard someone tries to concentrate on a memory task, irrelevant noises will intrude (Barbury and Macken).

Professors Nash Unsworth and Matthew Robison at the University of Oregon study the movements of our pupillary and how it correlates to lapses of sustained memory. Our ability to stay focused on task and hold attention may be compromised by our attention systems faltering. Our attention systems falter and causes memory lapses when we are focused on external stimuli or internal thoughts. The professors tracked how individuals are distracted by their environments and how their external environments may contain stimuli that causes fluctuations in attention. This means that while someone entering a room may fully intend to carry out a task, new visuals can be very distracting and may cause their brains attention to shift from their tasks to something new (Unsworth and Robison).

Our brains tend to bundle our memories into packages which may not necessarily by categorized by their content but under specific headings which would be the places in which they occurred. Consequently, in moving from one location to a next, although to perform a singular task, our brains move from the package assigned to one room or environment to the one assigned to our new environment which is the culprit behind memory lapses. After researching this I now know not to be hard on myself and understand that my forgetfulness is not a sign of me having poor memory or even my inability to keep on task but the brain's natural response to doorways. With that, I conclude just as Radvansky did; "doorways are bad avoid them at all cost."

Works Cited

Banbury, Simon P., et al. "Auditory Distraction and Short-Term Memory: Phenomena and Practical Implications." *Human Factors: The Journal of the Human Factors and Ergonomics Society*, vol. 43, no. 1, 2001., pp. 12-29.

Coyle, Jim. "Danger Lurking in Doorways; Memory Falters when we Cross through them, Researcher Finds." *The Toronto Star (Toronto, Ontario)*, Torstar Syndication Services, a division of Toronto Star Newspapers Ltd, Toronto, Ont, 2011.

Lawrence, Zachary, and Daniel Peterson. "Mentally Walking through Doorways Causes Forgetting: The Location Updating Effect and Imagination." *Memory (Hove, England)*, vol. 24, no. 1, 2016., pp. 12.

Radvansky, Gabriel A., and David E. Copeland. "Walking through Doorways Causes Forgetting: Situation Models and Experienced Space." *Memory & Cognition*, vol. 34, no. 5, 2006., pp. 1150-11561.

Radvansky, Gabriel A., Sabine A. Krawietz, and Andrea K. Tamplin. "Walking through Doorways Causes Forgetting: Further Explorations." *Quarterly journal of experimental psychology* (2006), vol. 64, no. 8, 2011., pp. 1632.

Unsworth, Nash, and Matthew K. Robison. "Pupillary Correlates of Lapses of Sustained Attention." *Cognitive, Affective, & Behavioral Neuroscience*, vol. 16, no. 4, 2016., pp. 601-615.

Hannah Arendt wrote: "No human life, not even the life of the hermit in nature's wilderness, is possible without a world which directly and indirectly testifies to the presence of other human beings." To me, as a writer, that "presence of others" means that our ideas about the world, and much of the language we use to talk about them is something we inherit from others. We can't help it, we're social beings. This assignment will stress that, and yes, those "others" will be appearing in your essay in the form of properly documented research. But please, don't call this a "Research Paper." That always brings to mind to me a disinterested collection of information written in the third person. This is still going to be a story driven assignment, it's still going to encourage you to reflect on experience and form opinions, it's just going to use research along the way.

For this assignment you'll write a 5-8 page paper that connects a story to a larger social or political issue. In this case, you don't have to be the main character in the story. The story can focus on a family member or friend, can be set at your school or some other community. In fact, it might be better to think of this as an assignment about something that happened to "US" rather than to "ME," because your goal really is to talk about what this event means to you as a member of a group. As such, it may also be important to defer to the perspectives of others, public records, or newspapers in order to better flesh out your story.Like the first essay too, you'll be including your beliefs, but they'll be beliefs formed in the presence of others. They won't be yours and yours alone.

- Dr. Edward Fristrom

Angelina Gomez

Urban Decay: When Lives are Cut Too Short

It's a familiar sight: a sidewalk littered with roses and candles with the picture of Saint Joseph, the patron Saint of the happy death. Every night, someone would light a new candle when the old one burned out or put a few more roses or stuffed animals out on the sidewalk. In many areas of Philadelphia, especially in Olney, an inner-city neighborhood of Philadelphia, it's customary for people to light candles at the sites where people were murdered. Some nights, there would be gunfire outside, and there have been times when, as I walked home from school, I had to run the opposite way to avoid active shootouts that were happening outside my front door. New memorials popped up on almost every street corner: one for my older cousin's best friend, one for the family who ran the bodega near my grade school, one for my neighbor from around the corner. Still, Olney is in no way Philadelphia's worst neighborhood, but it was tough nonetheless. Almost every week, I would hear that someone was shot or killed, but I never thought it could happen in my family. Gun control never seems like that important of an issue until someone you love is dead.

It was eleven o'clock pm when my mother got the phone call. I remember her screaming my cousin's name and not being able to understand the rest of what she was saying. When we made it to my aunt's house, she and my cousin's girlfriend were screaming.

"They shot Diego!"

At that time, I had little concept of what getting "shot" meant. I had heard gunshots and even seen guns, but I did not understand the difference between being shot with a BB Gun and being shot by an actual firearm. I did not know what to expect upon arrival to the hospital.

There were doctors and nurses running around everywhere. My mother, brother, aunt, and cousin all were waiting in the hallway near the OR for some word on the condition of Diego. After a few hours, the doctors determined there was nothing left that they could do. My family went in to say goodbye, and my younger brother and I sat at the door of one of the elevators. My brother slept, but I remember crying to my mother to convince someone to let me say goodbye to my cousin. The hospital did not allow children under the age of 12 to visit patients. Diego was like an older brother to me, and even though I did not completely understand death, I knew that he was not going to be okay. After waiting on the floor for what seemed like days, while the rest of my family were off talking to some doctors about life support options, I spotted a few doctors rolling a bed from one room to another. That was the last time I saw Diego.

That night, there were roses, teddy bears, and candles with pictures of Saint Joseph on them, planted on my aunt's porch. This was not the first death in my family that I encountered; my grandmother had died just months prior. Yet this death was completely different. My grandmother had suffered with cancer for almost thirty years, and when we learned that the cancer had spread to her brain, we all began preparing for the end. My cousin was only 24 years old, which made it so unexpected. Although he was older than I was, his mind was more like that of a teenager as the result of a drowning accident when he was a young child. He and I grew up together, played together, he even lived with us when I was very young. He was like an older brother. In 2009, he was murdered. He left behind four children, including a son he'd never met because he was born not long after his death. His life was cut short due to gun violence.

No one ever got arrested or charged with his murder. There were no suspects. No one who knew anything about what happened would talk. My cousin was shot at point blank range in the head because some man was jealous that his girlfriend said she liked my cousin. This was over seven years ago, and

to this day, Diego's case remains unsolved because no one wants to "snitch" and give the detectives any information on who my cousin's killer is. There will be no justice for Diego, just as there will be no justice for many of the victims of gun violence. Still, at least one person is murdered each day in our city, many times with a firearm. As reported in "Murder in Philadelphia: No Single Solution," in 2007, by April 11, 108 murders had already been committed in Philadelphia, 80% of which were the result of gun violence. Such high numbers would lead a person to believe that gun control laws would be stricter in such a place where so many people are dying. Yet, according to "How Pennsylvania, New Jersey Gun Laws Compare to Rest of Country," Pennsylvania still has very lax laws on gun control; Pennsylvania has no laws banning large capacity magazines and allows for open carrying of handguns in public, even without a license.

We are often unaware of the number of children who die as a result of gun violence. The article "Preventing Gun Deaths in Children" states that in 2010, 6570 young people (ages 1 to 24) died because of gun related injuries. Gun related injuries caused twice the number of deaths than cancer in people 24 or younger in that year. Too many times we hear of teenagers and children being accidentally shot because they were outside playing, or young men being mistaken for gang members and being killed just because they were in the wrong place at the wrong time.

Gun violence plagues Philadelphia. There are so many people in our city dying; I cannot understand why no one has brought about change. There have been no great reforms to help stop the deaths of so many young people. The most I've seen as late was a huge mural dedicated to the victims, but a mural isn't enough. There is a Philadelphia Gun Violence Task Force, but according to the article, "Officials Decry Cuts in Gun-Crimes Task Force," its budget was cut from 5 million dollars to 2 million dollars in 2010, even though the number of homicides in the city was still high. Each day we hear of the violence, whether it be on the news or in the Drexel Alert texts warning us to stay off certain streets because of shootings. With the outcome of this past election, I with many others cannot help but fear the situation getting worse. A study done by JAMA Internal Medicine, which was referenced in the article "Preventing Gun Deaths in Children," states with stricter gun laws have lower rates of gun related deaths, yet those who are about to become the leaders in our country believe in relaxing our gun laws even more.

It appears that this problem with gun violence in urban areas is being ignored. People are dying, adults and children alike, yet there is no change. Until our lawmakers decided to put the safety of our people first, I only see more innocent people dying. Just this past summer, three boys ages 14, 15, and 16 were shot on the way back from a basketball game. The 15-year-old

was fatally injured. The 15-year-old was my younger cousin, Joshua. Just like that, my family lost another member. My brother who was with me when Diego passed away is now 16 years old and I worry about him every day because at any moment, he could be at the wrong place at the wrong time, just as both my cousins were. I can't help but ask myself, "How many more young people must die before someone makes a change? How many more of my family members will be killed?"

*names have been changed

Works Cited

Babay, Emily. "How Pennsylvania, New Jersey Gun Laws Compare to Rest of Country." *Tribune Business News*, Washington, 2013.

Clark, Vernon. "Officials Decry Cuts in Gun-crimes Task Force." *Philadelphia Inquirer*, 24 Mar. 2010.

Currie, Donya. "State Gun Laws Linked to Lower Death Rates." *The Nation's Health*, vol. 43, no. 4, 2013, p. 22.

"Murder in Philadelphia: No Single Solution." Editorial. *Philadelphia Inquirer*, 11 Apr. 2007.

Jacobson, Joy. "A Cure for Gun Violence." American Journal of Nursing, vol. 115, no. 4, 2015, pp. 19-20.

Palfrey, Judith S., M.D., and Sean Palfrey M.D. "Preventing Gun Deaths in Children." *The New England Journal of Medicine*, vol. 368, no. 5, 2013, pp. 401-403.

Write about something that gives you a reason to write. What your writing will look like: You shall discover an organization that suits both your purpose for writing and the content of what you write.

- Professor Jan Armon

Joshua Jager

The Tinker

FADE IN:

INT. DIMLY LIT ROOM - CONTINUOUS

A small room, there is one window, slightly open, with the curtains tightly drawn.
It's dark outside.
A small wind moves them.
On the floor are various electronics and mechanical parts.
Abandoned.
Tossed aside and useless.

A large file cabinet against the wall with several drawers pulled open and papers lying on the ground around it.

More robotic pieces, wires, humming electronics.
Against the far wall is a

DESK — VIEW FROM BACK

The back of an old man, TINKER, sitting at the desk.
Hunched over a project.
Several lamps focus on the table as TINKER works

A trash on the floor can overflowing with more drawings and blueprints.
On the wall in front of him are many large papers.
They are covered in more blueprints and drawings.

DESK - FULL VIEW

The desk is littered with small electronics, wires, tools.

Held in TINKER's hand is his project, a small ROBOT.
Eyes lightless, lifeless.
Cute.
He finishes a few final touches to it.
Admires his work.

As he sits back, he catches sight of a

FRAMED PHOTO

sitting on the desk.
A younger TINKER next his son.
The latter proudly sporting a military uniform.

A small tear forms in TINKER's eye.
He blinks it away.
Sighs.

EXT. DESK

TINKER holds the robot softly.
Moves his hand over the delicate workmanship.
Gently places the ROBOT back on the desk, and opens a small door in its back.

He hooks several wires into ROBOT's back.
Careful...

Finished, TINKER hefts a large battery onto the desk.
A large switch on top, a red light on the side.
He connects the wires from ROBOT into it.

TINKER looks between his creation and the battery, and then reaches toward the switch.

Ready...
Grits his teeth.
Flips the switch.

THE RED LIGHT

Turns green.
On the table, ROBOT twitches slightly.
Its eyes flicker...
then go dark.
The battery light turns red again.

Disappointed, TINKER sighs.
Another crumpled blueprint is tossed into the overflowing trash can.

TINKER picks up his cup of tea and rises from the desk.
Takes one final look at ROBOT.
He exits through the door.
Leaving it open just a crack.

INT. ROOM WINDOW - CONTINUOUS

A small gust moves the curtains.
A larger gust blows them inward.

A small zap comes from the desk.

A spark comes from ROBOT.
Then another.

A light glows from inside ROBOT.
His eyes open.
ROBOT sits up.
Looks around the room.
Looks down at...
Hands?

He gets to his feet.

ROBOT begins to walk forward to explore.
...and is pulled onto his back by the battery connectors.

ROBOT sits up and struggles with the wires.
Disconnecting them...
Whew, free at last.

CUTS OF ROBOT INTERACTING WITH THE DESK

-ROBOT picks up a pencil.
 Tries to swing it like a sword.
 But he falls on his bottom.

-ROBOT finds a small flashlight.
He pushes the button to turn it on
...And immediately turns it off, it is very bright.
ROBOT doesn't care for the flashlight.

-ROBOT finds a drill, stuck into the desk.
Gets on it and turns it on.
It spins him fast.
He is very dizzy

Stumbling away, ROBOT bumps into a box full of screws, spilling them everywhere.
He accidentally steps on one.
Rolling and sliding across them until he is at the edge of the desk.

ROBOT teeters on the edge.
Can't get his balance.
The framed photo is nearby, ROBOT grabs at it.
He and the photo topple off the desk.

EXT. DIMLY LIT ROOM. - VIEW ON DOOR

TINKER is sitting in a chair, reading.
A loud crash comes from the room.

What was that?

TINKER quickly sits up and shambles towards the door.

INT. DIMLY LIT ROOM

The door opens slowly.
Reveals...

...a broken ROBOT, in pieces on the ground.
Next to him is the photo, its frame shattered.

TINKER gasps.

Rushes up.
He looks from the desktop to broken ROBOT

...how?
TINKER quickly gathers up ROBOT's broken pieces, and places them on the desk.
He hurriedly screws parts together, making repairs. Finished, TINKER places the battery connectors with shaking hands.
Quick breath.
Flip the switch.

BATTERY

A small fizzle...
...The light remains red

DESK

TINKER's face begins to show uncertainty.
Flip the switch again.
Frustration, desperation.
He continues flipping the switch, more quickly.
Still the light is red.

Unable to take the strain being put on it, the battery emits a loud *POP*
Smoke rises from it.

TINKER, defeated, places his face on his hands.
Sitting silently for a moment.

He looks toward still lifeless as ever ROBOT.
Grunts angrily.
Dashes tools and stray parts from the desk.

Calm again, TINKER picks up ROBOT.
Looks into its unlit eyes.

Lifeless.

He sighs, and drops ROBOT into the trash can.
ROBOT is buried underneath the many blueprints and papers.

TINKER turns off the desk lights.
He picks up the photo.
Brushing away the broken glass.

He slowly walks toward the door.
Begins to walk out.
CLOSE ON TRASH CAN

TINKER's shadow falls over the trash can as he leaves.
He closes the door until only a sliver of light is left. Just before the door is fully closed...

ZAP

A light flickers and begins to emanate from the trash...

THE END

First, review the chapters "Writing as Inquiry" and "Reflections." Then, focus in on a specific idea that emerged for you this term. Write a reflective essay that uses some of the strategies from both chapters. Then, either as part of your reflection or as an appendix, list at least three sources you have found that might enhance your thinking about the idea that you have identified.

- Professor Donald Riggs

Shelby Jain

A Competitive Life

Since 1923, the six high schools in my school district have used a ranking system that leads to the naming of a valedictorian and a salutatorian. But after much deliberation among the school board, they have decided to rid the district of the decile ranking system, removing the disastrous number that is seen as ultimately indicating a student's worth.

4.0000, 3.9999, 3.9998. These were the three top GPAs of the graduating students in my high school class. The twelve GPAs that followed differed by the same amount of .0001. It is easy to think that this high school produces the brightest and most intelligent students, especially since almost all of them have near perfect GPAs. While the students were intelligent, these numbers do not show what the students had to go through in order to achieve their ultimate success.

In eighth grade, I applied to a specialized magnet high school for students who were interested in pursuing a career in medicine. I was under the impression that I would be surrounded by students who had the same goals and aspirations as me, and that we would work in a collaborative environment where we would learn the advanced course content, but at the same time help each other throughout the program to eventually succeed. As it turns out, this was not the case. Students were cold and competitive. They did not help when you had questions. They kept their notes and studying materials private. And the most shocking realization was that students would compromise their moral integrity and cheat on exams to make sure they were receiving a better grade than anyone else. It did not matter if you knew the subject material as long as the answer was right and full credit was being received for it.

School was supposed to be a place of learning, where students could cooperate with one another and help each other grow as individuals. So why were students attending an institution meant for education, when all

they cared about was the grade they were receiving, as opposed to actually comprehending the subject matter?

I learned in my developmental psychology class this year that there are two different motivational approaches that individuals may adopt when they are children and use to accomplish goals in school and otherwise. The first is mastery motivation. Those who adopt mastery goals view abilities and talents as changeable qualities which can be improved with hard work. These individuals have a growth mindset and thus are motivated to put forth the effort to learn and increase their competence or knowledge. Failure motivates the individual to perform better. The second approach is performance motivation. Those who adopt performance goals try to prove their ability in order to appear smart. These individuals have a fixed mindset, meaning they believe they either have an ability or they do not. There is no concept of improvement. The individual is concerned with monitoring his or her performance in comparison to others in order to outperform them and increase their own status. Failure in subject matter leads to anxiety and shame because individuals are discouraged by their outcomes and believe they are "dumb" (Sigelman and Rider, 311). The latter approach is what I have noticed in myself and my peers and in all of the other students I know who attend competitive magnet programs.

The constant need to outperform others in school has created an incredibly stressful learning environment, which is leading to a higher degree of mental health issues for students. While it is difficult to admit, I experienced a large number of panic attacks during my junior and senior years and found myself visiting the guidance office multiple times a month. It is these high levels of chronic stress that are impeding academic abilities and compromising mental health functioning, which can lead to risky behavior such as substance abuse. A study done by Noelle Leonard and her team of NYU researchers conducted an exploratory study to assess the mental health symptoms of students who attend high-pressure high schools. A quantitative survey was administered. Results showed that fifty percent of the students experienced a lot of stress on a daily basis. Factors that contributed to stress were grades, homework, and preparation for college (Leonard et al. 1028).

Students are experiencing a greater degree of anxiety and stress. Levels of depression and suicide rates are increasing. And all for what? Because we are told from the very beginning that everything we do now will affect what will happen to us in the future. The grades we get now will dictate what colleges we will get into. The colleges we graduate from dictate what type of job we will receive. And the job we receive will dictate the type of life we will live. This was the ultimate mentality that was imprinted in every student's mind in my high school and is probably seen all across the country. The thought of attending the most prestigious colleges ran in every student's mind, and thus it heavily impacted the way we all interacted with one another.

A study done that tested cooperative versus competitive efforts in problem solving found that in four different types of problem-solving categories--which included linguistic, nonlinguistic, well defined, and ill defined--members of cooperative teams outperformed individuals who were competing with each other. In fact, these results held for individuals of all age groups. Those who worked in cooperative teams were also found to have performed better academically as individuals. If multiple studies have shown similar results, why have magnet schools not promoted a more collaborative learning environment?

While I understand that competition on a small scale is healthy for students, the degree of competition experienced by students today, in my opinion, is unnecessary and ridiculous. When I was in twelfth grade, the students in my class were preparing for the college application process. This was a time when everyone became extremely sensitive to those around them, as this was a time we were all competing to get into the same top ranked schools. In the beginning of the year, I had found out that my rank had dropped from 10 to 11, and I was visibly upset for weeks because I was no longer in the top ten of my class. It was not until the end of the year that I realized that minute differences in my rank number and grades in comparison to my peers did not make a significant difference. Students who had lower ranks than me were accepted into Ivy League schools. People who were ranked higher than me, did not get into some of the schools that I was accepted to. While my grades were essential, it was not as important as what I offered as an individual, what extracurricular activities I was involved in, or how I wrote my essays. I spent four years worrying about the number instead of actually learning in school. But once again, I only realized this at graduation. So while my school has decided to remove its decile ranking system, will the idea of being "number one" ever go away?

Works Cited

Leonard, Noelle R., Marya V. Gwadz, Amanda Ritchie, Jessica L. Linick, Charles M. Cleland, Luther Elliott, and Michele Grethel. "A Multi-method Exploratory Study of Stress, Coping, and Substance Use among High School Youth in Private Schools." *Frontiers in Psychology* 6 (2015): 1028. Web. <http://journal.frontiersin.org/article/10.3389/fpsyg.2015.01028>.

Qin, Zhining, David W. Johnson, and Roger T. Johnson. "Cooperative versus Competitive Efforts and Problem Solving." *Review of Educational Research* 65.2 (1995): 129. Web.

Sigelman, Carol K., and Elizabeth A. Rider. *Study Guide: Life-span Human Development.* Belmont, CA: Wadsworth, Cengage Learning, 2012. Print.

What is a question that you want to explore about yourself? Is there something that you'd like to know more about in your life? Perhaps you were adopted and want to research that topic as it relates to you, or maybe you are an artist and want to explore what tends to "make" an artist. The sky is the limit. Guidelines: Include yourself. Remember that YOU are at the center of this research; make sure your audience knows this. Address our class; your audience is the 19 people who have been talking together each week. You know us; write to us. Include at least 3 secondary sources, one of which must be scholarly.

- Dr. Karen Nulton

Kate Medrano

Is It Used and Abused, or Abused and Used?

What do you do when the monster with the capability to make your whole world crumble lives inside of you? It's waiting there, compelling you to give into it, much like how the serpent tempted Eve. What are you supposed to do when your arch nemesis is your own nature? All throughout my life, I have struggled with attempting to silence the monster inside called addiction.

Addiction runs stronger in my family than cancer, heart failure, or any other physical impairment. My father suffered the worst in our little family of four, but if you follow the family tree up to the very top on either parental side, you'll see broken branches and fallen leaves from where addiction has reared its ugly head. Although my mother and sister were skipped over by the toxic addiction gene, I can feel its ominous presence in my bones with every move I make. I try to hold myself back from anything that is slightly addicting, but I always feel an aching desire when I'm around alcohol, certain substances, food, sex, or anything that has previously made my body or mind say, "Oooh I like this." I fight my ultimate antagonist with all I have because I watched my father's life get torn apart by his addiction, and I never want that to happen to me. My father's addiction broke our family for a long period of time, and in some ways, it'll never be the same again. I had to painfully watch as addiction ripped my parents' marriage apart, and I personally suffered the excruciating pain of not being able to look a parent in the eye without bursting into tears or an outburst of anger. Seeing what giving into addiction could do to a person and those around him or her made me swear to myself that I'd never fully give into that awful monster. I promised myself that I would never hurt my future family like my father hurt ours. I never want my children to have to know what it is like to live with an out of control addict. Therefore, I made the decision to dive headfirst into research on the science and biology behind addiction as to

sleuth out a way to protect my future family and self from falling victim to the horrifying addiction-monster.

For too long, I was under the false impression that a person only becomes an addict because he or she is weak-minded. When I began my research, I discovered that this was not in fact true. A counselor at the rehab center my dad stayed at for a couple months once told me that addiction is half due to a poor state of mind and half due to a genetic and biological predisposition to addiction. At first, I swore she was just making excuses for my father's weakness. It sounded ridiculous to me that a person's biology could be what was hurting them, but further research into the biological world of addiction proved to me that what this counselor told me was actually the truth. When I did a little digging, I found an article written by Dr. Steven M. Melemis, an addiction specialist, that confirmed what the counselor tried to explain to me. In fact, Dr. Melemis began his article with that very fact in bold lettering. Dr. Melemis informed his readers about the reality behind addiction, and he explained how everyone has a predisposition for addiction because "there is an evolutionary advantage to that" (Melemis). This statement completely contradicts what I previously believed about addiction since it defines addiction as a gene all humans have, meaning that whether or not a person is weak-minded isn't the only factor at play if he or she is an addict. After reading Dr. Melemis's article on how the addicted person's stability is not the only reason for his/her addiction, I began to hypothesize on how biology as a whole is intertwined with addiction.

In general, I have always known that addiction is deeply rooted in the brain, yet I never truly knew how much. I knew addictive substances made the brain think it needs that fix, but I still couldn't grasp why people were still addicted even though the actual act of giving into the addiction was no longer a pleasurable feeling. With some research, I discovered that the chemicals being released in my brain while giving into one of my addictions are what the brain is actually craving, not the euphoric effect of the addictive act (Hyman and Malenka). This basically means that the brain thinks that activities such as drinking, doing drugs, or having sex are what it needs to function. After a period of time, the addiction to these initially pleasurable acts becomes deeply rooted in the brain's chemical composition, so when the addictive act is performed in the beginning, the brain releases neural substances, such as dopamine, that then partner with the pleasurable effect of the act (Hyman and Malenka). These substrates are what are tricking the brain into thinking that the addictive acts are a great idea, so the brain is inclined to make the release of such chemicals happen again. The brain registers the feeling from the chemical releases in the same way that it registers the chemical release while fulfilling other natural needs, like eating, so this feeling, unfortunately, gets locked into the long-term memory (Hyman and Malenka). I had always

wondered how it was possible that my father so easily relapsed after over twenty years of sobriety, and this bit of information explains just that. I thought that learning about how addiction occurs in the brain and how addiction isn't totally caused by a weak state of mind would ease my worries about my future with addiction, but if anything, this new information has only made me more anxious about what addiction could do to me. Therefore, I made a plan for myself.

I need to be ready. I know it's coming, and there's no way to avoid it. Addiction is like a train barreling down at me as I'm trying to fruitlessly untie myself from the cold, hard tracks. It'll be easier to escape if I have easy access to the knot in the ropes binding me down, so I need to leave myself access to it before I get tied down. The way to do this will be to devise a plan so I will always have an escape route available for when I get trapped by my own mind. When I arrive at the dark abyss where my family members have been infamously lost before, I know I'll first have to realize that I've landed in this abyss.

Initially, I will be frozen by my addiction. I won't be able to budge from my damaged state of mind, as if my brain was frozen solid in my point of view. I won't be able to see the affects of my actions on others or myself, and I won't be able to stop myself from recklessly going after what I want. I watched as this happened to my father when he relapsed, and I watched as he groped to find himself in the pitch black darkness. From watching him deteriorate right in front of my eyes, and having gotten caught up in addiction before myself, I have tried to memorize exactly what it feels like when I have fallen down the rabbit hole. After watching my father's mistakes and feeling the horrible pain of watching a loved one flail first-hand, I have devised a mock dialectical behavior therapy (DBT) method for myself as a last saving grace.

Within typical dialectical behavior therapy, the patient is typically someone who needs help coping with various mental illnesses, especially addiction. DBT is a beneficial format to follow because this kind of therapy aims to help build a patient's confidence and teach him/her a range of coping methods that will allow him/her to handle stressful situations, plus they even teach strategies to encourage healthy coping skills for when times get tough (Smith). These strategies include directing patients on how to seek out environments and peer groups that discourage giving into addictions; encouraging patients to remove addiction triggers from their lives, such as unhealthy relationships or a detrimental environment; and upping the patient's self-esteem and confidence to encourage sobriety during hard times (Smith). The way DBT is crafted to teach the patient how to cope with the core problem at hand instead of just teaching he/she drugs are "bad bad bad" is the greatest benefactor of this therapy method for me. My greatest problems with

addiction have always arose whenever I underwent a wave of depression, so my addiction problem evolves from a completely separate issue. DBT targets that separate issue and teaches me how to manage it so that the problem is cut off at the source. Researching DBT showed me that my problem could be solved by looking within myself to heal my real wound, as opposed to just laying down a couple of bandaids on the surface of a superficial scar. As with all styles of therapy, I had to adjust the DBT plan of action according to my personal needs.

In order to figure out what my core problem is, I have had to dig deep into my own mind to discover what were my "triggers" for addiction. Immediately, I found that my addictive personality wasn't an issue until some outside factor triggered a wave of depression in me. Although depression doesn't stick out quite like a sore thumb in my family tree like addiction, depression is another mental illness that plagues my genes. Both of my parents, my mother's mother, and my father's mother all suffered from depression at some point in their lives. As for myself, I have struggled with severe depression and suicidal thoughts since my early middle school days. This constant battle within me was what first weakened me to addiction. Scanning through my memories, one in particular screamed out to me as a sign that my depression was the link to my problems with addiction.

In order to understand this memory, a little background knowledge on my past is needed. When I was in elementary school, I was bullied by nearly all of the other children in my class. The girls I thought were my friends were actually using me for my big house, wide yard, and quick, easy access to our town's lake. They were more interested in the material objects my parents could provide to them than any of the friendship I could ever offer up. I would always invite every last girl to my parties and, in school, they would all kiss up to me, but whenever one of their birthdays would come around or there was a special event that they were hosting a party for, I would never get invited. In fact, the girls would hide it from me that there was even a party at all. I felt alone and like I wasn't good enough for anyone or even worthy of having friends at all. These nasty little girls conned me into believing that I was the problem. My parents hated how I was treated by my "friends, and one day when my mother found out that one of the girls had purposely not invited me to her party, she called the girl's mother. My mom tried to convince the mother to tell her daughter to let me come, but the mother just replied that the girls didn't like having me around because I was "weird" and told "weird girl" jokes. My mother never leaked a word of this to me until many years later for fear that this bit of information would crush me. However, she never had to tell me: eventually, the other children in my class came to openly mocking me during recess and on the bus, saying that I was an "ugly, fat weirdo." I even remember one boy telling me that my parents should take me back to the hospital I came

from to get their money back. Unfortunately, I was stuck with these people all throughout middle school, as well. I hoped that when we transitioned into middle school, maybe my situation would get better, but if anything, it just got worse. Now that we were "big kids," other children felt cooler, which just made me even weirder. Constant humiliation and vicious verbal abuse from my fellow classmates permanently warped my mind and perception of myself, and my young, impressionable age didn't help.

I carried this weight with me throughout middle school, into high school, and I even carry it with me now in my early days of college. After all of this abuse, all that was left of me for what felt like an interminable length of time was a shredded, hastily taped together version of the girl I should have grown up to become. I have struggled with depression since around seventh grade, and during the worst of times, I would become suicidal. Farther down the road, specifically during my last few years of high school, these dark times would pair with my addictive personality to invoke even more chaos in my life. As I got older, I discovered the alluring euphoria I could attain through drinking, and then later I discovered the indescribable thrill I got through sex. Whenever I became depressed, I would become addicted to these two highs, and as my depression would progress, I would lose all respect for myself and my body. These times of depression and addiction are almost exclusively jump-started by situations that remind me of my childhood trauma. The memory where the connection between my depression and addiction is most prominent is exactly this kind of situation.

Two years ago, on New Year's Eve, I had plans to go to a party at my close friend's house. For privacy reasons, we're going to call this friend Jane. I had just begun letting my guard down when it came to social situations, so I allowed myself to get excited. At around six, Jane texted me to tell me she wasn't having a party anymore. She gave me an excuse about her mom wanting just the family around that night, so although I was disappointed I didn't blame her. I started texting our other friends to see if anyone else was doing anything that night, but everyone said they were either with family or at an event that was special, exclusive, and planned far in advance. However, as the clock grew closer to midnight, I started seeing videos and pictures all over social media, such as Instagram and Snapchat, of my friends partying and having fun. Many of these pictures and videos seemed to have been taken in the same place, so I texted a couple of the girls to ask what was going on. All of their replies were essentially the same: apparently they were all just at a really fun family party! Where there were drinking games... and loud music... and lots of teenagers. I immediately knew they were all lying to me, but I couldn't understand why. I texted Jane to see how her night was going, but after she took an hour to reply, she then replied with a brief statement without her usual flair of personality. It wasn't long before I saw her post pictures with two of

her other friends celebrating the New Year. Upon seeing these pictures, I felt that all too familiar feeling of isolation and darkness creep into my heart, weighing it down like an iron anchor in water. I didn't have the strength to text her for an explanation because it felt like cement had begun flowing through my veins, turning me into an empty, stone-cold shell of a person. Disturbed thoughts swarmed by mind, and I heard my friends' voices in my head telling me that I was worthless and that I deserved to be abandoned. I could feel the hot sting of tears behind my eyes and the hollow pressure in my chest from a rising sob. Instantly, my urgent desire to banish all of these feelings arose like a vampire in the night, ready to suck all the life out of me. An aching heart and a twisted mind held up no defensive line at all against my rising need for my favorite addictions. Although I felt like I didn't even have the strength to lift up my phone to text my "friend," I rose automatically and swiftly to act on these irresistible urges, like my addiction was a puppetmaster manipulating my strings. I stole alcohol from my mother, brought it all up to my room, and then proceeded to lock the door and gulp down drink after drink. Before I knew it, the outlines of my vision were blurred and I couldn't sit upright. Yet my pain was still there, like a sharp blade through the center of my soul. That night I did what 2.2 million out of 8.3 million suicidally depressed people do: I wrote out a plan for how to end my own life (Pappas). That night, I became a statistic.

This is the darkest moment in my time with depression. The night I created that first entry in a journal, which came to be where I wrote down all of my most wretched thoughts and feelings, I gave into my urges of addiction. I was forced to pay the price for this decision in the following weeks. Every time I saw any of my friends after New Years, I would feel an irresistible need to give into one of my worst addictions. For about a week, whenever those feelings I was overwhelmed with on that night crept into my mind again, I would go home after that school day to either takes sips out of the large bottle of lemonade and vodka I stashed in my closet, or go recklessly hookup with a guy I barely cared about. Since my school work load was practically nonexistent due to just coming off the holiday break, and since my family was too busy with the new year to notice their daughter drowning in her depression, I had nothing and no one stopping me from destroying myself through my addiction.

To this day, I am unsure what it was exactly that saved me from myself. I don't know if it was me finally looking at myself in the mirror and not liking the girl staring back at me, if it was almost getting caught stealing the alcohol, or the need to behave normally again because of an increased workload; but I remember that one day I finally threw out the bottle and took a defiant step back from hooking up. I put myself back together not because I was told to do so by someone who loved me, but because I thought about all that was important to me, and somehow I was able to muster up the strength to help

myself. I decided I wanted to love myself, and once I made that decision, I knew I could get out of the hole I dug then threw myself into.

Depression is my core issue here, not addiction. Therefore, my plan of action against future addiction will be to attend to the broken mess left by depression in order to properly heal from the inside-out. The purpose of using a DBT-like approach will be to give myself an option other than to be strapped down on the train tracks with the addiction train barreling down at me. I won't be able to know exactly what coping mechanisms I will need when I get to that dark, scary place, but I do know that what has gotten me through the worst of times before, and what raised my father from his own perdition, was love. For my father, what he needed the most was the love from my sister and me, as his family, to let him know that he wasn't alone in this scary world. However, for me, the love I needed was my own. My childhood trauma left me feeling like I was worth less than discarded gum on the sidewalk, and like no one could ever love me. I hated myself, so I disrespected my body and soul because of it. I was able to recover from that terrible New Year's Eve because I made the choice to love and take care of myself instead of letting the monsters in my head convince me I shouldn't get to have any love in my life. Love for myself is what I need the most in my times of sorrow. While the love and support of others would only help me during my trials, the hole I try filling with alcohol or sex was left there by my own self-loathing, so the only thing that can fully fill that hole is love for myself and a reminder to myself that I am, in fact, worthy of love and joy. This can't be found at the bottom of a bottle or attached to some guy that seems irrelevant to me, and I need to remember this. My DBT will be a devised method where I remember that I need to love myself through all of my struggles. My escape route will be to let myself love who I am, for all of what have been through and have become. As long as I can remember this when I need it most, I will be okay.

Overall, I now know more about what is going on between my ears, I am able to make a plan that will prepare me against the alluring qualities of addiction. I have learned from my father's experiences, taken into account the advice of others on the subject matter, and studied my own past experiences, so I know I am ready to apply what I have learned to my own life. I pray to whoever's up there that my children will never have to see me struggle with the addiction that caused my father to falter, but at least now I have hope that even if I do fall down the long, windy path of depressed addiction, I will be able to get myself out of there.

Works Cited

Hyman and Malenka. "Addiction and the Brain: The Neurobiology of Compulsion and Its Persistence". *Nature Reviews Neuroscience*, vol. 2, no. 10, 2001, pp. 695-703, http://www.nature.com/nrn/journal/v2/n10/full/nrn1001-695a.html?cookies=accepted. Accessed 27 Oct 2016.

Melemis, Steven M. "The Genetics of Addiction". Understand Addiction, Addictions and Recovery.org, 20 May 2016, http://www.addictionsandrecovery.org/is-addiction-a-disease.htm, Accessed 27 Oct 2016.

Pappas, Stephanie. "Suicide: Statistics, Warning Signs and Prevention". Health, LiveScience.com, 16 March 2015, http://www.livescience.com/44615-suicide-help.html, Accessed 14 Nov 2016.

Smith, Kayla. "Understanding Dialectical Behavior Therapy (DBT)". Dialectical Behavior Therapy, AddictionCenter.com, 22 Jan 2016, https://www.addictioncenter.com/treatment/dialectical-behavior-therapy/, Accessed 7 Nov 2016

[In your map or profile], you will develop, research, and analyze a topic related to your previous essay or posts with input from primary as well as secondary (scholarly and popular press) sources... **Exploratory research aims to teach you something you don't already know, and it often begins with a question to which you do not know the answer.** Though you may have an idea, or hypothesis, about what sources will reveal to you, you aren't completely sure of your goal until you've read, analyzed, and synthesized the data you collect.Writing in this process acts not just to record what you already think, but as a tool of inquiry that helps you to determine what you really think.

- Dr. Deirdre McMahon

Julian Zemach-Lawler

Villains of Our Own Story

In Hip-Hop there are undisputed moguls. Artists such as 2pac, The Notorious B.I.G., N.W.A., and Nas all hold a spot in the metaphorical pantheon of rap for their success in the industry. However in terms of innovation, Kanye West's influence is indisputably unrivaled.

It is December 14th, 2012 and West is performing live at The HP Pavilion in San Jose.[1] The stadium is pitch black as the iconic minimalist piano melody plays to his track Runaway. A section of the stage, the one West is standing upon, rises out of the ground and stands alone as a red glowing cube. West is on an island, both physically and metaphorically throughout the dramatic rising and falling of the song. On the track, West deconstructs the rap clichéd facades of money, sex, and power, and reveals the grotesque reality of his fame. Seven minutes and thirty seconds in to the nearly eleven minute song West ad-libs, singing out, "The one place I f***** up, I thought I thought I thought I thought you'd always be mine... If I ever said I didn't love you I was lying, I swear to God I was lying". The regret, and wistfulness practically ooze out of the lines as West stands on his island of a stage, entrapped in a musical fight to the death between himself and his torments, with an audience egging on the downfall. And that is exactly what one of Kanye's greatest innovative leaps has been — **his creation of tragic rap.**

---

[1] channel, SonicAmbulanceTV's. "Kanye West - Runaway/heartless (live at the HP Pavilion in San Jose) (12/14/12).

When West claims to be "Shakespeare in the flesh"[2] the tabloids go wild, but there is a profound truth within what he is saying. Just as Shakespearean tragedies such as *Macbeth* and *Romeo and Juliet* tug at the strings of the audiences' hearts, West's music is able to do the same. Both *Runaway* and *Romeo and Juliet* play on the tragic theme of mistimed love and the destruction it causes, and in doing so create the potential for the cathartic experience that is unique to Kanye West's brand of Hip-Hop sound.

Perhaps before delving too deeply into the ways in which West changed the sound of hip hop it is necessary to discuss what hip hop sounded like before West. I sat down, and over the course of three days listened to a sampling of pre-Kanye hip-hop artists, as well as all of West's albums start to finish. Rappers such as Snoop Dogg, Dr. Dre, and Ice Cube arguably made up the "Golden Age" of hip hop. Their beats were simple. They usually consisted of a loose bass drum beat that held a single consistent pace. The rappers delivered their lyrics in a monotone inflection with a predictable pace. There were many references to violence such as N.W.A.'s lyric from the song *F*** tha Police*, "young nigga on a warpath, and when I finish it's gonna be a bloodbath."[3] Additionally, there was a competition across the industry for the status of alpha male, which led to a very specific central message. According to Matthew Oware, "Many rappers construct a black male subjectivity that incorporates the notion that masculinity means exhibiting extreme toughness, invulnerability, violence and domination".[4] Oware's claim perfectly describes the general message and tone of the most successful rap artists of the time and their music in the industry—as famous rappers, we are invincible.

Compared to his predecessors, Kanye West's music feels very dense. It is packed with intricate drum beats, layers of synthesizers, extensive sampling, a wide variety of paces, rhythms, and orchestral and symphonic elements.[5] It incorporates an emotional spectrum that West glides across while delivering his lyrics. Kanye West created a new genre in effect. One that employs sounds of the likes of Bon Iver. It is a niche section that is built on depressed, dark, self loathing soundscapes, woven with distorted samples, and muted autotune lyrics. For Bon Iver's Justin Vernon, one of Kanye's more unique collaborators, this sound is characterized best by songwriter Bruce Hornsby who describes Vernon as, "a soul singer who creates these unique and beautiful sonic landscapes on which to perform."[6] For Kanye, it is his monopolized empire of sound in the hip hop market.

---

[2] Barker, "Every Preposterous Comparison Kanye West Has Made Between Himself and These Cultural Icons"

[3] Independent case study of Kanye West and pre-West hip-hop.

[4] Oware, Journal of African American Studies, pp. 22–39.

[5] Independent case study of Kanye West and pre-West hip-hop.

[6] Pareles, "The Blessed, Cursed Life of Bon Iver".

Complex magazine claims that aside from sound, "His revolution was also ideological. He stressed relatability and an accessible, regular-guy middle-class sensibility in a time when hip-hop still reflected a streets-oriented consciousness." [7] This relatability can be seen when Kanye raps, "I'm so self-conscious, that's why you always see me with one of my watches" [8] on his first studio album *The College Dropout*. At a time when artists were flexing their invincibility, Kanye West introduced a sensitivity unheard in hip-hop music. Instead of his watch being a symbol of his fame and wealth, like most rappers of the era, it is used as symbol of his personal struggles with self-confidence—and his tragic vulnerability is a relatable one. However, *The College Dropout* was only the beginning of West's experiments with sensitive and emotional music.

Screaming fans blare out as the somber piano starts, and Kanye West's voice comes in, "Wise men say... you'll never figure out real love". He is free styling verses during a live performance of a song that would later take the name "Pinocchio Story" [9] from his fourth studio album *808's & Heartbreak*. Its obvious that although it is just a saying, West takes this one personally, in the heart. The fans's screaming swells and with it West's voice comes in again, forceful this time, "Do you think I sacrificed real life, for all the fame of flashing lights?" This is the paradox of Kanye West. His desperate cry for help goes unnoticed behind the veil of his own celebrity. The stanchions of his fame—Heartbreak, misunderstanding, loneliness, and isolation—torment this man and fuel his music. The music itself is tragic, and that is exactly what separates Kanye West's music from the rest.

After the release of *808's & Heartbreak*, Robert Christgau wrote about West's emotional music in his review of the album. Christgau states, "Altogether as slow, sad-ass and self-involved as reported, this is a breakup album there's no reason to like except that it's brilliant." [10] The album, from its sorrowful melodies to its auto tuned lyrics about broken love, spills out of the speakers as nothing else but a tragedy. As Christgau puts it, "although West couldn't hit the notes without Auto-Tune, his decision to robotize as well as pitch-correct his voice both undercuts his self-importance and adds physical reality to tales of alienated fame that might otherwise be pure pity parties". In this quote from his review, Christgau indirectly mentions another special quality of Kanye's kingdom of sound within the rap industry— his ability to "add physical reality" to human feelings using musical sounds. As Christgau mentions, on *808's and Heartbreak*, Kanye's use of the voice altering technique of Auto-Tune conveys

---

[7] Drake, "The 10 Major Influences on Today's Rap Sound".

[8] Independent case study of Kanye West and pre-West hip-hop.

[9] Kanye West - Topic. "Pinocchio Story (Freestyle Live from Singapore)."

[10] Christgau, "Robert Christgau: CG: Kanye West".

his disconnected feelings from himself and others without having to issue a single lyrical word. This could be one reason West's celebrity is just as big as it is. For people with feelings of sadness from the loss and isolation that Kanye dives into within his own music, being able to contextualize those feelings through their physical representation in music could potentially lead to the cathartic experience similar to Shakespeare's tragic plays.

In Kanye's "Artist's Talk" at the School of the Art Institute of Chicago (SAIC) he says, "There's drugs that make you tell the truth, there's drugs that make you happy, drugs that make you sad, there's different types of moods it can put you in... and music is like a drug." [11] Kanye's apparent recreation of intoxication in his music once again adds physical reality to despondent emotions people often struggle to describe. In West's song "Hold My Liquor" The blurry and distorted slow intro verse delivered Justin Vernon mimics the depressant effect of alcohol on sensory perception. Additionally, Kanye's lyrics from the song "Hold My Liquor," "You love me when I ain't sober, you love me when I'm hungover, even when I blow doja" mimic the self-destructive feelings associated with substance abuse. Many people turn to substances as a temporary release from their torments. Similarly, West's music, especially in its relatable representation of intoxication and the tragic circumstances that lead to substance abuse, can provide a cathartic and releasing experience for its listeners, substance free.

Kanye West has influenced the sound of the Hip-Hop industry greatly through his creation and popularization of tragic rap. His ability to create opportunities for cathartic experiences for his listeners through his revealing music is innovative and unique to his brand of sound. Additionally, by introducing a sensitive and relatable lyrical personality, West has set the path for the up and coming wave of Hip-Hop, as well as opened the door for artists to experiment in similar soundscapes within different genres of music. One such artist is his collaborator Justin Vernon, who is blazing a similar trail in the soul and folk genres. Thus, West has revolutionized both the physical sound, and the intrinsic message delivered by Hip-Hop, and proved that famous rappers are not indeed, invincible. Whether you think he is insane or a musical genius, one thing is undeniable; there will never be another Kanye West.

---

11 School of the Art Institute of Chicago (SAIC), "SAIC Artist Talk: Kanye West (HON 2015)".

Works Cited

Barker, Emily. "Every Preposterous Comparison Kanye West Has Made Between Himself and These Cultural Icons." Photos, NME, 6 Oct. 2015, http://www.nme.com/photos/ every-preposterous-comparison-kanye-west-has-made-between-himself-and-these-cultural-icons-1421468. Accessed 30 Nov. 2016.

Channel, SonicAmbulanceTV's. "Kanye West - Runaway/heartless (live at the HP Pavilion in San Jose) (12/14/12)." *YouTube*, 20 Dec. 2011, https://www.youtube.com/ watch.. Accessed 22 Jan. 2017.

Christgau, Robert. "Robert Christgau: CG: Kanye West." Robert Christgau Dean of American Rock Critics, 1990, http://robertchristgau.com/get_artist. php?id=5260&name=Kanye+West. Accessed 30 Nov. 2016.

Drake, David. "The 10 Major Influences on Today's Rap SoundMF Doom." Complex, Complex UK, 20 Oct. 2013, http://www.complex.com/music/2013/11/major-influences-todays-rap-sound/mf-doom. Accessed 30 Nov. 2016.

Kanye West - Topic. "Pinocchio Story (Freestyle Live from Singapore)." *YouTube*, 28 Jan. 2016, https://www.youtube.com/watch. Accessed 22 Jan. 2017.

Oware, Matthew. "Brotherly Love: Homosociality and Black Masculinity in Gangsta Rap Music." Journal of African American Studies, vol. 15, no. 1, 20 Mar. 2010, pp. 22–39.

Pareles, Jon. "The Blessed, Cursed Life of Bon Iver." Music, 4 Oct. 2016, http://www. nytimes.com/2016/09/25/arts/music/bon-iver-justin-vernon-22-a-million-interview. Accessed 30 Nov. 2016.

School of the Art Institute of Chicago (SAIC). "SAIC Artist Talk: Kanye West (HON 2015)." *YouTube*, 10 Feb. 2016, https://www.youtube.com/watch. Accessed 30 Nov. 2016.

Citations, Quotes & Annotations

Barker, Emily. "Every Preposterous Comparison Kanye West Has Made Between Himself and These Cultural Icons." Photos, NME, 6 Oct. 2015, http://www.nme.com/photos/ every-preposterous-comparison-kanye-west-has-made-between-himself-and-these-cultural-icons-1421468. Accessed 30 Nov. 2016.

Channel, SonicAmbulanceTV's. "Kanye West - Runaway/heartless (live at the HP Pavilion in San Jose) (12/14/12)." *YouTube*, 20 Dec. 2011, https://www.youtube.com/ watch. Accessed 22 Jan. 2017.

Christgau, Robert. "Robert Christgau: CG: Kanye West." Robert Christgau Dean of
American Rock Critics, 1990, http://robertchristgau.com/Kanye+West. Accessed 30
Nov. 2016.

Drake, David. "The 10 Major Influences on Today's Rap SoundMF Doom." Complex,
Complex UK, 20 Oct. 2013, http://www.complex.com/music/2013/11/major-
influences-todays-rap-sound/mf-doom. Accessed 30 Nov. 2016.

Kanye West - Topic. "Pinocchio Story (Freestyle Live from Singapore)." *YouTube*, 28 Jan.
2016, https://www.youtube.com/watch. Accessed 22 Jan. 2017.

Oware, Matthew. "Brotherly Love: Homosociality and Black Masculinity in Gangsta Rap
Music." Journal of African American Studies, vol. 15, no. 1, 20 Mar. 2010, pp. 22–39.

Pareles, Jon. "The Blessed, Cursed Life of Bon Iver." Music, 4 Oct. 2016, http://www.
nytimes.com/2016/09/25/arts/music/bon-iver-justin-vernon-22-a-million-
interview.. Accessed 30 Nov. 2016.

School of the Art Institute of Chicago (SAIC). "SAIC Artist Talk: Kanye West (HON
2015)." *YouTube*, 10 Feb. 2016, https://www.youtube.com/watch. Accessed 30 Nov.
2016.

Drexel Publishing Group
Essays

Introduction

Researching, thinking, and writing are at the core of the College of Arts and Sciences. No matter what field students are in, they must be able to find and evaluate the best evidence and information on a topic and, most of all, keep an open mind. Students must be able to think, to form original ideas, and take a fresh approach to a problem or question. And, of course, they must be able to write. After reading and thinking about the work of others, students make their own contributions by writing.

The following works were selected from student submissions to the Drexel Publishing Group Essay Contest. The contest was judged by faculty from a wide range of disciplines in the College of Arts and Sciences. The essays in this section of *The 33rd* explore diverse topics in a variety of disciplines in the arts and sciences and demonstrate originality and skill.

To honor the stylistic requirements of each field, we have reproduced the essays and articles in their original forms.

- The Editors

Samantha Stein

Closet Voters, Junk Food, and the American Dream: Education's Invisible Ties

On Tuesday, November 8th 2016, United States citizens (and according to President Trump, millions of illegal people as well) went into the voting booths to cast their say in American governance; the result of that election would defy all predictions from previously acclaimed polls, and would shock a nation in which Trump supporters had seemed obsolete. In the days after the election, with the results reverberating wildly through troubled academic circles seeking to understand how the polls could have been so off, the people who did not endorse Trump in social groups nor express favoritism for him in surveys, yet checked Trump while behind the safety of voting booth curtains became known as "closet voters." The world marveled at the grand-scale illumination of people who had thought different things than they said, and acted on their thoughts rather than their claims. But while the world reveled in this unexpected turn of events, I was all but shocked.

History, of which I am an unashamed fanatic, has a lot to tell. The election, though perhaps one of the most visible instances of people expressing their innermost thoughts rather than those they claimed to have, was far from the first instance of this phenomenon. Democracy and its relation to economics epitomizes the gap left when it is mythologized that pragmatics and theory align. While the United States was founded on the idea of the American Dream, the American Dream has proven contradictory to itself, and infeasible over extended periods of time since the moment the ideology was put forth. When given the opportunity to succeed with hard work, the minor advantages of a few quickly become exponentially advantageous leading a few to rise to the top, systemically barring others from social mobility. Consequently, a proletariat which struggles for survival and self-fulfillment emerges and begins to grow (Marx 36-45). This prediction has manifested in reality, and continues to do so. Yet, over again and again in American elections, capitalism has proved favored. Welfare has been bitterly disputed, and neoliberal ideologies have prevailed. But in a system with so many people bearing the negative consequences of capitalism in all its interdisciplinary essence, why is it continually favored in votes? Perhaps this phenomena is a testament to the futility of democracy in accurately representing the needs of the people, and illuminatory of a deeper issue which renders people incapable of competently making decisions for themselves as requisite by democracy. Thus, while true theoretical democracy,

unaffected by lobbyists and structured inequality represents people's desires in a utilitarian manner, it does not necessarily represent need as it is only so good as the majority voting within it.

Often, the needs of the people and people's desires do not correspond. So, after thirteen years spent in the American school system, and nearly a decade of watching family, friends, and the larger community be disappointed by the materialization of their political nominees' promises, I had a strong suspicion that American education just may be exacerbating, if not wholly fostering, and maybe even creating these unsubstantiated visionaries most recently termed "closet voters." To test the perilous waters of my suspicions, I distributed a survey to two classes: an Eastern Philosophy class (which made little to no direct reference to current inequality in the U.S.), and a Wealth and Power class (which was financially educative and focused on the stratification of American society, and the limited nature of social mobility). In the survey, I inquired about students' reasons for taking the class to determine potential perceptiveness to information and natural interests. I inquired about students' experiences in secondary school, asking what types of materials were utilized in the classroom to foster growth (specifically whether or not questions were encouraged, whether or not textbooks were used, and whether or not worksheets were designed by individual teachers or professional education companies), what types of information was emphasized (such as how communist countries were portrayed, and what financial education classes asserted if any were taken), how growth was measured (via tests, projects, or other means), and how students perceived themselves and others within society (asking whether students believed there could be such a thing as a self-made man, where they rated themselves/their families on a socioeconomic scale now, where they predicted themselves to be in ten and fifty years, and whether or not their parents were better off than their grandparents). In my survey, I also asked where people learned specific information (if it was learned at all) to determine what types of environments foster what types of learning. And, I asked whether my subjects identified with groups they felt had been discriminated against, and if so whether they thought the discrimination had increased or decreased over time (because as Jay MacLeod asserts, seeing a decrease in discrimination against a group with which one identifies leads to higher aspirations regardless of potential for attainability) (379-381).

The results of my survey bewildered me. Out of the 50 students who responded to the survey, not one student predicted that he/she would be poorer in either 10 or 50 years than he/she was now. While a few students predicted that they would maintain their places on the socioeconomic spectrum, most students predicted they would gravitate upwards. This overarching trend of perceived ability to move upwards in society is completely contradictory to what statistics say about social mobility. A study conducted by the Institute

of Fiscal Studies (along with several other studies) reveals that "Working-age households are at risk of being less wealthy at each age than those born a decade earlier" (BBC Staff). So, I was shocked to see that my peers, even the ones in financially educative Wealth and Power (despite acknowledging and appearing in class discussions to accept what statistics said) believed themselves to be the exceptions to the trends of socioeconomic decline and reduced social mobility when allowed to express their views in the safety of an anonymous survey. Perhaps this irrational view of place within society is what has caused people to continually vote for politicians who ultimately fail to work within utilitarian interests. And, perhaps people's voting for those who they feel are most likely to enable them to rise exceptionally should they choose to do so, is also the reason why the proletariat continues to grow, and those who thought themselves able to rise wind up the non-exceptions, fallen to the proletariat. So why is it that even once fallen among the proletariat people still feel themselves capable of rising exceptionally (as indicated by tendency to reinforce capitalist ideals through votes)? Perhaps my study holds some clues.

I was shocked to see that despite having received an extensive financial education (which revealed the ways of capitalism and the eventual resultant social immobility) in the Wealth and Power course, study participants still refused to believe the facts applied to them and consequently expressed thoughts of potential for individualized upwards mobility. Essentially, it is not just that people maintain irrational perceptions of their potentiality, but that people are also resistant to financially educative messages delivered in the post-high school years of education, granted a portion of the population never receives collegiate education. When made available, to accept the financially educative message as applicable to oneself requires developed critical thinking skills (because of the need to presuppose symbolism into transposable results on oneself). Thus, as school is a primary place for intellectual development, I believe much of the reason democracy proves continually devastating as people prove continually illusioned results from American education.

Jean Piaget, a biologist turned self-trained psychologist offers some insight as to the importance of fostering development of critical thinking skills in primary and secondary school. "Only 35% of high school graduates in industrialized countries obtain formal operations; many people do not think formally during adulthood" studies consistently conclude (Huitt and Hummel). Piaget believed that the mind develops formal operational capabilities around the age of twelve and that those capabilities then extend into adulthood. But, as people are unperceptive to messages requisite of critical thinking in college, it is evident that not even the more minor means of development necessary for students to progress on to critical thinking are being developed. So, why are schools not fostering critical thinking? And, what are students actually doing in school?

James Loewen, a historian, conducted an in-depth study of 12 American textbooks. Through this study he identified that references to class and social mobility were not made past discussion of the colonial period. In my survey, too, people expressed having learned little of class and social mobility in secondary school. In financial education classes, though most students had not taken any, students were taught to write checks, balance budgets, and engage in contracts, but were taught nothing of their actual economic potentiality (319-327). In my own high school financial education class, I was asked if I wanted to be a millionaire on the first day, and then subsequently told that if I stayed in school and worked hard afterwards, I too could achieve the much sought after status. I was taught that I could succeed on my own if only I tried hard enough, and that I could overcome whatever barriers I would be presented with. And in my survey, nearly all students regurgitated a similar ideology. Most students expressed a belief in the notion of a self-made man. And, they believed that they were to be him. They could rise above the others, they believed. Except "they" could not; only "he/she" could. It is critical to recognize that textbook companies maintain large holds on American education. By providing textbooks at discounted costs, companies maintain the ability to promote the views which best fit their objectives – namely squelching creativity to maintain the social hierarchy off of which capitalism, and they themselves, thrive (Cleese).

The documentary *Inside Job* also provides insight into why education is skewed away from bipartisan financial education. "Inside Job" delineates the ties many college professors at top economic institutions have outside of the classroom which lead to self-centered motivations behind in-class interaction. These professors, the documentary asserts, sit on the financial advisement boards of massive corporations in addition to teaching. Thus, they opt to promote deregulation in class. As their students mature and become the nation's new financial leaders, they in turn advocate deregulation. Thus, a cycle emerges each time leading to disaster of increasing proportions (the growing proletariat Marx speaks of) (Fergusen et al.).

Another driving factor behind education is the food industry. In his piece, "Between Obesity and Hunger: The Capitalist Food Industry" Robert Albritton details the immense funding schools receive from the junk food industry (particularly soda companies). In exchange for this funding, schools promote these company's products. Essentially, industries seek "'pouring rights,'" claims to fund particular underprivileged schools, in exchange for promotion opportunities (346). Perhaps, this is why in health class I experienced a tirade against fats while the negative effects of sugar were blissfully glossed over. In examining other curricula besides that of my high school, I have found similar results.

As exemplified, education has become a method for furthering particular economic agendas rather than educating students wholly. It is most logical to conclude that as schools rely heavily on and are composed of the funds of textbook companies, the junk food industry, and the employment of morally-compromised professors, all of these entities being capitalism-driven, schools cannot promote the critical thinking necessary for people to gain class consciousness and initiate revolution to reform the system (Marx 36-45). With the "doctrine of consumer sovereignty" being the dominant ideology taught in school, people are deceived into believing they have the free will to act autonomously, and like those who rose to great riches at the founding of the nation, to achieve social mobility (Albritton 343). Thus, the American Dream appears attainable to people, who in turn vote according to their aspirations, not in response to their current states. Thus, people, as high-aspiring beings who look to the future, are rendered unfit to vote in accordance with their needs as they tend to vote in ways which neither improve their current states, nor allow their aspirations to materialize (as the capitalism-pervaded system, an inevitable function of human nature, will never allow for their aspirations to materialize). In accordance with that logic, to propose "[bringing] about radical changes [to the American system] via long-term democratic planning," as Albritton and others propose doing to enact reform, would prove futile. Democracy is only so good as the self-consciousness and forward-thinking abilities of the people behind it. And so education, as a means of shaping these people, must first be reformed.

As a more appropriate solution than simply having blind faith in democracy as a system, rather than as a contextualized (human affected) entity, I propose promoting increased interdisciplinary education in schools, which I hope will lead to the realization that as people, regardless of the titles we put in front of our names or the corporations we shield ourselves with, we will all eventually succumb to the conditions we have created. But, to teach in this manner is not adjacently possible. With the funding of the junk food industry among others, schools must teach that which those companies promote; and, without that funding schools run dry and are unable to teach anything at all. Essentially, schools are currently being forced to choose between teaching incomplete information and no information at all. Thus, a revolution is necessary to completely renovate the system. This system has reached the horizon point. So many inequalities have been structured within it, that it is no longer feasible to attempt to compensate for those inequalities via minor adjacent possibles. Instead, the system must be overthrown if we wish to have any hope for universal eudaemonia. And, as human nature always prevails history tells us, it must be overthrown constantly or continual, perfect challenges which prevent authority from ever taking hold must be maintained. Either way, it is crucial that critical thinking be fostered in the masses, school being the vehicle through which to do so.

Works Cited

Albritton, Robert. *Let Them Eat Junk: How Capitalism Creates Hunger and Obesity*. Pluto Books,2009, www.jstor.org/stable/j.ctt183pbv8.

Ferguson, Charles H, Audrey Marrs, Chad Beck, Adam Bolt, Matt Damon, Paul A. Volcker, George Soros, Eliot Spitzer, Barney Frank, Dominique Strauss-Kahn, Svetlana Cvetko, Kalyanee Mam,and Alex Heffes. Inside Job. , 2011.

Huitt, W. and Hummel, J. "Cognitive Development." Jan. 1998. 1 Mar. 2017. Online.

Johnny V. "Cleese on Creativity." Online video clip. YouTube. Google, 15 Apr. 2015. Web. 1 Mar. 2017.

Loewen, James. "7/The Land of Opportunity." *The Practical Skeptic: Readings in Sociology*. 6th ed.New York: McGraw-Hill, 2014. 319-28. Print.

MacLeod, Jay. "Ain't No Making It: Leveled Aspirations in a Low-Income Neighborhood." The Inequality Reader: Contemporary and Foundational Readings in Race, Class, and Gender. 2nd ed. Boulder: Westview Press, 2011. N. pag. Print.

Marx, Karl. "Classes in Capitalism and Pre-Capitalism." *The Inequality Reader: Contemporary and Foundational Readings in Race, Class, and Gender*. 2nd ed. Boulder: Westview Press, 2011. N. pag. Print.

"Young 'to be poorer than parents at every stage of life'" *BBC News*. BBC, 19 Nov. 2015. Web. 16 Mar. 2017.

Sharee DeVose

African American Literature & Urban Life: *A Raisin in the Sun* by Lorraine Hansberry

One of the most critical historic events that contributed to the cultivation and growth of African American literature was World War II, which preceded the Great Migration of African Americans in the United States. In the one decade between 1940 and 1950, nearly 1.5 million Black Southerners migrated to the North in the hopes of encountering better social and economic conditions than existed in the South; the absence of white Americans drafted into the army created a need for more industrial workers, thus providing the incentive that brought on the Great Migration of the 1940's ("Migration" 538-539). Expectedly, the conditions of this time period and the decades after influenced the construction of African American literature. Accordingly, one work in particular captured the current climate in a presentation of Black life in the new North: Lorraine Hansberry's *A Raisin in the Sun*, which debuted on Broadway in 1959.

Lorraine Hansberry expresses through her writing the issues of the era and the manifestations of said issues through characterizations and relationships between persons and entities within her literary works. Accordingly, the mode of expression varies at times depending on the character in focus, as each responds to the pervading socioeconomic challenges of the 1950's in a manner distinct from each of the other characters. For these same reasons, along with the text's presentation of Black life being true to form, Lorraine Hansberry's *A Raisin in the Sun* is the quintessence of reality's and history's being reflected in African American literature.

The events of *A Raisin in the Sun* present to the audience an image of an African American family in South Side, Chicago, one region in which Black Southerners resettled in urban areas of the Northeast and, in this case, the Midwest. The play surveys the life of the Youngers, a family which spans three generations beginning with the matriarch who had left the South some 40 years before. Lena Younger, or "Mama," heads the household comprising her son and daughter, daughter-in-law, and grandson—a typical familial unit in urban, post-Migration cities that lived mostly in the close quarters of tenant buildings, sharing facilities with any number of other families. The neighborhoods which housed these buildings were, by way of institutionalized racism, highly Black-concentrated areas that prevented the integration of higher-end, white-dominated neighborhoods. In the play, the Younger family

is seen facing the inevitable struggle of African American life as a family that is striving to emerge from poverty and ultimately purchase their own, beautiful, single-family home and together move toward a more fulfilling life. With this picture as the basis of Hansberry's production, the play delivers several themes through issues that the Younger family faces individually and collectively. This paper will explore three of these issues, including family dynamics, education, and economic prosperity.

Throughout the length of the play, a solid distinction is made between the construct of the Younger family and that of the nuclear family—a mother, father, and their children—which, before and during the time, had been the standard structure of the American family. Be that as it may, the institution of the African American family is one that has been contested and degenerated, yet reconstructed since the beginning of the United States' involvement in the Trans-Atlantic Slave Trade ("Family, African American" 308). And due to the impact of slavery, the traditional African family was no more, but it had become a blend of blood and non-blood relatives, with households often including close friends as well as extended family members who often adopted the roles of close family members amid the separation of Black families in the proceedings of slavery. Furthermore, developing alternative family structures was a mechanism for surviving social and economic trials ("Family, African American" 311). In the chosen text, the Youngers make up a family of similar form, comprised of Lena, Walter Lee, Ruth, Beneatha, and Travis Younger— respectively, the matriarch Lena, Lena's son, Walter Lee's wife, Lena's daughter, and the son of Ruth and Walter Lee. The Youngers are like most other African American families in the urban North in the 1950's suffering economic hardships.

In addition to barriers caused by external forces, the Younger family faces weighty conflicts which are, in part, due to the power struggle between Lena, mostly named throughout the play as "Mama," and her son Walter Lee, or by role, he who is positioned traditionally as head of the home. While Walter Lee struggles to fulfill his dream of opening a liquor store and leaving his job as a chauffeur, he is at the same time failing in the roles that he plays for each member of the household, hence the pervading conflict that upsets the state of the entire household. In referring to African American history, this is a clear illustration of the plight of the Black man who fails in his duties as husband and father, often resulting in the collapse of marital relationships ("Family, African American" 311). Granted Walter Lee's internal and external family conflict, Mama is reluctant and at first seemingly incapable of allowing her son to come into his manhood by allowing him to try, to fail, and become molded into the man that his family needs, which further degenerates his ability to grow in what proves to be a vicious cycle. In one scene of *A Raisin in the Sun*, one very succinct line from Walter Lee encapsulates the imbalance of power

as well as the mental and emotional impact of his situation: "I'm a grown man, Mama," after which she silences him and commands him to be seated (1.2.201-2). Ultimately, Mama gives way for her son to lead the family and trusts him to make decisions in their best interests, which in the end comes into fruition. For the Youngers, family dynamics which challenge the American standard show to be a strength that helps to extract them from their financial situation, reconciles their bonds with one another, and restores the hopes of pursuing their dreams.

In the next case, Hansberry mirrors in her Broadway production the nature of African American life in the 1950's in the area of education. During this time, the idea of education was still a false ideology for many, as it often proved to require a large investment for far-off, unguaranteed results. On the contrary, finding employment was viewed as a more sensible course for socioeconomic prosperity because, if employment was secured, earning wages was evidence of invested time becoming reaped benefits. Although there did exist a value of education among African American people, many in the older generations, particularly those who had migrated from the South, saw the need of education extending simply to secondary education; as time passed, the prospect of attaining higher education became more appealing as opportunities for Blacks increased. Consequently, what had once been the desire for basic education among African slaves became then, in the 1950's and 1960's, a tangible reality which Blacks could strive and fight for in their communities and institutions of higher education (Duncan 681-683). Still, the attitude of some was marked by dismissiveness to dreams that seemed too large for an African American.

Within the context of *A Raisin in the Sun*, the character who faces notable barriers in pursuing education is Beneatha Younger, a young woman with many aspirations. With the primary goal of becoming a doctor, Beneatha receives the support of her mother and mostly the rest of her family: while Mama is intent on using the expected $10,000 life insurance check of her late husband in part to pay for Beneatha's schooling, Walter Lee cannot embrace her dreams in the same way. For Walter Lee, the desire to become a doctor is irrational and seemingly one of Beneatha's passing interests, whereas his dream of opening a liquor store is more concrete because of the increased likelihood of its coming to pass. Even more, her goals of a university education fall subject to ridicule and scorn for which she at one point dramatically and sarcastically begs her brother to "forgive [her] for ever wanting to be anything at all" (1.1.123). In this same spirit, Beneatha holds to her dreams and becomes more self-involved and with other intellectuals such as Joseph Asagai in her attempts to come into the young, educated women she hopes to be. Beneatha Younger's character signifies the current and emerging generations of African Americans who would seize opportunities for educational advancement,

moving further away from others like Walter Lee who still only saw ready employment as a worthy expense of African American hopes and capabilities.

Finally, the issue of economic prosperity is illustrated extensively in and by the chosen text, further painting a vivid image of African American life. Together, the issues of obtaining economic prosperity and the embodiment of the American dream act as one of the major driving conflicts of the entire play. Lower wages earned by Blacks in America, along with a higher rate of joblessness among the population than for white Americans, made the prospect of attaining steady employment and wealth less of a reality. The case remained the same so that more academic experience could not even diminish the impact of racial differences (Darity 673). Expressly, with the rise in Black literacy in the early 1900's, Blacks became increasingly more qualified in occupational fields dominated by white Americans. And, in contest, discriminatory practices intensified in order to exclude them from certain employment opportunities, reinforcing the wealth gap between them and the white population (Darity 674). As a result, Blacks were at a disadvantage when seeking quality education for their offspring, financial security for any instance of emergency, and of course homeownership—the latter was the leading possession of value to the African American family as well as a mechanism for transferring wealth to subsequent generations—further solidifying the wealth gap (Darity 675-676).

Essentially, the fixation on wealth and the American dream is the underlying cause of each principle character's challenges: without this ultimate goal in mind, there would not exist those issues aforementioned, involving African American family dynamics and higher education in America. Still, in *A Raisin in the Sun*, poverty's greatest implication is seen in the Youngers' living conditions and the inability to change them. For this reason, whether or not the family will receive the life insurance check of Lena's deceased husband "Big Walter" is a defining factor in their fates. To explain, it will be the source of the funds needed for Beneatha's medical school, Walter Lee's business venture, and, majorly, Lena's down payment on a new home in a better neighborhood for her family. As Mama says in the second act of the play, "it makes a difference in a man when he can walk on floors that belong to him" (2.1.270). In this line, directed at Walter Lee, Mama speaks to the reality that homeownership in the 1950's was in the United States a symbol of economic stability and independency. Although the Youngers do face some opposition in purchasing a home in a white neighborhood, Walter Lee makes the decision for his family to purchase the home despite his reservations. Consequently, the independent and joint conflicts that pervade the lives and wellbeing of the Younger family begin to move toward an end.

As can be seen in the discussion of the social climate of the urban North in the decade of the 1950's, the effects of the Great Migration were seen in African American family structures, educational interests and endeavors, and economic prosperity. These issues, illustrated by the work of Lorraine Hansberry, *A Raisin in the Sun*, were major forces that defined and directed the lives of African Americans. For this reason, the Broadway production has made a significant contribution to the wealth of African American literature, as it speaks to the hardships faced by Blacks in the North in major cities like Chicago and, therefore, exemplifies a work of literature that reflects real African American life.

Works Cited

Darity, William, Jr. "Economic Condition, U.S." *Encyclopedia of African-American Culture and History*, edited by Colin A. Palmer, 2nd ed., vol. 2, Macmillan Reference USA, 2006, pp. 673-676. *Gale Virtual Reference Library*, go.galegroup.com/ Accessed 13 Nov. 2016.

Duncan, Garrett Albert. "Education in the United States." *Encyclopedia of African-American Culture and History*, edited by Colin A. Palmer, 2nd ed., vol. 2, Macmillan Reference USA, 2006, pp. 680-688. *Gale Virtual Reference Library*, go.galegroup. com.ezproxy2.library.drexel.edu Accessed 13 Nov. 2016.

"Family, African American." *Encyclopedia of African American Society*, edited by Gerald D. Jaynes, vol. 1, SAGE Reference, 2005, pp. 308-312. *Gale Virtual Reference Library*, go.galegroup.com. Accessed 13 Nov. 2016.

Gates, Henry Louis, and Valerie Smith. *The Norton Anthology of African American Literature*. 3rd ed., vol. 2, New York, NY, W.W. Norton and Company, 2014.

"Migration." *Encyclopedia of African American Society*, edited by Gerald D. Jaynes, vol. 2, SAGE Reference, 2005, pp. 538-539. *Gale Virtual Reference Library*, go.galegroup. com. Accessed 13 Nov. 2016.

Yih-Chia Lam

Reflection: Halden Prison

During the winter break of 2016, I participated in "Crime and Justice in Scandinavia" – an Intensive Course Abroad (ICA) in Sweden and Norway led by Dr. Jordan Hyatt, a professor from the department of Criminology & Justice Studies. Over the course of 10 days, four students and I were given the chance to examine Scandinavian facilities, policies, and theoretical frameworks, both as individual entities and also in comparison to their American counterparts. We focused on the concept of Scandinavian exceptionalism – a term used to describe the institutional divergence from the traditionally punitive functions of criminal justice systems (Pratt, 2008).

In Sweden we visited SiS Ungdomshem Bärby, a juvenile correctional facility run by the Swedish National Board of Institutional Care, also known as Statens institutionsStyrelse (SiS), an independent government agency that provides compulsory care for troubled youth. In Norway we visited Halden Fengsel, the second largest prison in the country with 258 male inmates; an indescribably unique facility aptly known as the most humane prison in the world (Gentleman, 2012). As per the suggestion of my professor, I did as little research as possible prior to our visit to Halden, although it wouldn't have mattered either way. Neither articles nor photographs could have prepared me for what we saw that day.

Upon our arrival on the prison premises, Are Høidal, the warden of Halden, graciously gave us a tour of the facilities. Immediately, the differences in correctional philosophies between the American and Scandinavian systems were glaringly apparent. The men who were incarcerated in the facility wore their own clothes, which helped minimize the "us vs them" mentality as well as the social stigmas attached to incarceration. Uniforms were reserved for correctional officers only – almost half of which were female – who could be seen mingling and conversing with inmates on a casual and personal level. The interactions between inmates and staff were more amicable than I would have ever expected to see in a correctional facility. There was mutual respect and even trust between the inmates and prison staff, the latter opting to keep order with interpersonal connections rather than with weapons and intimidation. We later learned that aside from providing security, correctional officers also helped inmates in planning for their reintegration into society by setting up post-release support networks and helping with job searches.

As we were led down pastel-colored corridors and through daycare-like waiting rooms on our way to the warden's office, I had to keep reminding myself that I was touring a prison – not a hospital, not a college campus, but a prison – a maximum security one at that. And yet, the prison grounds were beautiful, full of greenery and art installations – some of which were commissioned from Dolk, a popular Norwegian graffiti artist (Leung, 2014). There was barely any barbed wire in sight and the facilities' windows gave view to open sky and forested paths rather than metal bars. Individuals were entitled to as much freedom and privacy as permissible in a closed facility and prison cells were thus treated as private property in that respect. 10 to 12 inmates shared a communal kitchen and living space, complete with furnishings and an entertainment system, picturesque living units comparable to Ikea displays.

Not only were the prison dwellings much more preferable to even the dorms on Drexel's campus, the visitor housing was nicer than most apartments (and kid-friendly as well), complete with bedrooms with and without cribs, a fully-equipped kitchen, a flat screen TV and gaming system, and a yard with playground equipment and a playhouse. The accommodations in Halden were meant to be as close to, if not more comfortable than, life outside as possible, minus the freedom. It is what Time describes as "home away from home." An inmate we passed by facetiously called Halden a "five-star hotel" in response to our gawking and verbalized fascination. Sarcasm aside, during certain parts of the tour, it didn't even feel appropriate to call Halden a prison. Without the ever-looming six-meter concrete and metal prison wall, one could have easily mistaken Halden for a peaceful college campus in the countryside.

In addition to the residential accommodations, Warden Høidal openly disclosed Halden's three solitary confinement cells, none of which has been used since institution's opening in 2010. As an American, this was astounding to me (then again, the U.S. still practices capital punishment, so my threshold for fair treatment was arguably low to begin with). From a more international perspective, aversion to the usage of restrictive housing is a common sentiment throughout most European countries (Lamb, 2015). Except for keeping extremely violent or dangerous felons away from the general prison population, solitary confinement serves little purpose outside of punishment. Such severe isolation is known to exacerbate existing mental conditions, and Dr. Raymond Patterson, a forensic psychiatrist, found that prisoners in California who are kept in solitary have a 33 times greater risk of committing suicide as compared to the general prison population (Collier, 2014).

Not only is solitary confinement seen as cruel and degrading, being subjected to it beyond a 15 day period is considered torture (UN, 2011). The U.S. seems to have no qualms about its liberal use of solitary confinement despite this, as an estimated 80,000 to 100,000 American inmates are currently in

held in solitary confinement throughout state prisons, not including jails, military, or juvenile facilities (Rodriguez, 2015). In addition, the U.S. has been known to confine individuals for decades at a time – one such case is Albert Woodfox, who spent 43 years in solitary confinement for 23 hours a day while at Louisiana State Penitentiary – on accusations lacking forensic evidence for both the initial and continued reasons for segregation (Aviv, 2017).

Unlike the negligent American justice system, Norway's contribution to Scandinavian exceptionalism manifested in Halden's extensive services that provided necessary means to help inmates rejoin society as productive citizens. The correctional facility took an active role in offender rehabilitation by providing countless programs and workshops in art, education, woodwork, pottery, and even a music studio (cleverly named Criminal Records) where prison staff helped mix and produce music videos alongside prisoners. The prison library was stocked full with novels, movies, and the latest magazine issues for inmates to enjoy, and the gymnasium bustled with sporting activities and games that both prisoners and correctional officers participated in. Halden also boasted a renowned culinary program in which individuals enrolled for training and degree certifications, showcasing their abilities for the warden's guests at the prison restaurant in the form of unforgettable multi-course meals. The program has been so successful it even released an internationally acclaimed cookbook called *Ærlig mat i Halden fengsel* or *Decent Food in Halden Prison.*

It was one thing to read about Scandinavian exceptionalism and the influences of cultural egalitarianism on correctional systems, but another thing entirely to see it executed in a functional manner. True to the works of academics, the facilities in Scandinavia focused sincerely on the rehabilitation of the inmates, rather than severe retribution like the American system. The amount of skill and talent we saw in the prison population were mere glimpses into the constructive impacts Halden's programs were able to facilitate in the men's lives.

Fyodor Dostoyevsky, who was once a prisoner himself, said, "The degree of civilization in a society can be judged by entering its prisons." This quote is relevant in any social or political climate; the treatment of a nation's prisoners – who are arguably society's most destitute and vulnerable population – can provide immense insight into a society's values and perceptions of righteousness. Based on expectations I had gained from the American correctional system, it was astonishing to see offenders being helped and treated like respectable human beings. Halden was nothing like the American prison model – in all the best ways possible.

References

Aviv, R. (January 2017). How Albert Woodfox survived solitary. *The New Yorker*. Retrieved from http://www.newyorker.com/magazine/2017/01/16/how-albert-woodfox-survived-solitary

Benko, J. (March 2015). The radical humaneness of Norway's Halden Prison. *The New York Times Magazine*. Retrieved from https://www.nytimes.com/2015/03/29/magazine/the-radical- humaneness-of-norways-halden-prison.html

Collier, L. (2014). Incarceration nation: The United States leads the world in incarceration. A new report explores why — and offers recommendations for fixing the system. *American Psychological Association Monitor on Psychology*, 45(9). 56.

Gentleman, A. (May 2012). Inside Halden, the most humane prison in the world. *The Guardian*.Retrieved from https://www.theguardian.com/society/2012/may/18/halden-most- humane-prison-in-world

Justice Policy Institute. (2011). *Finding direction: Expanding criminal justice options by considering policies of other nations factsheet: Sentencing*. Retrieved from http://www.justicepolicy.org/uploads/justicepolicy/documents/sentencing.pdf

Kamrany, N. M., & Boyd, R. J. (April 2012). U.S. Incarceration rate is a national disgrace. *The Huffington Post*. Retrieved from http://www.huffingtonpost.com/nake-m kamrany/incarceration-rate_b_1423822.html

Lamb, K. (November 2015). Beyond solitary confinement: Lessons from European prison reform. *Brown Political Review*. Retrieved from http://www.brownpoliticalreview.org/2015/11/beyond-solitary-confinement-lessons-from-european-prison-reform/

Leung, J. (August 2014). Halden Prison (Erik Møller Architects & HLM Architects). *Design and Violence*. Retrieved from http://designandviolence.moma.org/halden-prison-erik- moller-architects-hlm-architects/

Pratt, J. (2008). Scandinavian exceptionalism in an era of penal excess. *British Journal of Criminology*, 48. 119-137. doi:10.1093/bjc/azm072

Rodriguez, S. (2015). *Frequently asked questions*. Solitary Watch. Retrieved from http://solitarywatch.com/facts/faq/

Time. (2010). *Inside the world's most humane prison*. Retrieved from http://content.time.com/time/photogallery/0,29307,1989083,00.html

UN News Centre. (October 2011). *Solitary confinement should be banned in most cases, UN expert says*. Retrieved from http://www.un.org/apps/news/story.asp?NewsID=40097

Sharee DeVose

The Painful Irony

It was a summer evening, a few years back. As I headed home with my older, ridiculously tall (6'5") brother on this warm and dimly-lit evening, we approached a couple walking in our direction; I'll simply say we did not share the same color of skin. And as they laid eyes on my brother and me—two disheveled, well-tanned, dark-skinned youth returning from a day of play— what I saw was two gestures so absentmindedly done but so significant that I realized something I could never unlearn. The man's quick motion to pull his companion in at the waist was totally in sync with her attempt to bring her purse any number of inches closer to her body as possible.

I was then eight-years old. And I did not exactly understand what I had just learned, until it became more apparent in the following years. But what is the saddest aspect of these experiences? I've often found myself doing the very same. Drawing on immediate biases when encountering particular categories of people is an act taught in society that is not only essentially unjust; but it is also one that impacts those on the receiving end.

To behave protectively when encountering an African American individual is a very common act of automatic prejudice, and sometimes reasonableness. With my brother, at the age of 12, already towering over the unknown man, one might automatically assume that he is a volatile young man with intent to harm. Moreover, this display of bias can affect all Black people regardless of age. To explain, Black schoolchildren, Black customers in a clothing store, any Black passersby, and even Black men who may work for corporate companies are all susceptible to similar treatment. And it is difficult and truly shameful for me to admit that I have thought twice about walking on the same side of the street as a group of Black teenagers or made sure to tuck away my iPhone just as I approached a Black man. Ideas that African Americans, most often men, have some form of malicious intent are passed on through mere visual experience (Amodio 6). These ideas become so widespread that they seem impossible to reverse. Part of the reasoning behind this spreading of ideas is that stereotypes arrive through cognitive components, and therefore, the defining of a certain group by culture or social standing develops psychologically (Amodio 6). Consequently, every day, children and friends who may not have ever expressed prejudice before learn stereotype-based behaviors from others, from some prejudicial act a child

sees committed by his grandfather to an insensitive slur a teenager or adult is exposed to in school or in the workplace.

Moving forward, I also want to emphasize that the African American race is not the only minority group that faces stereotypes every day, particularly by me. Plenty of other groups who are minorities by race, socio-economic criteria, gender, religion, and sexual orientation experience an array of prejudicial attitudes (Jackson 1). Individuals who identify with the Islamic faith, for instance, are too often victimized by unfair expectations of hostility and violence. Though following a traumatic event for our nation, Muslim United States citizens were viewed in an entirely new light due to the terror attack which occurred on September 11th more than a decade ago. And despite the fact that many people began to think and behave out of fear, countless law-abiding and perhaps longtime Muslim-American citizens were faced with the actions of other Americans who were willing to incriminate any Muslims of "suspicion." They could not proceed in the workplace as usual, travel with ease and trust, or practice their faith with safety and peace of mind. I remember sitting rows behind a Middle Eastern man and woman on my first flight and the nervousness that followed; I let prejudices I had heard of as well as seen on television programs, like the series "Homeland," for example, influence me. When I realized my thoughts in that moment, I had to laugh at myself for shame of entertaining that ignorant thought. Returning to present day, people with the appearance of Middle Eastern origin in a Western world with steadily increasing diversity are met with sometimes unconscious, other times intentional, manifestations of prejudice.

The final and less political set of biases that I will focus on pertains to the general female population. For centuries, being female has been the equivalent of incompetency, in so many respects, from women in the workforce to women's roles in the home, and even women as drivers. I cannot say that I share the beliefs surrounding these stereotypes, but they often do cause me to question my capabilities and others' interpretations of who I am as an ambitious young woman, in comparison to any ambitious young male. For some time, I have been thinking about what my experience will be like in my co-op position this fall, and any difficulties I may face, or whether I will be seen as fit for hire. This kind of doubt even extends to how I view the competency of women as professionals in businesses or healthcare facilities. Honestly, though, if it were not for the thought that my ability to perform well on this job will be questioned, as well as any in the future, I would not have such a feeling of anxiety. I know that I will have to put forth great effort in order to exceed expectations and make an exceptional contribution to my place of employment during my internship.

With this said, I unwillingly acknowledge the fact that females in general will most likely always have to prove their worth and enforce the truth that women are not simply to be confined to the home. Even more so, it is necessary for me to reevaluate my beliefs and expectations of women in the professional world, because I certainly do understand that a woman physician or financial consultant, to name two examples, may possess the same level of skill as any of her counterparts.

Although the recipients of the common prejudices described above are the three that I have chosen to discuss, there are innumerable examples of people who are affected by prejudicial ideas. Immediately discrediting any individual or community of people because of gender, race, or creed is an attribute I need to improve because it is important that we all work towards empathetic attitudes, especially in intergroup relations (Tropp and Mallett 1). Accordingly, I hope for many others to acknowledge the same faults within themselves, because we can only continue rationalizing our failings by attributing them to society for so long: there is a point at which we must take responsibility for our own thoughts and actions in attempt to end them.

Forming instant biases and assumptions against people we encounter is not simply an unjust approach; but, even more, it profoundly impacts those on the receiving end in countless ways. Widespread negative views of various minority groups affect both formal and informal relationships, occupational opportunities and success, personal safety, and belief in oneself and one's ability to thrive. I have chosen to be honest with myself and with others by admitting that I have at times displayed the same stereotypical attitudes that I have come to despise. Going forward, I have decided that I will not pass on such prejudices to coming generations, an effort that will only be successful if I improve my actions as an individual as well as speak out on the ones that I may often witness other people committing.

Works Cited

Jackson, Lynne M., and EBSCO Publishing (Firm). "The Psychology of Prejudice: From Attitudes to Social Action." Washington, D.C: American Psychological Association, 2011.

Tropp, Linda R., Robyn K. Mallett, and EBSCO Publishing (Firm). "Moving Beyond Prejudice Reduction: Pathways to Positive Intergroup Relations." Washington, D.C: American Psychological Association, 2011.

Samantha Stein

Interdisciplinality: The Solution to Integrating the Populace into the Ever-Deviating Scientific Disciplines Commandeered by Executives, Reinforced by Journalists, and Fed by Researchers

In his book, *The Structure of Scientific Revolutions*, Thomas Kuhn makes it remarkably clear that cultural change does not simply coincide with the patterns of scientific discovery. Instead, Kuhn asserts, a public understanding of science must be garnered in order to elicit change (Kuhn 1996). In his book *Medical Writing – A Guide for Clinicians, Educators, and Researchers* Robert Taylor delineates the surface hindrances to public understanding of science. Particularly, Taylor examines the market for dense scientific writing which has popularized the production of work which is barely accessible to the budding clinician, let alone the public (2011). And in her book *How to Read a Paper: The Basics of Evidence-Based Medicine* Trisha Greenhalgh dispels the many preventable tragedies that have permeated medicine as a result of the aforementioned poor communication between researchers, educators, doctors, patients, and the general populace (2003). Although the results of stratified, single-faceted agendas manifested within an entangled world are particularly visible in medicine, the issue is far from confined to any particular discipline. In fact, it is exacerbated by the often incompatible perspectives offered by most disciplines as individual entities, and originates from the complex human agents whom further the disciplines theoretically, while traversing reality. The objective condition knows no borders; its repercussions know no mercy. At hasty glance, the issue seems to have a simple solution: Provide the public with more information about science. But, upon further examination, many infrastructural, logistical, and ethical issues appear evident.

On October 12th, 2016 *Outside Magazine* tweeted "The Great Barrier Reef of Australia passed away in 2016 after a long illness. It was 25 million years old" along with a cartoon picture of the reef in its prime behind a headstone. This extreme tweet evoked international outcry in ways previous climate-related propaganda had not (Lewis, 2016). Both researchers and the populace alike banded together to initiate conversation on the topic, eventually coming to the conclusion that no, the reef is not dead, but yes, it will be should we continue in our current ways. While the tweet had been misleading in its content, it

facilitated the necessary intersectoral conversation traditional articles had been trying to provoke to no avail for decades. The science web content producer particularly popular on Facebook, I F****** Love Science (IFLS), has been accused of similarly facetious operational tactics. Entire Reddit threads are devoted to picking IFLS owner Elise Andrew apart and many technical writers who produce the dense material favored by prestigious publications have expressed disdain for Andrew's popularity which they believe is unwarranted. They claim that IFLS creates ridiculously exaggerated headlines in order to lure in readers from Facebook who typically would not seek out science information independently. This, they believe is not only dangerous to the scientific hierarchy currently established, but to the readers themselves who may take, and act upon partial information misinterpreted as absolute. But others, such as Alexis Sobel, a journalist who esteems Andrew, say that the ends in case of watered down science writing to provoke public interaction often justify the means. Of Andrew, Sobel claims "To some extent, she is guilty of what plagues science-writing generally: the need to simplify and ignore the endless caveats that would otherwise make the stuff impenetrable to all the but the most specialized reader" (2014). Essentially, Sobel, as do others including Taylor and Greenhalgh, recognizes the dangers diminished communication between the information seekers (researchers) and the result receivers (the populace) poses and believes that slightly misleading information and the subsequent interest it spurs may be superior to utter ignorance. The singular example of the uproar over IFLS illuminates many of the issues surrounding communication between researchers, executives, journalists, and the populace.

In order to examine the conflicting agendas which pervade the world and manifest in complex, and oft devastating ways, it is necessary to dissect the conflicting positions of stakeholders, and the general climate in which they exist. It must be noted that the world is dominated by capitalist culture. This culture, regardless of form of governance, is a manifestation of human nature which inclines humans towards a desire for superiority. As humans, generally, have moved past the era of brunt force and raw strength as a means for achieving superiority, superiority is often sought in the form of wins (be they monetary, argumentative, political, etc). And thus, humans are resistant to revolutionary change, but inclined towards normative progression which ultimately manifests merely in exponentially furthered deviation between betterment of human causes and increases in technological advancement. As technologies initiated by a few accumulate, permitted by policies and marketed by publications, success becomes increasingly easier to those few, and disparity increases. In other terms, the more wins one accumulates, the more capable of achieving more wins he becomes, leading to exponentially furthered inequality and its dismal effects. Those at the bottom of the pyramid are left incapable of foraging their way to the top, and those at the top become

unmotivated to do things which better those at the bottom. However, those at the top are also rendered those most infrastructurally afforded to seek advancement and impose them upon those at the bottom, or at least render the bottom dwellers the indirect recipients of the effects. Essentially, progress occurs two-dimensionally – horizontally across time, facilitated by the vertical rise of a few, rather than multi-dimensionally (as would be most conducive to worldly eudaemonia).

Behind the aforementioned two-dimensional progress, a social hierarchy lies. Those at the top of the pyramid are the executives. They set standards for journalism, endorsing those expressions which further their goals, and condemning those which prove threatening. Subsequently, utmost influence is maintained. Researchers, in order to promote their own survival, are compelled towards topics which are publishable, and thus compatible with the executives' master narratives. In medicine, this phenomenon is particularly evident as researchers more often study topics which prove financially profitable, rather than those most beneficial to utilitarian welfare. Controlled studies, the driving force of maintenance to evidence-based medicine, focus on groups who can afford treatment, leaving the poor disadvantaged in health. In medicating those able to pay, treatment is favored over cure as treatments which must be applied consistently over long periods of time indebt patients to the pharmaceutical industry, rendering the industry financially almighty. Where vaccines are possible, pain pills are distributed to soothe those suffering. There is little motive to cure, and infrastructural barriers run rampant as immediate concerns for individual welfare supersede concerns for the goodness of the system, the very system attempts at self preservation reinforce. And thus, the populace suffers at the mercy of those at the top of the hierarchy, and those who choose to feed into it to survive. Ultimately, we are in a normative period of human exploitation. We are technologically capable of improving human quality of life, but logistically unable to do so as the intersecting worlds of researchers, executives, and journalists have become so entangled that the larger purpose has been lost, if not changed entirely.

This system is further supported by the lack of transparency which inhibits the populace from understanding the mechanics they promote, despite the counter agenda the mechanics pose to the populace's welfare. Social closure pervades academia. R. Taylor quotes D.A. Rew, a scientific writer, as saying "A fog has settled on scientific English. Well-written English effortlessly communicates the writer's intent to the reader. Unfortunately, far too often, science is written in a form that renders the content hard to understand and which makes unreasonable demands on the reader" (2011). In her book *Scientific Writing and Communication: Papers, Proposals, and Presentations 2nd Edition*, Angelika Hoffman details the specific way in which scientific writing must be executed to make it publishable. There are particular words

which should be used, and words which shouldn't be used. There are queues to be ingrained in the text, specific places within sentences where references are included, the place contextualizing the reference and granting meaning to the sentence. In certain types of citations, abbreviations are requisite over expanded phrases (Hoffman, 2010). While these caveats are often justified in that they improve the speed of evidence write-up and thus increase the pace of scientific advancement, even a brief observation of the guidelines delineated by Hofmann illustrates the inaccessibility of the material to the populace, on whom the medicalized reactions to the evidence is often projected. This leaves people unable to participate in their own care.

Medicine is in need of rekindling with the human roots it has deviated drastically from since its origins. Periodically, there have been attempts to reign medicine in. For example, after the exposure of the Nazi experiments, the Nuremberg code was produced. Later, in responses to further ethical breaches, the Belmont Report and Common Rule emerged in the United States. But, none of these referendums served to influence medical culture and drastically revert it as a first order study to humanitarian endeavors. Ideally, there should be a duality in which human life is nurtured by scientific innovation, not in which scientific industrial complex is fed with human life. While promoting interdisciplinary collaboration through more widely accessible communication could prove a hindrance to the pace at which scientific writing is produced, the benefits could prove worthy of the costs. Communication is not truly communication if there is no recipient of the idea. While it has been systemically ingrained that the only people necessary to completing the communication pathway are those already within the inner circle, or able to afford a place within it, the populace has borne the repercussions to a devastating extent. For multi-dimensional, utilitarian progress to be achieved, it is critical that the populace be brought into the realm of the executives, researchers, and journalists who dominate the system with their individualized, yet overlapping roles. In order to act autonomously, people must be able to access the material which factors into their care. Although the pace of scientific writing may be slowed to materialize this prospect, progress would prove more conducive to utilitarian eudaemonia. Thus, change is justified.

It is critical to understand that accessible does not simply mean reachable, but perceivable. And, there are a multitude of ways in which this change can be affected. In their paper "Thinking Across Perspectives," Matthew Miller and Veronica Boix Mansilla make some suggestions for bridging information across disciplines. These suggestions include "reasoning through analogies, creating compound concepts, building complex and multi-causal explanations, advancing through checks and balances, and bridging the explanation-action gap" (2004). Essentially, these ideas are intended to maintain the content

of jargon, while stripping its highfalutin merit by transforming ideas into parallel, contextualized concepts accessible to the layman. By taking the time to translate the caveats of science into publicly understandable terms, people are mobilized to play greater, more educated roles in their own care, and as citizens of the world. The validity of the concern surrounding IFLS and like sources, as sources of simplified, and consequently hazardous material dissipates as people are not forced to obtain the entirety of their perspectives from a singularly over-simplified source (as IFLS must be when not supplemented by a culture of scientific accessibility), but enabled to form well-rounded perspectives by synthesizing a multitude of sources.

In welcoming the populace into the realm of executives, journalists, and researchers, synergy is promoted. The barrier of socioeconomic status as a hindrance to health, environmentalism, and participation in the world is deconstructed. Transparency promotes truthfulness and justice. Incentives to research only that which is financially profitable disappear because the populace challenges visible inequalities. Honesty and fairness are favored and rewarded by reverence from the masses. Though the horizontal progress of science may be slowed, sciences comes to possess greater depth, breadth, and potential for goodness when reduced from lofty scientific aspirations and political agendas to human roots. If science is to coincide with and reinforce human existence, it must promote multi-dimensional, eudaemonia growth.

Kuhn illustrates the necessity of the populace in effecting revolutionary change. Brian Cox, a physicist warns of the potential for total collapse of civilization if technology and political agendas continue to evolve independent of humanitarian concerns, unchanged in direction (Williams, 2016). It is most definitely time to return science to its human roots. We must begin to communicate in an interdisciplinary manner to promote universal well-being and save society from the inevitable annihilation we threaten to inflict upon ourselves should we continue to exclude the populace from everything but the effects of the intersecting worlds of executives, researchers, and journalists.

Works Cited

Greenhalgh, T. (2003). *How to read a paper: The basics of evidence based medicine.* London: BMJ.

Hofmann, A. H. (2010). *Scientific writing and communication: Papers, proposals, and presentations.* New York: Oxford University Press.

Kuhn, T. S. (1996). *The structure of scientific revolutions*. Chicago, IL: University of Chicago Press.

Lewis, S. (2016, October 14). The Great Barrier Reef is not actually dead. Retrieved from http://www.cnn.com/2016/10/14/us/barrier-reef-obit-trnd.

Miller, M., & Boix Mansilla, V. (2004, March). *Thinking Across Perspectives* [Scholarly project].

Outside Magazine. (2016, October 12). *Twitter* [A tweet.].

Sobel, A. (2014, Sept. & oct.). Do You Know Elise Andrew?: The creator of the Facebook page "I f*cking love science" is journalism's first self-made brand . *Columbia Journalism Review*. Retrieved from http://archives.cjr.org/cover_story/elise_andrew.php

Taylor, R. (2011). *Medical Writing: A Guide for Clinicians, Educators, and Researchers* (2nd ed.).

Williams, O. (2016, October 30). Brian Cox Explains Why He Thinks We'll Never Find Aliens. *Huffington Post*. Retrieved from http://www.huffingtonpost.co.uk/entry/brian-cox-explains-why-he-thinks-well-never-find-aliens.uk.

Kimtee Dahari Ramsagur

The Voiceless

For more than 2 years in my late teens, I volunteered for an organization to rehome stray dogs and puppies in my country. Early morning every Saturdays, I would start my day with these puppies at the ELI WOOFF (Welfare Of Our Furry Friends) foster home, caring for them before they get adopted by their new families. My interest in advocating for animal rights started when I came across the cruel truth behind a government-funded organization in my home country that was supposed to care for nuisance-causing stray animals. However, although the dogs were not causing any nuisance on the roads or on beaches, they were cruelly captured and thrown in dog vans. The same day or the next day, these homeless puppies were being slaughtered inhumanely without any anesthetic (Hall, A).

To stop this painful cruelty, the non-governmental organization that I joined had a project of rehoming stray dogs. I met other people with the same compassion for animals and this is how my journey into advocating for animal rights started.

Having the zeal to volunteer for a good cause, I was subsequently elected the head of a beekeeping project to preserve bees and at the same time, I got involved in a group research project to sensitize people about animal cruelty in Mauritius. Animal testing was one of the major research areas we highlighted to the public.

Mauritius, a very small island, a holiday destination known mainly for its fauna and flora, is disreputable as one of the world's largest suppliers of monkeys for the research industry. Every year, ten thousand long-tail monkeys are exported from Mauritius to American and European research industries for $4,000 each (Bligh, Cherry). For each monkey exported, the government of Mauritius charges $70, and the main airline that transports the animals in small export cages, Air France, also benefits a lot from this trade. This shows how difficult it is to fight against the monkey trade since the revenue from it is $20 million every year. However, this amount is still insignificant when compared to the $1.35 billion Mauritius profits from the tourism industry (*Travel & Tourism Economic Impact 2015 Mauritius*). The money received from the monkey trade is less than 2% of the whole income from tourism. When the authorities were questioned why is Mauritius abstaining from banning this

cruel trade, the chief agro-industry officer ignored the issue by saying that this is the only way to reduce the 40,000 to 60,000 monkey's population in the forests (Ackbarally, N). Together with the communications officer of ELI WOOFF, some volunteers and I have been working on ways to stop capturing monkeys on the island, and an open letter was sent to the Prime Minister to address the dilemma and to question the fake promises he made when taking power in 2014 (Manoo). However, petitions and open letters to the Prime Minister have also been overlooked.

Most organizations have been helplessly trying to save those thousands of monkeys that have been captured from their natural habitats and separated from their families to be tortured inhumanely in laboratories in the U.S and U.K. Annual statistics from the U.K government revealed that more than 54% of the monkeys (1,343) that were used in the country in 2014 for medical research were from Mauritius island (Kite, S).

In addition to monkeys, more than 100 million other live animals including rats, mice, pigs, birds, rabbits, and reptiles (of which more than 50% are rats), suffer every year through animal testing (PETA). During investigations in biomedical labs around the U.S., a PETA spy questioned a mouse-lab worker about the treatment of animals and she replied – "How would you like to be sitting in a little square box with half your skin missing and your eyeball hanging out for a week, just shivering in trauma?" (Maffly).

People in the industry are aware of animal suffering but because of this trade expansion and employment opportunities, they simply ignore animal rights. All the animals have nervous systems and they feel just like we humans feel. They get panicked, stressed out, they develop phobias, and they suffer from mental illnesses from research that does not consider animal welfare.

It is not the animal's fault if people want to wear makeup, if people want to smoke and drink until they die of cancer or if people want to have designer babies. Unnecessary and inappropriate animal testing have been carried out with no positive results. For instance, penicillin is toxic to guinea pigs, aspirin is poisonous to cats, and the diet drug Fen-Phen caused no heart damage in animals, while it did in humans. In addition, chimpanzees, our closest genetic relatives, do not accurately predict results in humans; more than 80 HIV vaccines were safe and effective in chimpanzees but all failed in nearly 200 clinical trials to defeat the transmissible disease in humans. One of the vaccines instead increased a human's chance of HIV infection ("Limitations and Dangers" Society, New). Moreover, even though there are no laws that require animal testing for cosmetics and household products like cleaners, manufacturers for famous brands like M.A.C cosmetics, L'Oréal, Maybelline, ChapStick, Pampers, Vaseline, Febreze, Lysol, and Johnson and Johnson to

name a few, still test their products on animals before marketing them (PETA). For instance, rabbits are tested for eye shadows while holding their eyes open with clips. These tests have had adverse effects on them, like inflamed irises, blindness, bleeding and even death (PETA). Besides, through acute toxicity tests, lethal substances are injected into the animals' eyes, rectums, vaginas, stomachs or through holes cut in their throats, waiting for all of them or a huge percentage of them to die. This is not only cruel but ineffective and unnecessary. Millions of animals died in research, but we still do not have answers to AIDS, autism, cancer, Alzheimer's, Parkinson's disease, and many more which have been prevailing for nearly one century now. The alternatives are many and are reliable. Computer models, bioinformatic tools and in-vitro cell and tissue cultures have been effective in medical research and have proved to be less harmful to people. These methods are now being mainly used to monitor the effects of medical drugs toxic substances on humans, thus decreasing the number of live animals used for this research area (Doke, Shashikant).

Most animals have suffered because of biomedical research and despite knowing this fact, I am a Biomedical Engineering major at Drexel. I know that at some point during this career path, I will come across animal testing, and that that animal can probably be a species from my native island. However, I believe that like all the harmless alternatives developed through engineering, my field will undoubtedly allow me to create other alternatives to further decrease the number of animals used in medical research. Laws have been passed against animal ill-treatment in entertainment like dog fighting and in zoos, and I remain positive that animal testing will also stop being overlooked.

Animals are animals and people are people. Two different biological systems. Animals should not suffer for people's unnecessary or ineffective research. Global sensitization is needed to ban animal trade, hence animal testing in medical research. Biomedical engineering is a field in which human life is the most important aspect, and the way the cure is obtained might not really matter. However, it only needs one to have the right ethics and the courage to speak out for the voiceless in whatever way possible. Instead of depending on animals to get answers to our questions, it is better to use science and technology to engineer humane solutions for the overwhelming number of diseases. One thing that I can prove through my future medical research is that people can be cured without any animal tortured.

Works Cited

Ackbarally, Nasseem. "Mauritius: Tax On Exported Monkeys Pays For Conservation." *Global Information Network*: 1. Oct 12 2007. ProQuest. Web. 29 Jan. 2017 .

Bligh, Cherry. "Last Chance For Animals - Air France's Monkey Business." *Lcanimal.org*. N.p., 2017. Web. 30 Jan. 2017.

Doke, Sonali K. and Shashikant C. Dhawale. "Alternatives To Animal Testing: A Review." PMC (2015): n. pag. Print.

"Eli Wooff." *Eli Africa|Think different*. N.p., 2010. Web. 13 Feb. 2017.

Hall, Allan. "The Real Price of Your Paradise Holiday: Dogs Are Injected with Lethal Cocktail of Drugs – Cut With Cleaning Agents To Save Costs – To Stop Them Annoying Tourists." *Daily Mail* 2016. Web. 13 Feb. 2017.

Kite, Sarah. "Pressure Mounts On Mauritius To End The Monkey Trade | Cruelty Free International." *Crueltyfreeinternational.org*. N.p., 2015. Web. 13 Feb. 2017.

"Limitations And Dangers | Animals In Science / Research." *Neavs.org*. Web. 13 Feb. 2017.

Maffly, Brian. "PETA Spy Infiltrates U. Animal-Research Labs, Documents Alleged Suffering." The Salt Lake tribune 0746-3502 (2009): n. pag. Print.

Manoo, Pravisan. "Open Letter To Sir Aneerood Jugnauth: Ban The Monkey Trade." *eli - africa.org*. N.p., 2016. Web. 29 Jan. 2017.

"Monkey Experiments At Max Planck Institute, Germany | Cruelty Free International." *Crueltyfreeinternational.org*. Web. 13 Feb. 2017.

People for The Ethical Treatment of Animals. "Product Testing on Animals Is Cruel and Unnecessary." *Animal Experimentation*. Ed. David M. Haugen. San Diego: Greenhaven Press, 2000. At Issue. *Opposing Viewpoints in Context*. Web. 29 Jan. 2017.

"Stop Animal Testing - It's Not Just Cruel, It's Ineffective." *tribunedigital-baltimoresun*. N.p., 2017. Web. 30 Jan. 2017.

"These Companies Test On Animals. Which Brands Made The List?" *PETA*. Web. 13 Feb. 2017.

Travel & Tourism Economic Impact 2015 Mauritius. London: World Travel and Tourism Council, 2015. Print. The Authority on World Travel & Tourism. (*Travel & Tourism Economic Impact 2015 Mauritius* 3)

Sarah Julius
The Lobotomy: Surgical Procedure or Surgical Oppression?

Psychosurgery is a subset of surgery focusing on physically altering the brain in order to change the patient's personality, in an attempt to cure mental illness. Essentially, it is changing the structure of the brain to alter a person's symptoms or behaviors. Although psychosurgery, in any form, is rarely practiced today because of the controversy that surrounds it, it was popular at various times throughout history. It was often considered much more effective than alternate physical treatments of mental illness available at the time, therefore making it seem much more desirable [18].

It is unclear when the first psychosurgical procedure was performed, but there is much evidence to support that it was being performed as early as the stone age, in the form of trepanation. Throughout history, psychosurgeries have become increasingly complex, but generally showed only limited success. Although attempted for years, it was not until the late 19th century that psychosurgery entered the sphere of mainstream medicine. The first recorded surgical psychiatric procedure performed on humans resembling the modern lobotomy was pioneered in 1888 by Dr. Gottlieb Burckhardt. He was the first to perform the localized cerebral cortical excision, in hopes of decreasing symptoms of agitation in asylum patients [3,6,8,14,17].

Of his six initial patients, each diagnosed with chronic schizophrenia, most showed a marked improvement after the procedure, becoming less prone to outbursts and more likely to do as they were told. One patient died due to the procedure, and another later committed suicide, but the process was still considered successful enough to continue its use. The intention of this procedure was not necessarily to improve the state of the patients' minds but to make the patients more manageable for the asylum employees. Because the cerebral cortical excision had made patients calmer and less prone to outbursts, Burckhardt considered the procedure a success. With this, modern psychosurgery, and the obsession with what would become known as the lobotomy, was born [3,8,16].

In 1900, Ludvig Puusepp began to further Burkhardt's work. Puusepp cut nerves leading from the frontal lobes to the other parts of the brain in psychiatric patients. He hoped that the nerve firings that caused mental

illnesses would be stopped, curing the disease. His results were unimpressive. In the 1910's, he injected caustic chemicals into the frontal lobes of patients, to chemically sever the connections without requiring surgery. Once again, the results were inconclusive, but Puusepp remained optimistic. He continued his work in targeting the frontal lobes for the treatment of mental illnesses [14].

In the 1930's, American doctors Carlyle Jacobsen and John Fulton tested the first frontal lobe ablation in two female chimpanzees, Becky and Lucie. Their goal, like that of Burckhardt, was to make the subjects less prone to agitation. After the surgery, Becky's behavior seemed much improved, displaying less aggressive behavior or tantrums [9]. Lucie, however, did not show much improvement. In fact, her behavior may have worsened. Despite this, Jacobsen and Fulton presented their data in 1935 at the Second World Congress of Neurology in London, as though the experiment had been fully successful [3,4].

Dr. Antonio Egas Moniz attended the symposium and was inspired by the work of Jacobsen and Fulton. In 1935, Moniz developed a procedure like that of Jacobsen and Fulton. Ethanol was injected into the prefrontal cortex of humans to disrupt the neuronal tracts in the cortex. Moniz attempted his procedure on one of his asylum patients, and considered the procedure a success when the patient showed a marked decrease in paranoia and anxiety. A special instrument, the leucotome, was designed specifically for the surgery, replacing ethanol in disrupting the neuronal tracts [3,6,7,10].

Walter Freeman (and his lesser known partner Dr. James Watts) was greatly inspired by the work done by Moniz. He was intrigued and wanted to quickly begin work on this revolutionary new procedure [3]. Freeman was a well-respected psychiatrist working in St. Elizabeth's Hospital in Washington DC when his obsession with the lobotomy began [6]. Watts and Freeman performed over 620 lobotomies together, claiming good results more than 50% of the time. However, they did not give any reference as to what they considered good results for a lobotomy. The highly subjective term of "good results" could have meant anything from the patient becoming highly functioning after the procedure to the patient surviving the procedure. Whatever the results meant, Watts and Freeman believed that the lobotomy was the answer to the mental health crisis the United States seemed to be experiencing [6].

Freeman's procedure was much more efficient than previous methods, as it could be performed in as little as 10 minutes. This would allow it to be performed on many more patients. It also required much less postoperative care than previous lobotomies as there were no incisions made in the skull. When asked years later about his father's procedure, Frank Freeman stated that his father believed there had to be a better procedure.

Freeman's improved method, referred to as the trans-orbital lobotomy, involved entering through the upper portion of the orbital cavity and pushing up into the prefrontal cortex, eliminating the need to open the skull. The leucotome was inserted through the cavity and then forced through the thin bone and into the brain. Often, a hammer would be used to exert the force needed to push the leucotome into the brain. From here, the cortex could be "scrambled," effectively ending any debilitating symptoms.

Freeman initially practiced his methods on cadavers, and it soon became very clear that the leucotome developed for earlier lobotomies would not work well for his procedure. It was far too slim and would often break before it could penetrate the skull behind the orbital cavity. Because of this, Freeman picked a stronger, and eerily familiar tool: the ice pick. The ice pick was designed to exert a strong point force, making it ideal for Freeman's purposes. Using the pick, Freeman could perfect his procedure.

The procedure slowly altered until it could be performed regularly and efficiently. The first official trans-orbital lobotomy was performed on Sallie Ellen Ionesco in 1946. The operation was performed to reduce her suicidal tendencies. After the surgery, Ionesco lived a healthy and productive life. She died 61 years later at the age of 90 [3]. When asked about her mother's procedure, Ionesco's daughter, Angelene Forrester, said, "She was absolutely violently suicidal beforehand. . . It stopped immediately. It was just peace. . . That quick. So, whatever [Freeman] did, he did something right" [12].

After Ionesco's surgery, the procedure became extremely common for patients who had been diagnosed as chronically agitated or self-destructive. By the 1960's, Freeman alone had performed over 3,500 lobotomies [5], traveling from asylum to asylum, performing lobotomies for just twenty-five dollars per person. It had become a lucrative, full-time job for Freeman, and he taught many other mental health professionals to perform the procedure themselves.

Freeman understood that his procedure, which he considered to be life-saving and completely essential for many psychiatric patients, would be considered radical and dangerous by other medical professionals. In a 1979 interview, Dr. James Watts, who stopped work with Freeman when he decided the lobotomy was too dangerous, stated "I knew as soon as I operated on a mental patient and cut into a physically normal brain, I'd be considered radical by some people," [11] and he was right.

Freeman was quickly labeled a radical by some, but the public lauded him as a hero. He was the man who had given cures to the previously incurable. In an interview, Freeman's son, Walter Freeman III, said that his father made the procedure successful, unlike those before him. "In my father's hands, the operation worked. This was an explanation for his zeal" [11].

The lobotomy was soon seen as a cure-all for many different types of mental illness by the American public. Even though the science of how the brain works and what certain portions of it do was very new at the time, doctors believed that they could effectively manipulate the brain to cure mental illness. The brain is broken into four major components: the cerebrum, the cerebellum, the limbic system, and the brain stem. The cerebrum is where most of the higher brain functions take place, and is therefore the subject of most psychosurgical procedures.

Within the cerebrum, there are four lobes: the temporal, occipital, parietal, and frontal lobes. The frontal lobe, the area in question for the lobotomy, contains the centers for creative thought, intellect, judgment, physical reactions, and personality [13]. Histories of people who accidentally experienced brain injuries made it obvious that trauma to the frontal lobe could cause a change in personality.

Doctors like Walter Freeman believed that by cutting nerves in the frontal lobe, the doctor could prevent the brain from "over-acting." To them, it was obvious that the over-stimulation of the frontal lobe was causing the behaviorisms associated with mental illnesses. Modern medicine has since showed us that the brain is not that simplistic and that a person's personality is much more complex. It is now known that, yes, disconnecting a portion of the frontal lobe will change a personality, but it is not possible to correctly predict all the undesirable effects this might have on each patient.

Many patients who had been treated with trans-orbital lobotomies did indeed exhibit reduced agitation or anxiety, exactly as Freeman had claimed they would. Later, it was largely realized that along with these changes, patients also showed side effects such as apathy, inability to concentrate, and general emotional numbness. Some patients completely withdrew and were unable to take care of their own basic needs. They would often need to be fed, clothed, and bathed by nurses. Other side effects caused by the lobotomy included incontinence, eye problems, and lethargy.

Death was also a common occurrence; patients could die during the procedure or soon after if complications arose. Sometimes, the death would occur because the surgical instrument would penetrate too deeply into the brain. Other times, the patient might experience excessive bleeding within the brain. Because the incisions were not visible, and patients rarely received postoperative care [1], the bleeding within the brain would go unchecked. The hemorrhaging would cause pressure in the brain to build up, eventually killing the patient.

Despite the side effects and high mortality rate, doctors in asylums across the globe continued to perform the procedure. Most people still believed that being lobotomized was much better for the patient than suffering mental illness. Eventually the practice of the lobotomy had become so widely disseminated it became essential to the operation of hospitals everywhere.

Even though many asylums depended on Freeman's methods to "cure" their patients that displayed more severe symptoms, lobotomies in time became heavily criticized by American physicians. Doctors and psychiatrists alike seemed to hold a great distrust for Freeman's procedure.

In 1948, near the beginning of the lobotomy craze, Dr. Florence Powdermaker, chief of the VA's psychiatric education section stated that she believed that Freeman was too liberal with his surgery. Powdermaker said that she thought Freeman would treat anyone with a lobotomy, even someone who was simply a "pain-in-the-neck." She wondered if Freeman would ever come to accept that his lobotomy might not be the cure-all that can be used in any circumstances. In 1949, Dr. Harvey Tompkins of the VA said the agency had performed over 1,200 lobotomies, but could not definitively state whether the procedure had worked in any of the cases [11].

Others criticized Freeman for not making people aware of the dangers of his procedure. In 1948, Dr. Francis Murphey said that he was unsure of any procedure that did not come with a set of dangers and warnings. "So far as I know [Dr. Freeman] has published no article on the subject . . . I know nothing about the dangers, complications, or results" [11]. He warned other doctors about his concerns, stating that he could not approve of a method that couldn't allow a surgeon to see the area of the brain being altered.

Late in his life, even Dr. James Watts, the man who helped Freeman pioneer the lobotomy, stated that the lobotomy was a procedure that could not be completely trusted. "It's a brain-damaging operation – it changes the personality. We could predict relief. . . But we could not nearly as accurately predict what kind of person this was going to be" [11].

Despite the many problems associated with the procedure, the public continued for many years to view the lobotomy as something to be praised. For many of the individuals working in asylums, the procedure was not only a way of lessening the burden of care by easing symptoms, but it could also be a way of improving the quality of life for patients.

It was often believed by asylum employees that the lobotomy was a better alternative than other commonly used treatments, which included isolation, sensory deprivation, and straightjackets [1]. Effective chemical treatments

were extremely scarce at this point in history, so physical treatments and interventions were the only things available for severe mental illnesses. By performing a procedure known for its numbing effects, they were, in a way, helping the patients not feel as dismal or depressed about their situation.

Despite the dangers, the public, who saw the lobotomy as a cure for the "least of humanity," first viewed the procedure as a miracle. It wasn't until much later when it became apparent how awful the procedure was that public criticism developed. At first, all that was seen by the public was the great number of success stories, the great number of people whose lives had been saved and returned to them by the lobotomy.

The question then becomes, did the lobotomy actually improve the quality of life for those subjected to it? Quality of life is defined as "the general well-being of a person. . . in terms of health and happiness, rather than wealth" [15]. Individuals who had been lobotomized were often too numb to feel any emotions, let alone happiness. Individuals who could not take care of themselves and were resigned to life-long care in an asylum were rarely healthy. They were exposed to all kinds of communicable diseases. From this alone, it becomes abundantly clear that those who had been lobotomized rarely experienced a better quality of life [4].

Along with the many physical side effects of the procedure, lobotomies came with their own set of ethical issues as well [7]. The lobotomy was effectively used for cutting off a part of the brain, changing a person's behaviorisms and personality [4]. Because of this, the procedure should have been used sparingly, but it was not. It was often used on patients who had little-to-no previous treatment. It was seen as faster and easier than exhausting other methods.

Patients were often individuals who were diagnosed with mental disorders that could possibly be eased with talk therapy and mild medications, rather than intensive surgical interventions. Such mental disorders included bipolar disorder, depression, and PTSD [2]. While the lobotomy may have seemed warranted in some severe cases of these disorders, for newly diagnosed or less severe cases, alternate treatments should have been attempted before lobotomy was considered.

Another potentially disturbing issue comes from the fact that the lobotomy could alter a person's personality in unwanted or unexpected ways. Some people protested the lobotomy because of the effects it would have on who the patient was. The child of one of Freeman's patients stated, "I personally think that something in Dr. Freeman wanted to be able to take away who they were" [12]. The lobotomy gave doctors more of a chance to play

God than ever before. They could use the lobotomy to control those who were already extremely vulnerable.

Informed consent was almost never acquired before a lobotomy was performed [1,4]. Freeman believed that if a patient was in a condition where a lobotomy was considered necessary, they could not issue consent. Instead, he went to the patient's family, hoping he could receive consent from them. The patients almost never knew what was happening when they were taken into the operating room by Freeman.

The lobotomy remained popular for much longer than it should have. Many critics say that this may have been due to the rather large number of individuals in the public eye who were treated with lobotomies. Fortunately, by the 1950's, lobotomies were gradually replaced with medications and other therapies. Lobotomies are still used, but only in cases where no improvement is seen after all various other treatments have been tried and exhausted. Even though the procedure has been almost completely written off, this does not begin to make up for the pain and horror that lobotomy victims in the 1930's through 1960's experienced.

Freeman probably performed more lobotomies than any other surgeon in the world. After an estimated 5,000 procedures, Freeman performed his last lobotomy in 1967. The procedure was on Mrs. Helen Mortenson. Mortenson died of a brain hemorrhage, effectively ending Freeman's career and the popularity of the lobotomy. People finally saw that the lobotomy was dangerous and cruel. Concern about the procedure became less about the potential for curing individuals and more about protecting them from drastic surgical oppression. Freeman spent the rest of his life trying to redeem himself, but to most, he will remain a reckless doctor who performed terrible procedures [5].

In conclusion, the lobotomy was a horrific and unnecessary surgical procedure that gained acclaim and popularity through false claims of a cure for mental illnesses. It was an ethical travesty that was once lauded, but is now feared. Doctors, such as Freeman and Moniz believed that the lobotomy could help cure thousands of people, but there has never been scientific evidence to support such claims. The lobotomy is a history lesson that must be learned very well, because such travesties should never be allowed in the medical community again.

Works Cited

[1] - 10 Awful Realities Behind The Lobotomy Craze Listverse. *List verse*. 2014. Available at: http://listverse.com/2014/11/20/10-awful-realities-behind-the-lobotomy-craze/. Accessed June 30, 2016.

[2] - Bipolar disorder Treatments and drugs Mayo Clinic. *Mayo clinicorg*. 2016. Available at: http://www.mayoclinic.org/diseasesconditions/bipolardisorder/basics/treatment/con20027544. Accessed August 14, 2016.

[3] - Cutting of the Mind: The History of Psychosurgery. *DUJS Online*. 2008. Available at: http://dujs.dartmouth.edu/2008/04/cutting-of-the-mind-the-history-of-psychosurgery-and- its-application-today. Accessed August 6, 2016.

[4] - Fenton G. Neurosurgery for Mental Disorder: Past and Present. *Advances in Psychiatric Treatment*. 1999;5(4):261270. doi:10.1192/apt.5.4.261.

[5] - Freeman and Lobotomy. *Mcmanwebcom*. 2016. Available at: http://www.mcmanweb.com/lobotomy.html. Accessed August 16, 2016.

[6] - Guide to the Walter Freeman and James Watts Papers, 19181988 Collection number MS0 803.UA. *Librarygwuedu*. 2016. Available at: https://library.gwu.edu/ead/ms0803.xml. Accessed August 16, 2016.

[7] - Gross DSchäfer G. Egas Moniz (1874–1955) and the "invention" of modern psychosurgery: a historical and ethical reanalysis under special consideration of Portuguese original sources. *Neurosurgical FOCUS*. 2011;30(2):E8. doi:10.3171/2010.10.focus10214.

[8] - JL S. Dr. Gottlieb Burckhardt the pioneer of psychosurgery. PubMed NCBI. *Ncbinlmnihgov*. 2016. Available at: http://www.ncbi.nlm.nih.gov/pubmed/11446267. Accessed June 26, 2016.

[9] - Lobotomy: How An Explosives Accident Brought This Brain Surgery To Prominence. *Psychologistworldcom*. 2016. Available at: https://www.psychologistworld.com/biological/lobotomy.php. Accessed August 13, 2016.

[10] - lobotomy | surgery. *Encyclopedia Britannica*. 2016. Available at: http://www.britannica.com/topic/lobotomy. Accessed June 26, 2016.

[11] - Michael Phillips D. The Lobotomy Files: How one doctor steered the VA toward a lobotomy program. *WSJcom*. 2016. Available at: http://projects.wsj.com/lobotomyfiles/?ch=two. Accessed August 13, 2016.

[12] - "My Lobotomy": Howard Dully's Journey. *NPRorg*. 2005. Available at: http://www.npr.org/2005/11/16/5014080/mylobotomyhowarddullysjourney. Accessed August 13, 2016.

[13] - Parts of the Brain and Their Functions | MDHealth.com. *Mdhealthcom*. 2016. Available at: http://www.mdhealth.com/PartsOfTheBrainAndFunction.html. Accessed August 15,2016.

[14] - Psychosurgery children, therapy, person, people, used, brain, skills, theory, health. *Minddisorderscom*. 2016. Available at: http://www.minddisorders.com/ObPs/Psychosurgery.html. Accessed August 15, 2016.

[15] - Quality of life | Definition, meaning & more | Collins Dictionary. *Collinsdictionarycom*. 2016. Available at: http://www.collinsdictionary.com/dictionary/english/qualityoflife. Accessed August 14, 2016.

[16] - The rise & fall of the prefrontal lobotomy. *Neurophilosophy*. 2016. Available at: http://scienceblogs.com/neurophilosophy/2007/07/24/inventingthelobotomy/. Accessed July 3, 2016.

[17] - trepanation The Skeptic's Dictionary Skepdic.com. *Skepdiccom*. 2016. Available at: http://skepdic.com/trepanation.html. Accessed August 17, 2016.

[18] - What is Psychosurgery? definition of Psychosurgery(Psychology Dictionary). *Psychology Dictionary*. 2016. Available at: http://psychologydictionary.org/psychosurgery/. Accessed August 15, 2016.

Drexel Publishing Group
Creative Writing

Introduction

Creative writing is challenging. Creative writers take their experiences and observations and transform them into written journeys for their readers.

The following works were selected by faculty judges from student submissions (of fiction, poetry, non-fiction, op-ed, and humor) to the Drexel Publishing Group Creative Writing Contest. These varied and diverse pieces may make you laugh, cry, think, and marvel at the students who wrote them. The writers whose work appears in this section wrote because they *needed* to write, and they wanted to share their work. Please enjoy the writing they shared.

- The Editors

Nicholas Yurcaba

Cranes on a River Bank

I've never seen cranes eat
only build.
But romance isn't dead
my heart's still filled

in the summer city heat
I feel it;
Basquiat's crown on my head,
The primal halo

The endless highway too
I see it.
The nautilus spiral roads stretch
A path before me

And the wind blowing by rhymes
I hear it.
The ancient voices warm
Tell me it's all the same

And from glass capped peaks
Over steel canopies,
Brick skinned bushes,
And cement leaves
I see.

Jesse Antonoff

Overture

Sun soiled barren lot
becomes garden for the moment

behind a cloud
that barn red Toyota
rolls by

And parks saturated
stereo pulling heated bow
for shade again
the next draw somber

and the garden withers back
weeds and gravels
for breath, plunging mood
chamber blossom rocks
the swing
that hung there

James P. Haes

Smirk

I was eight-years old when I first heard it, sitting shotgun in my grandfather's teal '56 Chevy Bel Air. He slipped the cassette into the stereo without taking his eyes off the road. I leaned forward, wedging myself between my seat and the front of the car. I never wore a seat belt back then; no one did. Strategically, I lined my swamp green army men along the white, polished, leather dashboard. The somber drone of a harpsichord rang out through the speakers and caught my ear. I never heard anything like it at the time. My grandfather was strictly an Elvis man on road trips so the sudden deviation from the norm struck me. Puzzled, I turned to him.

"Who is this grand-" He cut me off, pressing his index finger to his wrinkled lips, then pointed to the stereo using the same finger, not daring to interrupt the orchestra.

I scooched back over in my seat, pressing my chest against the dash. An army man in each hand, I prepared each side for battle. As the music engulfed me, the war was waged. With every note a bullet fired, with every octave change a life was lost, with every drop in tempo a comrade was mourned. The engine purred down the highway like a Panzer and with each pothole in the road shocks of artillery brought the soldiers to their knees. The men slid across the dash as we made a left hand turn, others became lodged, crushed between the defrost vents. No one was making it out of this one alive.

Something about the music was pandemonious yet simultaneously peaceful. Even in my make believe war, amidst total fictional chaos, everything felt serene. Just as in an orchestral performance, each move in war is calibrated and methodical. One misstep, one wrong note, can ruin a score or lose a life. As my men laid scattered along the upholstery, the music soldiered on. While the tranquility of the song encapsulated me, I pressed my cheek against the cool glass of the window and absorbed every note like a sponge. I gazed through the glass as the red rocks of the Arizona desert sped by in a blur. From the corner of my eye, I watched my grandfather soak in the music. The white hairs of his mustache blew ever so slightly from the breeze that snuck in through the vents. I could have sworn his eyes were closed. This lullaby was having the same effect on him as it was me.

As the music ceased, my grandfather slowly turned down the volume knob of the stereo, fading the harpsichord into silence. No one spoke for a moment until the hypnosis wore off.

"George Frideric Handel." He broke the silence.

"What?" I responded confusedly. He caught me off guard. I had completely forgot I asked him the question just a few minutes earlier.

"That's the composer. Handel."

"I liked it. It was, different."

My grandfather allowed a crooked smirk through his rugged exterior, but he quickly regained composure. He was never one to express much emotion, but neither was I. I think that is why we got along so well.

The car slowed as we pulled off onto a dirt path, kicking up clouds of orange dust in our wake. We stopped maybe a mile down and both exited the car without saying a word. I followed my grandfather through a small clearing in the brush. It hadn't grown in much since when we here last year, so it was easy to navigate, just some briars and weeds that I knew better than to get caught on. Just a few hundred feet and we were back to martian like surface of the desert. We came here every year since my dad moved me to California. It was our favorite spot.

Nature's most majestic piece of architecture stood before us, the Grand Canyon. It was if Michelangelo carved the masterpiece out of the Earth's crust himself, using the Colorado River as his tool. Even though I had seen it from the same exact spot every year since I was three, the sight was still unfathomable.

Like the wrinkles on my grandfather's tanned, sun-worn skin, the layers of rock revealed the planet's age. Miles of treacherous mountains, valleys and gorges, each with their own tales to tell, created an inhospitable terrain. Yet, despite the harshness of the environment and the certain death that lingered below, it was the most indescribable, alluring sight I would ever see.

We stood side by side at the edge of the earth, the harlequin sky before us, and watched as the sun drifted beyond the horizon. My grandfather hummed a familiar tune. Handel. I peered up at him, beads of sweat dripped down his forehead. Glancing down from the corner of his eye, he caught me in admiration. I quickly diverted my attention back to mother Earth. He reached his hand in the pocket of his tattered, denim jacket and retrieved a small object. Still humming, he held it out in front of me, motioning me to take it. I

tilted my eyes downward and gently extended my open hand. It was a cassette. A small piece of white tape stretched across the contrasting dark surface and written in faded black marker it read "G.F. Handel." Focusing my eyes back on the Arizona skyline, I began to hum along.

Now, 20 years later with some wrinkles of my own, I sit on a cold mahogany bench in the front of a church. Swimming in a sea of black, the only thing that separates me is my dress blues. As the pastor ends his sermon, everyone stands in unison, including myself. The procession begins, granting us a final moment to pay our respects. As I take my first step, a familiar song echoes throughout the chapel. A tear streams down my face, but is caught by a crooked smirk.

Cindy Phan

Watchmaker

I started feeling for my husband again when April came.

We had an early spring that year, so by the time April came around, all the rains had stopped, the flowers were in full bloom, the air was gentle, and the sun was out. It reminded me of our first April together, when we'd first started seeing each other, talking and smiling on a stone bench in a quiet park where the trees had soft green dust that fell upon our heads.

We married two Aprils later, and I gave birth to our little boy on the fourth April we shared. We called him Junior, because we'd named him after his father, hoping he'd be like the great man, one day.

The three of us were happy together, living in our quiet little house in the middle of a cul-de-sac with a white picket fence and all. For years, it was day in and day out of running after Junior, asking my husband about his work at the thrift shop, and working at my office job in my same old cubicle. For years it was one day following another, weeks and months passing, and April's meaning nothing.

Junior is big enough to run around and talk now, and I started listening to his stories and his jokes more than I listened to my husband's talk of work.

Sometimes, I wondered if my husband noticed it too—how we didn't really talk anymore, or how we didn't even really look at each other anymore. We took care of Junior. We did that really well, I supposed. We love Junior more than anything. But we were just there, two bigger figures in the boy's life. I sometimes wondered if he even knew his dad and I had been inseparable souls before, not just two distant figures moving about in the same house.

One day, I'd left the house to drop Junior off at his best friend's house a few blocks away in another cul-de-sac. I came home to find that my husband was home early from work. He sat at our dining room table with this feverish look about him, staring over a pile of random little pieces I could only assume was a tiny broken clock. It turned out to be a pocket watch.

Apparently if you took a watch apart, it always seems bigger than it actually is. I told my husband this, and he laughed. The sound of his laughter was strange to me—like I was hearing it for the first time.

"That's like looking at Time, as well," he told me. "Just gleaning over it, Time is just *Time*." He shrugged, then looked at the working clock on our wall, and told me the time. "It's four in the afternoon," he said. "But if we start to unpack it, like break down Time, there's so much!"

I smiled at him. My husband had never been much into thinking about Time or looking at broken watches. But there he was, this familiar stranger smiling back at me, with a new and beautiful light in his eyes.

"Are you going to fix that?" I asked him. "Trying to be a person who fix watches?"

He nodded, then shrugged. "I guess. I've been feeling crazy nostalgic lately. Maybe I'll fix it, and then make it go backwards! Wouldn't that be fun?" I noticed a mischievous look come to his face. I noticed ideas turning in his head. "Oh, I could rework it. Maybe if I figure out how, I could make this watch better, not just fix it."

"So you're trying to be a quirky watchmaker?" I teased him. "Where did you find it?"

"Some funny-looking man came in a while ago. Dropped it off, and that was that."

"Was it already broken?"

"Yes."

"You took in a broken watch?"

"I'm going to be a quirky little watchmaker, like you said!"

"I never called you 'little'."

He smiled at me, then nodded and explained, "I didn't pay him for it. I just thought I'd take it off his hands."

That was the beginning of April. Days after, I watched him sitting at that dining table, poking at the delicate gears and cogs with tiny tweezers and a flashlight he'd wear on his forehead, like a ridiculous crown. He'd read all these

strange articles and books about how to fix a broken pocket watch, and he'd recount them to me. He'd tell me about how none of them gave him what he was looking for, however. None of them would tell him the secret to actually fixing that watch. So all that month, the watch remained in pieces on our dining table, and my husband remained a fixed statue there, trying to put it together.

I thought it was funny. By the end of April, I'd grown fond of seeing him always there, mumbling over the watch, and then mumbling to me. I supposed that nothing really changed, but in a way it all did. There was a brighter light to him now—like he had a purpose. I thought it was all so funny, how meticulous he was with the watch, and I took to teasing him endlessly.

He'd laugh about it. I remembered how great his sense of humor had been. I remembered how he could really take a joke, and make one right back at me without even thinking. Junior even joined in, and some nights the three of us would sit there, telling random stories and making jokes to each other.

It was the end of April, again, and I really felt for my husband.

Then one day, I came home after dropping Junior off. That time, I was dropping Junior off to school. I came home to feel a sudden emptiness about the house. I noticed that the dining table was empty, and my husband and the broken pocket watch were both gone.

It felt odd, to say the least. It didn't really scare me. It was just a bit of a shock, to have someone or something always be there, and then without warning it vanishes.

"Will?" I called, running around the house looking for him. "Will Bishop!" I shouted when I grew frustrated being unable to find him.

"Hey, hey. I'm here," he called, breathless and stupidly smiling from the top of the stairs.

"What happened to your watch?" I looked up at his beaming face from the bottom step.

My husband came hurrying down to me, holding a glass jar and not a watch in his hands. "Look what I did," he told me. He handed the jar to me, that bright smile still not vanishing, and the watch nowhere in sight.

Inside the jar there were two small twigs still with soft white blossoms clinging onto them, and seed-like leaves that looked hard and dead. Scattered around the bottom were a green dust that look almost like sand.

"Tree dust," he told me, grinning and meeting my eyes.

I hadn't made the connection then, so I just looked at him and raised an eyebrow.

"Tree dust from the park in April on our first date!" he explained, his voice a little hurried, a little impatient that I didn't understand, but endearing.

"You're kidding," I laughed.

"No." He was still grinning, and while I didn't know what to believe, I didn't dare take it away from him. "Really, the same dust that fell that day."

I relented, and went along with him. "The same ones that fell on our heads?"

"Exact same," he nodded. "I stole them right out of Time, right from April 30th of 1985. I don't know if I ever told you this, but I've always wondered how we looked. I've always wondered what you and I looked like, falling in love, just being together. I wondered how another person would have seen us, and if they could feel it too—all those feelings. So I figured I'd go back in time and check it all out, you know?" He shrugged at me, all plain and simple, and smiled.

"Brilliant!" I beamed, allowing the illusion.

"This is good, right? You want to see more?"

I hadn't thought much of it then, what he meant. I just nodded, and smiled. As shallow as I was, I didn't think much about anything, then. I was just delighted he remembered strange little things like that, and happier that I could really feel for him again like I once had—like on April 30th, all those years ago.

In the days following, my husband would bring me random little things from our past. Each time, he'd tell me how he'd stolen that item right out of Time itself for me, so I could keep it forever, and not have to worry about the turn of the world erasing all the memories we'd made.

My husband brought me a steaming cup of coffee from the coffee shop we once loved. The drink was still hot and I drank slowly it as he told me about the baristas who worked there, the people we'd since forgotten over the years. He told me about the concert they invited him to, so many years in the past. I remembered a hint of cherries and salt in the coffee I drank—just a gentle nod, not quite a taste—and it was exactly like the ones we'd drank so many times at that old coffee shop.

One time while I was out in the garden, ripping out weeds and grumbling at the stupid uneven dirt, my husband ran out of the house with Junior laughing and dangling from his neck. They both crouched down beside me, and presented me with a bouquet of fresh blue hydrangeas. I'd seen blue hydrangeas many times before in my life, but there was this one time when my husband and I had glimpsed upon a bush of blue hydrangeas the color of sapphire gems. They were the bluest flowers I'd ever seen. It was a long time ago, before we were married. My husband stealthily plucked a cluster out of the bush sitting on the edge of someone's yard. He presented me the stolen bouquet as a present, then held my hand and pulled me as we ran away. That was the day I remembered telling him I loved him, and I was in love with him. So years later, my husband presented me with blue hydrangeas as a reminder, and I didn't think much of it.

On a random day as spring was about to end, I walked up to my bedroom to find that a large glass bowl had magically appeared on my bedside table. My husband was sitting on the bed, putting something away tucked just under the pillow on his side of the bed. He looked over at me, then directed my attention back to the bowl. There was a lily pad floating in the center, moving steadily to the side as a scarlet red fish swam by it. It was a Siamese fighting fish. That exact same fish in the bowl reminded me of one we'd seen when we first moved in together, thinking we should add another life to our little apartment. We'd bought that brilliant red fish, and named him Noodles, because we were kids then and Noodles sounded like a good name.

"Is that Noodles?" I asked him, remembering.

He grinned at me. "The exact same."

I bent down to admire the fish. I couldn't tell if it was really Noodles, brought back from the dead or not. Noodles died shortly before we moved out of that old apartment, got married, and got our house. Our Noodles was dead long ago. But I figured I would accept this imposter, just for the sake of my husband.

"Did you steal him out of Time again?" I asked, just for the fun of it.

"Exactly," my husband nodded, his smile everlasting.

I hadn't thought too deeply into it then, my husband bringing back life from our past. I hadn't given much thought to any of it.

The day after, I came home from a long day at work, hoping I'd find my husband somewhere with another random little piece of nostalgia to show me. Junior was off at school, having had to stay late because the poor boy managed to get detention. I didn't even know they gave detention in the fifth grade.

I came home, and the house was empty. I wasn't about to call for my husband, thinking he'd show up somewhere smiling with a little knickknack from the history we shared. Instead, he was nowhere to be found, but on the empty dining table he'd left me with a single photograph.

The photograph was in black and white. It was a picture of us, when we were still very young. It was how we'd looked that day, when we went on our first date, April 30th, 1985. We were sitting on a stone bench in the sunlit park, and wind was blowing at us. You could see the leaves frozen by the photograph as they danced in circles on the flagstones. You could see the birds, mid-flight, against the breeze. That same wind blew the tree dust upon us, and swept a strand of my dark hair across my face. You could see my husband facing me, his eyes soft and dazed, a permanent smile etched upon his face. You could see us falling in love in that photograph, the way I looked at him, the way he looked at me.

We never took pictures that day. We'd been too shy then, to ask for pictures. Yet that photograph was there, in my hands, presenting me with a window into the very moment I remembered feeling for my husband for the very first time. I could remember the feeling. It was like a hand was playing with my heart, gripping one of the veins or heartstrings that made me feel, and tugging. It was at once frightening and ecstatic, and it made me vulnerable.

"Will?" I called, hoping he'd come bounding down the stairs.

I turned the photograph over, and found several words scrawled on the back in my husband's sloppy handwriting. He wrote: *This is us. I hope you like it. I'll be back soon with better things. I promise.*

He didn't come back after that. He left me with a bunch of stolen memories and a growing son, in late spring. I searched under his pillow and all over the house for that pocket watch, but I never found it either. I just knew that it'd gone off somewhere with my husband, taking the place that my son and I should have had.

I didn't call my son by Junior, anymore, after that year. I started calling him Will, because he was named after his dad. We named him that, hoping he would grow up to be like the man, and do great things. But I started calling my son Will, because I hoped he wouldn't be a *junior* to his father, a replication. I didn't want my little boy to be like his father and just leave one day without a proper, logical explanation. So I called him Will, not like his father, but as his own person, hoping he'd grow up to be someone different and not a man who smiles and leaves.

Samantha Stein

The Dying Game: An Allegory in the Chronicles of Stephen and Nick

Stephen sat up on the small cot he had slept on in a tiny cell of Arbitrate State Penitentiary. He rubbed his eyes groggily, smearing the sleepiness from them. "Morning," he yawned to his cellmate, Nick. Nick gave him a grim upturn of the lips from where he lay connected to a motley of tubes each hissing, whirring, and clicking as they mechanically simulated all of the functions his body could not execute on its own. GRUSM – that's what the doctors had called his disease. It was a terrible disease which debilitated him and made it so he could not dance, play the piano, or go on long walks in the city as he had once liked to do.

In another bubble, a man sat sternly at a machine which would have been referred to as a computer in Stephen and Nick's bubble. He typed furiously, setting up the system so that at 10:59 am he could press delete and eliminate Stephen from the the bubble. Stephen was one of the "bad guys" as they referred to his kind. He was convicted of murder several years back and thus, they had determined, he was undeserving of one of the country's houses or some of its overabundance of food. The country had more houses than people and food than hunger, and yet men still lined the streets begging for shelter and meals because they could not afford the homes which lie vacant around town and the food which the grocery store tossed out at the end of the day. This discrepancy, the man had always been told, was because of something called capitalism, a weird system in which people vied for nearly everything possible, from cars, to homes, to food, to these stashes of paper with strange green markings they kept in something called bank accounts, or so it was rumored. The man, however, had never laid hands on these green bills, but he had heard much about them in science fiction movies. They were no good, the movies said.

Nick blinked his eyes. "Typing, typing, typing . . ." his computer read out. It spoke for him since he was unable to speak on his own, picking up cues from his eye movements. Stephen looked up. "Are. You. Ready?" Nick's computer sounded out monotonously, except for a mere upturn at the end of the last word, the words themselves practically the only indication that it was a question. Stephen sighed.

"I'd do anything to trade places with you right now," he commenced, gesturing at Nick lying helplessly alive in the bed.

"Funny. I'd. Do. Anything. To. Trade. Places. With. You," the computer bleeped back a few moments later. The irony of it all was that Stephen, despite his desire to live and prospects for rehabilitation, was going to be forced to die in just a few hours at the mercy of the death penalty. Nick, on the other hand, who was miserable in his deprived state of life, was being forced to live on so long as machines were able to support him, as the state had outlawed physician assisted suicide for the past 50 years. It hadn't always been like that. But a new law was implemented after it became apparent that people had begun seeking death because they were unhappy in their lives – an idea incomprehensible to the government. "So what if people want to die because they're mentally suffering or because they're terminally ill, it's all about quality of life" Nick's computer blurted out practically reading Stephen's mind. Stephen perked up in realization that at least someone got it, someone understood. The fact was, most people got it, but the state was controlled by a small population of religious dictators, elected by the small percentage of people who could vote. People were required to pass a theology test before they were allowed to vote. This essentially eliminated all people who believed religion to be a frivolous waste of time undeserving of attention from government, leaving the government to rule freely based on anachronistic beliefs. It was quite strange indeed, the way it all worked, they mused frequently.

Then, in another spurt of revelation, Stephen began to laugh. It was all so ridiculously funny because none of it was real at all. It was all just one giant simulation. They were fretting over things which did not even exist. In a flurry of emotion, Stephen pummeled across the room, ripped the tube from Nick's mouth, and stabbed it into the side of his neck. *Better to press delete myself*, he thought as the blood spurted steadily from his carotid, *it's all I can do*. Nick sputtered for breath, unable to grasp at the air which moved shallowly in and out of his nose. And then their brains melted into the bliss of nonexistence, merging into the possibility of simulation.

The guy on the computer watched as the screen turned black and began to flash. *Oh well*, he thought, *those ones got away. Better luck next time, Jeff.*

Neida Mbuia Joao

Telling College Stories

There is a sepia-toned picture of my father hanging up in my living room. He's about forty-years old in the photo, which was taken in the seventies, about ten years after he first arrived in the United States, bright-eyed and ready for new opportunities. In it his eyes are twinkling as they did and he's smiling broadly, too broadly and I can that tell he's laughing at his own joke. At his funeral one of his friends asked me what my favorite thing about my father was. I smiled at him shyly through my tears and answered, "His sense of humor. He was one of the funniest people I knew." A look of confusion crossed his friend's face. Like my father, he was a blunt man, assured that his thoughts and opinions were vital to the world. "Really?" He said. "I didn't know he had one."

In truth, I wasn't surprised that my father's friend was shocked that he had a sense of humor. My father was a reckless volcano of a man. His anger was such that any slight thing anyone said could set him off in an instant and once the eruption began, it didn't end until it had destroyed something. There would be swearing, yelling, tossing of projectiles. Countless plates, lamps, picture frames, couches and Chinese food menus in the wrong place at the wrong time were lost to my father's wrath. When he came down from it he was usually sorry and willing to make amends with a trip to the mall and free use of his debit card. But in the midst of an eruption he was the most terrifying thing I had ever seen. As a result, throughout the years, me, my mother and my sister got very good at tip-toeing.

Though he sometimes terrified me when I was young, mostly his anger never seemed to turn on me directly. There would be the odd instance, like when I broke his toilet with my childhood curiosity, where his eruptive anger would be focused me and I would be subject to the "belt of knowledge." But those were few. Mostly, I noticed as I got older, I had a calming effect on him. My sister told me that when she was younger my father's rage had been much worse. He'd calmed down immediately after I was born, and starting coming home (and staying home) much more.

When I was a small child, along with being a volcano my father was an eclipse that took up most of the space in my mind. Everything he did fascinated me, from the way he tied his shoes to the sharp piney scent of the

Brut aftershave he wore. He lived his life in a strict routine. Every morning of my childhood he would wake up at 5 a.m., take his shower, have his coffee and then head to work. He'd be gone for nearly twelve hours every day, but when he came home, he always took the time to hang out with me.

There's an Abraham Lincoln quote, "All that I am or ever hope to be, I owe to my mother." That quote applies to me but in terms of my father. I have his eyes, his eyesight, his nose, his mouth, his intellect. People would always tell me how alike we looked, down to the faint dimple that appeared in our left cheeks when we laughed too hard. When he came home from work, we would sit in our living room surrounded by his library and read books together. When we weren't reading, he was telling me stories of his life before he'd had me and my sister. His favorite stories to tell were those about his college years. Learning was my father's favorite thing and he'd spent about 15 years in college at University of Illinois and Catholic University getting his doctorate. He would talk about college like it was Mecca, a holy land where knowledge and friends came together to make life perfect. He told endless stories about football games and tailgates, professors' antics, and wild stuff he'd done with his friends. He was most excited for me to go to college I think because out of my siblings I was the most like him. It didn't particularly matter to him where I went to school, just that I went and that I enjoyed myself.

All this talk about college made me think that my father was the smartest man alive. He'd owned and read more books than any person I knew and every question I asked him he had an answer to. My father was like Superman to me, about as broad as Clark Kent if not as tall. Just like everyone, I didn't ever really expect Superman to die.

No one told me my dad had been diagnosed with cancer until a year after it started eating him up. It was the summer before my junior year and the day my mother told me the news my father was lying in a hospital bed for fourth time in as many months. He'd been complaining of stomach pain for a long while, but me and my sister had chalked it up to his normal overreaction. We'd spent our childhood watching our Colossus of a father destroy people's worlds for looking at him sideways; we figured that no stomach pain could be so bad that he couldn't handle it.

And so I was sitting in his empty room watching his television and avoiding my homework when my mother got the call from his doctor. When she walked into the room, back hunched and eyes wet, I knew something was wrong. My mother didn't cry. In fact, she abhorred it. She prized strength over anything and even a single tear bore the threat of weakness.

But there she stood, crying in front of me, the strongest woman I knew falling weaker and weaker as she told me about the fall of the strongest man I knew.

"Daddy has cancer, mamita," she said. "That was his oncologist. He said it's getting worse."

I hadn't known that there was even a worse to begin with, and here it was in front of me, proof that the world was ending. *This must have been how Chicken Little felt when he realized the sky was falling*, I thought to myself in the shower later.

But I don't think I understood the gravity of the situation. There were little things about my father that would change over time. He stopped telling stories. He started sleeping in or not sleeping at all, resulting in the breakdown of the routine he'd cultivated over 35 years of working for the government. He got smaller, in height as well as weight to where he could hardly hold the door open for longer than ten seconds. His eyesight worsened, so that he could hardly read any of the thousands of books he'd spent so much time amassing. And towards the end, when it got really bad, he could hardly move to shave himself, so that his classic scent of Irish Spring soap and Brut cologne was quickly replaced with a vague aroma of urine and diaper rash cream.

I watched him change, grow weaker, thinner, more forgetful and less capable of his encyclopedic knowledge of history and still I thought little of the changes. If my father was really Superman, then cancer would be just a minor blip in his life story. He'd survived 78 years with a horrible meat based diet, little exercise, and an average of five hours of sleep a night. Surely he could survive this as well.

Even through the next year I never expected anything less than recovery. Through the year of endless doctor visits and rounds of radiation, every good day made me hope that he'd spring up and announce that he was only kidding. When he entered hospice care, and I spent nearly a month as his night nurse, changing diapers, holding his hand as his moans of pain filled our apartment, not sleeping, I never realized that this would be the end of him. His intestines turned to soup, organs failing through his mental resilience to live on, and still I didn't realize this would be the only battle that Superman would lose.

I think it's apt that my father, the raging volcano man, passed during the hottest time of year, in the most peaceful way possible. Two summers ago he went to sleep and just didn't wake up. And after months of preparation for the

inevitable, no one, least of all myself, was ready for it. Because, you see, nobody tells you how to handle losing the most important person in your life; there is no instruction manual for grief. No one can properly prepare you for the crushing emptiness of it, how it'll carve out your insides and leave you hollow to the point where any breeze too strong could knock you right over. No one talks about the overwhelming silence in the noise that follows.

College was always my father's place. Over the years, through all his stories about his time in school, I always pictured my own move-in day, my father carrying boxes, my mother giving orders, my sister lounging in a corner somewhere hiding from the work. The picture changed over the years, but in every permutation of the story that took place in my head, my father was there. I think I took it for granted that he would be here to experience this with me.

College is sort of a bittersweet victory for me now. I'm here and I'm learning, but being away from home is hard for me right now. I think what's been the hardest is realizing that when I go home for my first Thanksgiving and Christmas at home, my dad won't be there for me to tell college stories with.

Sarah DrePaul

Shared Language

My days always ended the same. Legs crossed, I would shift my weight backwards, straining the wood of the patio, and look up to the people in planes who come and go. I write about the lives of those people because back then that's what I did best: living off of others. I always had this sense of history about people and things; that there was a story behind everything we see. In my attempt to catch all those stories, or make them up, I started to understand the essence of poetry and how we believe it has something to do with us.

The root of that understanding started when my Dad's car creeped into the driveway and I'd leave the patio for the first time that day. He would stand at the bottom of the stairs, hand outstretched to start our walk to the mailbox. I always viewed our walks as the breathing form of a poem. We created the ground we walked on, a give and take of ideas we have known, used, doubted, and relied on in some part of the day— *Meetings, newly emptied hotel rooms, teachers who don't understand, skinned knees.* Our movement towards the mailbox belonged to the sound of our day — *the guttural, the drawn-out, the breathy.* The images we created by the time we reached the mailbox was our only way of seeing the others day — *a freckle, kettle, highway, chalkboard, a comatose boss.* I knew that life as a nine year old in New York City was a foreign idea to my father, similar to how his experience as an immigrant hotel manager was unheard of for me. I didn't like the way a tie looked on him; he spoke too much about bare knees and dirt brushed shirts for me to believe that he belonged in a suit. My Mom never liked talking about back home, flinching each time she saw the longing behind my Dad's eyes at the paved streets and manicured trees in the city. His distance always seemed longer than I could grapple with, and I only ever knew that I was my father's daughter because of the stack of books lining both of our rooms. His love for words was the one part I could latch onto. While I couldn't relay my day in the same Patois accent that creeped around his stories, or show him grass stained elbows, I offered him my words. I was never scared of how little I knew of my Dad, only scared if I would stop existing in his poems. We shared that unspoken fear every night we walked from the patio to the mailbox, but I loved that it was in our walks that I left my head for the first and only time of the day.

I grew up a lot faster knowing how I barely used my voice. I would tiptoe around conversations, and with those restrictions in my head. I mastered the

art of responding minimally. It wasn't a conscious decision; it was simply the effect of being such an intense observer. However, speaking with my dad was different because I only had such a short amount of time to explain my day. My most passionate and immediate responses to my environment were in these conversations. The heavy nod of his head and his deep growl of a laugh spoke for itself. He let me speak, unfiltered and unapologetic, and it was also in that way that he listened. That's what poetry is to me; someone listening.

There's no reason for me to feel close with my Dad, as I only ever saw him in the evenings, but it's precisely because of that constrained time period that I feel the closest to him than anyone else in my life. While our "poems" were an exercise of listening and empathy, it was also a frantic stream of questions and consciousness. The two of us, side by side, asking and receiving an outpour of the other's reality. The questions he asked me and the reactions he had to my "stanzas" gave me more insight into who he is and what stories he carried under his skin. I wouldn't have known that his dad died when he was seventeen or what a village from the top of a coconut tree looks like. All I wanted was to know this version of my Dad, the buckwild kid who I shared more than just wild hair with. That's the kind of information I couldn't have received by directly asking. It runs deeper than that, to a level neither of us may never be fully aware of, but it's something we shared. According to poet and teacher Deborah Cummins' article on the significance of teaching Pablo Neruda's *The Book of Questions (El libro de preguntas)* "The questions we ask and the way in which we ask them say much about who we are. As writers, we call it, in addition to our point of view, our stance on life" (Cummins). Speaking to my Dad helped me reach a level of self-awareness that, most times, was terrifying but necessary. I saw myself in him, in his quiet independence and in his stubborn attitude. I learned to love myself in a way that reached the rest of the world. I could look at something seemingly insignificant and feel its place in our world as I remember the interconnected nature of life, and no one could disprove that because my dad and I were proof: two separate existences coming together in our stories. I craved that personal relationship with any and everyone I encountered. When I recognized that craving, I threw myself into the poetry I found around me. Poetry became dutifully, wolfishly writing every moment down, and repeating it all back, like folklore. Poetry became so much more than the quick fix to a cultural and parental barrier: it became my answer to everything.

The subtlest and profound nature of our very beings go unnoticed but poetry lifts those things up, it defines us. It encourages us to unhinge the cautious parts of our mind, to surrender to wonder and awe. I'm never the same after reading a poem, just I was never the same after a conversation with my Dad because it showed me how similar his life was to mine. Poetry resonates with people the same way because its accessibility is its greatest

power. Having your feelings confirmed and clarified by a stranger's words is strangely comforting, just as every walk to the mailbox with my Dad was a comfort I never knew I needed. I can say that now because when those walks stopped, due to the destruction of our patio and a chunk of my memories, there was something missing; a sense of guidance that I never had. It was as if speaking in fragmented and urgent ways was showing me how to experience the world around me; the planes above our house and the people were so much more than just that. They were as significant as my being and once I realized that, poetry became my new sense of guidance.

When I come across a poem that resonates with me, I feel validated because I've always sensed a sort of truth to the world, but had no words for it. While it's both beautiful and overwhelming to feel clarified in this way, there's never an "ultimate" truth that poetry finds; poetry keeps giving. So when my Dad didn't show up to my first spoken word poetry performance when I was thirteen, I looked my hardest for some truth that would help me make sense of the situation. But no glorified poetry about being a "lost boy" with parents like mine changed the fact that all I needed was my dad looking back at me. It was an arresting moment, even with poetry all around me. While I felt naked on that stage and everyone could see the sting in my eyes, I let my words take control of the situation. Everything about that performance is blurry but the power and validation I felt in my voice is only as strong as it is now because of that night. My ability to trust and listen to myself are products of the poetry I created with my Dad. It was with him that I realized my words and my experiences were worthy of being told. And while there's no replacing what I lost that night in terms of faith, at least I have the stories and poetry of my father to understand why he made the choices he did. The literacy of poetry was never something concrete; I learned it by questioning and I still do. Neruda asks: "Where is the child that I was— inside of me still—or gone?" (Cummins). I will always have the answer to that question and anyone who reads poetry, religiously or for a few minutes, will have it, too.

Benjamin Folk III

Nine Thirty-Nine Post Meridian

Water cascaded down in condensed misty falls, clinging to mirrors and shower curtains and bare skin. Gone was the mid autumn cold, only the artificial sauna, a cocktail of gas heating and water halfway to boiling. Outside, hurricane wind whipped and howled, drenching the roof tiles and chimney stones and I soaked myself down to the bone in that stifling downpour, thankful to be out of the rain.

That was when the power cut out.

Showering in of itself is a mundane practice, but in complete darkness, it becomes more of a challenge. Finding the knobs for the faucets, keeping a mental note of the rim of the tub as to not stumble to an embarrassing and untimely death, naked on the bathroom floor. Groping around for a towel and pajamas, all the while swearing to myself all the way about some damn storm and global warming making life harder everyday.

It was the midst of Hurricane Sandy. Schools were suspended for the time being in preparation for the northern cyclone and the predicted damage it was said to cause. I was unconcerned. Hurricanes were only things to fear for people along the coast and in Louisiana or Florida. We lived sixty miles away from the shore and hadn't had any severe weather conditions since the early 1900's. What was there to worry about?

I sat the phone back down, unknowing that the next time I saw it, there would only be a puddle of crisp plastic glued to a ashen sink frame.

The lights flickered back on. Life was as it once was again.

Then I started coughing. Smoke was curling in through an open doorway, thick and gray. It was foul, not like the earthy smell of wood smoke, but more putrid and oily, an artificial chemical thing that in those few minutes of indecision probably took some odd number of months off of my total life expectancy.

My father rushed up the stairs, shirt tucked over his nose, coughing as he came up.

"What's going on?"

"I don't know." He went into his office, adjacent to my room and looked out the window, and mumbled some verbal epithet. I joined him by the window. Outside, embers danced and twirled across the roof and as the wind breathed into the flaming wound, the orange coals glowed white, crackling and breaking off as the storm sighed and heaved.

The house was on fire.

We all scrambled out of the house in pajamas and night clothes and a single laptop, going from shaking in fear to shaking in the rain. In hindsight, we had time to go back in and grab our things; precious irreplaceables and such. But that was a logical thought, and the fire blasting from the roof defied all logic. So we sort of stood there and watched. I had to be dreaming. I'd just wake up in a few seconds in my bed in a nervous sweat. This couldn't be real.

It looked like a climax out of some B-List horror film, the leafless trees groaning and moaning as the rain fell ins slanted sheets over the sidewalk with rolling thunder in the tar black clouds, all the while a hellish flame surged and roared and churned out smoke into the dark zenith above. Except, the fire and rain was all real, and the monster was nothing more than grim circumstance. My dad ushered us into the family car, keeping about as sane as anyone could, given the situation. My three brothers and I sat in darkness and noise as firefighter garble dissolved in the cacophony of the tempest and booming thunder all around us.

Looking up out the window, I could see my bedroom window, a vermillion hole that undulated and quavered in the gale, deep red fire spilling out along the walls and bringing light to the stormy night. I cursed to myself.

My younger brother piped up, "Oooh Benjy! You just said the f-word!" "Who gives a f***?" I didn't. What did it matter what I said here and now? Life was over. It was an incomprehensible thing that I felt, a helplessness and hopelessness beneath the wrath of the storm.

As the night trudged on, our neighbors opened their doors to us and we all huddled on their sofa, soaking wet and transient. I did not sleep for the long hours we spent there, eyes locked on a dark facet of ceiling, enraptured by the metronome of rain against window pane.

At some point during the endless night, my father asked "Is everybody alright?" I could muster a shrug. I was lost for words. "We're going to Grammy's house, ok?" Shrugged again. What difference did it make?

Here or there, anywhere. The house was still gone. Life would never be the same. The car tires squealed and we were off into all the wind and rain, leaving behind the reds and gold of firefighter lights. A yellow T-shirt from a Dr. Seuss play and burgundy plaid pants became my only possessions in the world. En route to my grandmother's house, I became aware of two revelations: I was homeless and there'd be no trick or treating this year.

As the four year anniversary approaches just a few weeks from now, the whole thing seems like a bad pipe dream in my mind, a dismal thing that changed my world forever. Time and insurance money seems to wash over the good and the terrible and smear them together like some ugly mosaic that leave you without thought, but just a feeling of solemn emptiness of what once was, until that hollow sort of feeling is all that you can remember.

See the thing about fires is that you come out of them like a phoenix; reborn, reinvented, an infantile thing spawned upon the world, and in my opinion, altogether more fit for it. But with that change, there also comes a loss. Insurance money can buy back a house, but it can't buy back a home. Where an Xbox or flatscreen stand, a baby picture or home movie is lost to the wind. A new phone might take photos in HD, but the albums from last summer were barely even memories. To be a phoenix is to have a new lease on life.

But to become a phoenix, one still has to die.

Pauline "Daisy" Good

Feed Him Once a Day

'Twas late summer in 2016 when bright young "adults" moved out of their parents' spacious, well-lit homes and into the blank, rectangular dorm rooms of Drexel University. I was one of these "adults." During the first week at Drexel, Welcome Week, no classes are held. Instead, freshmen have a week to make friends, get lost, and learn to forage for their own food.

It was Welcome Week, and that meant free stuff. All week, clubs, departments, associations, and organizations of every make and model scattered around campus, offering snacks, keychains, and pamphlets to every freshman in sight. Last year, hundreds of students were given identical T-shirts with the phrase "Be Different" stamped across the back.

In this storm of free merchandise, one giveaway stood out. For one Thursday afternoon, on a plastic folding table in the gymnasium, some organization I had never heard of was giving away free goldfish, the only pets allowed on campus. Each student willing to endure the endless line received a four-by-six-inch plastic fish tank, complete with gravel, seashells, and a fake palm tree. I waited with all the other wide-eyed freshmen, one behind the other, twirling their Drexel lanyards, sipping out of their Drexel water bottles, and clicking their Drexel pens absentmindedly. Ahead, I saw the table where two smiling women in cheery yellow polo shirts each held a small fish net. The woman on the right dipped her net into a tank of thousands of goldfish minnows, gathering them one by one and releasing each fish into the tank of a giddy freshman. I watched as the woman on the left quietly used her net to scoop handfuls of limp fish out of the big tank and into a nearby recycling bin.

When it was my turn, I took my tank to the woman on the right, who filled it with water and transferred a goldfish from the big glass tank to my quart-sized plastic one. The woman on the left handed me a tiny plastic bag containing about 25 pellets of fish food. "Feed him once a day," she said. As I walked away, I saw her start scooping out another round of lifeless fish and plopping them into the clearly labeled recycling bin, blind to the trash can right in front of her.

His little body was off-white, peppered with dark grey speckles and paired with a hazy complexion. His miniscule size toed the line between pitiful and

endearing, and he drifted through his rectangular palace with all the intention of a college sophomore ambling into his Math 101 classroom. And yet, there was something special about him. He was a goldfish with the nerve to be black and white? I was all about that. I named him Panda to match his unique coloring and impassive attitude. As we took the elevator up to the sixth floor, I lifted the tank up to my face, and looked him in the eyes. 'We are going to be best friends,' I thought to him. Through the tank, I watched the elevator doors part, opening into the sixth floor lounge. One step out of the elevator and a hopeful voice piped out "Yours is still alive!" I looked down at my son, holding his tank a little closer.

On September 15, 2016, exactly ten fish had been brought up to the sixth floor of Towers Hall. By the moment Panda and I stepped out of that elevator, six fish had already risen to a much higher place.

Over the next hour, cries echoed through the hallways as three other girls lost their fish one by one. Panda and I were the last ones left. I can't say why or how, but something told me that I would be the one to keep her fish alive. I was careful, I was lucky, and Panda was my everything. Together, we would make a miracle happen.

On September 15, 2016, a brave fish named Panda left this earth to join his fish brothers and sisters in fish heaven.

I carried the tank containing his little body into the common room, where I found a circle of girls pouting around a table. On that table sat nine rectangular fish tanks, arranged in an eerie mosaic. As I was invited into the circle and the girls made room for Panda's coffin, across the room, one girl added her fish's name to a list written on a whiteboard under the phrase "In memoriam, we will never forget." The memorial wall praised the names of such fallen heroes as Bruce, Ladyshark, Satan, and Finny. I rose to add Panda's name to the board.

The funeral was held at nine o'clock. Ten pallbearers processed solemnly into the communal bathroom. Mourners from other floors of the building heard news of the ceremony and joined us in support, each offering their condolences. Fish were lowered into the toilet two by two, so they wouldn't be alone. Suddenly, the pensive quiet was broken with the trill of a bugle as a boy from another floor stood outside the ladies' room, bowing his head and playing Taps on his iPhone. Laughter burst out amongst the girls in the bathroom. Though truly saddened by the loss of our fallen, we could not help but scoff at how thoroughly pathetic this situation was. The school gave out hundreds of fish that day. Who knows how many other freshmen were crowded around toilets at that very moment? Welcome to college! Enjoy the funeral. With one

grand, ceremonious flush, we sent our dear friends off into the great beyond, to swim in spaces larger than a four-by-six-inch plastic box. The deed now done, I retired to my room, sat the empty tank on my desk, and stared at it for a moment before scratching something into my planner:

"September 16, 2016- find a new fish"

Heather Heim

The Tomatometer

Preface

Eula Biss's essay wrote *about* and wrote *using* the pain scale. She compared it to other scales like the Beaufort scale for wind. There were other recurring comparisons in the essay as well, such as, *Dante's Inferno* and Hell, math and numbers, and comments from her father who is a physician. She used these main themes along with other pieces (comments from her mom and sister, pain of people in other countries, newspaper clippings, etc.) as she built up her own pain and suffering through the pain scale. In choosing my topic, I wanted to go with an existing measuring device, as Biss did, but I wanted my essay to be more light-hearted. I decided to write about the Tomatometer from the Rotten Tomatoes website, used for rating movies. This is different from Biss' pain scale in many ways, an important one being that it is not a scale that is based subjectively on the individual, but a rating system based on reviews done by professional critics. It represents the percentage of professional critic reviews that are positive for a given film or television show. I thought I'd comment on the tomatometer by drawing on past experiences, comments from family and friends, and other outside sources. The categories on the tomatometer are:

Fresh - The Tomatometer is 60% or higher.

Rotten - The Tomatometer is 59% or lower.

Certified Fresh - Movies and TV shows are Certified Fresh with a steady Tomatometer of 75% or higher after a set amount of reviews.

I also thought it'd be a nice touch to analyze the categories themselves in the way that Biss analyzes the numbers on the pain scale.

The Tomatometer

Rotten

The first recorded use of the word rotten dates back to the early 1800s. It comes from the old Norse word "rotinn." Some definitions of rotten include "suffering from decay," "morally, socially, or politically corrupt," and "extremely unpleasant." A tomato can be suffering from decay. And a movie can be morally, socially, or politically corrupt. But a movie can't be suffering from decay and a tomato certainly can't be morally, socially, or politically corrupt. Both can be extremely unpleasant. Is it fair to judge two things that are rotten differently by the same scale? If we can't even compare apples and oranges, then how can we compare tomatoes and movies?

I'm not a chef. I'm sitting in front of my computer trying to pick a movie based on its freshness. They say a rotten apple spoils that barrel. Does this translate for movies? Does one rotten movie spoil an otherwise fresh series?

There is no use for rotten eggs. Yet, the website *Maria's Farm Country Kitchen*, cites 10 uses for rotten bananas, some of which include banana muffins, banana smoothies, and banana icing. Is a rotten movie like a rotten egg or a rotten banana? Though it is rotten, can one still get enjoyment out of watching it?

The last movie I watched was *The Girl on the Train*. This movie received a 44% on the tomatometer, and was thus classified as rotten. I enjoyed this movie. I thought it was gripping and suspenseful. By no means did I find it extremely unpleasant.

Fresh

My mom used to call my sisters and me "fresh" if we misbehaved or talked back. But I've also heard men refer to women as fresh if they're being sassy or flirtatious. There are many uses of the word fresh. One that *could* apply to both movies and tomatoes is "not previously known or used; new or different." Thus, originality is a key factor in scoring high on the tomatometer.

18th century philosopher, Immanuel Kant, argued that true works of art are products of genius. And products of artistic genius must be original. By this logic, it makes sense that freshness should play a role in rating movies, which are works of art.

The movie *Sharknado* is considered fresh with a rating of 82% on the tomatometer. While it may be true that no other movie has been released about a shark tornado, I have to wonder if originality should be the most influential factor of a movie's rating. In the case of *Sharknado*, perhaps elements such as dialogue and feasibility should be more heavily considered.

Other movie rating sites judge movies based off of ratings from the general public. The Internet Movie Database (IMDb) rates movies on a scale from 1 to 10 using input from its members, and anyone can be a member if they get a subscription. *Sharknado's* rating on IMDB is 3.3.

Am I better off trusting the masses in making decisions on which movies to watch than the critics? To be fair, while the general public's knowledge of current events and politics is lacking, they are usually in the loop when it comes to matters of entertainment.

Certified Fresh

Many years ago, my oldest sister, Jackie, saw the movie *Fight Club* for the first time. She came home and aired her grievances about the movie's plot. "You're not gonna see it, right?" She asked, not waiting for an answer before she spoiled the big twist of the movie. "If you go back and watch it again, it doesn't make sense!" she said angrily. *Fight Club* is certified fresh with a 79% on the tomatometer.

Jackie is one of the smartest people I know. She went to an Ivy League school and is studying to be a lawyer. She's a little bit of a snob. If she can't agree with the critics, I don't know who can.

The movie *Sausage Party*, about food items shaped like sex organs, is also certified fresh with a rating of 83%.

Upon further research of the tomatometer, I have to think that critics account for originality too much in their assessments. Or maybe movie critics are just a lot more immature than we think.

Perhaps a better system would be a scale based on how much you'd rather be doing something else. For instance, I'd rather mow the lawn than sit through *Caddyshack* again. I'd rather take a calculus exam than watch *Urban Cowboy*.

I am surprised by how much I disagreed with the tomatometer, but I guess I can take comfort in the fact that we don't all enjoy movies the same way.

Stephanie Heim

The Necessity of Zoos

Human-fueled global changes, such as climate change, deforestation and habitat destruction, introduction of invasive species, and excessive hunting and fishing have caused many species around the world to become threatened, endangered, or extinct. As a result, zoos around the world focus on public education, animal conservation, and research to attempt to maintain and restore our environment. However, since completing an internship at the Philadelphia Zoo, it has come to my attention that many people adamantly oppose zoos due to incorrectly assuming animals are poorly cared for and serve no scientific purpose.

It is a growing trend that zoo and aquarium attendance is dropping, partially thanks to what PETA vice president Lisa Lange calls the "*Blackfish* effect" (CNN Wire). The 2013 documentary *Blackfish* outraged the public by exposing SeaWorld's deplorable treatment of their orcas. Since then, attendance has been declining at circuses, aquariums, and zoos. This year, SeaWorld has pledged to phase out orca shows as a result of public demand, and the Ringling Bros. and Barnum and Bailey Circus announced its plan to close after almost one-hundred-and-fifty years due to low ticket sales (Bowman). The biggest cause for public concern regarding these types of animal performance venues is that they exist to entertain and often do not have animal care standards. Although zoos and aquariums promote education and conservation rather than entertainment, the public's distaste for animals in captivity has resulted in a decline in zoo and aquarium attendance as well.

Many people consider it inhumane to keep animals in captivity because they think animals in captivity are unhappy or poorly kept; these ideas are usually based on misconceptions. For example, when I was stationed at the gorilla exhibit, I often heard the comment that the gorillas "look bored." I explained several times a day that humans misinterpret primate contentment as unhappiness, because content gorillas have relaxed faces, slouched posture, and aren't alert. There are many agencies that ensure the well-being of animals in captivity. The United States Department of Agriculture (USDA) and the Association of Zoos and Aquariums (AZA) are both institutions that inspect the welfare of animals in captivity to ensure their needs are met. The AZA has accredited over two hundred zoos and aquariums that meet the highest standards for animal care, which includes most major zoos and aquariums in America ("About Us"). Although animals may appear to be bored or unhappy,

zoos and aquarium staff are often animal care advocates and are very receptive to their care requirements.

Zoos and aquariums provide vital protection and breeding programs for species that are declining in the wild. AZA accredited zoos and aquariums have species survival plans for almost five hundred species ("Species Survival Plan Programs"). These plans identify animals in captivity that are able to produce healthy, viable offspring and create transfer plans in order for zoos to have prolific breeding programs. The Philadelphia Zoo alone houses over a dozen endangered species, including four species that are extinct in the wild, and has successfully bred endangered species such as lowland gorillas, orangutans, aye-ayes, giant elephant shrews, and more. A 2016 study by the University of Zurich also shows that mammals in captivity generally live longer than their wild counterparts (Gaillard et. al., "Comparative Analyses of Longevity...in Zoos across Mammals"). The Philadelphia Zoo provides many examples of animals outliving their life expectancy; it currently houses the oldest polar bear in America. Coldilocks is thirty-six years old, six years older than the average polar bear in captivity and sixteen years older than those in the wild.

Zoos and aquariums are also beneficial for research and educating the public. They allow scientists to study the effects of climate change, diseases, and pathogens on wild animals. This is particularly helpful for species that may be difficult to observe in the wild. In addition to being useful research hubs, zoos and aquariums inspire the public. They teach guests about wild animals and environmental issues and inspire them to donate and reduce their carbon footprint. Additionally, their revenue is often put into research and conservation efforts. By educating the public and raising funds for research and conservation, zoos and aquariums help to preserve and restore the environment.

Although some people oppose zoos and aquariums for keeping animals in captivity, the benefits far outweigh the negatives. The USDA requires that zoos and aquariums in the United States meet animal care standards, and many far exceed these standards and qualify for the AZA accreditation. The breeding programs and protection plans keep endangered species from going extinct, and research programs help us to better understand causes of species decline and their solutions. Zoos and aquariums educate people and inspire them to do their part in preserving the environment.

Works Cited

"About Us." *About Us: Association of Zoos & Aquariums. Association of Zoos and Aquariums*, n.d. Web. 23 Jan. 2017.

Bowman, Emma. "After 146 Years, Ringling Bros. And Barnum & Bailey Circus To Shut Down." *NPR*. NPR, 15 Jan. 2017. Web. 19 Jan. 2017.

CNN Wire. "After SeaWorld, a 'Blackfish Effect' on Circuses and Zoos?" Fox40. N.p., 19 Mar. 2016. Web. 19 Jan. 2017.

Gaillard, Jean-Michel, Laurie Bingaman Lackey, Olivier Gimenez, Marcus Clauss, Morgane Tidiare, VÃcrane Berger, Dennis W. H. Maller, and Jean-FranÃ§ois Lemartre. "Comparative Analyses of Longevity and Senescence Reveal Variable Survival Benefits of Living in Zoos across Mammals." *Scientific Reports* 6 (2016): n. pag. Web. 23 Jan. 2017.

"Species Survival Plan Programs." *Species Survival Plan Programs. Association of Zoos and Aquariums*, n.d. Web. 25 Jan. 2017.

Samantha Stein

Against the Adoption of Aramark; For the Upholding of Our Values

Drexel University staff, I am extremely disappointed in your selection of Aramark as Drexel's new food service provider. Aramark has an extensive history of human exploitation for corporate growth. Historically, the adoption of Aramark has proved devastating for many stakeholders across settings ranging from schools, to healthcare providers, to prisons. While I recognize that choosing a food service provider is an extensive task to which many factors weigh in, I ask that you revoke your decision to adopt Aramark, and if not possible, seek to terminate the contract in a swift manner for the sake of our university's people, and the values we strive to uphold. I suggest you instead opt to patronize a smaller, locally-contained organization (preferably non-profit). While to its credit, Aramark is a Philadelphia-based company, its services extend nationally, and its sourcing globally; as a result, it has accrued a multi-billion dollar status and much of the subsequent corruption consistent with large corporations. As a non- profit university, and citizens of the world, we have an ethical obligation not to support unethical business practices, such as those of Aramark, by patronizing them. Additionally, as a private university, we have the liberty to use our funds at our discretion. It is critical to the maintenance of our principles that we utilize the liberty that comes with being a private institution to materialize the ideals we seek to embody as a nonprofit. We must uphold the values of ethical business operation we so vehemently assert in the Lebow School of Business on an exemplary level. If we make exceptions to our values by patronizing companies such as Aramark, we deconstruct our moral high ground, and thus our abilities to preach ethical business practice; we must practice our tautology.

In addition to breaching our values in principle should we see through our collaboration with Aramark, we will potentially subject our students, staff, and Aramark's ground-level workers to much mistreatment and possible dangers. In 2009, at Northpoint Training Center, a Kentucky prison, a riot broke out over ""the quality of the [Aramark provided] food, the portion sizes and the continual shortage and substitutions for scheduled menu items"" according to state officials. In this situation, Aramark exploited a vulnerable population to increase profits, promoting prison industrial complex. In another instance of the exploitation of vulnerable persons, Aramark distributed "smaller-sized sack lunches instead of hot meals for nearly seven months"

causing inmates to suffer malnutrition and weight loss as told by one inmate "Malik" who chose to be recognized by a pseudonym (Lavender, 2014). Malik's accusations are reflected in an ACLU lawsuit Indiana has since settled (Kovac, 2014). In 2012, Niagara Health Services severed ties with Aramark after ""Aramark contributed to the C. difficile outbreak by cutting corners, using cheaper cleaning chemicals, and reducing staffing levels,"" asserted Sharleen Stewart, Service Employees International Union Canadian sector president (Boyle, 2012). And, in another example of Aramark's cost-cutting measures resulting in disease, a survey of the Chicago Teachers Union revealed that "Aramark's cost-cutting measures . . . overburdened custodial staff, resulting in classrooms going uncleaned for days at a time," subsequently initiating respiratory illness amongst the students, and exacerbating asthmatic signs and symptoms (Kovac, 2014).

Personally, I also experienced the malevolence of Aramark's practices throughout the duration of my time in the Cherry Hill school system. In elementary school I witnessed Aramark's slow service resulting in kids having to throw away lunches immediately after receiving them, as well as Aramark workers taking and trashing full lunch trays from kids whose parents had forgotten to, or were unable to put money in their accounts, leaving them hungry and crying until their parents added money, sometimes weeks later. Additionally, in high school I experienced Aramark placing a ban on food sales by the non-profit cultural groups within the school as kids began to opt for the home-prepared food over Aramark's highly processed food. This left the cultural clubs destitute and impeded their abilities to put on the Multicultural Day production loved by all.

Furthermore, Aramark's sleazy financial tactics and their repercussions on the general public delve deeper into humanity. These sleazy tactics are mirrored within the treatment of the company's 269,500 human assets. Not only does Aramark shortchange patrons, it does so not out of necessity, nor for the overall good of its employees, but for the fiscal benefit of CEO Eric Foss. It was reported that Foss took home $32.4 million of Aramark's $14.8 billion revenue while Aramark cashiers made only a smidgen over $9 an hour, respectively earning Foss the title of highest paid Philadelphia executive, and his company a place on the list of lowest paying companies in the United States (Frohlich et al., 2015). Essentially, Foss exploits patrons to preserve his own aristocracy and a vastly stratified social hierarchy. Is this a company whose tactics we want to endorse?

As exemplified, Aramark has an extensive history of taking on responsibilities, and profiting off of its failure to handle them acceptably as a function of its current bureaucracy. Despite Aramark's for-profit status, it has the ethical obligation to operate at socially responsible standards, and

to turn down opportunities if it cannot satisfy humanitarian needs; however, Aramark has proven itself unable to make those socially responsible decisions. We, Drexel, must instead take control of the situation and rid them of the opportunity to further their scandal-riddled history within our university setting before it is too late (or at least until they renovate the ethicality of their operations). A.J. Drexel, a man from humble roots, who sought a subsequently philanthropic implementation of his great fortune, would likely not approve of the adoption of Aramark and its morally reprehensible practices (Falcone, 2016). In an effort to pay homage to him, the values we seek to instill within our teachings, and the ethical observation we strive to promote in practice, it is advised that we sever our ties with Aramark promptly, and opt for a more socially responsible food servicer.

Sources:

Boyle, T. (2012, March 27). Niagara Health System cuts ties with Aramark, U.S. firm that managed housekeeping. | Toronto Star. Retrieved December 08, 2016, from https://www.thestar.com/news/gta/2012/03/27/niagara_health_system_cuts_ties_with_aramark_us_firm_that_managed_housekeeping.html.

Falcone, A. (2016, August 24). Who Was A.J. Drexel? Retrieved December 08, 2016, from http://drexel.edu/now/archive/2016/August/Who-Was-AJ-Drexel.

Frohlich, T. C., Sauter, M. B., & Stebbins, S. (2015, April 9). The 10 Companies That Pay Americans The Least. Retrieved December 8, 2016, from http://www.huffingtonpost.com/entry/the-10-companies-that-pay-americans-the-least.

Kovac, M. (2014, October 07). The Top Five Aramark Scandals You Haven't Heard Of - Progress Michigan. Retrieved December 08, 2016, from http://www.progressmichigan.org/2014/10/top-ive-aramark-scandals-havent-heard/

Lavender, G. (2014, January 30). Private Contractor Accused of Skimping on Prisoner Food - The Prison Complex. Retrieved December 08, 2016, from http://inthesetimes.com/prison-complex/entry/16206/private_contractor_accused_of_skimping_on_prisoner_food.

Literature
Essays

Introduction

The essays in this section are the winners (first place, second place, third place, and honorable mention) of the Literature Essay Contest. Essays must be submitted by (or nominated by) faculty teaching literature courses. Literature faculty are asked to select no more than two essays per class that demonstrate excellence in writing. These essays explore a variety of literary topics. The editors are pleased to include the winning literature essays in *The 33rd* for the very first time.

- The Editors

Zachary Stott

"London": A Comparative Analysis

William Blake's "London" is a masterpiece in its own right, one that resonates with all who read it. Simultaneously a historical snapshot and prophetic premonition, it offers itself as a realistic depiction of the often-romanticized city of London as well as a cautionary tale of the perils of classism, elitism, and greed that may befall any metropolis. Blake had an incomparable mind, ear, and tongue when it came to the English language and used these in concert to pen some of the most controversial and provocative works of his time, which still serve as an impetus for social discourse across all nations and stratifications. Just as Rome was not built in one day, this masterpiece was not written overnight and there were drafts that preceded the final, polished version we revere today. When any author is considered, drafts aid us in understanding a writer's process and Blake is no exception. Blake's drafts demonstrate very carefully chosen words and phrases, many of which evolved over time in order to convey better-articulated intent or reinforce his cleverness, with final selections of terminology producing the jarring effects he so desired when attempting to penetrate the minds of his readers. The pages that follow are an effort to execute a comparative analysis of the final version of "London" with a draft by analyzing a sample of initial word choices, word changes, and final word choices. With any luck, researching the meanings of particular words, especially in historical context, may lead to the discovery of some reasoning for a word change and the final choice of a word. This may also aid in demystifying Blake's fondness for the use of polysemy, "the fact of having several meanings; the possession of multiple meanings, senses, or connotations," and bring heretofore unrealized significance to a particular word change or choice.

Initial word choices, word changes, and final word choices begin very early in "London," as Blake makes an audacious choice in changing the fifth word (also the tenth word), proving that even the "strong start" of any draft is eligible for editing. This particular change is from the initial choice of "dirty" to "charter'd," the contracted form of "chartered." To begin by analyzing the initial choice of "dirty," one must consider that, as an adjective, dirty can have two possible senses – the first example of Blake's employment of polysemy. Obviously, the first sense is "characterized by the presence of dirt; soiled with dirt; foul, unclean, sullied," which is likely intended to convey Blake's dissatisfaction with the cleanliness (or lack thereof) of the streets of London

and of the River Thames. Yet, the second sense can convey "morally unclean or impure," "that which stains the honor of the persons engaged; dishonorably sordid, base, mean, or corrupt," "earned by base or despicable means," "an epithet of disgust or aversion: repulsive, hateful, abominable, despicable," or "tinged with what destroys purity or clearness." Those definitions of the latter sense are certainly much more pointed and articulate a more subtle judgment of not only the cleanliness of London, but also of its leaders, inhabitants, and all of their corruption and depravity.

Dr. Linda Freedman, Lecturer in British and American literature at University College London, wrote an article for "The British Library" titled "Looking at the Manuscript of William Blake's 'London'." In it, she explains, "'Dirty' was quite an accurate description as the late 18th-century London streets that he knew so well were piled with filth of all kinds. It also suggests the fallen state of contemporary society. Blake saw a world in turmoil: blood running down palace walls, prostitutes suffering from sexually transmitted diseases, children forced to become chimney sweeps and innocent babies born to mothers who couldn't look after them. 'Dirty' describes this state of moral and physical degeneration..." Evidently, Dr. Freedman and I are in agreement regarding the weight of the term and its dual implications. Nonetheless, Blake saw fit to change this word – perhaps the designation itself was too simple, despite its insinuations.

"Charter'd," the contracted form of "chartered," was the ultimate locution of choice and, to modern readers, possesses historical connotation no longer in use today. The "Oxford English Dictionary" offers two pertinent senses of the word. The primary is "founded, privileged, or protected by charter," but the secondary is "privileged; licensed" and directly references its use in this poem as an example by citing "1783–94 W. Blake London in Songs Exper. 3 Near where the charter'd Thames does flow." A footnote in "Blake's Poetry and Designs" offers some insight by noting that "The "chartered rights of Englishmen" ultimately derive from the Magna Carta of 1215, but the ancient charters of London, which grant certain liberties, did not extend to most of the inhabitants. As Paine noted in *The Rights of Man* (1791), a charter actually operates by "taking rights away"." While this footnote reveals employment of the primary sense of the word, it, unfortunately, does not reveal very much about the secondary sense, which is the one, in the OED, directly referencing the poem. This is, perhaps, due to the fact that the primary definition does not subtly imply the privilege experienced by those who benefit from the practice of chartering. Dr. Linda Freedman, again, explains it best by stating "Chartering was an 18th-century process of corporate ownership, effectively transferring public land to private hands. Blake's readers would quickly have recognized the political implications of the word. Supporters of chartering claimed that it gave people rights over the land. Those against claimed that

it took rights away from the many in order to give them to the few." This offers a better explanation for the secondary sense of "chartered," as well as concisely explaining the historical context of the word, as it would have affected Blake's readers. Chartering, explained as giving "people rights over the land" is propaganda favoring the privatization of public land for the benefit of corporations and their wealthy owners in many of the same ways in which privatization benefits corporations and their wealthy owners in capitalist America. Thus, Blake conjures up imagery of London streets and the River Thames, which are implicitly dirty, but they are privately owned by people who care very little for their states of cleanliness. The dissenting sentiment that chartering "took rights away from the many in order to give them to the few" reflects much of the political upheaval currently experienced in America as well as conjuring up shock at the idea that in a city like London, or Philadelphia, someone could privately own the streets and sidewalks, which are within the public domain and are used prominently for protests against privatization, among other struggles faced by those who are not members of the elite. Part of the privilege of the elite was that they, as owners of the streets, were not required to spend very much time in the vicinity of the streets – unperturbed by the rising piles of malodorous garbage, nor by the people who must be in the streets because they worked there, must travel on foot to work, or were simply living and sleeping there because they were homeless. This is a direct link to the next important locution alteration made by Blake in his editing.

Blake, still within the first stanza, conscientiously changed the fifteenth term, "see," to "mark." This was a very wise choice on Blake's part because it became yet another opportunity for him to demonstrate his shrewdness when utilizing polysemy, as he changed the verb "see" to the verb "mark," then used the noun "marks" twice in the line that immediately follows. This sort of word play can only be truly appreciated when one acknowledges the fact that this was not the poem's original construction. The verb "see" has two senses, the first being "to perceive with the eyes; to behold in imagination, or in a dream or vision." The second is "to perceive mentally; to apprehend by thought, to recognize the force of; to have a particular mental view of; to perceive, apprehend, or appreciate in a particular manner; to perceive in a person or thing." It is of interest to consider "to behold in imagination, or in a dream or vision" because it could suggest that this poem is merely a dream the speaker is divulging. However, given historical records of this time in London, we know these descriptions to be much more real than simply a dream. While these definitions are straightforward, they do not convey the subtle nuances of the different senses of the verb "mark." In its various senses, "mark" can mean "to put a mark on; to identify or characterize with or as with a mark; to designate as if with a mark; to characterize," "to make perceptible or recognizable, by some sign or indication," "to take notice of mentally; to consider; to give one's

attention to; to notice or perceive physically; to observe; to look at or watch; to take notice of, reflect on, consider." In the first sense, we imagine the speaker wandering the Streets of London and, when they come across a person, they are choosing some physical or other feature with which to characterize or identify the assortment of people they encounter. In the second sense, the speaker would have their eyes drawn toward people on the street based on visible and noticeable indications. In the third sense, the speaker is having their attention drawn to certain people on the street, considers and observes them, and makes a mental note of them. The idea conveyed by the poem seems to be an amalgamation of these senses because, surely, the speaker has their attention drawn to certain people on the street, considers and observes them, and makes a mental note of them. The reason their attention is drawn is that the people have visible and noticeable characteristics, which the speaker is using in order to identify them. These barely-detectable nuances of "mark," when compared with "see," while important are not as interesting as the difference between "dirty" and "charter'd." However, the intrigue lies within the choice of "mark" over "see," in order to facilitate the polysemy of the verb "mark" and the noun "mark."

Now, compared with the verb "mark," the noun also has several senses. These include "an indicator, symptom, or omen (of something); a quality, occurrence, etc., indicative of something," "a characteristic property; a criterion; a distinctive or distinguishing feature or characteristic (of something); an attribute," "a vestige, a trace; a visible trace or impression on a surface (esp. skin), produced by nature, an accident, etc., as a stain, blemish, scar, fleck, stroke, dot," or "a target for a malign force, public opprobrium, etc.; the object at which a blow or thrust is aimed." The senses of the verb are quite monotonous, but there is much more interpretive freedom in the senses of the noun. In the first sense, which is very straightforward, "mark," such as one of weakness or woe, means an indicator, symptom, or omen. These could very well be those physical characteristics, which are indicative of some misfortune – making the inclusion of the word "omen" particularly captivating. The second sense reinforces the sense of the verb that is occupied with distinctive and distinguishing features as marks that will result in one being marked. The third sense is enticing because it begins to describe truly physical indications produced by accident, such as blemishes and scars – obvious symptoms of misfortune. These visible marks are signs of struggle which are unique to each person who suffers and toils in their own way and are contrasted with members of the elite who are unlikely to be sullied by any of these marks because they do not experience the sufferings of the common people found on the streets. The fourth sense is, like the third, much more pointed in its description of physical effects with the additional implication of emotional and mental abuse. The people on the streets of London bear the marks of physical suffering,

but they experience these sufferings at the hands of the elite, the elite being the ones targeting the people with malign force, resulting in emotional and mental abuse. It is likely the elite are also targeting the people with blows and thrusts, thus leaving distinguishing, indelible physical marks, which serve as reminders of encounters.

Emotional and mental abuse, previously explained as invisible marks, are pertinent once more when one considers the line "the mind-forg'd manacles I hear." Originally conceived as "the German-forg(d/ed) links I hear," these two versions do not require lexical explanation so much as they require historical explanation. Lexical explanation will be slightly more critical when "links" and "manacles" are considered, but, for now, it suffices to say those words are intended to convey the notion of imprisonment or enslavement. Beginning with the draft version, "the German-forg(d/ed) links I hear," the most notable feature is the use of "German" and its change to "mind" – very different concepts, indeed. In "Blake's Poetry and Designs," a footnote explains, "Reference to the Hanoverian and Hessian mercenaries brought in to withstand a French invasion or maintain public order in the event of mob rule." The historical context for this passage is that, at the time of Blake's writing, George III was king. George III was king during the American War of Independence, but, in a matter closer to home, he was also embroiled with revolutionary and Napoleonic France and allied with Germany in order to ensure protection. The presence of German forces was intended to protect from French invasion, but also quell a revolt by the people, displeased with their treatment at the hands of the elite, which was ultimately inspired by the revolution in France. This historical version stands in contrast to the later change to "mind," which is intended to demonstrate that the imprisonment or enslavement by links or manacles is not literal, nor is it due to the physical presence of Hessians, rather it is due to constraints levied on the minds of the people being oppressed by the elite. Dr. Linda Freedman explains that Blake's decision to shift focus from "German" to "mind" "reflects a shift in emphasis from externally imposed political oppression (in the form of hired mercenaries paid to suppress revolutionary spirit) to internally imposed restrictions on the mind." While both are important, especially the former when modern readers are concerned and unaware of the historical context, Blake deemed it less necessary to directly reference current events. Instead, he thought it more crucial to inform his readers that the oppression of the people was not physical, rather it was mental – they were allowing themselves to be controlled by the elite, not by chains, but by mental enslavement. Those chains, however, represent another calculated word choice on Blake's part and are reflected in his decision, during editing, to alter "links" to "manacles."

"Links" was a soft choice, one that requires some interpreting, but it seems clear that it was mostly a placeholder until a better word came along.

The definition, "one of the series of rings or loops which form a chain," is a bit ambiguous because it does not do much for describing the likes of handcuffs. It is much more abstract, like the concept of "mind" over "German," and seems to imply that each link, like each person, is a part of a larger chain, or society – in this society, the elite are not a part of the chain. Rather, the people of the streets are the links making up the chain and the elite have control of the chain and use it to further enslave the people. Still, the people, like the links, are all connected and all experience suffering at the whims of the elite. This is much too interpretive, even for Blake, and "links" is a term we, as his readers, should all be grateful gave way to "manacles." "Manacles," "fetter for the hand; (more generally) a shackle; a bond, a restraint," is a much more effective word choice, assuming the reader knows the definition. "Manacles" paints a much more vivid and jarring mental image of the mind, an abstract concept, being chained. The elite have usurped so much of the lives of the people of the streets, and have no doubt put a great many of them in literal chains, that it comes as no surprise that they have managed to burrow so far into the minds of the people and find yet another way by which to enslave them. Langston Hughes asked "what happens to a dream deferred?" Blake has now shown "what happens to a mind manacled." Dr. Linda Freedman has some further insight into this and its historical significance where authorities, likely Hessians, and radicals, likely revolutionaries, are concerned. She writes "by replacing 'links' with 'manacles', Blake made the poem more subversive. 'Manacles' was one of the code words directed at oppression by the authorities. Radicals used it to convey their sense of an enslaved society."

While there are numerous examples in which Blake selects a new word in lieu of a previously chosen term in a draft, especially if the new vocable is polysemous, there is also an important example of a polysemous term that survived from draft to final cut. "In every voice; in every ban" contains an example of polysemy, which many may not even recognize as polysemous. Thanks to a footnote in "Blake's Poetry and Designs," this is brought to the reader's attention and adds historical context as well as a world of meaning to a single syllable. Most readers are aware of the different senses of the word ban, which can be an "authoritative proclamation; a public proclamation or edict; a formal and authoritative prohibition; a prohibitory command or edict, an interdict; a proclamation issued against any one by the civil power; sentence of outlawry," a "sentence of banishment," "a formal ecclesiastical denunciation; anathema, interdict, excommunication; practical denunciation, prohibition, or outlawry, not formally pronounced, as that of society or public opinion," "a curse, having, or supposed to have, supernatural sanction, and baleful influence," or "an imprecation of a curse, an execration or malediction expressing anger." The last sense is exemplified in the OED by the line "In every ban, The mind-forged manacles I hear," presumably designating this definition as the one to which special attention should be paid. Given the

knowledge that the privatization of the streets of London awards power to the elite, it comes as no surprise that they would subsequently declare authoritative proclamations or prohibitions, much like when alcohol was banned in America in the 1920's. This application extends once more when one considers that these authoritative proclamations or prohibitions are issued as commands from the elite to the people of the streets. Much like the previous example of alcohol in America in the 1920's, the banishment sense of the word is quite clear. In these religious times, when the Church had its hands in State matters, excommunication was a dreadful fate and one that would have been readily bestowed upon undesirable persons. The matter becomes a bit more complex when the final two senses are concerned because they seem to be of a more archaic sense and involve magic, which was a very troubling subject during these "holier" times. A curse, which most know to be a type of magic that produces ill effects, and an imprecation, which is the act of cursing, are the intended senses of "ban" in this line. This produces the modern interpretation of "in every voice and in every curse," which could possibly allude to witchcraft. This poem is dated sometime between 1789 and 1794 and we all know what happened merely one hundred years earlier in an American town by the name of Salem. Perhaps, one hundred years later, accusations of witchcraft were not quite so serious, but they were likely undesirable and unhelpful regarding the general state of being as a member of the common throng. The historical polysemy of this word comes from the church and stands in stark contrast to the allusions to malevolent magic. "Banns," always in the plural, were "a proclamation or public notice given in church of an intended marriage, in order that those who know of any impediment thereto may have opportunity of lodging objections." The footnote in "Blake's Poetry and Designs" states "also "marriage banns," the required three-Sunday notice of forthcoming weddings in Anglican churches." The banns were the equivalent of today's "if anyone has any reason why this couple should not be joined in matrimony" and were an opportunity for a woman to escape from a potentially abusive union or for a man to renege upon learning his bride-to-be was not a virgin. In this instance, "in every voice; in every ban" could mean "all of the voices objecting to this marriage" and the following "mind-forg'd manacles" could imply that support or opposition to a marriage is likely rooted in some societal "rule." The "rule" is simply something humans made up and to which we have become enslaved, much like the concept of marriage – and that it is all futile. This is a very nihilistic and cynical perspective, but it is just as valid as any other perspective – Blake seems to have believed that most people are the proverbial "sheep" who blindly follow what the "shepherd," elite society, dictates without question.

Word changes and polysemy abound in "London" and its drafts and this was merely a sampling of the many that are ripe for analysis. When one

considers initial word choices, word changes, and final word choices, along with words possessing multiple meanings and senses, as well as historical context, there is a great deal to uncover about the specific vocabulary of a literary work. A resource, such as the Oxford English Dictionary, is helpful in pinpointing etymology and evolution of a word and its definition(s), as well as revealing significant examples of a term's employment at different points in history. It was a remarkable discovery coming across so many edits between the draft and final product of "London" in addition to learning more about polysemy and just how many polysemous words one can use in a four-stanza poem. The concept of polysemy is one many are familiar with, but are unaware that there is a word to describe the phenomenon, much less that it is a fascinating writing tool to employ.

Works Cited

"ban, n.1." *OED Online*. Oxford University Press, September 2016. 28 November 2016.

"banns, n." *OED Online*. Oxford University Press, September 2016. 28 November 2016.
Blake, William. "London." Ed. Mary Lynn Johnson and John E. Grant. *Blake's Poetry and Designs*. New York: W.W. Norton, 2008. 41.

"chartered, adj." *OED Online*. Oxford University Press, September 2016. 28 November 2016.

"dirty, adj." *OED Online*. Oxford University Press, September 2016. 28 November 2016.

Freedman, Linda. "Looking at the Manuscript of William Blake's 'London'" *The British Library*. The British Library, 20 Mar. 2014. 28 Nov. 2016.

"link, n.2." *OED Online*. Oxford University Press, September 2016. 28 November 2016.

"manacle, n." *OED Online*. Oxford University Press, September 2016. 28 November 2016.

"mark, n.1." *OED Online*. Oxford University Press, September 2016. 28 November 2016.

"mark, v." *OED Online*. Oxford University Press, September 2016. 28 November 2016.

"polysemy, n." *OED Online*. Oxford University Press, September 2016. 28 November 2016.

"see, v." *OED Online*. Oxford University Press, September 2016. 28 November 2016.

Chandni Lotwala

The Full Circle of Shakespeare's Rosalind

From Rosalind in *As You Like It* to Lady Macbeth in *Macbeth*, there is no shortage of powerful women in Shakespeare's plays. Rosalind, however, has an advantage over Shakespeare's other strong-minded female characters- she doubles as a he. As Ganymede, a young, effeminate man, Rosalind experiences freedom of speech and action. She is emboldened by the power society offers a man and embodies the role from the instant she conceives the idea of her transformation. It is perhaps this gender change that allows her to avoid the fate ambitious, strong willed women like Kate in *The Taming of the Shrew* and Lady Macbeth in Macbeth suffer. Ultimately, however, Rosalind retains no power: her male counterparts retain ownership over her and her speech is demure. The only power she really ever has in the play is over Celia, and even that is usurped by Oliver by the end of *As You Like It*.

Rosalind is introduced in *As You Like It* as a powerless victim in a patriarchal world. Saddened after her father, Duke Senior, is banished, Rosalind is convinced by Celia to be happy and acquiesces to " . . . devise sports" in order to maintain happiness (1.2.20). This frivolous solution to Rosalind's dilemma plays at the supposed simplicity of women. In Act 1, scene 2 of *As You Like It*, the complex exchanges between Rosalind and Celia are marked by the entrance of the fool, Touchstone. Celia states in 1.2.47-49, "[Nature], who perceiveth our natural wits too dull to reason of such goddesses, and hath sent this natural for our whetstone," marking self-deprecation of the female mind and wit.

In the setting of the court and as a female, Rosalind remains meek. In her exchange with Duke Frederick in Act 1, she begins her conversation with "I do beseech your Grace . . ." and, while demonstrating strength as she briefly argues with him, she resigns the conversation to a submissive, "then, good my liege, mistake me not so much" and allows Celia to finish the fight for her (Frye 120; 1.3.39,59). Rosalind possesses little power in the Court and is dominated by others.

Once Celia suggests the two of them escape, Rosalind instantaneously takes charge, taking the first step towards her transformation as a man in patriarchal society. "Rosalind's suggestion that she dress herself as a man to aid their escape is the first moment of agency that the play allows her . . . the

configuration of power in [Celia and Rosalind's] relationship shifts (Frye 120)." Rosalind's transformation is necessary because "the perspective of the play is precisely that of Orlando's half sonnet, in which Rosalind is the "unexpressive she" (3.2.10). She is, as Orlando intends . . . unable to express herself." (Green 42). While Orlando experiences a momentary lapse of speech during his conversation with Rosalind, he maintains his power as a male by expressing himself throughout his exile. Throughout the play, he characterizes Rosalind as "the fair, the chaste, and unexpressive she" (1.2.219-221; 3.2.10).

Continuing her transformation from the unexpressive female to the powerful male, Rosalind, as Ganymede, assumes her new identity. While tired from her trek to Arden, she does not readily admit to fatigue, claiming "I could find in my heart to disgrace my man's apparel and to cry like a woman, but I must comfort the weaker vessel, as doublet and hose ought to show itself courageous to petticoat" (3.4.4-6). As Larkin mentions:

> Ultimately, Rosalind was empowered by her masquerade because disguise inscribed her with greater self-confidence. Although the initial motivation for the character's gendered masquerade was to provide safety, Rosalind also suggested that: "Were it not better, Because that I am more than common tall That I did suit me all points like a man, A gallant curtal-axe upon my thigh, A boar-spear in my hand, and in my heart, Lie there what hidden women's fear there will." (1.3.108-113; 6-7)

Perhaps a part of Rosalind's transformation to Ganymede has to do with Freud's ideas of males in society. Zajac explains one of Freud's theories described in *Civilizations and Its Discontents* in a footnote, stating that society is simply the product of a man attempting to obtain the object of his sexual desire. Taken out of context of the court and into a pastoral setting, Rosalind, as Ganymede, can make the forest of Arden her own medium to obtain the man she desires, Orlando.

Simply by donning the attire of a male, Ganymede, Rosalind takes on the role of the homosexual fantasy her namesake commands (Zeitlin). As Ganymede, Rosalind is able to challenge Orlando's love and show him her wit. Ganymede proclaims, "Come, woo me, woo me," a command Rosalind would not be allowed to make while living in the court as a woman (4.1.58). As Susan Baker has mentioned, " 'the young women who dress as men gain a freedom of movement denied them in their women's weeds' (315). . . . because Rosalind (in the guise of Ganymede) could secretly uncover Orlando's feelings for her undisguised self'" (Larkin 6). Her disguise enables Rosalind to act outside of societal norms and court Orlando in a nontraditional manner that would characterize her as a loose, immoral woman otherwise (Larkin 6-7). A simple

comparison of the reactions to Ganymede's "Nay, an you be so tardy, come no more in my sight" and to Kate's scolding of males in *The Taming of the Shrew* demonstrates Rosalind's newfound freedom as a man (4.1.45).

Her repeated outbursts of "And I am your Rosalind," fall to Orlando's deaf ears because Ganymede, while effeminate, is still a man (4.1.56). He has the power of speech and wit, seen through the banter between a clever Ganymede and slightly witless Orlando. Rosalind might be empowered by her power of speech as Ganymede but even as Ganymede, Rosalind herself is still constricted to a feminine identity. Orlando repeatedly characterizes Rosalind as 'his' Rosalind, as virtuous, and of a quiet disposition (4.1.55). He is blinded by his perception of an obedient woman. "Even as a boy... Rosalind is circumscribed by patriarchal institutions, conventions, and perspectives-like the original Ganymede, she is the beloved and the servant of the all-powerful male, whether father or lover (Green 46). The biological male can give up power to the pretend male pretending to be Rosalind, but will not give up his power over the female Rosalind. "She could be a threatening figure if she did not constantly, contrapuntally, reveal herself to the audience as the not-man, as in actuality a lovesick maid," maintaining that the real power in *As You Like It* is ultimately held by the males (Howard 434).

This constriction, seen in Orlando's inability to identify Rosalind, can also be noted in Rosalind's interaction with those who know she is posing as Ganymede. While talking to Celia, she acts as a weaker vessel, unable to contain her excitement (3.2.165-185; Eddleman 69). An interesting point to note, however, is Ganymede's stereotyping of females in his male form (Eddleman 69). He disparages females, asking, "Do you not know I am a woman? When I think, I must speak" (3.2.227-228). Rosalind, overcome by the freedom a male has, frowns upon females and their emotions and supposed duplicity. Jardine, in *Still Harping on Daughters: Women and Drama in the Age of Shakespeare*, notes the change in views between Rosalind and Ganymede, stating that as Ganymede, "She 'keeps decorum' in slandering women . . ." (20). Celia notes this, yelling at Rosalind because "[she has] simply misused [their] sex in [her] love-prate . . . and [Celia must] show the world what the bird hath done to her own nest" (4.1.174-177). Even as the same person, Ganymede, the male, wins over Rosalind, the female. The male view about females is vocalized by Ganymede/Rosalind rather than a more empathetic view Rosalind should have.

Celia soon realizes the unforeseen consequence of Celia and Rosalind donning the roles of Aliena and Ganymede. As the sister to a male, Celia has to relinquish the power she held over Rosalind as Duke Frederick's daughter. Frye mentions that Celia has to be submissive when in the company of two males, Ganymede and Orlando, agreeing to pose as a minister at Ganymede's

request (120). Ganymede's sex allows Rosalind to "[leave] behind the feelings of inferiority and submission that being female entailed in the world of the court," with a juxtaposition between what a female disguised as a male can do and what a duke's daughter disguised as a common woman can do (Edd¹⁻man 71). There is a drastic switch in power between Rosalind and Celia. Even while alone in the forest, Rosalind still exerts power over Celia simply because in the forest, Rosalind is known as Ganymede.

In scene 4, Rosalind tells Celia "let [Orlando] be judge how deep I am in love. I'll tell thee, Aliena, I cannot be out of the sight of Orlando" (4.1.188-190). Rosalind refers to Celia as Aliena, speaking as Ganymede to his submissive, female sister rather than Rosalind's female counterpart. Referring to Celia as Aliena in this dialogue exemplifies Celia's alienation from Rosalind's world as Ganymede. The powerful, male authority and presence that Ganymede experiences are something Celia, as herself or as Aliena, will never get to experience. Though the pastoral setting allows characters to resolve problems outside the context of the court, Rosalind's transformation causes any homosexual tension between Celia and Rosalind to dissipate, resulting in an alienated Celia and a freed Rosalind.

Unfortunately for Rosalind, as she is freed from her constrictive bond with Celia, she is bound yet again, but this time by the shackles of her gender. As she begins to resume her femininity after her peak as a well-spoken, witty male, she loses that part of her identity. This relapse begs the question of the purpose of Rosalind's transformation to Ganymede. Initially taken upon as a means to travel from the court in safety, Rosalind gains self confidence and freedom of speech, both of which seem to dissolve upon her transformation back to Rosalind. As written by Green:

> Thus Rosalind has no identity except as Other to a socially constituted, male Self; she is the periphery brought centerstage. Finally she rejoins the ranks of women in her society-limits her protean character to the traditional roles of daughter and wife in what Peter Erickson calls a "benevolent Patriarchy." The engaging heroine of *As You Like It* simply disappears, disintegrates into the improved, but nonetheless reestablished, masculine domain of court and marriage. (41)

Further emphasis of Rosalind's quick loss of power occurs immediately after her complete alienation of Celia. When Oliver arrives with a handkerchief stained with Orlando's blood, Rosalind faints. Oliver immediately questions Ganymede's masculinity, exclaiming "Be of good cheer, youth. You a man? You lack a man's heart," implying a woman's frailty compared to a man (4.2.191-192). This display of weakness on Ganymede's part, though attempted to be

played off as an act, strips Rosalind of her power as a man. Her weakness peaks through her macho exterior and after that point, "Rosalind may continue to plot, but the plot she organizes is one that will perforce subsume the heroine within the identity of her husband and silence her voice" (Kinney 313). As quickly as Rosalind's ascent to power and freedom of speech is, her loss of control occurs just as rapidly.

The interplay between the versions of Rosalind: the weak female in the court, the female assuming the rôle of a male, the female assuming the role of a male playing a female, and the female bound by marriage, can be interpreted by a cultural critique view of feminism (Nielson). Green highlights Shakespeare's use of a temporarily powerful female to entertain the male, misogynist audience that is ruled by a Queen.

> The heroine of Shakespeare's *As You Like It* is an example of woman conceived and represented by and for men-the "you" who "like it." Shakespeare's "you" is the Self associated with the dominant male powers of Elizabethan society, insofar as it reflects and reproduces the ideology of those powers and that society. (46)

Rosalind's ultimate role of pleasing the audience correlates to the female's role of pleasing her husband, brother, and father in Shakespearean society. Kinney argues that once Rosalind slips back into the role of Rosalind, she resumes the role of Orlando's "heavenly Rosalind" (313; 1.2.251). Hymen, the God of marriage, has to 'present' Rosalind once she retains her female form. She pledges herself to both her father and to Orlando, stating, "To you I give myself, for I am yours" (5.4.107-108). Rosalind is once again property, stripped of the wit and power Ganymede once held. Howard interprets this as closure within the play, with all characters in their proper social positions (435).

A drastic change occurs in *As You Like It* after the marriages that signify Rosalind's reemergence as "the fair, the chaste, and unexpressive she" (1.2.219-221). A play filled with lines by Rosalind, whether as Ganymede or as Rosalind, is abruptly shifted to a play with predominantly male lines. While the closing scene is marked by a soliloquy by Rosalind, the dialogue is, in fact, delivered by the male actor playing Rosalind as himself. This is evidenced by the lines,:

> I am not furnished like a beggar; therefore to
> beg will not become me. My way is to conjure you . . .
> If I were a woman, I would kiss as many of you as had
> beards that pleased me, complexions that liked me,
> and breaths that I defied not." (5.4.205-215)

The male actor dominated his feminine role of Rosalind at the end, emphasizing the recurring theme of male dominance over females. In addition, he alludes to bewitching the audience because he was dressed as a woman. Rather than trying to please the audience through a woman's wit, displayed by Rosalind as Ganymede, the actor immediately correlates women to bewitching and conjuring men.

Shakespeare's Rosalind in *As You Like It* temporarily gains power while she is disguised as a man. Ganymede has freedom of speech and can engage in a battle of wits. He is able to express his desires and chastise Orlando and other females in the play. Regardless of the wit and confidence that Rosalind displays while she acts as Ganymede, in the end Rosalind must return to her role as a subservient female. Once Rosalind gives up her role as Ganymede to marry Orlando, she becomes property of the males in the play and loses her independent voice. While her societal position is elevated, she will end her journey in the Forest of Arden as a wife in a patriarchal society.

Works Cited

Eddleman, Stephanie (2013) "The Transforming Power of Breeches: the Merging of Rosalind's Two Selves in *As You Like It*," The Oswald Review: An International Journal of Undergraduate Research and Criticism in the Discipline of English: Vol. 4: Iss. 1, Article 7

Frye, Susan and Robertson, Karen. *Maids and Mistresses, Cousins and Queens: Women's Alliances in Early Modern England*. New York: Oxford UP, 2010. Web.

Green, Douglas E. "The "Unexpressive She": Is There Really a Rosalind?" *Journal of Dramatic Theory and Criticism* 2.2 (1988): 41-52. University of Kansas Libraries. Web. 4 Mar. 2017.

Jardine, Lisa. *Still Harping on Daughters: Women and Drama in the Age of Shakespeare*. New York, N.Y.: Harvester-Wheatsheaf, 1990. Electronic.

Kinney, Clare R. "Feigning Female Faining: Spenser, Lodge, Shakespeare, and Rosalind." *Modern Philology*, vol. 95, no. 3, 1998, pp. 291–315., www.jstor.org/stable/438878.

Larkin, Sinead. "'The Weaker Vessel'?: Disguise and Empowerment in Postmodern Shakespearean Performance." Quest 4 (2007): 1-11. *Drexel Summons*. Web. 3 Mar. 2017.

Nielson, Christopher. *English 325 Shakespeare's Women Syllabus 2016*. Philadelphia, 2016. PDF.

Shakespeare, William. *As You Like It*. Ed. John Crowther. SparkNotes LLC. 2004. Web. 23 Feb 2017.

Zajac, P. J. "The Politics of Contentment: Passions, Pastoral, and Community in Shakespeare's *As You Like It*." *Studies in Philology*, vol. 113 no. 2, 2016, pp. 306-336. Project MUSE, muse.jhu.edu/article/614012.

Zeitlin, Froma. "Configurations of rape in Greek myth." *Rape: An Historical and Social Enquiry* (1986): 122-151.

Caitlin McLaughlin

Beyond Catherine Barkley: Analyzing the Writings of WWI Nurses

Men are the center of discussion in discourse of WWI. If women are brought up, it is typically in their role on the homefront. During this time, the women's suffrage movement had just begun in Britain, and with the war brought the opportunity for women to work as nurses close to the front. Women's role in society was changing, and women like May Sinclair wrote poetry to describe this newfound freedom from the societal expectations of women in this time period. Other women like Mary Borden wrote vivid accounts of the horrors of war through the eyes of women. These women were not passive as male writers at the time had categorized them. Borden and Sinclair subverted gender norms by writing accounts of women as active participants in the war.

War is a masculine topic; it is difficult to imagine a feminized version of war. Yet with the presence of nurses in the war, women experienced some of the most horrific elements of battle through the gruesome injuries of men who were cared for by female nurses. In her anthology, *Her War Story: Twentieth-century Women Write about War*, Sayre P. Sheldon notes that authors like Borden "had ventured into a 'forbidden zone' for women at the time. They wrote about bodies and their hitherto unmentionable functions, about mutilation and appalling suffering..." (Sheldon 5). It was not ladylike for women to discuss the horrific details of war, yet women were actively experiencing these elements of war. Mary Borden in particular details her experiences as a nurse in her short story "Blind." She does not shy away from describing internal organs or bodily functions. She describes the man that came into her care as " something that was not very like a man. The limbs seemed to be held together only by the strong stuff of the uniform. The head was unrecognisable. It was a monstrous thing," and later goes on to describe another patient whose "brain came off on [a] bandage" (Borden 1-2). In describing the raw, grotesque details that a nurse experiences during the war, Borden takes away the gendered element of suffering often applied to the war. Borden shows a woman experiencing the same monstrosities that a man would experience seeing the injured, and positions women in a role where they cannot show emotion. A nurse has to do her job regardless of the horrifying details. When the "masculine" experience of war is applied to women, constructed gender roles lack the meaning they once had.

Little was known about PTSD at this time period, but what little was known was typically applied to male soldiers returning from the front. Yet, as Sheldon notes, " 'Blind,' ends with Borden showing symptoms that would not yet have been recognized as shell shock--the same disorder afflicting thousands of men at the front and causing widespread desertion and hospitalization" (Sheldon 5). Borden illustrates that women were not passive in the war, they were equally affected by the experiences of seeing men injured and dying in their care that male soldiers were on the battlefield. In "Blind" when the nurse comes face to face with the blind man, her "body rattled and jerked like a machine out of order. I was awake now, and I seemed to be breaking to pieces" (Borden 7). The nurse in the story had been carrying out the functions of her job, despite witnessing human suffering consistently. She could not afford to stop and experience her emotions. Masculinity values stoicism, while femininity values emotion, yet Borden's writing shows a woman who has removed herself from emotions and stepped into a masculine role. Borden's description of the nurse being "awake" implies that she is now unable to overlook the horrors around her. The realization of what she is seeing causes her to "break to pieces" in the way that soldiers returning from the front suffered as they coped with their experiences at war. Borden shows that women, although not in combat, were still affected by the war in the same way as male soldiers with PTSD.

May Sinclair, another WWI nurse, further explored women's role in the war through her poetry. Sinclair was excited by the war, because it gave her opportunities that she would not have had back home, yet Sinclair was also aware of the horrors of war. Laurel Forster, in her article "Women and War Zones: May Sinclair's Personal Negotiation with the First World War," notes "It was wrong to enjoy the war [...] wrong merely to devote oneself to one's children [...] It was right for men to go to war to fight for 'freedom', wrong for women to nurse or drive an ambulance to help to fight for the same freedom" (Forster 231). Women who were involved in the war would not gain the same glory coming home that a man would. Women would still be expected to follow society's plan for a woman at the time. They would come home, still be expected to marry, have children, and perform domestic tasks. Sinclair devotes herself completely to the war for some of the same reasons as men, to give back to her country, but also to experience the freedom she would not have back home. In Sinclair's poem "Dedication" she expresses her upset at not being invited back to serve in the ambulance corps, which granted her a great deal of freedom. She writes of her fellow nurses, "You have taken my dream/And dressed yourself in its beauty and its glory" ("Dedication" 4-5). Sinclair's "dream" was to help the soldiers fighting for her country through nursing, to make a difference in a way that women's passive societal role did not allow until this point. The "beauty" and "glory" she could have received was given to other women. Sinclair would have to return home to a life where she would not be afforded the same freedoms.

Through her writing, Sinclair unpacks the masculine elements of war, and expresses the polarity that a woman in a masculinized setting feels. In Sinclair's poem "Field Ambulance in Retreat," she discusses the retreat of an army through the eyes of a nurse, detailing the disconnect between nurses and the soldiers. Sinclair writes:

"Our safety weighs us down
Safety hard and strange, stranger and more hard
As, league after dying league, the beautiful desolate land
Falls back from the intolerable speed of an Ambulance in Retreat"
("Field Ambulance in Retreat" 22-23).

The lyrical speaker in this poem is aware that in the ambulance she is safe in a way that the men who battle every day are not. Her distinctly female experience causes her to have safety, but also to be weighted down by this safety. And as more men die, it becomes harder to experience the safety of her role in war.

Women experienced war at a distance, even close to the front. Sinclair further explores this distance in her poem "After the Retreat." The speaker looks "Through windows blurred like women's eyes that have cried/too long" in a town she passed on the ambulance's retreat (9-10). Women at home were mourning the loss of their sons, and Sinclair is thinking about these women even as she is participating in a different role, figuring out how to navigate this war zone as a woman. This represents the internal conflict between life at home for women and their new role as nurses in the war.

Women writers like Mary Borden and May Sinclair wrote to express the uniquely female experience of war in a society where women's role was actively changing. Still, these women writers were not widely accepted until after their time. Sheldon notes that, "Many of these outspoken and revealing accounts were either withdrawn or not published until long after the war's end in 1918" (Sheldon 5). In a time where women did not yet have the right to vote, a woman writing about her experiences was a radical act. Sinclair and Borden wrote to understand their own conflicting emotions about the war, but also to show that women's experiences were as diverse as male experiences. From Borden's depiction of female PTSD in her story "Blind," to Sinclair's conflicted thoughts about the freedoms the war granted her, these women were deeply impacted by their war experiences in ways women at home were not. This is not to say that women at home were not liberated or that domestic work should be valued less, but Borden and Sinclair entered a world typically closed off to women. Women's writing in WWI, fueled by the women's movement in England, enriched our understanding of the female war experience.

Works Cited

Borden, Mary. "Blind." Print.

Forster, Laurel. *Spatial Practices: An Interdisciplinary Series in Cultural History, Geography and Literature, 4 : Inside Out : Women Negotiating, Subverting, Appropriating Public and Private Space: Women and War Zones: May Sinclair's Personal Negotiation with the First World War*. Editions Rodopi, 01/01/2008. Web. 11 Feb. 2017.

Sheldon, Sayre P. *Her War Story: Twentieth-century Women Write about War*. Carbondale: Southern Illinois UP, 1999. Print.

Sinclair, May. "Field Ambulance in Retreat" *Poetry of the First World War*. Oxford: Oxford University Press, 2013. 17-18. Print.

Sinclair, May. "After the Retreat" *Poetry of the First World War*. Oxford: Oxford University Press, 2013. 18. Print.

Sinclair, May. "Dedication" *Poetry of the First World War*. Oxford: Oxford University Press, 2013. 19. Print.

Heather Heim

Literary Devices in Gray's "Elegy Written in a Country Churchyard"

In Thomas Gray's "Elegy Written in a Country Churchyard," the author uses numerous literary devices to emphasize themes of death. He uses anastrophe and inversion, making his syntax purposefully vague, and creating a confusion between subject and object that reinforces his theme of uncertainty in life and death. The idea of death is further pronounced in his use of diction. While Gray's word choice sets up a pastoral feel at the beginning of the poem, his shift in diction leads to a shift in tone as well, bringing the idea of the graveyard's inhabitants nearer to the forefront of the readers' minds. Moreover, Gray's use of personification also does work in the poem to strengthen Gray's themes of the dead and his memory (or lack of memory) of them.

Gray's use of anastrophe in the poem stands out more than any other literary device used, but why does he use it? In *The Poetry Toolkit: The Essential Guide to Studying Poetry*, author Rhian Williams defines anastrophe as "a scheme in which the parts of a sentence appear in an unusual order" (234). Williams further notes that anastrophe can provide emphasis in the poem or allow "disturbing acts to be suggested" (234). One such example of a "disturbing act" occurs in Robert Browning's "Porphyria's Lover," in the lines: "Her hair / In one long yellow string I wound / Three times her little throat around" (Williams 234). Williams notes that the lines "would have far less impact if anastrophe had not been used to perform this action by making 'little throat' sit suffocated between the rhymes of 'wound' and 'around'" (234). The anastrophe in Gray's piece also serves to emphasize and disturb, although in a much subtler way than Browning's piece.

To begin, the syntax in Gray's poem serves to emphasize uncertainty. In his article "Syntax of Death: Instability in Gray's 'Elegy Written in a Country Churchyard,'" W. Hutchings suggests that there's an instability in the poem brought about by "fluid," "indeterminate" syntax, and that understanding this instability is key to understanding Gray's "Elegy" (496). For instance, Gray jumbles grammar and semantics to be purposefully unclear. While a normal sentence has one subject and one object, Gray's lines make knowing which words are subjects and which words are objects complex.

Hutchings notes "In the case of 'all the air a solemn stillness holds,' neither grammar nor meaning dictates which is the subject and which the object. It is not clear whether it is more likely that an abstract noun should hold or be held by something which is insubstantial..." (500). This unclarity on Gray's part makes the subject and the verb interchangeable, thus, creating a "lack of syntactic definition" (Hutchings 500). The lack of syntactic definition is important because the instability of Gray's form mimics an underlying theme of Gray's poem, the instability of life as a whole. Hutchings believes it demonstrates that Gray's world is one in which "subjects and objects are losing their fixity, where stability is being undermined" (502).

In her essay "Elegy Unto Epitaph: Print Culture and Commemorative Practice in Gray's 'Elegy Written in a Country Churchyard,'" author Michele Turner Sharp further comments on Gray's syntax and its significance, she says "The difficulty that the poem takes to get to the point places the poet's uncertainty about his rapport with the ignoble dead, together with his uncertainty about the resources of poetry to bridge this gap between the poet and the subject of his poem" (3). However, Sharp believes that the "gap" between poet and subject extends beyond just those elements. She believes that it represents a gap between speaker and "any and all potential hearers" (3).

Supporting Sharp's theory is Hutching's idea that "The syntactic confusion of subject and object has been used to render the nature of death" (505). As previously mentioned, the subjects and objects of Gray's sentences are jumbled, demonstrating that things that are usually active can become passive. This represents people, and how those who are active will become passive in death. Hutchings takes this idea further, suggesting that the speaker himself also becomes part of this pattern, because while Gray begins as the poem's subject, he eventually shifts to become the poem's object when he mentions "Haply some hoary-headed swain may say / 'Oft have we seen him at the peep of dawn...'" (97-98). The "hoary-headed swain" now becomes the subject and muses about the speaker, making him the object. Hutchings notes, "The 'Elegy''s uncertain relationship between subject and object allows us to accept that the writer of a poem could end up as its object. The fact of death's inevitability demands that such a transition take place" (505).

Lorna Clymer, author of "Graved in Tropes: The Figural Logic of Epitaphs and Elegies in Blair, Gray, Cowper, and Wordsworth," is in agreement with Sharp and Hutchings, noting that Gray's displaced subjects create "an intersubjectivity between the deceased and those involved in commemoration," which is "increasingly displaced from the grave to the ongoing life of the community that remembers the dead" (356). Thus, Gray's syntax represents the uncertainty of death, showing within the poem how subject becomes

object, and how even the speaker can go from active to passive. This implies that the reader will also someday fit into the pattern of inevitable passivity, or death.

Furthermore, while the arrangement of Gray's words is important, the words themselves do work in the poem as well. Sharp discusses the diction that Gray uses to open the poem. Words like "slowly" (2), "fades" (5), "droning" (7), "drowsy" (8), and "lull" (8) set a "slow motion" pace, draining the scene of urgency" (Sharp 3). This sets the poem's tone to be one of "timelessness" and the speaker's voice to be "lethargic" (Sharp 3). At the same time, the lines "The lowing herd wind slowly o'er the lea / The plowman homeward plods his weary way" (2-3), magnify how alone the speaker is, as men and animals alike leave him isolated in the graveyard. The diction at the beginning of the elegy sets a tone of reflectiveness and oneness between the speaker and the graveyard. Furthermore, the line "And leaves the world to darkness and to me" (4) represents death, and the speaker's eventual death.

However, Sharp suggests a tonal shift when "the hard consonant sounds of 'molest,' 'ancient,' 'solitary,' and 'mantled tow'r'...contrast with the pattern of rhythmic tolling of long vowel sounds in the preceding stanzas" (Sharp 3), which suggests a mounting "uneasiness" (Sharp 3). Sharp argues that the word "molest" itself "intensifies the poem's distress" and thus "heralds the rising of the village dead in stanza four and their power to disturb both poet and poem" (3). So, just as the lifeless, passive objects of the poem, the dead, creep up through syntax, their presence is also felt through Gray's word choice.

Clymer further comments on Gray's representation of the dead by discussing the author's use of personification, which is used in the lines "Let not Ambition mock their useful toil" (29) and "...Nor Grandeur hear with a disdainful smile" (30). Clymer believes the personification provides distance between the dead and their past lives (351). She notes that this literary device helps "make abstract any distinct accomplishments or qualities, or within generalizations that reduce individuals to a collective whole" (352). This idea ties in with one of Gray's overarching themes that " The paths of glory lead but to the grave" (36).

Upon closely reading Gray's "Elegy Written in a Country Churchyard," readers discover that each word, word placement, and literary device that seems unstable or awkward is actually serving as a *momento mori*, meant to bring the idea of death to mind. It is in this purposeful instability that Gray draws out the uncertainty of life and death. Syntax that sounds disturbing is meant to disturb, just as personification that sounds vague is meant to sound vague.

Works Cited

Clymer, Lorna. "Graved in Tropes: The Figural Logic of Epitaphs and Elegies in Blair, Gray, Cowper, and Wordsworth." Poetry Criticism, edited by Michelle Lee, vol. 80, Gale, 2008. Literature Resource Center, Accessed 14 Mar. 2017. Originally published in *ELH*, vol. 62, no. 2, Summer 1995, pp. 347-386.

Gray, Thomas. "Elegy Written in a Country Churchyard." *The Norton Anthology of English Literature. The Restoration and the Eighteenth Century.* edited by Stephen Greenblatt, New York: Norton, 2012. p. 3051-3054. Print.

Hutchings, W. "Syntax of Death: Instability in Gray's 'Elegy Written in a Country Churchyard'." Poetry Criticism, edited by Michelle Lee, vol. 80, Gale, 2008. Literature Resource Center. Accessed 14 Mar. 2017. Originally published in *Studies in Philology*, vol. 81, no. 4, Fall 1984, pp. 496-514.

Sharp, Michele Turner. "Elegy Unto Epitaph: Print Culture and Commemorative Practice in Gray's 'Elegy Written in a Country Churchyard'." *Papers on Language & Literature*, vol. 38, no. 1, 2002, p. 3. Accessed 14 Mar. 2017.

Williams, Rhian. *The Poetry Toolkit: The Essential Guide to Studying Poetry.* 2nd Edition. Bloomsbury, 2013. Accessed 14 Mar. 2017.

Davina Lee

Contextual Analysis in Poetry

For most readers, evaluating context—both immediately in surrounding text and in a wider historical or cultural sense—is one of the first key steps in any critical analysis of literature, since it serves to clarify authorial intent and help prevent misinterpretations of meaning. This is an invaluable tool for analyzing prose works, but several things call into question the usefulness of context analysis as a tool for understanding poetry, particularly poetry from the twentieth century and beyond.

In the first place, many poems are written to stand on their own and do not necessarily benefit from being placed in collections with other poems. Furthermore, much of modern poetry is either not overly concerned with the cultural or physical realities of the time, or sufficient context is provided within each poem for understanding. These points, however, have numerous and notable exceptions, which is ultimately a testament to the extraordinary diversity of poetry in both style and purpose, and the subsequent variety of analytical methods that poetry demands.

Arranging poems into a book usually differs significantly from writing a book with chapters. The prose book is a progression of thought, chapters building upon one another, and this is not necessarily the case with adjacent poems in a collection. For example, a work such as Li-young Lee's "The Cleaving" derives little meaning from anything set before or after it. The poem begins with the man who "gossips like my grandmother" ("Cleaving" 1) and ends with the same man, "this immigrant, / this man with my own face" (335-336): it is a complete thought within itself, and most poems tend to follow a similar philosophy of self-sufficiency.

Here the exceptions abound. One thinks of works like John Berryman's *Dream Songs*: each Dream Song functions well as an individual poem, but new dimensions of fractured identity, haunting memory, and other thematic elements only arise when the songs are read together. The characters—Mr. Bones, Henry, the minstrel-voiced friend, Henry's father—need the space of many poems in order to take on their full personas, as difficult to parse and perplexing as they are.

One might also point to *The Wild Iris* by Louise Glück and note how the flower poems together say more about Nature and humanity and spirituality than any poem does on its own, though each is exquisitely beautiful in its own right. In "The Red Poppy," the reader is prompted to consider the difference between the poppy and the human— "were you like me once, long ago, / before you were human?" (13-14)—and what it means to speak the way the human does, to speak "because I am shattered" (20). The poem is one complete thought, but only by reading more of these does the reader learn of the flowers' fixation with the act of speaking and how it relates to life, to living. "I tell you I could speak again," marvels the speaker in "The Wild Iris" after experiencing something akin to both birth and death (18), and the reader is invited to revisit her original questions in a new context, which allows for additional nuance in exploration.

Does analyzing the context of surrounding text (in this case, surrounding poems in the same book) add value to the meaning of a particular poem, then? The answer perhaps depends on whether the poems were written together as subunits of a whole or were written separately and only later assembled into a collection. Both are equally valid styles of poetry and simply exhibit the versatility of forms for expressing a variety of meanings.

As for cultural or historical context analysis, the concept of usefulness is less clear. On one hand, knowing certain details about the time in which a poem was written can be the key to unlocking an otherwise inscrutable piece. Frank O'Hara's "The Day Lady Died," for instance, is difficult to fully understand without knowing who Billie Holiday was and her significance as a cultural icon. On the other hand, the common form of poetry as stand-alone pieces means that many poems simply provide as much cultural context as is necessary within themselves.

Self-contextualizing poems may explicitly refer to a specific location, as in "Facing It" by Yosef Komunyakaa, wherein the speaker directly tells the reader, "I'm inside / the Vietnam Veterans Memorial" (10-11). Some poems do this more subtly, as in Sylvia Plath's "Tulips," which suggests a mental hospital as the speaker's surroundings through the repetition of "white" as a descriptor, references to nurses and surgeons, and sentences like "they bring me numbness in their bright needles" (17). Other poems can be even simpler. William Carlos Williams and his minimalist imagery come to mind, with works such as "The Great Figure" focusing entirely on several small but vivid parts; in this case, the rain, the fire truck, and the dark city are all the context the poem needs.

Also fitting under the self-contextualizing banner are those poems that seem unconcerned with physical reality in the first place. This includes poets

like Wallace Stevens and John Ashbery, who may use familiar objects in their poetry— "the veritable ocean" ("Key West" 7), "train rides / and romance" and "starched white collars" ("Worsening" 21, 31)—but mostly construct worlds that only exist within the poem. For this kind of poetry, the world around the poem is not particularly important to the world inside the poem, so cultural contextual analysis adds very little value.

As with textual context, the answer here is again rather ambiguous. Historical and cultural context is sometimes a useful tool for analyzing poetry, but its helpfulness depends on whether the poem invites consideration of its context or seeks to build its own world separate from reality.

It is worth noting that there is a component to all literature that should be considered apart from historical or cultural context. Mary Ruefle points out in one interview that "it often never occurs to the reader to simply read literature as an act taking place in the present, not having a context other than the present moment as the text unfolds" ("Life-Long Sentence"), which gets at something in the mystery of writer and reader interacting over literature even when separated by time, distance, and context. This is not to say that context is never important, but perhaps that it should occasionally take a backseat in the experience of reading and analysis.

Works Cited

Ashbery, John. "Worsening Situation." *The New Yorker*. The New Yorker, 12 Jan. 1975. Web.

Glück, Louise. "The Red Poppy." *Poets.org*. Academy of American Poets, 26 Feb. 2015. Web.

Glück, Louise. "The Wild Iris." *PoemHunter.com*. PoemHunter, 31 Dec. 2003. Web.

Komunyakaa, Yusef. "Facing It." *Poetry Foundation*. Poetry Foundation, 2001. Web.

Lee, Li-Young. "The Cleaving." *Poetry Foundation*. Poetry Foundation, 1990. Web.

O'Hara, Frank. "The Day Lady Died." *Poetry Foundation*. Poetry Foundation, 1995. Web.

Plath, Sylvia. "Tulips." *Poetry Foundation*. Poetry Foundation, 1992. Web.

Ruefle, Mary, and Tony Leuzzi. "The Life-Long Sentence." *The Brooklyn Rail*. The
    Brooklyn Rail, 15 July 2014. Web. 23 Mar. 2017.

Stevens, Wallace. "The Idea Of Order At Key West." *PoemHunter.com*. PoemHunter, 03
    Jan. 2003. Web. 17 Jan. 2017.

Williams, William Carlos. "The Great Figure." *Poets.org*. Academy of American Poets, 24
    Aug. 2016. Web. 24 Jan. 2017.

Faculty
Writing

Introduction

Faculty writing reflects current, published work by professors in the College of Arts and Sciences. These texts have previously appeared in academic and scholarly journals, books, conferences, magazines, and websites. They are often thought-provoking, poignant, and funny, and they serve as a powerful demonstration of the many forms that writing can take. *The 33rd* is enriched by the interests and passions of these writers.

- The Editors

Lloyd Ackert

Origin of Life

Keywords: spontaneous generation, bacteria, stomata, , Catastrophism, Gradualism, Linnaean classification system; Microbe, Uniformitarianism, Vitalism, Archaeplastida, Spores, Meiosis, Mitosis, Haploid, Diploid, Gametophyte, Sporophyte, Zygote, Colloid, Photochemical, Reducing atmosphere, Primeval Soup, Coacervate, Biogenesis, Darwinism

Key figures: Svante Arrhenius, Aristotle, Henry Charlton Bastion, Titus Lucretius Carus, Thomas Cech, Carol Cleland, Andrew Ellington, J.B.S. Haldane, Hermann von Helmholtz, Fred Hoyle, James Hutton, Jean-Baptiste Lamarck, Carl Linnaeus, Antonie von Leeuwenhoek, Marcello Malpighi, Thomas Malthus, Lynn Margulis, Stanley Miller, Hugo von Mohl, John Needham, Aleksandr Oparin, Louis Pasteur, Felix Pouchet, Francesco Redi, Theodor Schwann, Matthias Schleiden, Erwin Schrödinger, Lazzaro Spallanazani, William Thomson, John Tyndall, Harold Urey, Carl Vogt, Chandra Wickramasinghe, Carl Woese

Introduction

The history of the 'origin of life' question covers an era that spans from its roots in ancient philosophy to ongoing research today. It was a central aspect of a wide range of philosophies, belief systems and scientific investigations, including in the modern period, the experimental physical and life sciences. This essay explores only several of the periods and approaches to this question.[1] At its core, the search for the elusive answer(s) to this question defines our understanding of our place on the Earth and in the cosmos.

Origin of Life in the Ancient Period

One of the earliest conceptions of the origin of life is found in Aristotle's (384-323 BCE) description of spontaneous generation. He believed that life is created out of a melding of the elements air, earth, water, and fire. In *Generation of Animals* he wrote that, "[a]nimals and plants come into being in earth and in liquid... in all air is vital heat so that in a sense all things are full of soul. Therefore living things form quickly whenever this air and vital heat are enclosed in anything. When they are so enclosed, the corporeal liquids

---

[1] For an excellent review of recent works on the origin of life see, James Strick, "Essay Review: The Cambrian Explosion (of Books on the Origin of Life), *Journal of the History of Biology*, 09/2000, Volume 33, Issue 2.

being heated, there arises as it were a frothy bubble" [2] Aristotle believed that this "vital heat" contained the soul, or *eidos*, which was necessary to animate otherwise nonliving matter. It is the soul, which forms the matter into its necessary shape, providing an ancient explanation for the adaptation of species to their environment.[3] Recently, some have tried to relate Aristotle's *eidos* to the modern genetics, seeing it as an early forerunner to DNA.[4] He realized that in sexual reproduction the role of sperm in fertilization, yet he believed that the generative power was in its "vital heat" and that "the semen, if cold, is not generative."[5] The details of the reproductive cycle, remained outside his observing powers--for example, he concluded that in "testaceous" creatures (mollusks), "one does not generate in another; but they are formed and generated from a liquid and earthy concretion."[6]

The Roman philosopher Titus Lucretius Carus (99-55 BCE) proposed a similar doctrine of spontaneous generation. In his epic natural historical poem, "De Rerum Natura" (On the Nature of Things), he did embrace the Epicurean idea that human suffering is caused in part by a dread of the gods, but yet advocated for spontaneous generation, stating that the world takes form without the intervention of the gods.[7] He claimed "they feign/ That gods have established all things but for man."[8] Though accepted the existence of the gods, Lucretius thought they played little role in the "ordering or continuation" of the world.[9] Following Democritus and Leucippus, Lucretius held a materialist atomist view of nature that informed his view on the origin of life. Although, as Robert Wardy argued, a belief in an "atomic microstructure" alone does not "compel the theorist to adopt any particular ontology of macroscopic objects."[10] Lucretius, however, explained spontaneous generation due to the constant clashing of atoms that created cascades of combinations and eventually life.[11]

---

[2] Aristotle, *On the Generation of Animals*; Book III, Part 11.

[3] Nigel Williams, "Aristotle's Lagoon," *Current Biology* 20, no. 3 (February 9, 2010): R84-R85.

[4] Vinci, Tom, and Jason Scott Roberts. "Aristotle and Modern Genetics." *Journal of the History of Ideas* 66, no. 2 (April 2005): 201-21.

[5] Aristotle, *On the Generation of Animals*; Book I, Part 7.

[6] Ibid., Book I, Part 23.

[7] Ada Palmer, "Reading Lucretius in the Renaissance," *Journal of the History of Ideas* 73, no. 3 (July 2012); 397.

[8] Lucretius. *De Rerum Natura.* Translated by William Ellery Leonard; Book II, "Atomic Motions."

[9] Palmer, 397.

[10] Robert Wardy, "Lucretius on What Atoms Are Not," *Classical Philology* 83, no. 2 (April 1988): 115.

11 Lucretius. De Rerum Natura. Book II, "Atomic Motions."

17th Century Thoughts and Discoveries on Spontaneous Generation

During the early modern period, debates on the origin of life reevaluated ancient assumptions about spontaneous generation in terms of origins from non-living matter and initiated the experimental period of its investigation.[12] Natural philosophers conducted small-scale biological experiments challenging the idea that organisms could arise from sources other than similar organisms—e.g. that worms could generate out of decaying meat,[13] or parasites out of dust. Francesco Redi (1626-1697), for example, conducted a series of experiments proving that worms and maggots formed not spontaneously, but rather from another biological source. Covering meat with gauze and a perforated dome, he observed that eggs and maggots appeared on the gauze, but not the meat. He claimed that insects such as mosquitoes and flies deposited eggs that lead to the generation of new organisms.[14]

Due to his inconclusive studies of plant galls, however, Redi continued allow for the origin of life by spontaneous generation in other cases. The discovery microorganisms defined a new era in investigating the origin of life. Redi's contemporary, Marcello Malpighi (1628-1694), for example would explain their cause of galls. Using the newly invented microscope, Malpighi observed the action of microorganisms in them, eventually tracing them to cynipid gall-wasp eggs.[15] The still controversial observations of Antonie von Leeuwenhoek (1632-1723), the discovery of bacteria and their biological origin offered scientists a new material category of life to consider in the experimental investigation of origin of life.[16]

Spontaneous Generation and Uniformitarianism in the 18th Century

18th century developments of spontaneous generation research stemmed from the work of the early 17th century vitalists who, based on observations of toads being born out of "slime" and maggots out of wheat grains, believed that life could arise out of nonliving matter.[17] Belief in the theory of spontaneous generation began to wane in the 17th and 18th centuries due to observations

---

[12] Paweletz, N. 2001, "From Galen to Golgi: birth of the life sciences in Italy," *Nature Reviews.Molecular Cell Biology*, vol. 2, no. 6, pp. 478.

[13] Mazzarello, P. 1999, "Achilles and the maggots", Nature, vol. 402, no. 6759, pp. 237. (Mazarello 1999, p. 237)

[14] Hawgood, B.J. 2003, "Francesco Redi (1626-1697): Tuscan philosopher, physician and poet," Journal of medical biography, vol. 11, no. 1, p. 30.

[15] Corrington, J.D. 1961, "Spontaneous Generation," *BIOS*, vol. 32, no. 2, pp. 65-66.

[16] Corliss, J.O. 2002, "A salute to Antony van Leeuwenhoek of Delft, most versatile 17th century founding father of protistology," Protist, vol. 153, no. 2, p. 187; Corrington, p. 66

[17] Pommerville, JC 2012, *Alcamo's fundamentals of microbiology: Body systems*, Jones & Bartlett Publishers, Burlington. P. 10.

of sperm and embryo development (Leeuwenhoek) and controlled biological experiments with negative results (Redi). Following Leeuwenhoek's work in 1677, British clergyman and naturalist John Needham (1713-1781) conducted a series of experiments by boiling and stoppering mutton gravy discovering that: "the gravy swarm'd with life, with microscopical animals of most dimensions."[18] The Italian cleric and naturalist Lazzaro Spallanazani (1729-1799) criticized this work, proposing that Needham had insufficiently heated the broth, and established a new protocol using open, stoppered, and sealed vials. Spallanazani's open vials teemed with bacteria, the stoppered vials had many fewer, and the sealed vials had none.[19] He argued that this experiment discredited the theory of spontaneous generation, others (Needham) countered that excessive heating destroyed the vital force, a debate that would persist into the late-19th century.

In 1735, Carl Linnaeus (1707-1778) published *Systema Naturae* a classification system for organisms from kingdoms to species. Built on the idea that organisms are more closely related to some than others, his system became a key to determining ancestral relationships in the fossil record.[20] James Hutton (1726-1797) in *The Theory of the Earth* (1795) developed the geological concepts of gradualism and deep time, which together comprised uniformitarianism, or the idea that "the present is the key to the past."[21] This notion that the geological record provided "no vestige of a beginning, and no prospect of an end," challenged creationist theories of the origin of life.[22]

19th Century Materialism and Cell Division

Naturalists exploring the origin of life question in the late-18th-mid-19th century argued from a wide range of materialist frameworks. They considered matter the fundamental substance of nature and all phenomena the result of material interactions. Others favored vitalism, the idea that life is defined by the existence of a "vital spark" (soul) that separates it the realm of the inorganic or nonliving.[23] For the materialist Carl Vogt (1817-1895), for example, the human soul is only a function of the brain, and thoughts the products of the brain, just

---

[18] Wayne, RO 2009, *Plant cell biology: From astronomy to zoology*, Academic Press, Burlington. P. 299.

[19] Pommerville. Pp. 10-11

[20] Holmes, T 2008, *Early life: The Cambrian period*, Infobase Publishing, New York. Pp. 134-136.

[21] Thomson, KS 2009, *The young Charles Darwin*, Yale University Press, New Haven. P. 47-48.

[22] Ibid.

[23] Bunge, Mario. 1981. *Scientific Materialism*. Vol. 9. Springer Netherlands. P. 17; and Normandin, Sebastien. 2006. "Visions of Vitalism: Medicine, Philosophy and the Soul in Nineteenth Century France." Order No. NR25222, McGill University (Canada). P. 6.

as bile is a product of the liver.[24] In materialistic views of nature, the existence of soul does not differentiate living from nonliving objects. Among those who believed in materialism were scientists such as Jean-Baptiste Lamarck (1744-1829), who supported the notion that all organisms have an innate ability to change over time.[25] This hypothesis suggested that supernatural abilities once reserved for God could instead be performed by nature, leading some to believe that matter was the only substance in the world and there was no need for supernatural explanations.

The turn of the nineteenth century witnessed a new wave of evidence that supported materialism. The work of the German physiologist, Theodor Schwann (1810-1882) helped define cell theory and garner support for materialism. In 1839, Schwann, informed by Matthias Schleiden's theory that the basic structure of plants consisted of cells, extended it to the animal world. An essential part of their research was the materialist notion that only cells formed cells.[26]

Schleiden discovered that daughter cells are created within the parent cell in 1838. Hugo von Mohl countered with a new theory that cells were not created within, but divided from parent cells to daughter cells. This concept of cell division was first introduced in Mohl's work with green algae in 1837. His investigation showed that cells would split then grow into full size again as separate cells. The idea that life could crystallize "out of an unspecific nonliving fluid, which can be regarded as a special case of the doctrine of spontaneous generation" was central to these novel theories of cell development.[27]

Alternation of Generations Streenstrup

A community of morphologists in the 19th century challenged the established ideas about the relationship between, and thus the origin of animal and plant life. Johannes Steenstrup (1813-1897) in his *On the Alternation of Generations* (1845) represents a pioneering achievement concerning biological development in the lower classes of animals. His investigations of the 'alternation of generations' in *Medusa* and other invertebrates, he argued, revealed the plasticity and progressive development of species.[28] His work

---

[24] Rupke, N. (2000). "Translation Studies in the History of Science: The Example of "Vestiges"." The British Journal for the History of Science 33(2): 219.

[25] Burkhardt, Richard W Jr. 2013. "Lamarck, Evolution, and the Inheritance of Acquired Characters." *Genetics* 194 (4): 796.

[26] Sander, K. 1996. On the causation of animal morphogenesis: Concepts of Germanspeaking authors from Theodor Schwann (1839) to Richard Goldschmidt (1927). Int J Dev Biol 40(1): 8.

[27] (Deichmann, p. 535).

[28] Steenstrup, J. Japetus Sm 1845, *On the Alternation of Generations; or The Propagation and Development of Animals through Alternate Generations.* 6th edn. Printed for the Ray society, London. P. 2.

highlighted novel ideas about the cellular origin, but yet complex development of plant and animal life, from its simpler to more complex forms.[29]

End of Spontaneous Generation

The ancient notion of spontaneous generation persisted into the late-19th century, when for much of the scientific community, they were resolved by the work of Louis Pasteur, John Tyndall and others. Working within a quasi-Darwinian framework, these biomedical experimentalists participated in a series of popular scientific debates with the notable figures serving as the opposition, including Felix Pouchet and Henry Charlton Bastian.[30] In 1862, Pasteur published the results of his experiments, in which he maintained a sterilized broth in swan-neck retorts that filtered out bacteria and dust particles, but yet allowed in air, proving that decomposition had a biological origin (biogenesis).[31] At the same time, Pouchet and Bastian provided convincing experimental evidence in support of spontaneous generation. Pouchet's research showed that bacteria growth occurred in "previously boiled and sealed infusions made from... hay, supporting Bastian's theory of heterogenesis--that germs and microbes originated only from inorganic material.[32] While these debates were resolved more politically than experimentally, others, for example contributed new evidence: John Tyndall's light scattering experiments supported the ideas that atmospheric dust consisted of organic materials and germs and likely contaminated Pouchet's experiment.[33] Pasteur's arguments, and long series of experimental evidence led to a consensus among the scientific community that biogenesis was the correct theory for the origin of life.

An alternate hypothesis based on the work of Thomas Huxley, Ernst Haeckel, Carl Nageli, August Weismann, Eduard Pfluger and others, called abiogenesis proposed that "life emerged during the course of the evolution of matter and life on earth was a natural product of terrestrial processes."[34]

---

[29] Ibid., 109-110.

30 Strick, 2000, *Sparks of life: Darwinism and the Victorian debates over spontaneous generation*, Cambridge, Massachusetts. P. 2

[31] Strick, 1999, 'Darwinism and the Origin of Life: The Role of H.C. Bastian in the British Spontaneous Generation Debates, 1868-1873', Journal of the History of Biology, vol. 32, no. 1, pp. 56.

[32] Ibid., Pp. 56-61

[33] Strick, 2000, *Sparks of life: Darwinism and the Victorian debates over spontaneous generation*, Cambridge, Massachusetts. P. 22.

[34] Kamminga, H. 1982, "Life from space — A history of panspermia", Vistas in Astronomy, vol. 26, pp. 67-68.

Panspermia

In the 19th century, physicists William Thomson (1824-907) and Hermann von Helmholtz (1821-1894) developed panspermia—from the Greek *panspermos* meaning 'containing all kinds of seeds'—a theory of the cosmic origin of life, in which "seeds of life were spread from star to star."[35] In *Worlds in the Making* (1908), Svante Arrhenius (1859-1927) proposed an evolutionary and thermodynamic version of panspermia that discussed the conditions of "bacterial spores and plant seeds" to determine the likelihood of survival in interplanetary and interstellar space. He was the first to discuss the "unearthly qualities" of bacteria and the mode of transportation of these cosmic voyagers (the force of starlight). More recently, Fred Hoyle (1915-2001) and Chandra Wickramasinghe (1939-), arguing from a neo-Darwinian perspective, asserted that bacteria (travelling on comets) could survive in space because they must originate from space. Thus, panspermia can explain the quick evolution of life on earth.

The Biogeochemical Hypothesis

Up to the 1920's, the question of the origin of life was discussed mostly in biological and chemical terms. The debate hinged on whether life was spontaneously created in one flash of organic synthesis, or whether life formed slowly by a combination of inorganic and organic reactions. The growing field of colloidal chemistry, or the study of homogeneous solutions suspended with microscopic particle, fueled this debate. Biochemists argued whether colloids would be able to effectively trap and concentrate organic precursors in such a way as to create life. The argument then proceeded into a familiar debate over spontaneous generation, which had yet to be resolved. Despite the lack of consensus, one general principle was agreed upon that profoundly changed the discussion going forward: the origin of life could be explained in purely chemical terms.[36]

This conception of a purely chemical origin of life gave J.B.S. Haldane (1892-1964) and the Soviet scientist Aleksandr Oparin (1894-1980) the opportunity to synthesize the prior debate into one clear hypothesis. In 1929, Haldane, discussing the role geological conditions played in the origin of life, he proposed the idea of an anoxic early earth, rich in proto-organic compounds.[37] In chemical terms, organic molecules could arise anew only

---

[35] "Panspermia" New Scientist 189, no. 2541 (Mar, 2006). 54.

[36] Farley, John 1974, The Spontaneous Generation Controversy From Descartes to Oparin, The Johns Hopkins University Press, Baltimore. Pp. 159-163.

[37] Kamminga, H. (1988) Historical perspective: The problem of the origin of life in the context of developments in biology. *Origin of life and evolution of the biosphere*. Springer Link. 18 (1-2) p. 7.

in the absence of oxygen, which permitted ultra-violet radiation (energy) to initiate the photochemical organic synthesis.[38]

Oparin extended Haldane's concept further, hypothesizing a series of steps in the chemical evolution of life. Drawing on geochemistry, astronomy, evolutionary biology and colloidal chemistry Oparin developed a grand origin theory.[39] In Earth's early history, inorganic molecules were broken down by UV rays to form organic molecules and a "primeval soup."[40] These molecules would then have coalesced into a coacervate colloid, which would concentrate organics, allow proteins to gradually form, and through competition eventually evolve into the first life forms.[41] This revolutionary synthesis of biology, chemistry, and geology would set the next stage in the experimental era of the study of life's origin.

What is Life?

During the 20th century, attempts to define 'life' came to bridge the physical and social sciences and the humanities. Debates became personal, emotional, and often mired in cyclical rhetoric and beyond the reach of practical explanations, no matter the philosophical and scientific contexts. A novel set of questions came from Erwin Schrödinger (1887-1961), who asked in a public lecture *What Is Life*, explored three important issues related to the origin of life: resistance to entropy, permanence of genetic material, and its replication—all of which occurred bounded in the living cell. His work was significant less for its portrayal of contemporary ideas in origin of life scientific research, but more for the influence it had on its investigation in the 1950-1970's, and especially molecular genetics.[42]

Origin of Life: Urey-Miller's Experiments

In 1952, inspired by Oparin's work and advised by Harold Urey, Stanley Miller (1930-2007), conducted a now classic experiment that demonstrated how amino acids and other organic compounds—that is, the basic building blocks of life—could be synthesized under primitive Earth conditions. Miller's idea was a prebiotic synthesis experiment in which an electrical energy source would be discharged on a mixture of methane, ammonia, water vapor, and hydrogen (replicating primitive earthly conditions). During the experiment, a

---

[38] Rutten, M.G. 1962, *The Geological Aspects of the Origin of Life on Earth*, Elsevier, NY. Pp. 48-49

[39] Kamminga, 1988, p. 8.

[40] Miller, Stanley L. & Orgel, Leslie E. 1974, The Origins of Life on Earth, Prentice-Hall, Englewood

[41] Kamminga 1988, p. 8-9.

[42] Robert Olby, "Schrödinger's Problem: What is Life?," *Journal of the History of Biology*, Vol. 4, No. 1 (Spring, 1971), pp. 130-135.

mixture of primitive earthly gases were circulated through a water solution and zapped with electric sparks (substituting for natural lightning). The results of the continuous sparking were "biochemically significant" compounds such as amino acids, hydroxyl acids, and urea.[43] Numerous scientists replicated and expanded these investigations since, finding a large number of amino acids that are integral to life, and many others that are not.

RNA/DNA Biochemistry

In the field of evolutionary biochemistry, two important questions exist; how did life originate, and how did it evolve. In particular, biochemists look at components of a cell to help make that determination. The cell's nucleic acids RNA (ribonucleic acid) and DNA (deoxyribonucleic acid) are necessary components in the formation of proteins; likewise, proteins are necessary in the formation of nucleic acids. In 1967, Carl Woese (1928-2012) attempted to determine which came first, nucleic acids or proteins, leading to the RNA World Hypothesis. He proposed that RNA was the precursor to life by mixing proteins, RNA, and DNA.[44] Following Woese, in 1982 Thomas Cech discovered a type of RNA that can act as a chemical catalyst was found, scientists did not know whether proteins or nucleic acids came first; however, with this discovery it was determined that some forms of RNA can replicate itself, thereby solving the question that RNA came first in the evolution of Earth's first life.[45]

In 1967, evolutionary biologist Lynn Margulis (1938-2011), an extension of the Russian tradition, published her theory of symbiogenesis, which added a new dimension to Darwinian evolution that allowed for the combination of existing genomes in a new symbiotic organism (at both the cellular and organismic levels).[46] Margulis proposed that a major transition in the origin of life occurred when nuclear information transferred between bacteria and eukaryotes.[47]

In the 1980's, Andrew Ellington noted that the chemicals that make up life have formed without living matter, by replicating themselves and later evolving into reproducing life forms. He investigated the evolution of

---

[43] Miller, S.L. 1953, "A Production of Amino Acids under Possible Primitive Earth Conditions", Science, vol. 117, no. 3046, pp. 528-529.

[44] Woese, Carl. The Genetic Code" the Molecular Basis for Genetic Expression. Harper & Row, New York: 1967; Zimmer, C "A tiny emissary from the ancient past" New York Times. Sept 25, 2014

[45] Gilbert, W. "The RNA World," Nature. P. 618

[46] For a discussion of the Russian context see, Khakhina, L.N. Concepts of symbiogenesis: A historical and critical study of the research of Russian botanists: by edited by L. Margulis and M. McMenamin, translated by S. Merkel and R. Coalson, with an appendix on Ivan E. Wallin by D.C. Mehos, Yale University Press, 1992., P.

[47] Margulis, Lynn. Symbiotic Planet: A New Look at Evolution. Sciencewriters, Amherst Mass: 1999.

dehydrogenase isozymes, enzymes found in single celled organisms that do not have a defined nucleus. Shortly thereafter he developed a method to engineer nucleic acid species known as 'aptamers' through repeated in vitro selection. Today Ellington is extending and accelerating his evolutionary engineering approach to whole organisms and biotechnologies.[48]

'Life' in recent philosophical debates

The question "What is life?" an abiding topic of philosophical debate has in recent years become an increasingly scientific inquiry. Carol Cleland, a leading psychologist at CU Boulder challenges the approach taken by philosophers and scientists in answer it; that is instead of looking for "definitions of life," we should develop a general theory of living systems that might exist in the universe—life on Earth is only one possible example of life.[49] Informed by recent work in philosophy and evolution, Iris Fry concludes that similarities in Earth's microbiology and biochemical make up, it has a point of common origin.[50]

Another issue is the Earth-centric view that pervades the scientific world. In the infinite universe it is a distinct possibility that life could form in-multiplicate, with non-living materials without necessarily being on Earth. Life arising more than once from nonliving materials could occur elsewhere than Earth, but it could also have occurred on Earth. It is within the realm of possibility that even with extraterrestrial life that all life could have a similar origin, or not. For example, Scientists believe that microorganisms could survive on interspace travel on meteors through contact with planetary bodies containing life.[51]

Astrobiology: the Past, the Present, the Future

The origin of life question, and it corollary the existence of intelligent life, is a primary focus of Exo/Astrobiology. [52]Applying the principles of natural sciences (biology, chemistry, and physics) to explain the mechanisms behind the origin and evolution of life, they are developing search parameters for

---

[48] Ellington, A. 'Q&A Andrew D Ellington.' *Current Biology*. Vol 18 (5). P. 184

[49] Cleland, Carol; Chyba, Christopher (2007) "Does Life have a Definition." Sullivan and Baross (eds.), *Planets and Life: The Emerging Science of Astrobiology*, Ch. 5. Cambridge: Cambridge University Press (2007): pp. 119-131.

[50] Fry, Iris. 2000 *The Emergence of Life on Earth: A Historical and Scientific Overview*, 5th ed. Rutgers University Press.

[51] Cleland, Carol E. Is a General Theory of Life Possible? Seeking the Nature of Life in the Context of a Single Example. Biological Theory, 06/2013, Volume 7, Issue 4, 368-379.

[52] Brack, A; Horneck, G; Wynn-Williams, D. "Exo/Astrobiology in Europe," Origins of life and evolution of the biosphere : the journal of the International Society for the Study of the Origin of Life, 08/2001, Volume 31, Issue 4-5. Pp. 459-480.

life on other planets. NASA leads the study of astrobiology, with roots dating back its first program in 1959. Ariel Anbar's team at Arizona State University exemplifies the great diversity of this work. They study the past, current, and future mechanisms that allow Earth to be a habitable planet and how those mechanisms can apply to extra-terrestrial life.[53]

Conclusion:

The history of the origin of life described above is a necessarily narrow view that excludes equally important perspectives that occurred in religion, literature (especially science fiction) and other humanities disciplines, and in many other scientific fields. A more complete account of this story would include the ideas of non-western science and philosophy, especially Islamic), and those of the very earliest civilizations (Babylonia, India, China, and African). It would also require a more thorough discussion of the philosophical debates on the origin of life during the early-Modern period, including Bernard Fontenelle (1657-1757).

Bibliography:

Aristotle. De Generatione Animalium. Translated by A. Platt. 8vo. Oxford: Clarendon Press, 1910.

Bunge, Mario. 1981. *Scientific Materialism*. Vol. 9. Springer Netherlands.

Burkhardt, Richard W, Jr. 2013. "Lamarck, Evolution, and the Inheritance of Acquired Characters." *Genetics* 194 (4): 793-805.

Corliss, J.O. 2002, "A salute to Antony van Leeuwenhoek of Delft, most versatile 17th century founding father of protistology." Protist, vol. 153, no. 2, pp. 177-90.

Corrington, J.D. 1961, "Spontaneous Generation", *BIOS*. vol. 32, no. 2, pp. 62-76.

Des Marais et al. 2008. Focus Paper, The NASA Astrobiology Roadmap. *Astrobiology*. Mary Ann Liebert, Inc.

---

[53] Des Marais et al. 2008. Focus Paper, The NASA Astrobiology Roadmap. Astrobiology. Mary Ann Liebert, Inc.

Ellington, A. 'Q&A Andrew D Ellington.' *Current Biology*. Vol 18 (5).

Farley, John 1974, *The Spontaneous Generation Controversy From Descartes to Oparin*, The Johns Hopkins University Press, Baltimore.

Hawgood, B.J. 2003, "Francesco Redi (1626-1697): Tuscan philosopher, physician and poet," *Journal of medical biography*, vol. 11, no. 1, pp. 28-34.

Holmes, T 2008, *Early life: The Cambrian Period*, Infobase Publishing, New York.

Kamminga, H. 1982, "Life from space — A history of panspermia", Vistas in Astronomy, vol. 26, pp. 67-86.

Kamminga, H. 1988, "Historical perspective: The problem of the origin of life in the context of developments in biology." *Origin of life and evolution of the biosphere.* Springer Link. 18 (1-2) p. 1-11.

Lucretius. *De Rerum Natura*. Translated by William Ellery Leonard. Accessed October 20, 2014. http://classics.mit.edu/Carus/nature_things.html.

Mazzarello, P. 1999, "Achilles and the maggots", *Nature*, vol. 402, no. 6759, pp. 237.

Miller, S.L. 1953, "A Production of Amino Acids under Possible Primitive Earth Conditions", Science, vol. 117, no. 3046, pp. 528-529.

Miller, Stanley L. & Orgel, Leslie E. 1974, *The Origins of Life on Earth*, Prentice-Hall, Englewood Cliffs.

Normandin, S. 2006, Visions of vitalism: Medicine, philosophy and the soul in nineteenth century France, ProQuest, UMI Dissertations Publishing.

Robert Olby, "Schrödinger's Problem: What is Life?," *Journal of the History of Biology*, Vol. 4, No. 1 (Spring, 1971), pp. 119-148.

Palmer, Ada. "Reading Lucretius in the Renaissance." *Journal of the History of Ideas* 73, no. 3 (July 2012): 395-416.

Paweletz, N. 2001, "From Galen to Golgi: birth of the life sciences in Italy", *Nature Reviews Molecular Cell Biology*, vol. 2, no. 6, pp. 475-80.

Rupke, N. (2000). "Translation Studies in the History of Science: The Example of "Vestiges"." The British Journal for the History of Science 33(2): 209-222.

Rutten, M.G. 1962, *The Geological Aspects of the Origin of Life on Earth*, Elsevier, NY.

Sander, K. 1996. On the causation of animal morphogenesis: Concepts of Germanspeaking authors from Theodor Schwann (1839) to Richard Goldschmidt (1927). *Int J Dev Biol* 40(1):7-20.

Steenstrup, J. Japetus Sm 1845, *On the Alternation of Generations; or The Propagation and Development of Animals through Alternate Generations*. 6th edn. Printed for the Ray society, London.

Strick, 2000, *Sparks of life: Darwinism and the Victorian debates over spontaneous generation*, Cambridge, Massachusetts.

Vinci, Tom, and Jason Scott Roberts. "Aristotle and Modern Genetics." *Journal of the History of Ideas* 66, no. 2 (April 2005): 201-21.

Wardy, Robert. "Lucretius on What Atoms Are Not." *Classical Philology* 83, no. 2 (April 1988): 112-28.

Wayne, RO 2009, *Plant cell biology: From astronomy to zoology*, Academic Press, Burlington.

Williams, Nigel. "Aristotle's Lagoon." *Current Biology* 20, no. 3 (February 9, 2010): R84-R85. - Woese, Carl. The Genetic Code" the Molecular Basis for Genetic Expression. Harper & Row, New York: 1967.

Zimmer, C "A tiny emissary from the ancient past" *New York Times*. Sept 25, 2014

Stacey Ake

Scientists in the Cosmos: An Existential Approach to the Debate between Science and Religion

Abstract: Walker Percy's use of the terms *Umwelt* (environment) and *Welt* (symbol world) as well as his separation of events into dyadic and triadic ones, where the latter involve human beings, is brought to bear on the relationship between science and religion with the upshot being that science (a dyadic enterprise) is not equipped to really understand or explain triadic entities (namely, human beings).

Keywords: *Umwelt*; *Welt*; dyad; triad; triadicity; sign; symbol; Helen Keller; euglena

Introduction

Much has been written about the conflict between science and religion. And much of it has been very interesting. But when we say such things, i.e., that there is a conflict between science and religion, we are actually using a euphemism. There is no conflict between science and religion. What do exist however are conflicts between practitioners of science and practitioners of religion. In other words, the only places where such conflicts can arise are among (and within) people. No one places a copy of the *Koran* on a table, places a copy of Newton's *Principia* across from it, and expects the two books to duke it out. Rather, we deceive ourselves when we talk about a debate or conflict between science and religion. The conflict or debate is actually ours. Given this, it seems appropriate to consider these conflicts as existential conflicts, conflicts about what science and religion ought to mean to individual human beings. And it is the individual wherein science and religion meet at a crossroads that interests Walker Percy.

For Walker Percy, practicing Catholic and non-practicing physician, the late 20th century (and in continuity, the 21st) is truly the era of science or of the scientist. "The scientist is the prince and sovereign of the age," he declares (Percy 1983, 115). In other words today the scientist has become "the secular saint of the age." (ibid 115) But what does Percy mean by this?

Percy has looked around himself and discovered that the average human being—or, at least, the average American—is in trouble. It seems to him, as it seemed to Augustine, that we know a great deal about the world around us (knowledge that is today accrued through science) but very little about ourselves. As Percy puts it at the beginning of *Lost in the Cosmos: The Last Self Help Book*:

How can you survive in the Cosmos about which you know more and more while knowing less and less and less about yourself, this despite 10,000 self-help books, 100,000 psychotherapists, and 100 million fundamentalist Christians.

or...

Why is it possible to learn more in ten minutes about the Crab Nebula in Taurus, which is 6,000 light-years away, than you presently know about yourself, even though you've been stuck with yourself all your life. (ibid. 1)

These are legitimate questions. Percy posits that this chasm between our scientific knowledge of the world and our lack of personal knowledge about ourselves drives many people to try and escape themselves. There are various methods for doing this: travel, drugs, sex, and the ultimate escape: suicide. But in this day and age, there exist two sets of people whose occupations allow them to transcend this existential problem: artists and scientists. Here we are interested in scientists. And according to Percy, the scientist's transcendence of the world is genuine. That is to say, he stands in a posture of objectivity over against the world, a world which he sees as a series of specimens or exemplars, and interactions, energy exchanges, secondary causes—in a word: dyadic events. (ibid. 115)

But this transcendence is true as long as the scientist is practicing science. What happens to the scientist when the existential world intrudes? Well, one manifestation "which always amazes laymen, is the jealousy and lack of scruple of scientists. Their anxiety to receive credit," says Percy, "seems more appropriate to used-car salesmen than to a transcending community." (ibid. 117) Moreover, one of the more distressing consequences occur[s] when the zeal and excitement of the scientific community runs counter to the interests of the world community.... The joys of science and the joys of life are not necessarily convergent. As Freeman Dyson put it, the "sin" of the scientists at Los Alamos was not that they made the bomb but that they enjoyed it so much. (ibid. 117)[1]

---

[1] Something similar is said by Richard Feynman. As he sat in a New York City café about a month after the bombs were dropped on Japan, he realized that the scientists at Los Alamos were so busy seeing whether they could build the bomb that they never asked whether they should.

Thus, it would seem that in matters of politics, just as in matters of religion, the scientist is an amateur. Hence, it is my contention that when the scientist goes to speak about matters like religion, he or she is no longer speaking from the point of transcendence of science. Rather, a scientist is speaking just as any other human being would, from a point of existential immanence. I have three reasons for this position that I have drawn from Walker Percy: 1) the difference between living in an *Umwelt* as opposed to a *Welt*; 2) the difference between a dyadic and a triadic relationship; and 3) the problem of making a human being, who is a subject, the object of scientific examination.

Umwelt versus Welt

Consider the euglena. It is a funny little organism. It is a single cell with a flagellum; it can live in fresh or salt water. It has the dubious distinction of being neither a plant nor an animal. It has chloroplasts that allow it to take nourishment from sunlight, just like a plant, and it can consume food through phagocytosis, rather like an animal. It was for organisms such as these that the kingdom *Protista* was invented.

It has a red spot (or stigma) just near its flagellum that filters out particular wavelengths of sunlight, allowing an organelle beneath the red spot to orient the euglena toward the light in a process known as phototaxis. In other words, the euglena responds to light by moving toward it. It also responds to food particles it runs into by surrounding said particles and consuming them. And the euglena is a very successful organism; there are over 800 species worldwide. From this it would seem that euglena are very adaptable organisms exploiting a wide variety of niches. They are thus very successful organisms in their environments.

And this is precisely what Walker Percy would stress about euglena and other non-human animals: they are organisms in an environment, where that environment is called an *Umwelt* (surrounding world). This is significant. Here Percy is making a distinction between communication—which animals, including euglenas, can do—and language, which is unique to the human condition. In having language, humans are symbol-mongers; they are the creators and interpreters of a certain class of signs.

In elaborating his position, Percy calls upon a variety of sign theorists or semioticians: Peirce, Saussure, Seboek, von Uexküll, for example, and he insists on calling them semiotists for reasons that are difficult to fathom. But, as Percy says:

I am grateful for the important distinction, clearer in the German language and perhaps for this reason first arrived at by German thinkers, between *Welt* and *Umwelt*, or, roughly, world and environment, e.g., von Uexküll's *Umwelt* as, roughly, the significant environment within which an organism lives, and Heidegger's *Welt*, the "world" into which the *Dasein* or self finds itself "thrown".... (ibid. 86n)

In understanding Percy's work and the role it might play in the relationship between science and religion, we must understand what this distinction between *Welt* and *Umwelt* means. An organism in an environment, in its *Umwelt*, is merely another element in that environment. No organism is privileged above another in an *Umwelt*. No organism transcends its environment. Moreover, the relations between an organism and its environment can be fully described in the terms and concepts of science. We can talk of reactions, energy exchanges, homeostasis, gravity, and so on. In none of these interactions is one part privileged over another. In the gravitational relationship between the earth and the moon, one cannot say that either the moon or the earth in more important. Likewise, in the chemical reaction that makes salt, no one prioritizes sodium over chloride.

But our euglena seems slightly more complex. It reacts to stimuli. It moves toward light. Somehow, it responds to the environment. It responds to the environment as if the environment contained valuable information in it. And so it does. The environment of the euglena contains those elements the euglena needs to stay alive. We, looking at this situation, privilege the euglena, probably because we, too, are alive, and thus are rooting for the home team. We say, "The euglena converted light into energy through photosynthesis." We don't say, "The photon, in a remarkable display of altruism, gave itself up to be turned into energy by the euglena." We, being alive, privilege the euglena. Even so, as a member of an environment, say a freshwater pond, the euglena is not a privileged organism. It is equal in importance to the bladderwort, the frog, the rushes, and the crayfish.

This interrelatedness of equality is what makes ecosystems both strong and fragile. This is why an intruder into an ecosystem can be so destructive. Until there has been time for the new entity to be equalized and balanced into the ecosystem, our intruder will upset this delicately balanced system. Essentially, the intruder has no "place" in the ecosystem or environment it has invaded, and this affects every member of the ecosystem. However, the interrelatedness of equality means that the euglena and the information it encounters in its environment are on par. Just as sunlight is "food" for the euglena, so, too, is the euglena food for some other organism.

Inasmuch as human beings are organisms in an environment, they are not different from the euglena. Some organisms are food for the human; for other organisms, the human is food. A human being is just another node in the food web. It is just another member of the *Umwelt*.

However, this is not the case for the relationship of the human being with its *Welt*. While a "sign-using organism takes account only of those elements in the environment which are relevant biologically," (2000, 202) the human, a *symbol*-using organism does much more than this. Following Heidegger, Percy speaks of a human's being "thrown" into the world. We all arrive *in media res*—the story has been going on long before we got here, and it will continue long after we have gone. For Percy, the way we cope with this "thrownness" is through language, through the use of symbols. It is not only that objects have significance for us (as light did for the euglena); objects also have *meaning*.

Consider an apple. For the human organism it is the sign of something edible, something that will quell hunger pangs. For the human being, however, it can symbolize (mean) the fall from grace of Adam and Eve, the oft-repeated story of Newton's enlightenment about the nature of gravity, or Thanksgiving at Grandma's when she made her old-fashioned apple pie. All of these meanings that are associated with an apple, but that do not directly follow from an apple (i.e., Adam and Eve could have eaten a peach, Newton could have been hit on the head by a chestnut, Grandma could have made an excellent pumpkin pie), are symbols. It is the endless number and infinite combinations of symbols that make up a human being's *Welt*. Thus, the human being is an amphibian, living simultaneously in two domains: its *Umwelt* and *Welt*.

For Percy, while science can tell us a great deal about our *Umwelt*, it cannot address those questions that belong to our *Welt*.

The Dyad and the Triad

The reason that science can inform us about our environment but not about our symbol-world is that science, according to Percy, can only describe dyadic relationships. It cannot speak of triadic relationships. Thus, for Percy, science and scientists begin skating on thin ice when they try to explain triadic phenomena in dyadic terms. When using the terms dyadic and triadic, Percy is using them as they were put forth at the turn of the 20th century by American philosopher, pragmaticist, and logician Charles Sanders Peirce.

Peirce believed that there were two kinds of natural phenomena. First there are those events which involve "dyadic relations," such as obtain in the "physical forces...between pairs of particles." The other kind of event entails "triadic relations"....

If A throws B away and B hits C in the eye, this event may be understood in terms of two dyadic relations, one between A and B, the other between B and C. But if A *gives* B to C a genuine triadic relation exists....

Dyadic events are, presumably, those energy exchanges conventionally studied by the natural sciences: subatomic particles colliding, chemical reactions....

Triadic events, on the other hand, characteristically involve symbols and symbol users. Moreover, a genuine triadic relation cannot be reduced to a series of dyadic relations.... (2000, 161-162)

It is the last part of this quote that is so important for our current discussion: "a genuine triadic relation cannot be reduced to a series of dyadic relations." But what, precisely, is a triadic relation?

Consider the example above: "A throws B away and B hits C in the eye." In this case, Mark (A) throws a ball (B), and this ball (B) hits John (C) in the head. This series of events can be broken down into two dyadic relations. One: Mark throws the ball. Two: The ball hits John. In other words, while Mark throws the ball and hits John, it is quite possible for Mark to throw the ball apart from his actually hitting John. However, the relations that obtain where "A gives B to C" or Mark gives a ball to John are different. There is no way to break this interaction into dyads for a soon as Mark gives the ball, John receives it. As a matter of fact, if John does not receive the ball, then Mark has yet to give it. All three of these elements are inextricably linked to each other. They form a triad. But it is not this type of triadicity that fundamentally interests Percy. His interest in triadicity lies with the human phenomenon of language, especially the human capacity to *name* things, for it is *naming* which makes us human.

Consider Helen Keller, whom Percy considers at length. He is interested in what happened to her in the well-house when she discovered the nature of language. In the summer of 1887, in Tuscumbia, Alabama, Helen Keller was walking to the well-house with her teacher, Anne Sullivan. When they arrived at the well-house, Ms. Sullivan placed one of Helen's hands in the stream of running water. Into the other hand, Ms. Sullivan spelled "w-a-t-e-r" using a finger alphabet. At some point, Helen realized that "w-a-t-e-r" *meant* water, the substance running over her hand. Heretofore, "w-a-t-e-r" had signified "get me a glass of water". It had been a command. It was simply one element of a dyadic relation. Signing "w-a-t-e-r" was merely a means to an end. In other words,

Helen signs "w-a-t-e-r" —> Helen gets water.

But after her experience in the well-house, Helen Keller knew that "w-a-t-e-r" meant/stood for/represented/symbolized a thing—the cool, wet substance running over her hand. In other words, Helen (A) came to know that "w-a-t-e-r" (B) is/means water (C). This is a triadic relationship. Helen can no longer spell out "w-a-t-e-r" without knowing that it *is* water, even if all she wants is a drink. She has become a symbol-user. She has become fully human. Previously, she had been a very successful organism in her environment. She could navigate the *Umwelt* of her home. But she did not have a *Welt*. Only after the well-house incident did Helen Keller have a world. And she had that world because she had acquired language.

...what is important to note about the triadic event [of language] is that it is there for all to see, that in fact it occurs hundreds of times daily—whenever we talk or listen to somebody talking—that its elements are open to inspection to everyone, including natural scientists, and that it cannot be reduced to a complexus of dyadic events...even though millions of dyadic events also occur: light waves, excitation of nerve endings, electrical impulses to neurones [sic], muscle contractions, and so on....

For once one concedes the reality of the triadic event, one is brought face to face with the nature of its elements. A child points to a flower and says "flower."... But what is the entity....which links the...two?... Peirce, a difficult, often obscure writer, called it by various names, interpretant, interpreter, judge. I have used the term "coupler" as a minimal designation of that which couples name and thing, subject and predicate, links them by the relation which we mean by the peculiar little word "is."...

Here is the embarrassment, and it cannot be gotten round, so it might as well be said right out: *By whatever name one chooses to call it—interpretant, interpreter, coupler, whatever—it, the third element, is not material.* (1991, 286-287)

Another way to look at this is to note that while the *processes* of thought and language are material (excitation of nerve endings, electrical impulses to neurons, release of neurotransmitters, and so on), the *content* of thought and language is not. Percy goes on to say that:

> Peirce's insistence on both the reality and the nonmateriality of the third element—whatever one chooses to call it, interpretant, mind, coupler—is of critical importance to natural science because its claim to reality is grounded not on this or that theology or metaphysic [sic] but on empirical observation and the necessities of scientific logic. (1991, 287)

Evidence of this is not simply the fact that humans have language, but that they have *languages*. Photosynthesis is ubiquitous. Gravity is ubiquitous. DNA is ubiquitous. And while human language is ubiquitous, languages, however, are not. Languages are specific and local. One speaks Cantonese or Twi or Sami; one does not speak language. Moreover, along with language comes culture. Language produces culture, and culture produces language. They are products of each other.

Consider the word "sick", as in the statement "He's sick!" For most of us that statement would imply that the person in question has an illness of some sort and possibly should be seen by a physician. However, to those thirty years of age and younger, the statement means that the person in question is awesome or great or cool. Youth culture has produced a new meaning to an old world, and only those who are part of that culture would recognize it.

This is also true for science. According to *Wikipedia,*:

> Diffeomorphism is an invertible function that maps one differentiable manifold to another such that both the function and its inverse are smooth.

A person unfamiliar with differential geometry, while recognizing such words as function, manifold, and smooth has no idea what those words actually mean in this context, much less what the statement itself means, because they are not part of the culture of mathematics. Another thing to consider about this statement is that it is an abstract statement about an abstract entity. In other words, this entity is both real and nonmaterial just like Walker Percy's coupler "is" is. This statement is, in fact, language about pure symbols, the ultimate in triadicity.

While science, too, has its cultures and, hence, its specific and local languages, when we speak of things scientific, we speak of products that are general and generalizable and, hence, universal. We assume, for instance, that the relationship between two objects that we call gravity obtains in all situations everywhere; thus it is universal. An exception to this (your car keys flying upwards when you drop them) would cause us to re-evaluate everything in search of a new universal. According to Percy:

> There is a secret about the scientific method which every scientist knows and takes as a matter of course, but which the layman does not know. The layman's ignorance would not matter if it were not the case that the spirit of the age had been informed by the triumphant spirit of science. As it is, the layman's ignorance can be fatal, not for the scientist but for the layman.

The secret is this: Science cannot utter a single word about an individual molecule, thing, or creature in so far as it is an individual but only in so far as it is like other individuals. The layman thinks that only science can utter the true word about anything, individuals included. But the layman is an individual. So science cannot say a single word to him or about him except as he resembles others. (2000 22)

For the human being, it is the existence of triadicity and his or her symbol-world, his or her *Welt*, that underpins Percy's claim. For example, scientists can tell me the average or "normal" side effects of a medication, but they cannot tell me how I, individually, will react to the medication. Scientists can make statements about what the average American is doing at 10am on a Tuesday morning, but they can make no such claim about what I, particularly, might be doing. The claims of science consist of statements about generals (most birds fly) and universals (f = ma), but it cannot speak to the individual and particular.

An excellent example of this problem is the problem of pain. We cannot quantify pain. We can make pseudo-measures of pain ("On a scale of 1 to 10, how strong is your pain?"), but we cannot actually understand what it means when a person says, "My finger hurts." There is no dyadic way to estimate pain. Blood sugar we can estimate dyadically or protein content in a person's urine but not pain, and for the following reasons. One: we cannot feel that individual's pain directly. Two: we must rely on metaphors and similes ("It's a burning pain." Or "It feels like heavy pins and needles.") in order to understand. We must rely on the person's triadic communication to convey to us the nature of their pain. We rely on symbols; we rely on words. It is this aspect that makes evaluating the pain an animal is in so difficult. They cannot tell us in *words* (symbols) how they feel.

Is it any wonder, then, that science cannot quantify religious experience?

Subject as Object

There is a problem in English with the words subject and object; they can be used almost interchangeably: as in "The object I held in my hand was the subject of my study." We know from experience and context that the item in the person's hand is both the subject and object mentioned in the sentence. So, how do we distinguish them? For the purposes of this essay, I would like to use simple, grammatical definitions. A subject is something (or someone) who does something while an object is something (or someone) that has something done to it.

Furthermore, when we use the term subjectivity, we usually mean the unique and individual perspective of a subject, namely a human being, or

the simple experience of being an individual human being. But the term objectivity causes some consternation. It is often presented as a value-free understanding of the world, the strange belief that a subject, with a particular and individual perspective, can understand the world in some way separate from his or her own experience of the world. Given this, it seems odd when scientists speak of their objectivity. Percy himself asks, "Having achieved the transcending objective stance of science, has [the scientist] also transcended the mortal condition?" (2000, 108)

The answer, of course, is no.

The entire spectacular history of modern science seemed to bear out [scientists'] unspoken assumption that there was indeed something to be known out there [in the world] and it was worth the effort to try to find out what it was.

Yet the natural scientists, with all their understanding of interactions, energy exchanges, stimuli, and responses, could not seem to utter a single word about what men did and what they themselves were doing: observing and recording, telling and listening, uttering sentences and hearing sentences, writing papers and reading papers, delivering lectures, listening to the six o'clock news, writing a letter to one's daughter in college. (2000, 34)

In other words, science could address the situations of human organisms in an *Umwelt*, undergoing dyadic relations, but science could not address the experience of a human being in a *Welt*, an individual in a world of triadic relations. It seems that scientists (subjects) had a hard time understanding objects (their fellow human beings) because those human beings were also subjects. For Percy, this led to a kind of incoherence in science, especially the human sciences.

There are...incoherences in [the] sciences of man. Sociology and cultural anthropology have to do with groups and cultures, with people; this is to say, human organisms. But sociology deals with such things as self, roles; anthropology with such things as sorcery, rites. But how do you get from organism to roles and rites?" (1991, 276)

This, for Percy, is the elephant in the room, the great unspoken or unremarked problem: how do you get from descriptions of the human being as organism (physiology, anatomy) to descriptions of the human being as an individual that takes on roles and engages in rites? How do you transition from

the dyadic description of a human being to a triadic description of a human being engaging in triadic behavior?[2]

This is extremely difficult, if not impossible, because science, an undertaking that elucidates dyadic relationships, is not sufficiently equipped to elucidate triadic relationships. Any attempt to do so leads, according to Percy, to incoherence, an incoherence that arises "when the natural sciences, so spectacularly successful in addressing the rest of the cosmos, address man himself. I am speaking of such sciences as psychology, psychiatry, linguistics, developmental anthropology, sociology." (1991, 273) Here, I, the author, would add neuroscience.

Neuroscience is the contemporary attempt to bridge the gap between the dyadic and the triadic, between neurotransmitter levels (dyadic) and human behavior (triadic), between biology (dyadic) and psychology (possibly triadic). But consider what we study in a freshman psychology class: "neurones [sic], signals, synapses, transmitter substance, central nervous system, brain, mind, personality, self, consciousness, and later such items as ego, superego, archetypes." (1991, 273)

The words early in the list refer to things and events which can be seen or measured, like neurones [sic], which are cells one can see through a microscope, or signals, which are transmissions of electrical energy, which one can measure, along a nerve fiber. The later words, like "self," "ego," "consciousness," refer to items that cannot be seen as things or measured as energy exchanges. They can only be described by some such words as "mental" or "mind." (1991, 273-274)

We have all read books that purport to show us how anything "mental" can be reduced to some kind of brain activity. Now, everything a human being does or experiences is *correlated* to brain activity. The question is whether it can be *reduced* to brain activity. Is "mind" nothing but the brain in action?

In our age of science, the first answer that comes to the fore is "Yes, mind can be reduced to brain activity. In fact, it is nothing more or other than brain activity." And here, Walker Percy would vehemently disagree. He would posit that science and scientists cannot say such a thing because they do not come equipped to do so. To stretch the dyadic process of science into the triadic

---

[2] According to Walker Percy, one "semioticist defined the subject of his study [the human being] as the only organism which tells lies." (1983, 108) How is this fact quantitatively taken into consideration when one is undertaking a survey or studying a culture? We trustingly accept that neither the scientist nor the informant nor the research subject are lying in their communications.

realm of things such as mind and language is scientism. As he himself says, what he opposes "is the imperial decree of scientism (not of science) to discredit other ways of knowing." (1991, 194) Science is expert at examining and elucidating dyadic entities and operations: photosynthesis, chemical bonds, black holes, and so on. However, it overreaches itself when it attempts to reduce the triadic to the dyadic and moreover undermines its own integrity by positing the dyadic explanation as a complete explanation of a triadic event. As Percy remarks:

> My purpose here is not to challenge science in the name of humanism. Scientists are used to and understandably unimpressed by such challenges. No, my purpose is rather to challenge science, as it is presently practiced by some scientists, in the name of science." (1991, 272)

It is a concern for the integrity of science that moves Percy to write what he writes. He is not an anti-evolutionist nor a religious radical.[3] He is certainly not anti-science. But he is concerned that science is losing its way as science. Furthermore, I think he would add that part of certain people's strong reactions against science result from scientists overstepping the boundaries of their sciences. The first example of this that comes to mind is, of course, Richard Dawkins. He may be qualified to talk about biology, but he is in no way, shape, or form qualified to talk about religion *qua* scientist. He is, however, qualified to talk about it inasmuch as any private citizen is qualified to talk about religion.

Conclusion

The purpose of this paper was to show three ways in which the thought of Walker Percy, Catholic, physician, and novelist (although we did not talk about his novels here) is relevant to religion and science.

The first of Percy's contributions was his distinction between *Umwelt* and *Welt*. The upshot of this idea is that while the natural sciences are qualified to talk about a human being as an organism in an environment (*Umwelt*), the natural sciences are not equipped to deal with a human being as a symbol-user in a world of symbols (*Welt*).

---

[3] Although he does observe that difficulties "arise when triadic creatures (scientists) try to explain [human] evolution through exclusively dyadic events." (1983, 161)

The reason for this limitation on the part of natural science was its inability to describe events in any terms other than dyadic ones, such as cause and effect. According to Percy (and Peirce), as a result of language (especially the capacity of naming), humans engage the world through symbols, thus creating a triadic relationship among human, event, and name. A fairly simple example of this is the statement "That is bread." The dyadic response to the presentation of bread is to eat it. The triadic response to the presence of bread is to name it.

Finally, and perhaps most importantly for Percy, this failure to understand the difference between dyadic and triadic behavior in human beings causes extremely grave problems for the human sciences (psychology, anthropology, and so on) because these scientists, who are triadic creatures or subjects, are trying to study and understand other triadic creatures (human beings) as if they were objects and thus reducible to dyadic interpretation when, in fact, the human being can only be understood triadically.

Thus, one might picture the conflicts that arise between practitioners of science and practitioners of religion as a conflict between triadic creatures that are trying to explain the world dyadically (i.e., scientists) and triadic creatures that are trying to explain the world triadically (such as a practitioner of religion). Perhaps by acknowledging these conflicting perspectives, a new discussion about or between "science" and "religion" can begin, because then we will really be talking about human existence.

- Stacey E. Ake would like to thank Justin R. Warren for his help in writing this paper.

References

Percy, Walker. 1983. *Lost in the Cosmos: The Last Self-Help Book*. New York: The Noonday Press (Farrar, Straus & Giroux).

Percy, Walker. 1991. *Signposts in a Strange Land*. New York: The Noonday Press (Farrar, Straus & Giroux).

Percy, Walker. 2000. *The Message in the Bottle: How Queer Man Is, How Queer Language Is, and What One Has to Do with the Other*. New York: Picador USA (Farrar, Straus & Giroux).

andré m. carrington

Spectacular Intimacies: Texture, Ethnicity, and a Touch of Black Cultural Politics

An early scene in a documentary on the life of amateur scientist and entrepreneur Madam C.J. Walker, *Two Dollars and a Dream*, features Helen Humes performing "Nappy Headed Woman." She laments, "You can't comb it, don't you try," and "Straighten it or burn it, makes no difference I don't care." As is so often the case in the blues, what may initially come across as nihilism gives way to a more complicated, even indulgent performance of the will to tolerate pain. As integral as suffering is to her experience, the speaker pleads in the last verse to Madam Walker and offers her a $50 bill to "Help a poor girl if you will."[1] The song is not a document of black women thriving with their hair in its natural state, nor a lament for the pain of struggling against it. Rather, through her relationship to another black woman, the speaker transforms her pain into a commodity: a demand for which Madam Walker can supply satisfaction. In order to observe how Walker and Humes's performance valorizes straight hair, we must conceive of "nappy hair" as "hair that fails to be straight." By the same token, we assign value to our natural hair by recognizing that it resists straightening and deciding whether and how to meet that resistance. The objective of this essay is not to rationalize the subjection of black features to white supremacist beauty standards or to polemicize the current movement toward natural hair among black American women. Instead, my animating impulse is the energetic tension that exists between black skin, often defined as an immutable distinguishing feature of "the race," and black hair, for which alteration serves as a defining experience.

Conceptualizing nappy hair as something other than hair that "fails" to be straight occurs to me as a fruitful opportunity to reassert the centrality of black bodies—considered in whole and in part—to articulating both the power relations that structure society in dominance and the critical practices that impel contemporary scholarship on forms of subjectivity, subjection, and possibilities beyond their limitations. Here, I hope to position this essay as a gesture in concert with efforts by Chandan Reddy, Judith Halberstam, Sharon Holland, and Alex Weheliye in recent years to problematize theories of the subject in favor of more thoughtful attention to the complications involved in falling outside normative regimes of citizenship, gender, sexuality,

---

[1] *Two Dollars and a Dream*, DVD, directed by Stanley Nelson (New York: Filmmakers Library, 1989).

and humanity.[2] The studies above share some prerogatives with the work of Kandice Chuh, whose *Imagine Otherwise* first posited the possibility of Asian American Studies as a critique without a subject, which is in turn informed by queer theory's productive elaboration on the significance of sex/gender, sexuality, and desire beyond their function as identity markers.[3] In the same vein, I hope to explore the ramifications of thinking about black hair and black skin, not so much in the absence of black people, but in terms that regard the facts about blackness purportedly evidenced by these bodily features in light of their failure to define black subjects.

In this essay I forward an appraisal of the cultural politics of black hair texture and black skin, apprehended in visual and tactile terms, in order to stimulate critical conversation on the role of the act of touch and the realm of the haptic in the propagation of knowledge about race and ethnicity. In turn, I explore how the developments in knowledge production examined below are germane to the articulation of racial power. This discussion proceeds from an analysis of current cultural interventions concerned with black hair (and their histories) to an assessment of the transformation of skin color's significance that is taking place under a new regime of colorblind racial ideology. I focus on two examples: a performance titled "You Can Touch My Hair" and an emergent system for the classification of black hair textures, the Andre Walker system. Through these examples, I argue that hair and skin texture may come to supplant skin color as a reified property of racial difference. Accordingly, interrogating of the act of touch attests to the need for a critical orientation toward quasi-scientific practices that are currently constructing knowledge about skin texture in racialized and gendered terms. This exploration involves a steady engagement with fundamental questions about the human and the object that have been initiated in recent years by interlocutors in black and American Studies such as Alex Weheliye, Darieck Scott, and Sylvia Wynter.

The salience of Critical Race Theory resonates throughout the perspectives I am drawing into conversation in this essay, as it prefigures and encompasses the concerns of the scholars above. The topics under investigation below form part of an antiracist critique of everyday life: treating

---

[2] Judith Halberstam, *The Queer Art of Failure* (Durham: Duke University Press, 2011), Sharon Holland, *Raising the Dead: Readings of Death and (Black) Subjectivity* (Durham: Duke University Press, 2000), Chandan Reddy, *Freedom With Violence: Race, Sexuality, and the U.S. State* (Durham: Duke University Press, 2011) and Alex Weheliye, *Habeas Viscus: Racializing Assemblages, Biopolitics, and Black Feminist Theories of the Human* (Durham: Duke University Press, 2014).

[3] Kandice Chuh, *Imagine Otherwise: On Asian Americanist Critique* (Durham: Duke University Press, 2003) and David Eng, Judith Halberstam, and José Esteban Muñoz, eds. "What's Queer About Queer Studies Now?" Social Text 23.4-5 (Fall/Winter 2005): 1-17.

race as a discursive formation that is materially present in the world, learning not to take for granted what constitutes racial discourse, questioning how race, class, and gender influence their respective forms of appearance, and linking black vernacular intellectual practice to interdisciplinary efforts to reckon with what race has meant and what it has done.

Performance is a useful heuristic for this analysis, because it allows us to describe how the defining power of race inheres in doing (and undoing) identity practices and social relations. In this sense, qualities typically described in terms of "ethnicity" might be reconsidered as performance. Here, I am not using ethnicity to refer to ritualized or traditional customs and habits enacted by persons in real time, but rather, in a slightly more pointed way, I refer to physical features determined to have identificatory implications within and across racial categories. Ethnicity may invoke skin color and hair texture, two overdetermined and overtaxed signs for racial identity, but it also involves the many ways of presenting the skin and hair, maintaining them, altering them, and submitting them to or withdrawing them from interaction. Ethnicity, as a way of naming the differences between and among phenotypes within a racial category and the way phenotypes are used to differentiate between racial groupings, links the determination of what comprises physical evidence of racial identity to the consequences of making that determination. As it is organized by racial discourse, ethnicity is not reducible to the presence or absence of physical signs any more than racial identity, but instead, considered as a performative dimension of race, it describes how the presentation and reception of distinguishing features makes the body meaningful in racial terms. In a purportedly colorblind society wherein biological definitions of identity seem to be obsolete, we should beware the ways in which race as a regime of powerful knowledge reasserts itself in "flexible" terms by using ostensibly benign knowledge about the body to maintain the racial power of ethnic distinctions.[4]

The cultural interventions I examine and my interpretation take place in the critical space made available by women artists whose works dethrone vision from its integral role in maintaining the masculinist imaginary. Scholars including Donna Haraway, Laura Mulvey, and Kaja Silverman mark this as a crucial priority for feminist cultural criticism. French filmmaker Agnès Varda is one artist who contributes to this project; according to Kate Ince, she employs "haptic visuality," composing shots that "caress the skin" and reflexively "'film one hand with the other,'" in an ongoing negotiation with phenomenology.[5] Marina Abramovic and Francesca Woodman provoke similar considerations

---

4 Emily Martin, *Flexible Bodies* (Boston: Beacon Press, 1995).
5 Kate Ince, "Feminist Phenomenology and the Film of Agnès Varda," *Hypatia* 28. 3 (Summer 2013): 604.

in the work of Premi Prabhakar for undertaking performances that place their skin in contact with exterior surfaces including the bodies of spectators and the walls of the spaces around them.[6]

Feminist knowledge practices intersect with and augment race thinking throughout Sarah Ahmed and Jackie Stacey's collection *Thinking Through the Skin*. In her contribution to the anthology, Shirley Tate examines the abjection of blackness, typically enacted through figures of speech and visual constructs such as stereotype, as a paradigmatic construction of the skin as a site of subordinating difference. Tate explores a tradition from Frantz Fanon to bell hooks that demonstrates how "negotiating discourses of Black skin lead[s] to alternative identity positionings."[7] In search of those alternatives, she works through the notion of hybridity to describe how relationships instantiated in speech implicate the speakers in constructing the meaning of blackness in their shared discursive space.[8] The aforementioned artists and critics destabilize the power of vision to define subjectivity, and I would like to extend their endeavors by questioning how we might politicize the power of touch to construct knowledge about race.

A labored genealogy of black hair straightening

The lessons that black feminists have drawn from exploitative situations in which the construction of knowledge regarding hair texture takes place are critical to understanding how black subjects negotiate with and resist bourgeois conventions of self-fashioning. In that sense, its legacy comprises "thinking through the hair." I am currently working at the confluence of two black feminist intellectual traditions that operate within and outside the academy. The first of these extends at least as far back as Madam C.J. Walker and regards hair texture—especially the texture of black women's hair—as an integral part of the performance of class and ethnicity. In this discussion, I will move from reconsidering Walker's interventions in historical perspective to an account of the questions her legacy poses for negotiating intimacy with black hair in the present. The second stage in my discussion questions the implications of some contemporary practices that revalorize the production of knowledge regarding black hair and skin.

---

[6] Premi Prabhakar, "Invoking the Spectral Body: A Study of Potential Corporealities in the Work of Marina Abramovic and Francesca Woodman," *Excursions* 1.1 (June 2010): 91-101.

[7] Shirley Tate, "'That is my Star of David': Skin, Abjection, and Hybridity," in *Thinking Through the Skin*, ed. Sarah Ahmed and Jackie Stacey (New York: Routledge, 2001), 209.

[8] Ibid, 220.

Some of the most significant contributions of black American and African Diasporic subjects to the repertoire of identity and cultural practices in the modern world have begun in the domain of self-fashioning. The woman who would become Madam C.J. Walker, Sarah Breedlove, born in 1867, became a historical prototype for black women's traditions of invention and entrepreneurship. The significance of her contributions to black subject formation—most notably, her popularization of the hot comb and her role advancing black women's employment in the commercialization of beauty products—continue to resonate far beyond the quotidian and individual level.[9] The competing interests brought to bear on maintaining and altering black hair textures that Walker emblematizes can be traced back to demands placed on the bodies of black women working at the intersection of social mobility, desire, and ethnicity in the shadow of American slavery.

Walker's innovations attained substantial breadth because of the significance of waged work in the everyday lives of black women moving into the 20th century. The parochialization of the middle-class home as a site of leisure and "feminine mystique" in the United States, which excluded black women from normative gender ideology, relied on labor saving techniques and accumulated wealth, and these developments took place against the backdrop of economic shifts that favored white men. Bourgeois femininity took shape for married white women under conditions in which a white "family wage" ameliorated poverty; high wages for white men became possible, in turn, through the marginalization of their black competitors as well as their white wives and children in the labor market.[10] The black intelligentsia encouraged women in their communities to approximate their white counterparts by supporting their husbands with uncompensated reproductive labor and training for "jobs that could be performed in the home," such as taking in laundry. Noliwe Rooks points out that Madam Walker's ethos of self-sufficiency situated black women as the primary stakeholders in their own self-fashioning. In her study of the political economy and cultural politics of black hair, in which Walker and the black women who became haircare professionals like her example play major roles, Rooks writes, "Walker broadened 'acceptable' public representations of working-class African American women by urging them to join her in careers outside of the domestic sphere."[11] While the aesthetics of black women's pursuit of social mobility converged with white femininity superficially via straight hair, it is important to examine black women's efforts

---

[9] Noliwe Rooks, *Hair-Raising: Beauty, Culture, and African American Women* (New Brunswick: Rutgers University Press, 1996), 16.

[10] Kathleen Nutter, "Family Wage," in Robert Weir and James Hanlan, *Historical Encyclopedia of American Labor* (Santa Barbara: ABC-CLIO, 2004), http://www.credoreference.com/entry/abcamlabor/family_wage, (Accessed April 1, 2015).

[11] Rooks, 16.

to transform the meaning of hair texture in material terms. Circumventing discriminatory labor practices, making cost-effective personal investments, and achieving financial independence from men factored into black women's decision to participate in the emergent hair straightening enterprise in ways that uncannily prefigure the contemporary movement toward natural haircare.

The exploitative practices that accompanied black Americans' incorporation into the labor force in the 20th century gave rise to invaluable legacies of resistance. As scholars from Dorothy Roberts and Jacqueline Jones to Carole Boyce-Davies and Adrienne Davis note, black women facing up to white supremacy conceptualized cultures of work in ways that exceed the limits of Western hegemonic feminism and conventional labor history.[12] Confronting the ubiquitous hazards of heteropatriarchy and racism, black women at work envision ways of life beyond the bifurcation of work and everyday life that defy the cultural logic of capitalism. Investigations oriented toward black women's agency in articulating the meanings of labor and capital, like Rooks's social and economic appraisal of hair straightening, have led to new theorizations of what constitutes politics. Considering the centrality of expressive culture to legacies of black resistance, as scholarship on black radical traditions continually suggests, returns our attention to the significance of hair texture as a matter of cultural politics.

While I argue in concert with the thinkers cited above that we might enrich our perspectives on black women's roles in capitalism by reappraising their efforts to make their own fortunes, my turn toward expressive culture, and performance in particular, is also informed by Roderick Ferguson's suggestion that critics "disidentify with historical materialism."[13] Rather than interpreting the gender performances and class trajectories enacted by black women's involvement in hair straightening as either anomalies peculiar to their position on the margins of dominant social structures or evidence of their capitulation to normative standards of beauty, I would follow Ferguson's insights to ask whether the cultural politics of black hair texture demonstrate the simultaneous "normalization of patriarchy on the one hand, and the emergence of eroticized and gendered racial formations that dispute

---

[12] Jacqueline Jones, *Labor of Love, Labor of Sorrow: Black Women, Work, and the Family, from Slavery to the Present*, Revised Edition (Philadelphia: Basic Books, 2010), Dorothy Roberts, *Killing the Black Body: Race, Reproduction and the Meaning of Liberty* (New York: Vintage, 1998), Carole Boyce-Davies, *Left of Karl Marx: The Political Life of Black Communist* Claudia Jones (Durham: Duke University Press, 2008), and Adrienne Davis, "Don't Let Nobody Bother Yo' Principle: The Sexual Economy of American Slavery," in Sister Circle: Black Women and Work, ed. Sharon Harley (New Brunswick: Rutgers University Press, 2002).

[13] Roderick Ferguson, *Aberrations in Black: Toward a Queer of Color Critique* (Minneapolis: University of Minnesota Press, 2003), 4.

heteropatriarchy's universality on the other."[14] In light of Ferguson's queer of color critique, informed by women of color feminism, we might perceive hair straightening as a disidentificatory practice: a practice that embodies the ideal of straight hair as an aspect of white bourgeois femininity while redefining what that embodiment means in relation to blackness. In the example set by workers who defined haircare as a uniquely black female business, hair straightening comprised part of an emancipatory strategy that allowed them to separate their economic interests from bourgeois leadership and domestic intimacy with men. Insofar as hair straightening comprises a spectacle that elicits mixed responses today, situating its significance within the lives of black women who have a unique and original claim to its value helps us recognize its disidentificatory potential.

You can't touch this

The tension with which contemporary race relations are charged manifests in the lives of black women in many ways that involve the sense of touch directly. This tension haunts many of us as we move through social worlds in which the tangible signs of our blackness beg the question: "Can I touch it?" When I wore long locks, in college, an older white woman once asked, "Can I touch it?" from behind me in a video store. I wrote about the interaction for my school newspaper. I wondered how one might stage that confrontation through the looking glass: what would it take for me, as a younger black man, to speak the phrase "Can I touch it" to an adult white woman whom I did not know? Part of my disquiet at moments like this, I now recognize, is the sensation of racism shearing away the cloak of male privilege from my black body. Being black, male, and cisgender in a white supremacist society entails experiencing, occasionally, a fraction of what black women experience constantly. Notwithstanding our common humanity and shared struggles against racism, black men's experiences with alienation from dominant gender ideologies can yield the conditions of possibility for empathy across genders. This empathy sometimes becomes tangible in the context of kinship, friendship, and other sites of intimacy.

Particularly for those of us with recognizable signs of ethnicity on our bodies—"natural" hair, dark skin, marks of scarification—our blackness takes on a worldly value that others can only realize through their sense of touch. Whereas Frantz Fanon's analysis of the "epidermalization" of racial identity helps articulate how blackness is always already defined by white supremacy

---

[14] Ibid, 11.

according to the sense of sight, the meaning of race according to the sense of touch is speculative in everyday life. The features that distinguish black bodies from whiteness look different, but differences in texture are merely inferred by sight; only the sense of touch can confirm them. In the visual register, the stereotyping of racialized features can make strangers appear familiar: when seen as the properties of a collectively-known blackness rather than the private parts of a whole black individual, kinky hair and fascinating skin no longer belong to their bearer but to the race.

I think this was the assumption at work when a stranger once (more than once) called out "M.C. Hammer!" at me, apparently provoked by the resemblance between my haircut at the time and that of the rapper. On another occasion, I was almost flattered to hear someone intone, in a quiet falsetto, "Maxwell!" as I walked by. These stylized microaggressions accost black women all the time, with the extemporaneous citation of the celebrity's name determined by her respective hairstyle: hey Jill Scott! and so on. Like the question, "Can I touch it," directed at natural hair, these misrecognitions rehearse an objectifying script in which all bearers of racially-distinctive features become indistinguishable from one another as individuals, rendered instead as collective expressions of a given phenotype.

The question "Can I touch it?" restated in the second person and answered affirmatively, was the subject of a performance and short film, titled "You Can Touch My Hair" staged in New York in June 2013 by un'ruly. The un'ruly project and lifestyle brand, founded by Antonia and Abigail Opiah with several other black women as collaborators, frames black hair from the purview of black women's investments in their own bodies and images of themselves. Un'ruly engages black women in consumer culture vis-à-vis natural hair by evaluating haircare products and practices. By positioning women with natural hair as agents in capitalism rather than passive subjects of its machinations, it reiterates the dynamics of Madam Walker's earlier movement in the context of an economy increasingly driven by consumption rather than the production and distribution of goods.[15] The cultural politics of un'ruly reconfigure the relationship between cultivating natural hair and hair straightening by identifying "black hair experience" in pluralistic terms that lend themselves to celebrity, stereotype, social mobility, and everyday life.[16]

The performance, which un'ruly called an "exhibit," took place over two days in New York City's Union Square, is an object lesson in the cultural

---

[15] Susannah Walker, *Style and Status: Selling Beauty to African American Women, 1920-1975* (Lexington: University Press of Kentucky, 2007).

[16] Antonia Opiah, "A Place for Black Hair," Un'ruly (2013), http://www.un-ruly.com/about-us, (Accessed April 1, 2015).

politics of racialized curiosity. For two days in June 2013, small groups of black women posed with signs that announced "You Can Touch My Hair," and invited onlookers (of all backgrounds) to do so. One at a time, an individual from the gathered crowd would approach and greet the women with the signs, then put their hands on each of their hair briefly, sometimes running their fingers through the strands and locks, sometimes holding a portion of hair between their fingers, sometimes patting hair that lifted itself away from the scalp with their palms, usually moving from one woman's hair to the next. Some of them took photos of themselves with the women holding signs. Throughout the process, the participants conversed with one another, sharing their observations, asking and responding to questions in dialogue with the women recording the event. Along with the women who were affiliated with the production, other people who participated carried smartphones and recorded what was happening, apparently without any restriction from the organizers. The format of this event comprises part of un'ruly's strategy of blending "curated" and original content on their website. It makes use of public space, accesses an existing site for urban cultural and political gatherings, and lends itself readily to observation by the general public as well as other producers and consumers of specialized media. Un'ruly thereby maintains live performance as a distinct form of cultural and critical practice. The short film produced to accompany the event showcases the aforementioned engagements in addition to interviews that were recorded on separate occasions. Other elements woven throughout the film include coverage of the simultaneous recordings, conversations, contestations, street noise, and counter-discourse taking place alongside the exhibit.[17]

Taking exception the spectacle was a group of women filmed nearby, at the same site where women with "You Can Touch My Hair" signs stood. This group held signs reading "I Am Not Your Sarah Baartman," "Touch My Hair With Your Hand & I'll Touch Your Face With My Fist," and "You Cannot Touch My Hair," making their own critical cultural intervention through live performance. One of the contestatory presences was cultural critic and social media strategist Nicole Moore, founder of the blog The Hotness.[18] Moore's counter-performance and her later writings on the experience problematize the curiosity that was a driving force in the exhibit. By speaking to the specter of Sarah Baartman at the event, Moore's critique expands the relevance of the interactions taking place beyond the occasion of the performance and situated

---

[17] "You Can Touch My Hair", directed by Antonia Opiah and Abigail Opiah (2013; New York: Un'ruly, 2013), http://www.un-ruly.com/you-can-touch-my-hair, (Accessed April 1, 2015).

[18] Nicole Moore, "But Ain't I a Woman? Badu, Serena, and Hair Touching," The Hotness (2013) http://thehotness.com/2013/06/19/but-aint-i-a-woman-though-badu-serena-hair-touching, (Accessed April 1, 2015).

their meaning in the genealogy of knowing racialized and gendered difference through exhibition and touch, reminding participants and observers that patriarchy and imperialism have enabled spectators to satisfy their curiosity at black women's expense.

Moore's blog chronicling her participation in the counter-performance alongside the exhibit takes exception to its content as well as the mode of address employed by un'ruly's signage. "Why Do You Want to Touch My Hair?" and "How Does My Hair Make You Feel?" might have "questioned rather than acquiesced" to the desires of onlookers, instead.[19] By affirming the validity of the question "Can I Touch Your Hair?" Moore argues that the language through which un'ruly invoked the occasion failed to prioritize its participants' agency as black women. The potential impact of the event was similarly questionable, in Moore's view, insofar as it sustained existing tendencies to scrutinize black women's hair rather than initiating any new dialogue. The knowledge made available through touch on the occasion of the performance might not change the way non-black participants felt about black women, and it would not alleviate "intra-community biases" among black women regarding different choices with respect to hair texture and self-presentation. The counter-performance thus calls the conditions of possibility for the exhibit into question and reframes the politics of touching black women's hair in a context that presumes their right to deny permission instead of offering it.

Pointedly, one woman who stood with Moore was depicted in the film holding a sign reading, "What'll It Be Next...My Butt?" She posed the rhetorical question of whether an observer needed to touch her to know "why she was genetically predisposed to having a larger backside." Her question insinuates that the desire to touch black bodies is a prerogative of sexual power, and not just a matter of benign curiosity, reminding the viewer/participant that an ostensibly benign, invited touch can nonetheless elicit coercive, even violent connotations. This critique insists that the act of touch has historical and structural features that can be felt in the present.

Antonia Opiah addresses some of the critical perspectives on "You Can Touch My Hair" in the film by the same title produced by un'ruly. Notably, her comments acknowledge the ways in which the interaction evoked the spectacle of Sarah Baartman, thus incorporating the response to the performance by its detractors into her account of the event. Opiah also explains the organizers' choice to name the event an "exhibit," conceding that it deliberately calls to mind the ways in which black bodies have been displayed in order to illustrate their difference from whiteness.

---

[19] Ibid.

Sexology, comparative anatomy, and ethnographic displays from World's Fairs to museums have all relied on strategies for exhibiting the living and dead bodies of black and indigenous people.[20] The "Year of the White Bear" performance by Coco Fusco and Guillermo Gomez-Peña, in which the artists enact a satirical representation of a couple from an undiscovered Amerindian island culture, addresses this legacy most memorably by incorporating fabulist language play, costume, and dance into a counter-spectacle that mocks the audience of the racial diorama. Naming "You Can Touch My Hair" an exhibit ironically posits the possibility of touch as a counter-discourse to visual display that might disrupt myths of black inferiority: if appearances lie, touch might tell the truth. While the visual field dominates the exhibit as such, in live performance, a combination of stimuli shapes the meaning of the occasion. The smoke from the "inauthentic" cigarettes that Gómez-Peña enjoys in the aforementioned collaboration with Fusco (and an audience member's attempt to burn him with same) along with other responses, from shaking their stage/ cage to ogling and touching them sexually, presented each moment as a discordant combination of visual, aural, olfactory, and haptic impressions. [21]In "You Can Touch My Hair," vision elicits the desire to know, and touch fulfills that desire. The knowledge of texture attained through touch promises to demystify the appearance of black hair. Implicitly, touch does more than produce a unique observation: it constitutes a unique relationship between subjects.

While the interaction at the center of "You Can Touch My Hair" yields an immediate transition from ignorance to a knowing state for the observer/ participant, the follow-up discussions joined by bystanders and recorded in the film provide further edification and critical exchange. Participants are encouraged to examine their motivation for accepting the invitation to touch a black woman's hair, and they are debriefed about the experience after the fact. One white woman's report in the film about what she learned through the experience of touch is particularly intriguing. Asked if there were questions about black women's hair that touching it answered, she replied that there were not; what the experience provided was "getting a chance to touch it."[22] The notion of the exhibit as a "chance" or fortuitous circumstance in which touch was expressly permitted communicates an awareness of the risk involved in

---

20 Donna Haraway, "Teddy Bear Patriarchy: Taxidermy in the Garden of Eden, New York City, 1908-1936," Social Text 11 (Winter 1984-1985): 20-64, Siobhan Somerville, *Queering the Color Line: Race and the Invention of Homosexuality in American Culture* (Durham: Duke University Press, 2000), and Adam Green, *Selling the Race: Culture, Community, and Black Chicago, 1940-1955* (Chicago: University of Chicago Press, 2007).

21 Guillermo Gómez-Peña and Coco Fusco, Interview by Anna Johnson, *BOMB* 42 (Winter 1993): 36-39.

22 "You Can Touch My Hair".

trying and potentially failing to touch black hair without an open invitation; under other conditions, making the attempt might have elicited infelicitous consequences.

Herein lies the competing discourse made manifest by the presence of black women at the exhibit who denied onlookers permission to touch their hair: there was not only a confrontation between the knowledge made available to participants' hands and ignorance about the telling difference that texture conveys, but also a contestation over the different purposes for which one might legitimately, ethically seek to know the touch of an Other. Said one protester, "I'm not interested in having a conversation where I make people feel better about their hair or they finally get to learn what my hair texture feels like. Have an intimate relationship with a black person, have a black friend... and ask them." By voicing this alternative way of knowing the black body through touch in a performative fashion, enjoining the person addressed to "*have* an intimate relationship, *have* a black friend," the speaker invokes an alternative situation—a relationship that must begin long before one poses the question, "Can I touch your hair"—as the setting in which coming to know the texture of black hair might take place. The suggestion that permission might be granted by a trusted friend or other intimate whose relationship to the observer already includes occasional or habitual physical contact also entails the risk of rejection, of course. This possibility underscores the agency of the individual to whom black hair belongs, and reminds the observer that in the context of interaction with a stranger, the risk of rejection does not pose the same threat as the potential loss of a friend, the disappointment of a lover, or the judgment of a respected peer. The possibility that we might violate the boundaries of a stranger is risky, with respect to social mores, but we reconcile ourselves to the vulnerability involved in putting ourselves at risk of rejection when we seek to touch someone with whom we are intimate.

The skull beneath the skin

Circumstances in which black people allow our bodies to know and become known through mutually desirable touch make it possible to comprehend blackness as something other than abjection. The phenomenal significance of a caring, careful touch that entails risk and requires permission—the intimate touch—occurs across racial lines and within them, as well. When black subjects touch one another, we encounter our shared humanity and vulnerability as well as our individual differences. Amongst ourselves, we practice what Michelle Wright has identified as a "negation" of the very negation that defines blackness as only and always merely "Other to the

white subject."[23] By rejecting certain constructions of ourselves that make our identities meaningful only as antithetical to whiteness, installing whiteness as normative for the human, we arrive at unique forms of self-definition that belie the normative regime of human subjectivity. Wright and Roderick Ferguson point to the politics of recognition and self-fashioning found in black feminism as crucial, in this regard, because they entail a refusal to be only and always Other to whiteness or manhood, or otherwise limited to a singular definition of the human.[24] One way of finding significance in encounters between persons who are circumscribed within the same set of racial boundaries by shared phenotypes and heritage is to perceive them as crossing the internal borders that exist among our racialized bodies: differences of age, gender, class, ethnicity, nationality, or individual life experience.

The concluding portion of this essay will introduce an analysis of racialized differences in skin texture. My readings of scientific discourse on skin and previous interventions in performance studies suggest that racialized skin texture is the inchoate subject of a benign differential that is currently under construction, paradoxically, at a post-biological and "colorblind" moment in the history of race thinking. The cultural politics of intimacy vis-à-vis racialized skin texture have yet to be explored thoroughly in scholarship, but the present analysis of hair texture and skin color may provide touchstones for the challenges and opportunities this area presents.

Haircare is, for reasons enumerated above, both labor- and capital-intensive within black communities. As an illustration of what Foucauldian theorists term "power/knowledge," the reproduction of black hair textures through commodity-driven practices lends itself to the expression of power dynamics, including relations of dominance and subordination, as well as the ostensibly benign process of disseminating information.[25] Up to this point, I have deliberately framed the conversation on hair texture in quotidian terms, but there is a robust knowledge economy organized around black hair texture as a form of physical difference that can be observed, analyzed, and manipulated by professionals as well as amateurs and individuals engaged in self-care. Over time, the construction of hair texture as a site of intraracial difference has lent itself to the formation of folk taxonomies in black communities: "good" versus bad hair; desirable and undesirable textures and styles; critical perspectives

---

[23] Michelle Wright, *Becoming Black: Creating Identity in the African Diaspora* (Durham: Duke University Press, 2004), 9.

[24] Ibid. See also, Ferguson, "Something Else to Be: *Sula*, the Moynihan Report, and the Negations of Black Lesbian Feminism," in *Aberrations in Black*.

[25] Linda Martín Alcoff, "Foucault's Normative Epistemology," in *A Companion to Foucault*, ed. Christopher Falzon, Timothy O'Leary, and Jana Sawicki, (Somerset, NJ: Wiley, 2013), 207.

on the heritability, manageability, and expense of textures, styles, and habits of care; debates regarding "professionalism" and presentability that intersect with and contest the politics of black respectability. These considerations make the knowledge of black hair texture powerful in everyday life.

The development of ostensibly objective knowledge about black hair, however, situates it on the same discursive plane as skin color, in some ways. If skin color and hair texture are both subject to becoming known, through touch or through sight, in terms of their "true nature" prior to modification, then knowledge about them can be made to function more authoritatively. While in some ways, refining knowledge about black hair might make self-care more legible for non-specialists who wish to cultivate the self-knowledge necessary to make decisions about their bodies, the example of skin color shows us how facile it can be to portray physical features with racial significance in terms of a simple dichotomy between the unvarnished truths they might yield, on the one hand, and their liability to contrived performances, on the other.

The discourses of identity that inform contemporary state practices in the United States, for example, tend to portray superficial qualities like skin color and secondary sex characteristics as "accidents of birth" about which authoritative knowledge can be attained while insisting that they are not causally linked to differential outcomes and life chances among the people defined by them. At the same time, claims to "colorblindness" plead ignorance about the material differences that persist between groups who are disempowered by irrational racial distinctions and those who are empowered by them by claiming that observing the distinction is invalid and inherently suspect. Scholars like Lawrence Bobo and Eduardo Bonilla-Silva extend this critique to note that contemporary accounts of the same racial disparities that were once rationalized on the basis of immutable characteristics like skin color are reiterated in arguments that "rely on cultural rather than biological tropes to explain blacks' position in this country."[26] These discourses on race correlate the cultural traits that prevail among members of minoritized racial groups—speech patterns, naming conventions, styles of dress, sexuality and childbearing—with these groups' collective experiences of social disadvantage; rather than structural change, they favor policies such as the promotion of marriage that incentivize normative behavior and punish deviance.[27] Color-blind racism thus assumes that racial minorities themselves continue to drive inequality by maintaining their distinctiveness. In this fashion, it leverages the "truth" that differences in skin color are superficial into a means to argue

---

26 Eduardo Bonilla-Silva, *Racism Without Racists: Color-blind Racism and the Persistence of Racial Inequality in the United States* (Lanham, MD: Rowman and Littlefield, 2013), 7.

27 Vivian Hamilton, "Will Marriage Promotion Work?" *The Journal of Gender, Race, and Justice* 11.1 (September 2007): 15.

that racial differences observed in culture are profoundly meaningful, and it thus "works to obscure the role that truth claims play in the reproduction or transformation of power relations."[28]

If we conceptualize racial differences as differences of power, however, physical and cultural criteria are equally suspect as explanations for persistent disparities between racial groups. Furthermore, accounting for the ways in which we perform our racial identities entails observing how we bring "culture" into being, sometimes fashioning it into the form of "ethnicity," using our bodies and the objects, space, and other persons in the world around us as raw materials. For this reason, I find it important to conceptualize ethnicity in ways that comprise phenomena that blend phenotype and cultural practice, like the presentation of hair and skin, because attempts to disaggregate them can easily play into reductive and disingenuous arguments that legitimate injustice. Hence, it is not simply the truth-effects of racial distinctions but also the priority placed on them that demands scrutiny. If the truths the body is compelled to tell and the truths embodied in cultural practices are equally subject to interrogation as aspects of the performance of racial identity, we might understand both their natural variation and their susceptibility to transformation as *political.*

The rhetorical invocation of "skin color" as a proxy for race in colorblind racial ideology strikes me as one instance in which truth claims regarding race masquerade as apolitical. The contemporary cultural logic that might claim race does not matter invokes "skin color" to stand in for race in order to signal the putatively inconsequential quality of racial classifications based on such arbitrary factors. This gesture, however, attempts to disaggregate skin color from an ensemble of other features, including political, historical, and material factors, to which a structure of difference articulated in racial terms remains quite relevant. The rhetorical gesture that reduces race to skin color and insists skin color does not matter suppresses our capacity to recognize how colorblindness itself reinstalls the skin into the dominant structure of power/knowledge by fortifying its capacity to articulate objective truths. In a similar fashion, the propagation of objectifying knowledge regarding hair texture, against the backdrop of assertions that differences between textures are real, but superficial, rather than fictive and political, opens onto the same horizon of possibilities as the reappraisal of skin color. While no one wants to oversubscribe to reductive versions of black cultural politics (i.e. assuming that dark skin and natural hair form the embodied conditions of possibility for antiracist praxis), we might employ performance as a framework that militates against the reifying tendencies of truth claims about race by bearing witness to the scenarios in which these claims achieve their efficacy as truth.

---

[28] Alcoff, 219.

As an example of a contemporary knowledge project that offers opportunities to enact the cultural politics of blackness in a variety of ways through self-fashioning, I would identify the Andre Walker hair classification system. The Andre Walker system is a quasi-scientific method for categorizing texture according to the shape, appearance, and structure of individual strands and full heads of hair, including the hair's resistance to normative beautification practices.[29] The first notable feature of the Walker system is that it takes for granted that women are the presumptive subjects of cosmetic haircare and that hair subject to prescribed forms of care belongs to women. This concession to the gender ideology of market capitalism is one of several contradictions that I will point out. Nonetheless, Walker's system has come to my attention because of its manifest value in the lives of black women who employ it within a regimen of self-care.

Walker's schema conjoins visual and haptic properties in ways that blur distinctions between the processes involved in growing, styling, and caring for hair (or leaving it alone) and their product: hair as an aspect of physical appearance that can only hypothetically be touched. Andre Walker, a celebrity hairstylist, came to prominence as the man behind Oprah Winfrey's hair in the 1980's.[30] Walker's photography-intensive 1997 book *Andre Talks Hair* articulated a four-part hair classification system (Type One: Straight, Type Two: Wavy, Type Three: Curly, Type Four: Kinky) with subtypes within each class that describe physical properties such as reflectivity, compressibility, heat tolerance, and moisture retention. While these properties are discernible within the everyday experiences of people across racialized and gendered lines, it is notable that intimate contact with black women's hair is the Walker system's point of departure. Oprah Winfrey ranks alongside Angela Bassett and Whoopi Goldberg with Type Four hair.[31] That the preponderance of black women inhabit Type Four, in the illustrations to his book and his examples, while white women and East Asian women populate Type One, is an apparently immaterial coincidence, according to Walker: "You can be African-American with naturally stick-straight hair, or you can be a kinky-haired Irish-American. And because our country is becoming such a multiracial hybrid, it just doesn't make sense anymore to stick to such rigid definitions."[32]

Walker rationale for disclaiming rigid racial classifications relies on a "grass-is-always-greener" hypothesis, which rests on a false equivalency. The parallelism in his statement above equates one set of the many national origins

[29] Andre Walker, *Andre Talks Hair* (New York: Simon and Schuster, 1997).
[30] Robbin McClain, "As Seen on TV: Andre Walker, *The Oprah Winfrey Show, American Salon*, June 1998, 85-86.
[31] Andre Walker, 34.
[32] Ibid, 26.

submerged within American whiteness with the complex, recombinant blend of ethnicities that makes up African-American (and, by extension, black and African Diasporic) racial identity. Because of the traumatic fragmentation of our knowledge regarding the ethnic heritage of our ancestors and the coerced patterns of reproduction that have produced our range of phenotypes, African-American descendants of slaves do not enjoy the same benign indeterminacy regarding the historical roots of our various hair textures, eye colors, and other phenotypes that Irish-Americans might. In the course of becoming African-Americans, black captives and their enslaved progeny experienced a conversion, en masse, from paradigms of identification grounded in ethnicity to a regime of subjection ordered by race.[33] Within this same regime, due to the conventions of hypodescent by which "one drop" of "black blood" can identify a person as black rather than white, the unlikely presence of kinky hair might have engendered life-changing shifts in racial belonging for an Irish-American and her or his descendants, at one point in history. Many historians would further emphasize that Irish-American is hardly interchangeable with "white" to the degree that African-American functions with respect to the term "black," in the same national context.[34]

To acknowledge that the Walker system is in fact grounded in pre existing understandings of racial identity, regardless of its author's intentions, is not the same thing as asserting that this system is necessarily serviceable to white supremacy. The naturalization of hair texture according to the Walker system unsettles racialized conventions, in part, because it ascribes the manageability and resistance of hair—that is, discipline—across a range of phenotypes. By making racialized differences in hair texture a matter of universal knowledge and subjective problem-solving, it demystifies haircare for the market as well as the individual. By revalorizing differences in ostensibly apolitical terms, the system elides some of the political significance of the acts performed in and through black hair—political significance that is made legible by other self-styled identity practices. Even in its efforts to evacuate hair texture of its racial, political meanings, therefore, the Walker system recalls how black women perform disidentification through self-fashioning: enacting a variety of relationships to power through the selective deployment of the various meanings that the popular imagination ascribes to the choices they make about their features.[35]

---

[33] Michael Gomez, *Exchanging Our Country Marks: The Transformation of African Identities in the Colonial and Antebellum South* (Chapel Hill: University of North Carolina Press, 1998), 3-4.

[34] Matthew Frye Jacobson, *Whiteness of a Different Color: European Immigrants and the Alchemy of Race* (Cambridge: Harvard University Press, 1999).

[35] José Esteban Muñoz, *Disidentifications: Queers of Color and the Performance of Politics* (Minneapolis: University of Minnesota Press, 1999).

At the very least, the Walker system takes part in undoing the pathology that describes varieties of black hair in its unvarnished state as inherently problematic by insisting, instead, that they can thrive with or without modification. On the terms of the dominant culture, however, "nappy" hair comprises as a demand for specific forms of care. In the same fashion, Ahmed and Stacey note that skincare regimens ultimately enumerate the ways in which "skin surfaces will always fail to be smooth" instead of attending to the various states, with or without modification, in which the skin acts as an interface with the world.[36] Knowledge made available through the hair and skin is only available insofar as it is touched by power, and it cannot escape politics. The studies and ongoing practices cited here demonstrate how skin and hair become overdetermined signs of racial, gender, age, and class identity when their meanings are constructed without deference to their bearers' agency.

Blue tone

Hair texture travels alongside and apart from skin color as an embodied and occasionally mutable phenotype subject to racial marginalization. Like skin color, hair texture has been fashioned into a shibboleth of essentialism, an archetype for resistance, and a site of self-care. Reifying these qualities has produced disastrous results in the lives of racialized and gendered subjects marked by them, including internalized oppression and violent pressure to conform. At the same time that the Walker system demonstrates how acts that reproduce authentic, authoritative knowledge about benign differences do not necessarily undermine racism, not all modes of self-fashioning that alter the embodied experience of identity are violent. Like haircare, skincare is often conscripted into the cultural politics of race, gender, class, and age in ways that construct the surface of the body as a source of information that must be disciplined into telling the truth. Emerging clinical discourse on differential skincare practices highlights how presenting moisturized skin functions as a means of performing health and self-knowledge in everyday life. By reifying the skin as the "true mirror of the age of a human being," research driven by corporations like L'Oreal, Procter & Gamble, and Unilever compel the skin to attest to its demand for treatment.[37] Some studies aim to reconcile the feminized practice of adhering to skincare regimens with the market imperative of expanding their consumer base by establishing criteria that mark untreated skin as a hindrance to the presentation of healthy masculinity.[38]

---

[36] Sara Ahmed and Jackie Stacey, "Introduction: Dermographies," in Thinking Through the Skin, 2.

[37] Hans Junginger, "Preface—Human Skin: The Medium of Touch," *Advanced Drug Delivery Reviews* 54, Supp. 1 (November 2002): S1.

[38] Keith Ertel, "Gender Differences in Attitudes and Practices Toward Body Skin Care," *Journal of the American Academy of Dermatologists* 60.3, Supp. 1 (March 2009): AB85.

Others incorporate black knowledge about skincare into treatment regimens by appropriating black vernacular—namely, using the term "ashy" to refer to dryness—as a way of performing the internalization of a value system that places a premium on the presentation of moisturized skin.[39] While apparently shedding the negative connotations of terms like "nappy" and "ashy" by recuperating their descriptive value, these gestures also deactivate the terms' power to invoke an intimate, intra-racial discursive space in order to place them in an objective, disciplinary frame of reference.

Whereas the practices of moisturizing and natural haircare are fraught with the risk of losing racially-specific knowledge and techniques of self-care as they become commoditized, the practice of skin bleaching has a powerful legacy that extends beyond the violence it performs to the capacity of the body to tell truths about racial identity. As patterns observed in the history of hair straightening would suggest, skin bleaching is driven by economic and political forces that operate at the structural level where racial formation takes place as well as the individual and sub-individual scale on which self-presentation occurs. In the course of presenting and mediating discernible ethnic features, individuals employ ethical, medical, cultural, and intimate frames of reference to negotiate the racial systems that lend their physical features social significance.[40] Though it is challenging to reconcile a critique of the gendered structural racism that incentivizes light skin with the attention to the tactical and subjective priorities of the individuals who pursue these advantages, deference to these individuals' agency demands that we construct knowledge about skin bleaching in the same conscientious way that has proven viable for understanding hair straightening.

In literature, George Schuyler's prescient satire *Black No More* and memoirs by Toi Derricotte and Marita Golden speak to color complexes at the level of the skin.[41] These and other texts attest to dark and light skin as sites of knowledge production within blackness, and it would be compelling to explore them in another venue as counterpoint to the quasi-scientific knowledge that currently seeks to stake truth claims regarding skin color and texture. At present, it should be possible to draw some inferences that link the politics of

---

[39] Anthony Jeralis, Greg Nole, and Jamie Regan, "Effect of Moisturizing Treatments on Dry Skin of Whites and African Americans," *Journal of the American Academy of Dermatology* 60. 3, Supp. 1 (March 2009): AB68, and Li Feng and Stacy Hawkins, "A Novel Lipid-Rich Moisturizing Body Wash Reduces Clinical Ashiness in Skin of Color Subjects," *Journal of the American Academy of Dermatology* 64.1, Supp. 1 (February 2011): AB59.

[40] Yaba Blay, "Skin Bleaching and Global White Supremacy: By Way of Introduction," *Journal of Pan African Studies* 4.4 (June 2011): 4-46.

[41] Toi Derricotte, *The Black Notebooks: An Interior Journey* (New York: Norton, 1997) and Marita Golden, *Don't Play in the Sun: One Woman's Journey Through the Color Complex* (New York: Doubleday, 2004).

hair and skin texture to skin color by drawing on the lessons learned from the inquiries above. Black hair, in its natural state or as the subject of alteration, resists its construction as "hair that fails to be straight." Similarly, as dark skin resists its construction as "skin that fails to be light" on the bodies of persons who present it, it also becomes skin that yields to bleaching, on the bodies of other persons. It may do both for the same individual, as skin-lightening products have been marketed for the purpose of concealing blemishes or rendering the skin's color uniform across an individual's face or body parts.[42] By transposing the significance of part of the body onto the identity of the whole individual, marking him or (more often) her as "fair," "healthy," "typical" or "atypical," or even "natural," alterations to skin color and hair texture alike highlight how racial identification depends on the mediation of ethnic signifiers situated on the surface of the body.

The politics of skin texture are not only vexed by the troubled past of skin color and hair texture but also by the future. Differentials in the biophysical properties of the skin may come to supplement differentials of color among the ways in which we perform racial identity through our bodies.[43] As science works toward a concept of the skin as a "smart biological interface", what practices will militate against the legacies of oppression bound up in the construction of smart subjects and "dumb" matter?[44] The clinical studies that portray "ashy" skin as a need for treatment tend to use the term interchangeably with the word "ashen," recapitulating an obstacle to communicating knowledge about skin texture and appearance in racially differentiated language communities.[45] As many black writers who have worked with white editors and publishers can attest, "ashy" is not a synonym or corruption of "ashen," yet the disciplines that propagate knowledge differentiating language communities in racial terms and the commodity-driven knowledge practices that produce skincare products seldom speak to one another. Finally, when it comes to the capacity of skin to register pain and the capacity of subjects to tolerate it, medical discourse reveals sharply racialized differentials in white practitioners' willingness to perform empathy with black people's need for

---

[42] Blay, 30.

[43] Neelam Muizzuddin, Lieveke Hellemans, Luc Van Overloop, Hugo Corstjens, Lieve Declercq, and Daniel Maes, "Structural and Functional Differences in Barrier Properties of African American, Caucasian, and East Asian Skin," *Journal of Dermatological Science* 59.2 (August 2010): 123-128.

[44] Shekhar Bhansali, H. Thurman Henderson, and Steven Hoath, "Probing Human Skin as an Information-Rich Smart Biological Interface Using MEMS Sensors" *Microelectronics Journal* 33.1-2 (January 2002): 121-127.

[45] Judith Nebus, Geoffry Smith, Ellen Kurtz, and Warren Wallo, "Alleviating Dry, Ashen Skin in Patients with Skin of Color" *Journal of the American Academy of Dermatology* 50.3, Supp. (March 2004): P77.

care.[46] These and other quandaries continue to politicize black skin—the skin of black individuals—as a substrate for haptic practices of racial knowledge, even as political rhetoric disavows the problems associated with observing race in the visual field by pronouncing colorblindness. Although colorblind ideology eschews knowledge about the skin's appearance by disavowing its reliance on visual perception, knowledge of skin texture proliferates with an undertheorized vigor. Perhaps knowing the skin through the sense of touch seems to evoke situations involving intimacy, reciprocity, and agency, rather than distant, disconnected visual surveillance? The process of apprehending knowledge about hair texture for public use suggests otherwise.

Like knowledge of hair texture and knowledge of skin color before it, constructing power/knowledge about skin texture involves staking ever more precise truth claims about deeply contested identity formations while marginalizing other ways of knowing through touch. Practices of self-care and vernacular frames of reference, such as intimacy, insofar as they allow racialized subjects to contest the defining power of meanings inscribed on our bodies, remain indispensable as venues for critical responses to dominant discourse on what blackness is and what it does. Thus, in the future, our critique of the biopolitics of race may benefit from cultural interventions inspired by considerations of skin texture, as the sense of touch attains a greater role in the propagation of racial knowledge and power.

Performances like "You Can Touch My Hair," the inspired counter-performance that enacted a live critique of its presumptions, the movement among black women to cultivate their natural hair, and haircare practices from Madam Walker to Andre Walker demonstrate that whom you allow to touch your body matters. Black women's interventions in culture and commerce have proven indispensable to confronting the forces implicated in the cultural politics of texture and resistance to certain forms of touch. The "Nappy Headed Blues" is a valuable touchstone for the cultural construction of the way it feels to be black, historically, but it has greater interpretive value in the present alongside performances that attest to the pleasure of having type four hair, kinky hair, hair that resists straightening. Whether our hair texture characterizes us in whole or in part, some of us are "happy to be nappy." [47]Likewise, there is pleasure in black skin, particularly when its texture becomes known through intimacy, but it likewise bears witness to pain. It breaks, bleeds, and scars. As a complement to pleasure and pain, there is a repertoire of resistance in the texture of our skin that makes the blues

---

[46] Sophie Trawalter, Kelly Hoffman, and Adam Waytz, "Racial Bias in Perceptions of Others' Pain," *PLoS One* 7.11 (November 2012): 1-8.

[47] Lola Ogunnaike, "Some Hair Is Happy to be Nappy," *New York Times*, December 27, 1998, and bell hooks, *Happy to Be Nappy* (New York: Jump at the Sun, 1999).

an appropriate idiom for its presentation. From its resistance to the sun to its whip-scarred history and propensity to keloids, the ways in which the skin covering our black bodies yields and does not yield attests to its commonly human yet uniquely individuated texture. To know that our skin is black is only to define a part of our bodies and a part of our blackness. By emphasizing what it means to know our touch, I insist that knowledge about our bodies belongs to us, as people who may choose to make our touch known or to deny that privilege.

Ted Daeschler

Invited Remarks at the Public Rally for the March for Science PHL

April 22, 2017
The Great Plaza at Penn's Landing

It is a great honor to be here with each of you for this wonderful celebration of science, and to discuss the immense impact that science has on the human condition. My name is Ted Daeschler. I am a paleontologist at the Academy of Natural Sciences and a Professor of Geosciences at Drexel University.

I study the earth and life on earth within a particularly long, evolutionary timeframe. In that context, mankind is a very recent player in a very long story. We are certainly unique animals – bipedal primates with large brains and dexterous hands, with a capacity to reflect on and synthesize information about our world.

But my interests lie deeper down the tree of life – beyond the origin of the primate body plan, beyond the origin of mammalian endothermy and reproductive strategy, beyond the branching point in the tree where mammals and reptiles share a common ancestor, to the beginnings of the evolutionary lineage of all limbed animals. Yes, the iconic "fish" coming out of the water..... Your inner fish!

Research into evolutionary history makes sense of biodiversity and places us within the beautifully complex tree of life. This knowledge has innumerable applications for medicine (things like genetics, anatomy, physiology, and developmental biology). Evolutionary history documents how life has interacted with changing environments informing issues of sustainability and adaptation, conservation, and even philosophy.

An evolutionary perspective also demonstrates that we are threads in the tapestry of life on earth – interconnected to the complex ecological interactions of all life on this verdant planet.

Scientific inquiries into the patterns and processes of biological change, ecological change and geological change are especially relevant to sustaining living conditions for mankind, and all life. It is clearly in our own self-interest to maintain the diversity of life that underpins the planet's ecosystems and supports us in so many ways.

These fundamental truths (derived from scientific inquiry of our connections in the tree of life and our co-evolutionary history with life-sustaining earth systems) comes with a relatively small public investment in science and education, but, I would argue, brings foundational knowledge and perspectives for shaping the quality of the human condition.

I get to do my science at field sites across the world and within the walls of the Academy of Natural Sciences at 19th and the Parkway. The Academy is a library of life and laboratory of environmental change built during more than 200 years of enlightened science focused on exploration, description and preservation of the natural world.

I am fortunate to work in such an esteemed institution in a remarkable city for science. Just outside my office are two gleaming white cabinets with Thomas Jefferson's Fossil Collection. Among his many interests, Jefferson sought to document the variety of life in North America, even from the unusual fossil remains of animals that no one had ever seen alive.

Jefferson's political rivals belittled his interest in scientific inquiry of these prehistoric remains. To those critics Jefferson answered as follows:

"Of all the criticisms brought against me by my political adversaries, that of possessing some science has probably done them the least credit. Our countrymen are too enlightened themselves to believe that ignorance is the best qualification for their service."

"Ignorance" is this context seems to be the inability or unwillingness to hear evidence-based inquiry that can inform issues of the day.

Did Thomas Jefferson have more confidence in his fellow citizens to recognize the importance of science than we have today? Although I believe most people today would acknowledge the importance of science, they, and many scientists, may not concede that science has a social and political component. As much as we want to believe that the value of science is self-evident, it seems we cannot take that for granted!

To encourage better understanding, all of us need to communicate our science and its impact to our fellow citizens. No ivory towers, we need to get out into the classrooms, town halls and corridors of democracy to join public debate and inform others about the impacts of our work.

To conclude, the most important thing to me about science is the perspective it brings that we are part of something so much larger than human society. Science connects us to the earth and life on earth in profound ways. As such, science is critical for understanding the past, managing the present, and ensuring a healthy future for all.

Thank you.

Timothy Fitts

Does Anything Beautiful Emerge?

Jackson was intent on catching a bullfrog. He said it was easy. All you had to do was estimate the direction of the frog's leap and time it to the exact moment of the frog's reaction. Then you had it. You have to sneak up on it, but once you do that, all you had to do was predict the time and direction.

"No shit," Fisher said.

"You got a better plan?"

"Yeah, a net."

The three boys had gotten sidetracked at the pond while walking to the school. They had decided on the location after Marlon told them that the janitors always left the side door open on the far end of the church. He and his neighbor had gone in last week. They had taken the shortcut by the soccer field and walked up Old Tyler Road. They had made their way into the girl's locker room, rifled through the desks of all the teachers, and even found a chamber above the pulpit where you could observe the congregation on Sunday mornings without anybody knowing. Once you got into the church, all you had to do was wander through the halls to the back, and the door connecting to the school didn't even have a lock. It was that easy, Marlon told them, and they headed off. But after they trekked down Savoy from Jackson's house, they turned up on South Saunders Road and heard a water sound where the drain from the pond emptied into a ditch. "Shit," Jackson said. "Those are bullfrogs," and jumped down to have a closer inspection.

Jackson said if they could get one bullfrog, they could cut it up, tie the pieces to milk jugs, and catch a bunch of snapping turtles. They could all sneak out at night and meet up. They could jump the fence and put the jugs out into the water. Come back in the morning and get the turtles.

"What are we going to do with snapping turtles?" Fisher asked.

"Sell'em," Jackson said. "Plenty of people would buy snapping turtles. Everybody wants a snapping turtle."

Marlon said nobody's going to catch a bullfrog with their bare hands, and nobody's going to catch a snapping turtle. You could try your whole life and you wouldn't be able to do it. If you wanted a bullfrog, you had to come out at

night with a gig and a flashlight, and then you look for beady red eyes, and the light beam paralyzes them. That's when you stick them. But you have to have your bucket and your jugs all ready. You don't do one thing on one day then the other thing another day. Plus, you don't do any of it unless you have a *market*. If you know somebody who wants a snapping turtle, then you do it. You do it if the price they are willing to pay is worth the time and effort and your expenses. "You don't go to all the trouble with the vague hope that you *might* find somebody willing to buy a snapping turtle. Sure, people out there want to buy snapping turtles, but do you know them personally?"

"I'll figure out who," Jackson said.

"Besides," Marlon said, "we come here at night, walk around with flashlights, somebody's liable to start shooting at us with rock salt."

"Marlon's a p***y," Jackson said.

"You two are small time," Marlon said. "Bullfrogs. Snapping turtles."

"Forget about the bullfrogs," Fisher said, suggesting they keep on walking to the school. They should go inside and turn everything upside down. "We should steal all the chalk and erasers."

"Smash all the mirrors in the bathroom," Jackson said.

They thought about other types of mayhem. They mused upon going into the walk-in refrigerator, dumping milk on all of the carpets and making the entire building stink, turn over the library shelves, change all of the grades, or steal the gradebooks altogether, bend the legs of the chairs so they all wobbled. Fisher said they should steal some toilet paper from the janitor's closet and roll some houses. Buy a couple dozen eggs at the grocery store.

"Again, small time," Marlon said.

"Again, Marlon's a p***y," Jackson said.

Marlon said he wasn't a p***y, it's just that all of their ideas ended up making their own lives more difficult. Stinking up their own classrooms rooms with rancid milk, sitting in uneven chairs, making pissed off teachers regrade them. Marlon said he wasn't a p***y, but if he was going to do something at all, he was going to do it big. He wasn't going to trash any classrooms, break any mirrors or anything like that. If he was going to do anything, he was going to go big. All that stuff was petty vandalism. If he was going to f*** with them, he was going to f***with them. You could burn the whole school down in an hour.

"Less than an hour," Marlon said. "Guaranteed. All you have to do is pull the fire alarm, get everybody out, and burn the place down. I can get some sodium from my dad's lab. We could pack the sodium in a shell of sugar and flush a couple cubes down the toilet. By the time the sugar melts, all hell breaks loose. Or we could sneak in some gasoline, hide it in the janitor's closet on Friday, show up Saturday morning, climb up into the ceiling tiles and pour it down the inside of the walls. We do it on all four corners of the school. Keep the windows shut so the fumes build up. Flush the sodium, leave a trail of rubbing alcohol to the hallway. You could make the place one big bomb. Turn the place into an actual inferno." Marlon then presented the other two with an image. The school itself, three stories high, one hundred fifty feet in length, burning from all sides, flames catching wind and forming a vortex. He told them that it is entirely possible during forest fires for the wind to create small tornadoes consisting solely of flame. "Imagine that," Marlon said. "Our school, a monolith of fire licking the sky. It would be like the Earth opening up and swallowing that shithole," Marlon said. "If we do anything at all, we do something big, like that."

Just two years prior, the boys had practiced school spirit with nationalistic fervor. They wore their Shades Mountain Bible soccer uniforms all day after games, green Adidas jerseys with white shorts with the built-in jock and the three stripes down the side. The varsity team had won the State finals two consecutive years, and students at Shades Mountain Bible Academy walked with pride. In the autumn and winter they donned nylon green jackets with an Eagle patch sewn to the back and chevrons stitched to the sleeves signifying years of athletic service.

But then things took a turn. Newschannel 6 showed up one weekday morning at Shades Mountain Bible after Pastor Vincent had delivered a mandate that each student bring to school an item that causes him or her to stumble in their Walk with the Lord. And by stumble, Pastor Vincent explained that it could be anything – not just dirty magazines, chewing tobacco, televisions, or rock albums, but anything that distracted you from your quiet time, your tithing, your prayer life, your anything. It could be a bicycle, favorite shirt, favorite socks, favorite cereal. If you awoke in the morning thinking about cereal before Jesus, bring in the cereal.

In a single day, the school's fortune shifted. Newschannel 6 created a montage of images – students standing behind shimmering heat waves and smoke, teachers tossing baseball gloves and money onto the pile of char, a shot of Pastor Vincent observing his handiwork, standing stoic behind a sheet of white smoke. The exodus of normal students concentrated the children of fanatics, and those left behind could feel their skin bluing in the Appalachian foothills, the sounds of banjos emanating from the woods across the street.

The finances of the school also plummeted, and to make up the tuition gap, the school began taking on a disproportionate number of students who had been expelled from public schools, establishing an undercurrent of vice ranging from pot to pills, and even a sixteen year-old eighth grader who had caused one of the star cheerleaders to hemorrhage.

Marlon said they were better off walking around Bluff Park collecting deposit bottles and blowing their loot at Wizard's Palace, spending the afternoon playing *Dig Dug* or *Tron*. At least they would go home and not have to worry about whether or not they were going to JDC or some kind of bullshit like that – live their lives like criminals and worry all the goddamn time. "We go to the school, we burn it down, or we don't go at all," he said. "We can siphon some gas from the lawnmower at my house. We don't need much. Get the gas, we go."

Jackson pointed to a snout poking out from beneath a rock in the small pool where the drain emptied. "That's a bullfrog," he said. "Get it," he said to Fisher.

Jackson pointed to a spot where one of the rocks jutted out at the bottom, with a small crevice covered with algae. It was difficult for any of them to determine whether what Jackson saw was a rock or one of the bullfrogs. Fisher said if he wanted a bullfrog so bad, he could get it himself.

Jackson said he couldn't believe that he had friends that were such cowards and removed his socks and shoes, stepped in the water, and caught his balance on a piece of sandstone that crumbled to the touch, sinking Jackson immediately to his knees, muck halfway up his shins. Heightening his embarrassment, when Jackson looked up, behind Marlon and Fisher, he saw the open passenger-side window of his uncle Runner's Pontiac Sunbird Sport Coupe.

"What are you idiots doing?" the voice said from inside the Pontiac.

"Catching bullfrogs," Fisher said.

Jackson told Fisher to shut it and climbed out of the muck.

"Come on," Runner said. "Get in the car."

"What for?" Jackson said.

Runner stepped from the car and approached the three boys, Jackson's feet covered in black and green. "Wash those feet before getting in the car."

Jackson stepped back in the water and shook his feet. Runner told him to cut the crap, and forced Jackson into a sitting position and scooped water onto Jackson's shins, rubbing the grime from his feet and between his toes. Runner stepped back to the car and took a towel from the trunk and wiped Jackson's feet dry. "Now, get in the car. All of you."

"What I do?" Jackson said. "Did mom send you to pick me up?"

"There's a fight at the church," Runner said. "It's going to be big."

"Our church?" Jackson said.

"No. The Baptist church. Andy Moseman is fighting some guy that used to go to your school. We gotta get there before it starts. We have to see this thing."

Runner pulled a three-point turn and took off towards Savoy, passing Jackson's house on the back way to John's Convenience Store to pick up a pack of cigarettes. When he got back in the car, he packed his cigarettes and said that somebody at the fight was going to have a chain. That's what he heard. It could be Moseman. It could be the other guy.

"What kind of chain?" Fisher said.

"I don't' know," Runner said. "A *chain*."

"A bike chain?"

"Who cares?" Jackson said.

"Not a bike chain," Runner said. "Just a chain. Don't worry about it."

Marlon said that the Bible says that if you attack a country, you should destroy every single person in the country. You have to have a total cleanse. Otherwise, the war goes on forever. Runner said they weren't going to see a war. They were going to see a fight.

"You still don't show up to a fight with a chain. What is the person going to do with the chain? Is he going to kill the other guy?"

"Probably," Runner said. "Why else would you bring a chain? Why else would we go see it?"

Fisher said if you hit someone with a chain, the other person could just grab it and pull you closer.

Marlon said if you bring anything to a fight, you bring a gun. If it comes to it, you kill the other person. Otherwise, don't bring anything. But if you beat somebody with a chain, that person, and their friends, and their parents, and their children, and their children's children, are going to come back and exact revenge a hundred fold. You bring a chain, you win one fight, but the rest of your life is misery.

"Who are these guys?" Runner asked out loud to the three in the back, then hit the gas and drove toward the Baptist church.

Runner was ten years younger than Jackson's mother, almost young enough to look like her son. Runner had dropped out of high school after getting his girlfriend pregnant and had started working at a sheet metal factory in Bessemer. He used to show up at Jackson's house regularly for dinner. After his girlfriend had the baby removed and left him, Runner showed up less frequently and usually unannounced. When he did show up, he brought barbecue or a bag of hamburgers from Jack's and would talk about how much he loved his job as a sheet metal worker. He told Jackson's family that he was going to go into sales once he put his time in. Sheet metal was big business. He told Jackson's family sheet metal was his calling. He told them he knew this to be true when he first saw fresh stacks of aluminum slabs, and they shined so clear and alive that he ran his hands across the surface, and it was like the metal had spoken to him in secret code transmitted through his fingertips. He told them that when aluminum is molten, it does not glow like iron or steel, but holds its color. Jackson noticed that his uncle's eyes watered as he talked about this world. Runner said that he was not sure why, but this trait in an element was a thing to admire, and the smelting process is so hot and smoky and oppressive that you cannot imagine anything so beautiful emerges. He sat up and told Jackson's family that he didn't even feel normal unless it's a thousand degrees and he's dripping with sweat.

After dinner, Runner showed Jackson how to smoke pot. He told Jackson it was the best education you could get, but Jackson was unsure of whether Runner was referring to the weed or the aluminum.

"It's simple, and it's everything," Runner said. "You don't learn it from school, and you don't learn it from p***y. You almost learn it from p***y, but p***y burns you. It's this. This is what I am talking about," but Jackson was still unsure about what 'this' thing was; he felt as if a layer of film had been placed between his mind and his thoughts, and all he could think about was terror. He thought about botulism and wild dogs, and all the accidents at the plant Runner had told him about. Stifling heat and smoke, fingers snipped like putty, thumbs and raw skull against sharp edges and unmovable objects, whole patches of skin peeled from forearms and faces, the sight of raw bone.

The filter in Jackson's psyche, the film, remained fixed, and Jackson wondered if he would ever come down, or if this was just the new him.

At the Baptist church, cars had lined up around the perimeter, and a crowd had gathered in the middle of the parking lot like a rock festival. People walked around without aim, girls wearing concert shirts, tits on all of them. The crowd grew dense at the middle, but it was impossible to tell who was fighting, or if the people fighting were in their respective camps, or if they had even arrived. All three of the boys felt the tension of some great possibility. Many of the teenagers walked on tiptoes, straining to look over the heads of their peers, also trying to figure out who was where, and what was going to happen, and Runner told the three boys to climb a tree, or stay around the edges. Just get a good place to watch and stay out of the way. Somebody had already ambled up the angled concrete supports of the church, and crawled monkey-style up the rooftop at sixty degrees, all along the tiles to the apex, where the church suggested a steeple, but now featured a late teen in blue jeans, hands gripping the peak and legs dangling over the edge.

A couple of teenagers told the boys to stand on the hood of their car, a 1971 Dodge Dart, and the view opened up before them. Two cars, a sky blue Chevy Nova and rusted out red Volkswagen Rabbit, had been parked in the center of the crowd forming an impromptu pit. More girls in concert shirts. More tits. Moccasin boots laced all the way up with fritters. But then the crowd parted, and a tall preppie walked to the center. Marlon knew him from the way he walked, a slight bow in his legs. Nelson Hadley, the goalie of their varsity soccer team. State champ. Nelson had been a part of the exodus after the burning of worldly goods. Marlon recalled a moment during the bonfire, where Jimbo Parsons had emptied a sack of worldly goods onto the heap before the pile was ignited, including a can of beer he had drained on the way to school and a porno. The leaves of the magazine had flapped open, and Marlon remembered catching a quick glimpse of a blonde woman on her knees, hands tied behind her back while she performed fellatio on a man painted purple with an oversized helmet, looking part spaceman, part light bulb. Marlon remembered Nelson, too, taking offense to this and getting in Jimbo Parson's face, demanding to know exactly what Jimbo wanted to accomplish. Participate, or stay home, he shouted at Jimbo Parsons. *Participate* or stay home. This is not a game. This is not entertainment.

Nelson Hadley was considered by the students at their school, as well as the coaches and most of the parents, to be a true athlete. Once, during the semi-finals of the state soccer tournament, with the game on the line, the opposing team had kicked a corner. The ball veered way out to the edge of the penalty box, then turned inward. While players from opposing teams jumped to head the ball either direction, the figure of Nelson Hadley's torso had risen

above the players, scooping the ball to his chest, then somersaulting over the shoulders of his opponents, careless of whose head and feet and elbows might be out for him, then landed on his back, tightening into a fetal position, before rising and booting the ball deep into enemy territory. He spat a wad of blood to the ground. Marlon remembered seeing the blood bounce off the dusty surface of the soccer field, reflecting in the afternoon sun like a discarded jewel. Game over. Nelson Hadley also pitched Pony League baseball, ran cross-country, and had placed two consecutive years in the Vulcan Run. Now, he danced on bare feet with the sleeves of his Izod royal blue velour shirt pulled up to his elbows.

"Look at that," Fisher said to Marlon and Thomas, pointing to two people standing next to a green Kawasaki dirt bike. One of them stood tall, taller than Nelson Hadley. Marlon said the next guy, the small guy, was Andy Moseman, who was crazy. Small and stocky. Marlon looked at his friends and said that Moseman lived two blocks over, and once he saw Moseman getting high from the fumes of his bike. Marlon told the others that he had seen him in his driveway, staring at his grandmother, who watched him from their front porch while he huffed gasoline straight from the tank of his motorcycle, the siphon held to a single nostril until he passed out. Other things were common knowledge about Andy Moseman. He had fallen from the bluffs on Shades Crest Road, fifty feet to granite, cushioned by a layer of autumn leaves, only to get up and walk away with a chipped tooth. He had been hit by a car, and made the papers two years before after he had beaten up the father of two girls in the Skate World parking lot.

Moseman walked towards the parking lot with his helmet on, his eyes shaded by a black visor. His stocky frame waddled, swinging his hips awkwardly as he walked – his feet, in a pair of blue and yellow Nike LDVs, moved faster than his body. As he approached the pit and the two cars, he removed his helmet. Moseman's shoulder length hair fell out, framing a face impossibly packed with pimples – ridges and inflammation clear and defined from fifty yards away, a face pulsing and bulging with pus. Moseman held the helmet his with his right hand, then brought it down hard against Nelson Hadley's extended forearm. The crowd surged forth and turned into a sound of collective awe, terror and glee, while Moseman's arm swung with machine like precision, rapid fire, knocking down Nelson's arm and connecting with Nelson's orbital bone, driving him to the ground. The boys wondered if the blows had killed Hadley. He had fallen backward, and his head bounced on the pavement. Both of his arms raised in a slight begging position, as if his nerves had taken over.

The crowd reminded Marlon of the scene of the bonfire, the same intensity. He remembered seeing Pastor Vincent walking along the outskirts of the scene, his suppressed joy at Newschannel 6's appearance, and the

regional attention the event would garner. Marlon could see Pastor Vincent formulating a sermon in his mind at that very moment. People would jeer, people would ridicule them for their righteousness. Let them. First purification, then longsuffering. If people wanted to laugh, let them laugh. If people wanted to mock, let them mock.

However, later that day, after the burning, the look over Pastor Vincent's face had changed, and he had visited each individual classroom to speak his mind. He spoke to the students with frankness at his horror that morning, shuffling through their objects of worldly goods before dousing them with lighter fluid. "The level of your stumbling is frightening," Pastor Vincent had said to them. "Abhorrent. Prophylactics. Cigarettes. Rock albums. *Playboy*." Pastor Vincent looked at the classroom and seemed to make eye contact with each student simultaneously. "What troubles me is that you don't even know what you did today. My fear is that those who will mock us will be none other than yourselves."

Moseman turned around and faced the crowd of teenagers and grabbed himself. However, Hadley came to. The boys saw him vomit, then get to his knees and take in his surroundings. Blood covered the side of Hadley's face and neck, but still, he raised himself to his feet, and it was not until that point that he appeared to be aware of the situation, and the blood coating his face and neck, blackening his royal blue velour shirt, was his own. Somehow, he stood, but before he could land a punch to the side of Moseman's turned head, he was pulled back by a rush of teenagers, who slammed him against the side of the sky blue Chevy Nova. His velour shirt came apart in strips, and the boys saw that the blood and had soaked through to his torso as well. In the pocket of mayhem, the boys saw Runner make a move forward, delivering a few lightning fast body blows of his own to Nelson's ribs, followed by an open handed slap to the face. That's when the boys saw that Runner was right, Moseman did have a chain, a thin chain, five or so feet in length, designed as a dog leash. Moseman wrapped the around his hand like a whip, striping Hadley's back and shoulders, until the crowd was upon them, dense and pressing, then popped loose like wild atoms, punctured with the modulating pulse of a squad car.

That night, Marlon awoke to a scraping sound in his room. A soft grind, slowly scratched, as if someone stood in the dark dragging the edge of a sheet of typing paper against the surface of his dresser drawer. The sound stopped, and just before he re-entered his slumber, the sound picked up again. It was difficult for him to tell if the aural image resulted from a cockroach or a mouse, but the timbre struck a nerve that allowed neither sleep nor proper relaxation. The sound seemed to Marlon bigger than a cockroach but smaller than a mouse or a rat. The sound stopped again, but he had awoken. He looked at the ceiling and could see colors swirling in his vision, greens and yellows,

and orange and red and a flare of bright orange dots that shifted from defined patterns to a blur. When he closed his eyes, he found himself thinking about Nelson Hadley and replayed the scene in his mind from that afternoon. Marlon wondered if maybe was dead, maybe he was in a coma. He wanted to ask his parents if they had heard anything on the news but knew that question would lead to many other questions. He closed his eyes again and imagined Nelson at Parisian's walking around with his parents, trying on Izod velours. Marlon imagined Nelson's mother giving him a burgundy sweater, telling him to try it on, then handing him the same one in green, and then blue, then trying a size larger, then a size smaller, and his mother asking the salesperson fold the sweater in white tissue inside the cardboard box. But it probably didn't happen like that at all. Nelson's mother probably bought the velour sweater for him while he was at school without even mentioning it to him. She probably just brought home the shirt and hung it up in his closet. Who knows, Marlon thought. It could have been hanging there for weeks.

Valerie Fox

November Nightmare

My bag disappeared
with my passport, my keys
a little vial containing
a sliver of bone.

I was stalked by an ordinary man.

My bag reappeared on a table
like at an airport.
Stained. Light as air.
All that remained was a plastic comb
and some pennies.

I got separated from my daughter.
I had to sit across from a man
making super-small talk,
trying to keep me there
as long as possible.

It wasn't my trauma it was somebody else's.

I couldn't have my bag back
even though it was only a limp husk.
An official person went upstairs
and threw it overboard.

This happened. There was a splash.

Henry Israeli

Our Age of Anxiety

Many have taken off their white shirts
and are waving them in the air.
I've come so far I hardly have to talk
or walk anymore. Soon I'll be able to conduct
my business without leaving my bed. Still,
our very existence is endangered by one lonely rat
chewing on a wire. Turns out nothing so much as
the old country resembles the new country.
Turns out there are no ghosts, just pixelated .
monsters roaming our homes, our streets,
grinning, mocking, floating between us wherever we go.
It's all part of an algorithm generated in Moscow.
They tell me my love for the natural world threatens
the corporate dream of annihilation.
I long for the days I was oblivious as a dandelion.
Ever since I woke up on the floor
of a vacant factory I've felt myself entangled
in radio waves, in this aftermath.
I'm scared of the government's fear of me
for where do I stand on the most important issues?
I don't stand for anything; that's their point, isn't it?

Miriam Kotzin

Bluff Note: Desdemona's Handkerchief

Who would have thought that such a flimsy scrap—
though cleverly embroidered—would undo
so many caught in sly Iago's trap?
He took the straight and made it seem askew.

Iago killed directly, too. His sword
dispatched Roderigo (duped and then betrayed).
Emilia, faithful wife, though she adored
Iago? Skewered on his blade.

Othello smothered Desdemona who
was innocent though he believed that she
had screwed around with Cassio. On cue
O killed himself to end the tragedy.

They could have all been spared this bloody bother
had only Desde listened to her father

Miriam Kotzin

Emily

1.from the introduction to Emily Dickinson's letters by Mabel Loomis Todd

The lovers eager
(a passing mood),

she kept no journal.
Far-away

in her garden,
dark finger-tips

hold a shadow.

2. from the introduction to Emily Dickinson's letters by Thomas H. Johnson

The husbandry of mornings
and afternoons aside

delayed (perhaps a day or two)
approaching death.

She was still.

At the end of a tether.
habit, thread-tied, held.

3. from the Introduction to The Master Letters edited by R.W. Franklin

The heart a little distant
claims few Prerogatives—
nothing more destroyed.

To slant the Truth—
no mention
of obscured Uncertainty—
stray marks have been ignored.

Miriam Kotzin

Tiger Lilies

Across the woodland floor a flame
of tiger lilies flares, a distant blaze
I spot while passing by. What becomes
of fire drenched in watery light?

This afternoon the light streams
through trembling leaves. Below the canopy
a shadow darts, shakes out a dark
disturbance. Just a bird in flight?
What kind of bird could make its simple
passage through a clearing seem
a flash of coming night?

Miriam Kotzin

To a Man From Last Season
After William Shakespeare's Sonnet 18

Shall I compare thee to an Autumn's day?
No way, old friend. You are intemperate.
You stuff your face; swill down the suds. You may
go home with sluts who seek a paying date--
or maybe not, since you're so cheap. Sun shines
and lights what you would hide in shadows, dimmed:
Your life's in disarray. Your stock declines.
You leave your hair and graying beard untrimmed
and bleach your ripped blue jeans to shreds to fade
them to imagined fashion. You're the lowest
on any list of "extra" men. Your shade
spreads empty poolside. Is that weed that grow'st
along thy sill?
                    —I'd give my all to see
another perfect Autumn's Day with thee.

Miriam Kotzin
Upstream

Under the sand was something smooth and cool they said was clay. We liked to dig and hold it in our small fists, squish it through our fingers. I wondered how it could be molded into anything. I couldn't believe it would hold a shape. Still it was something to do, finding it. The clay wasn't everywhere, or if it was, we couldn't always reach it. I've never figured that out.

We liked to watch the small schools of minnows and the tadpoles that swam in the shallows. Even though the tadpoles grew legs we never saw any frogs.

The beach was about fifty yards long, Jersey sand. Pines and oaks surrounded the beach and across the river it was all woods. The river disappeared into woods to the right and to the left. We would have been amazed to see a canoe on our stretch of the river, though it would have had as much right to be there as we did.

The big kids danced in a wooden building, feeding nickels into the jukebox next to counter where a man sold food. My favorite thing to get was a pretzel stick with yellow mustard for two cents and a dime coke in a bottle that I had to return even though they didn't charge a deposit.

If it rained suddenly we all ran into the shack and heard the rain on the tin roof, but we hardly ever got caught in the rain. If it wasn't a perfect day, we didn't go there. So almost all I remember were summers of perfect days.

Here the Maurice River ran neither fast nor deep, though it got deeper where it curved out of sight in the woods. We were supposed to stay within sight of the beach, and not head upstream over towards what everyone called Dobie, but I don't know why. When we waded towards Dobie the cedar water came up to my chest and then my neck, and all but once I turned back.

Boys used to climb the trees across from the beach and jump into the water. They didn't dive, of course, just jump, and as far as I know none of them ever got hurt climbing and jumping. We would have heard because it was the sort of place where whatever happened, eventually, everyone knew about it even when it was supposed to be a big secret.

Birds. Of course. But most of the time I wasn't conscious of them. They were just part of the beach sound of people talking and the music floating out of the shack. Only once did I ever hear the birds. Marsha Cohen had talked me into going up towards Dobie. I'd turned twelve two weeks before and she was exactly six months younger, but we were in the same grade and were best friends. We walked single file. I went first.

It was July and hot. The cedar water was cool and the riverbed was smooth-even the rocks on the bottom were worn round. When we walked towards the first bend I turned and looked back. The beach wasn't that far away, but it looked like one world in the woods and another in the clearing where everyone was sitting. In the woods we could really hear the birds. I wouldn't say they were singing, just making bird sounds. The only one I recognized was a crow and I couldn't see it, just heard it calling from a distance.

The river here was different in that the bank was about a foot above the river, and the water, as I said, came up over the top of my suit and then up to my neck. If the river had been faster it might have been hard to walk upstream. It would have been easier to go in the other direction, but anyway we knew that going back to the beach would be easier when we went with the current. After we got out of sight of the beach, Marsha said maybe we should go back, but I didn't want to. We argued about it for a while, and I told her it had been her idea so she shouldn't be a baby now, and we kept walking upstream towards Dobie. Once or twice I asked her if she heard voices coming from ahead of us, but she said she didn't. It was my imagination. Marsha walked slower than I did, and she was getting farther behind me the longer we walked. I didn't mind, and I didn't think she did either. I'm sure she never told me to wait up for her or anything else like that.

The trees here reached all the way across the river. We could hardly see the sky, but what we could see was bright blue. The sunlight came through the leaves and made spotlights on the river. The cedar water was so clear we could see our feet. I wished I'd come here before. I liked walking upstream and not talking. It was like being alone but not as scary.

I held my hands out to the side and picked my feet up and let the current carry me back downstream. It was like sitting on the most comfortable chair ever. I floated that way, backwards. I thought I'd bump into Marsha unless she was floating too. But when I turned around she wasn't there. I hollered her name and I thought I heard her say something, but what I don't know. It didn't sound like an echo. I don't know if I was mad or scared or both. But I wasn't going to go back just because she did. I stopped floating and walked upstream again until I got to a place where there was more sun, a sort of clearing and

it was so pretty I forgot to be afraid. Even though I'd been hot before, after walking in the river for a while the sun felt good. I ducked under the water and came up. My hair stuck to my neck and shoulders and I held my face up to the sun.

I let the water carry my weight and I jumped up and down, bobbing for a while in one place trying not to go back down stream yet. I thought I'd walk just a little farther and then turn back before I got into trouble with my mother. I hoped Marsha wouldn't say where I was. This was her idea.

Up ahead the trees shaded the river again, and I walked looking at my feet because I'd seen a branch under water. I didn't want to get hurt. I figured I'd go just around the next bend to see what was there (more trees probably) though I'd heard of an old farmhouse along here, mostly fallen down. That's what the kids said though really I didn't know anyone who'd actually been here. I decided I'd give myself about ten minutes at most to get to the bend where I'd turn around. I'd have to guess about the ten minutes because I didn't have a watch.

And then a splash behind me, and as I was turning to see what, shouts and four more jumped out of the trees into the river. They were laughing and calling to one another. At first I was just glad they hadn't landed on me, but then they surrounded me. I didn't recognize them from the beach or anywhere else. They were naked and standing too close to me. One of them said something about my bathing suit and they all laughed. They started grabbing at me and the straps of my suit. One of them held my hair from behind so I couldn't move my head. I kicked at them. My fingernails weren't long and when I tried to slap them, the one whose arm I hit said I wanted to touch him. They tugged at my straps and held my wrists and pulled my bathing suit down to my waist, and they touched me and kept pulling at my suit until it was all the way down, and then they got it off me and tossed it up on the bank and did things to me that hurt, all of them hurting me until they got tired of it and left me standing naked in the river while they climbed up on the bank and put on their clothes, laughing, and ran off into the woods.

I could just reach my suit and got it on and went back down stream, running, pushed by the current right through the spot that had been sunny, but the sun had moved, and it wasn't sunny any more, and I kept going though I hit my leg against the branch and scraped my shin, but I didn't stop, and when I got near the beach a whole bunch of grownups were headed upstream with my mother and Marsha who was crying, too. I didn't want to say what happened in front of everyone, but I told my mother. And she made me go to a doctor probably because I was bleeding for a couple of days, not a period, but bleeding there. And after that things were different.

We didn't go to the beach for the rest of that summer or the next either. Marsha said she was sorry, but then after she apologized she didn't want to see me any more, and I didn't understand why. She hadn't been the one, I had. If it had been the other way around, I would have talked to her. I'm sure I would have. Besides, it would have happened sooner or later anyway. Or something would have. You're a woman, and you know what I mean. After all, even if you never told, you know what happened to you.

Lynn Levin

Baby and Gorilla

A new Spiffycuts has opened in town. They need someone to walk around the shopping center in a gorilla suit to spread the word, and I am the man for the job. Pay is off the books, less than minimum wage, a temp job, but I'm not choosy. My drug arrest makes it hard for me to pass a background check, and Spiffycuts hasn't asked too many questions.

On my first day, I shuffle to the back room where they store the towels and shampoo. The manager suits me up in my fur costume. One of the stylists fastens the yellow pinney that says "SPIFFYCUTS GRAND OPENING" in front and "CELEBRATION SPECIALS" on the back. I pull on the grinning gorilla mask.

"Hey, everyone, meet our newest associate," calls the manager. I practice my welcome wave as I big-foot it through the salon.

"Tell me I'm not going to leave here looking like him," jokes one lady.

"I think a vampire would attract a better class of customers. Don't you?" says another lady like she's a marketing expert or something.

I respond in character with some grunts and strike a fashion pose. Yeah, mock this big hairy beast all you want. He's going to do his monkey job and then wash dishes at the Greek diner afterward with the caballeros. I am practically a caballero myself, not very documented and working for cash.

I have a lot going for me as an ape. I like the outdoors, and it's April, so not too hot in the costume. The suit has a big plastic chest that makes me look mighty. Inside the big black pecs, my heart's a flat tire. I have a court date and a lame public defender. I could get sent upstate. Possession and receiving stolen property. Not that bad, but enough to f*** up the rest of my life.

Pointing to the announcements on my yellow pinney, wearing my big ape grin, I stroll up and down the shopping center, which also happens to be a drug hotspot. I see some of my old user friends. They have no idea it's me in the gorilla suit.

"Hey, Harambe," jeers a junkie named Weezer. "Where's Cecil the lion?"

I continue on my rounds, past the pizza shop, the pretzel place, the pay-day loans place, the hardware store, the urgent-care clinic. I wave to shoppers. Some wave back. Some even check out Spiffycuts.

You learn a lot about people when you're an ape. And the kids. Don't get me started on the kids. Some scream in terror when they see me. One kid hugged me. One kid kicked me. I acted wounded and wiped my gorilla eyes. "Be nice to the gorilla," the mom said. "There's a person in there."

Not that I see her very often, but with my mom it's always, "Grant, are you going to meetings? Grant, are you going to jail? Grant, are you still on methadone? Are you going to be on methadone for the rest of your life?"

So it's my last day as a gorilla. I'm waving my fond farewells to the shoppers when a teen mom appears. She's bug-eyed, jumpier than a grasshopper, higher than a drone. She's swinging a pink-and-blue-flowered diaper bag on one arm, and in the other arm, football style, she's carrying a tiny baby. Then she swings the diaper bag too high and twenty, maybe thirty, small wax paper bags fly out of her satchel. Plus a couple of diapers. She falls to her knees, puts the baby on the concrete, and scrambles to pick up her dope.

"What are you looking at?" she says. Her gaze is like the muzzle of a gun.

I hold out my arms for the baby and give what I think might be a gorilla daddy coo. I huff. I coo again. The girl figures out that she can give me the baby. It's a baby boy. He's wearing blue. He's crying now. I rock him. I've never felt so sad in all my days, or so human.

Richard McCourt

Life Finds a Way: Novel Algae in Reactor Cooling Pads

And we all thought that tardigrades were tough. These charming little Pok'emon-like creatures are able to withstand wide extremes of temperature and desiccation (Hengherr et al. 2009. ref). Their hardiness has elicited amazement, if not outright admiration, abetted by their adorable appearance. Now an alga has one-upped them. And not only that, this eukaryotic unicellular chlorophyte has matched the reigning world champion of resistance to nuclear radiation, the prokaryote *Deinococcus radiodurans*, also known as "Conan the Bacterium" (Huyghe 1998), which withstands 2,000 times the radiation dose that would kill any of us. Who would have expected a green alga could match that level of stress resistance?

In this issue of the *Journal of Phycology*, Rivasseau et al. describe an astonishing green alga that grows in the spent cooling effluent of a nuclear reactor (Fig. 1). These scientists had earlier reported the discovery of this microalga (Rivasseau et al. 2010, 2011, 2013), but here they give it a name and ask: how radiation tolerant is it? The short answer: very. Whether subjected to low levels of radiation for long periods or short bursts of extremely high levels of radiation, the alga survived and recovered after at most a few weeks of growth.

The authors named the species *Coccomyxa actinabi- otis*, whose specific epithet means, "able to grow in an ionizing radiation environment." They found it growing on the lens of a light used to illuminate the cooling pool of a nuclear reactor in Grenoble, in slightly acidic and very nutrient-poor water with a high level of ionizing metals—an environment the authors, in an understatement, call "peculiar." No kidding—radiation, oxidizing metals, and acid constitute a triple threat to the growth of anything, much less a green alga. Sequences of the 18S rRNA and the adjoining ITS1-5.8S rRNA-ITS2 region firmly position the new taxon within the Trebouxiophyceae, sister to other *Coccomyxa* species, so the phylogenetic position is clear. What is not clear is how *C. actinabiotis* can survive this harsh environment, and why it evolved the ability to do so.

In addition to some Archaea, some photosynthetic autotrophs are resistant to radiation, but they too are prokaryotes (cyanobacteria). Among eukaryotic organisms, fungi, tardigrades, and rotifers are known to be resistant to radiation to some degree. But the levels that kill the multicellular fungi and animals, or render them sterile, are an order of magnitude lower than that which *C. actinabiotis* can withstand. The authors provide a nice

review of the literature on how living cells can withstand high radiation doses. Possible outcomes include numerous breaks in double stranded DNA and damage to enzymes necessary for repair of damaged DNA. Possible protective mechanisms include a highly condensed nucleoid that would keep small pieces of DNA together, many copies of DNA so that damage to one or a few would not be lethal, or enhanced repair mechanisms—all of these have been demonstrated or suggested for bacteria. For the algae, Rivasseau and colleagues say the protective mechanism is unknown, but they suspect that protection and repair are involved.

In the end, the mind boggles. Why would the algae grow in this hostile environment? And how do they do it? Moreover, even though the early Earth was likely an unstable wasteland subject to high levels of radiation, eukaryotes were not there. Living in a maelstrom of radiation, where on Earth did these green algae come from? Though of course it was Earth where they were found. Perhaps an ancient prokaryotic mechanism was passed on vertically or laterally transferred to what would become a green eukaryote in the lineage bearing green plastids from primary endosymbiosis. The authors state that genomic sequencing is underway, and this may provide more clues into the origin and evolution of this lineage.

It's worth noting the lengths to which Rivasseau et al (2016). went and the risks they took to perform their research. The *Coccomyxa* cells themselves were exposed to so much radiation over a long period of time that the cells emitted their own radiation and posed a threat to the humans studying them, which necessitated special protective equipment for growth and observation. Kudos to this research team for a remarkable discovery in an unexpected place. As Jeff Goldblum's character in the film *Jurassic Park* noted with a sigh, "Life finds a way." In this case a green alga found it.

References

Hengherr, S., Worland, M. R., Reuner, A., Bruemmer, F. and Schill, R. O. 2009. "High-Temperature Tolerance in Anhydro- biotic Tardigrades Is Limited by Glass Transition."*Physiological and Biochemical Zoology* 82:749–755.

Huyghe, P. 1998. "Conan the Bacterium". *The Sciences* 38:16–9.

Rivasseau, C., Farhi, E., Atteia, A., Cout'e, A., Gromova, M., de Gouvion Saint Cyr, D., Boisson, A. M., F'eret, A. M. & Bligny, R. 2013. "An extremely radioresistant green

eukaryote for radionuclide bio-decontamination in the nuclear industry." *Energy Environ*. Sci. 6:1230–9.

Rivasseau, C., Farhi, E., Compagnon de Gouvion Saint Cyr, D., van Lis, R., Falconet, D., Kuntz, M., Atteia, A. & Cout'e, A. 2016. "Coccomyxa actinabiotis sp. nov. (Trebouxiophyceae, Chlorophyta), a new green microalga living in the spent fuel cooling pool of a nuclear reactor." *J. Phycol*. 52:689–703.

Rivasseau, C., Farhi, E., Cout'e, A. & Atteia, A. 2010. Une nouvelle micro-algue radior'esistante, FR 10/00578.

Rivasseau, C., Farhi, E., Cout'e, A. & Atteia, A. 2011. Une nouvelle micro-algue radior'esistante, WO 2011/098979.

Sean O'Donnell

Bushwhacked

The "white fang club" is made up of a cadre of field biologists who have been bitten by venomous snakes in the line of duty. My membership-qualifying experience may be a valuable lesson on how *not* to respond if bitten.

While teaching a tropical field course in a lowland rainforest in Costa Rica, I was following an army ant foraging column with a small group of students. When the ants entered a tangled tree-fall gap, I went around the mass of vegetation to try to pick up the ant column on the other side. Ironically, I avoided entering the gap with the students in part because of concern about snake encounters. On the far side, I noted a flock of birds attending the ant raid. As I raised my binoculars, I felt a sharp and tremendous pain in my left foot. I yelled out and removed my boot, thinking that a bullet ant or scorpion had fallen in and stung me. I removed my sock and saw a single bloody puncture wound on my heel. But there was no other evidence; I have no recollection of seeing a snake immediately before or after I felt the sudden pain.

Soon afterwards, I lost my vision and became dizzy, disoriented, and panicked. After sitting for a few minutes, however, I was able to get up and, with some support, walk slowly back to the lab clearing.When I developed a pounding headache, I raised the possibility to the gathering crowd that I had been bitten by a snake and hit by only one fang. I was assured by two fellow faculty members (including a herpetologist) that my wound and subjective experience were consistent with a bullet ant sting and not with a snake bite.We looked over my boot, and found no obvious punctures or venom.

I walked back to the dining hall, ate lunch, rested for two hours, attended a lecture, and consulted with students. After dinner, I participated in a night hike searching for amphibians and—again ironically— snakes in a nearby swamp. I had a great deal of pain in my foot and lower leg and a bad headache, but I was not otherwise compromised. Around 10:00 p.m., I noted a bruised swelling (hematoma) forming near the bite wound. When I used the bathroom, there was a small but noticeable amount of blood in my urine.

Upon my insistence, I was taken to the local medical clinic. Unfortunately, and surprisingly, the doctor who examined the puncture wound and hematoma also concluded it was not a snake bite. The doctor attributed the blood in my urine to a very rare but dangerous immune reaction that could occur in response to "any kind of venom," and he recommended that I seek care in Costa Rica's capital city, San José.

After a two-hour drive and a battery of tests, results came back, showing my blood cell counts and other vital signs were "off the charts." I had been bitten by a viper. Luckily, Costa Rica produces a polyvalent antivenin that is effective against all local vipers. The hospital promptly dosed me with ten vials. Once I had recovered,

I spoke with the attending physician, who confirmed that my situation had been very serious and I was lucky to have survived.

There are two important lessons to take from this experience. First, snake bites are not unitary in their presentation. Even people with extensive tropical field experience, and those who have seen viper bite cases, may not be in a good position to recognize a wound as a snake bite.

Second, if there is even a remote possibility that a person was bitten by a viper, bring the victim immediately to a fully-staffed hospital. Time is truly of the essence. Internal physiological distress is not always clearly manifested in the victim's demeanor or subjective state. Given my early suspicions that I had been bitten by a snake, I should have insisted upon treatment right away.

Upon returning home, I re-examined my boot under a strong lamp and found the two punctures apparently made by the snake's fangs, only one of which penetrated the sole. The punctures were twenty-seven millimeters apart, leading a Costa Rican herpetologist to estimate that the snake was over seven feet long and most likely a bushmaster. Even with treatment, human mortality rates to this species' venom exceed fifty percent. Before returning to field work, I purchased a very good pair of snake-proof boots.

Sean O'Donnell

Keep Your Distance

My fascination with other species and my compulsion to know more about them can sometimes draw me toward the bad-decision end of the judgment spectrum. On one occasion, a less-than-well-thought-out impulse raised the hairs on the back of my neck when I reflected on the real danger I had put myself in. I was nearing the end of a long and successful field season at the remote Tiputini Bio- diversity Station in Amazonian Ecuador. After nearly a month of hard work tracking and collecting army ants, I took an afternoon off to join a visiting student group and their instructors on a river float trip. On such trips, the group dons orange life jackets, is ferried upriver in a motorized launch, and jumps over the gunwales into the rippling café-au-lait waters of the Tiputini River. The idea is to float along toward home base, around the river's many graceful meanders, while gazing at the sunset-lit treetops, passing birds, and beautiful tropical sky. In the back of one's mind is the awareness that Amazon basin rivers are home to a fantastic diversity of aquatic creatures that are best appreciated from some distance and, preferably, from behind intervening glass walls. Unseen co-swimmers can include electric eels, anacondas, piranhas, black caimans, giant catfish, and freshwater stingrays. The station staff (who I note in retrospect stayed in the boat) assured us that midstream swimming and floating was safe They warned, however, to avoid the riverbanks and shallow edges.

As I floated along a rare straight stretch of the Tiputini, I was amazed to hear the distinctive squeals and growls of a group of giant otters (*Pteronura brasiliensis*) near the bank. I counted five of these sleek social hunters rolling in the shal- lows, each at least as long as I am tall. These are truly rare animals in Ecuador. I was thrilled at my good fortune and wanted a closer look, a watery communion, and I began to gently paddle toward the otters. They quickly noted my clumsy attempts at river travel and shifted into alarm mode. All five began periscoping— bobbing their shiny, wet heads two feet above the surface while emitting piercing squeals and shrieks that still echo through my memory. I was mesmerized, until a fellow floater gently noted that perhaps terror was a more appropriate response, that my behavior was not the best advised, and she encouraged me to slowly paddle back toward mid-stream. As I did so, the otters relaxed, staying put but keeping ten big dark eyes glued on my receding orange life jacket.

As often happens, a bit of post hoc analysis suggests some real risk was involved. A colleague who studied primates at a remote site in Peru, one with abundant black caimans and venomous snakes, told me the researchers'

greatest fear was encountering a family of giant otters as they migrated between streams on the station's trails; these are mammals not to be toyed with, even on land. They are known to rush toward threats as a coordinated screaming group. They are superb aquatic acrobats that make a living chasing fish; their formidable teeth and claws are reputed to be effectively deployed in defense as well. I shudder to imagine the outcome had the otter family been a bit less tolerant of my intrusion. Nevertheless, I feel immensely fortunate to have met such fascinating endangered animals in a way that may have been too close for our mutual comfort.

Donald Riggs

Building Epic Anticipation: Peter Jackson's Hobbit Videoblogs

If we take the term "epic" to mean "vast in scope," "surpassing the ordinary in significance," or, simply, "long," then Peter Jackson's film version of J.R.R. Tolkien's novel *The Hobbit* was intended to be an epic from the outset, a major challenge being that Jackson's previous Tolkien-based movie, *The Lord of the Rings* trilogy, was based on a trilogy of novels more obviously epic in scope, length, significance within the created world, complexity, and both number and diversity of characters than was the novel version of *The Hobbit*. This is in part because, having first made an epic trilogy from the matter of Middle-earth, Jackson could not make anything that seemed to be "smaller" for his second attempt. This inflationary spiral imposed upon *The Hobbit* because of *The Lord of the Rings* was not new to Peter Jackson's films, however; Tolkien himself revised the earlier novel to accommodate the evolution of Gollum's and Bilbo's ring of invisibility into the One Ring created by Sauron to Rule Them All in the larger universe of Middle-earth. As Adam Roberts points out in his *The Riddles of the Hobbit*, "[no longer a folk-story, [*The Hobbit*] now becomes a grand sacramental drama of incarnation, atonement, and redemption" (96). To resurrect the decade-old enthusiasm for the "original" *Lord of the Rings* film trilogy, to interest life-long readers of Tolkien in this new film, and to cultivate a fandom among those too young to have experienced LotR in the theaters (and probably not having read the novels), Peter Jackson released a series of videoblogs concerning the making of the film as a combined advertising and consciousness-raising campaign.

According to media theorist Vivian Sobchack, a by-product of the making of the 1962 historical blockbuster "How the West Was Won" was "a press book memorializing the production and release...of Hollywood's first narrative film made in Cinerama" (30). Cinerama was a filming and projection technique using three cameras side-by-side to capture and project a much wider visual field to enhance the audience's immersive experience of the film. Sobchack links the epic content of the film about the Westward expansion of the United States with the technological advances made to better capture the history in an appropriate aesthetic form. As Sobchack puts it, "Historical adventures of epic quality, quantification of the scope and magnitude of hardships and obstacles that had to be endured and overcome, heroic perseverance, appeal to national pride—at each rhetorical turn, these elements equivalently mark both the winning of the West and the achievement of its *appropriate* cinematic representation" (30). The press book extended the epic scope of the film's narrative to include the epic scope of the film's production, and much

of the same descriptive language could suit the production of Jackson's *The Hobbit* as well. The difference here is that, due to the technologies of digital photography and the internet, Jackson could release his "press book" directly to the public, without depending on any press as a medium, and he could do this before the release of the movie, thus cultivating a fanbase before the film was there to generate fans itself.

The videoblog series uses all three Aristotelian "elements of persuasion," with *logos*, or reasoning from evidence, especially prominent in the sections where technical advances such as shooting faster to obtain clearer definition are explored, and *pathos* in sections where the development of a feeling of community among the cast, crew, and others are featured, but the most brilliant use of one of these elements is that of *ethos*. While *ethos* is often translated in first-year composition textbooks as "credibility," the original meaning in the Greek is "character," as a person's character is the basis for his or her credibility (Clark 13). Ethos is central to Peter Jackson's 10-part video blog produced and webcast in anticipation of the release of the first installment of *The Hobbit: An Unexpected Journey*. At the beginning of the first blog, released on April 14, 2011—a full twenty months before the American release date of the film itself, on December 14, 2012—Jackson himself, in Bag End, addresses the camera—that is to say, the viewer—directly, establishing himself as a hobbit by inclination, if not stature. At the start of the second blog, he again addresses us from Bag End, but this time he is seated before a live fire in the fireplace. Jackson's presence is the link that ties together all of the various scenes and shots of the video blog sequence, which is over two hours in length, all told. However, he is inclusive: montages of cast and crew members, singly and in pairs or trios, pop up at various points in some of the blogs, giving us, the viewers, a sense of inclusion in the many aspects of the process of making the film(s), from casting, scouting New Zealand for locations, set building and design, visual concept creation, to training, acting, shooting, and such post-production activities as computer graphics to complement the visual footage and sound design and soundtrack to be coordinated with the film's visual aspect. During the limousine ride to the film's premiere in Wellington, New Zealand, Jackson comments on the fans who have been waiting for hours, in some cases camping out to have a good place to observe cast and crew walking up the red carpet to the theater, and he says, "It's pretty humbling, really, to think that, you know, one day I'll just think we're making a movie, a piece of entertainment, but then there's all this support for what we're doing, and I'm very very grateful that," at which point he looks directly into the camera (Video blog 10).

Jackson's use of ethos is not limited to establishing himself as hobbit-in-chief for the two film trilogies, but extends to his over-500 crew members and his extensive cast, and the fandom that is engaged in blog #8, where he

and several members of the cast appear at Comic-Con on July 14, 2012, in San Diego, California. He says, of fans who have been camping out in order to get in and see the *Hobbit* cast, "These are the people we're making the film for" (Video Blog 8). By extension, those of us who are watching the series of video blogs are part of the fandom as well, so one of the major themes of the campaign is to establish a sense of *inclusion* in the process of making the film, and a sense of identification of the viewers with a world-wide *Hobbit* film fandom. As Jackson says at the end of the eighth blog, "It's been a terrific atmosphere shooting this movie and I hope that the blogs have in some way given you all a chance to share in that and to experience it for yourselves."

The drive for inclusiveness is balanced by certain constraints against complete openness on the blogs, which Jackson alludes to at times when he says that he wishes he could show us certain scenes—evidently being shot as he is speaking to us—but he can't because they are for the second film. Certainly, what we see of the first film being shot is not the finished product, but is obviously done on set, with bright green in the background on which landscape will be imposed in post-production, and actors like Andy Serkis with an LED-studded rubber suit and helmet cam to allow post-production computer graphics to be imposed. At the same time, Jackson teases the viewers with allusions to the films, such as a brief discussion of the giant furniture in Beorn's house, letting readers of the novel know that that character will appear in the second film. So what Jackson is doing is balancing the drive for including fans in the process of making the films without including spoilers that will reduce the effect of, for example, first seeing the dragon Smaug on screen in the theater.

Tolkien and his novel are only mentioned once, when Ian McKellan—Gandalf—comments that, while the dwarves are not differentiated in the book (except for a few), they need to be all individualized in the film, since all of them are seen by the viewers, a problem not seriously addressed in the 1977 Rankin-Bass animated production. There is also a comment by Jackson about the difficulty of walking and running through the rough ground cover at certain locations—there is a close-up shot of some tangled and thorny brush—which is in the film to give the viewer a sense of the difficulty of actors' running across open land, but which, possibly inadvertently, evokes the narration of Tolkien's *Fellowship of the Ring*: "[Frodo] soon found that the thicket was closer and more tangled than it had appeared" and "the bushes and brambles were reluctant to let them through" (87), among many other examples. However, it appears that Jackson's inclusivity is directed more at the fans of the first film trilogy and others raised on digital and CGI-inflected films than fans of the novels.

Jackson's highly intelligent video-blogging campaign fulfills some of the predictions in media scholar Henry Jenkins's 2004 article "The cultural logic of media convergence," in which Jenkins sees a tension between a "top-down corporate-driven process and a bottom-up consumer-driven process" (37). Jackson, a world-renowned producer and director, having been knighted for his significant contribution to New Zealand's film industry, seems to be straddling the two sides of Jenkins's equation through his video-blog outreach to fandom; throughout the video blog he associates himself with the crew, asserting his own "bottom-up" credentials, reinforcing them with his references to the fans.

The sequence of ten video blogs provides a focused campaign of building anticipation for the release of the film(s) that can be studied in terms of intended audience, constraints on Jackson both as filmmaker and blogger, and different categories of what Henry Jenkins has called the "five logics" of media outreach to fandoms. Jenkins, a prominent scholar of "converging" media—through which communities of fans are developed via books, movies, television, online platforms, and others—has identified five "logics" underlying any such media's products to the readership, audience, viewership, or fandom as relating to: 1. entertainment, 2. social connection, 3. experts, 4. immersion, and 5. identification. An analysis of individual video blogs in the series suggests that all of these "logics" are in play, but the emphasis varies from one blog to the next. *Entertainment* is central to the rhetorical strategy Jackson uses, as the goal is to get the largest number of viewers possible to see the final theater cuts of the films themselves; the blogs are well edited, with a surprisingly extensive amount of information—about the sites, the casting, costuming, art direction, 3-D filming, and more—but this viewer was never bored during the presentation nor did he perceive the pace as bogging down. Jackson makes judicious use of Howard Shore's music, at first from the initial *Lord of the Rings* trilogy, which would evoke a sense of nostalgia in fans of the films, then gradually motifs from *The Hobbit*, to establish a sense of melodic continuity and progression linking the two groups of films.

The logic of *social connection* was accessed by having the Facebook options of "liking" and opportunities for comments, which were not all positive—among the comments to video blog 4, on December 20, 2012, Dries Schelfhout wrote: "personally, I despise 3D"—nonetheless, it can be argued that, of the 20,224 people who "liked" that video blog, many felt engaged enough to click on the "like" button, and thus in some way contribute to the momentum of the movie's progress towards completion.

The logic of *experts* is engaged by Jackson with his expositions of technical matters, such as the demonstration of how the 3-D cameras are built, of how the two cameras triangulate on an object to replicate bifocal vision, the

exhibiting of sets built inside studios, with their excessively intense colors—at one point, Jackson comments that the Mirkwood set is really a "psychedelic" forest with pink, purple, and other unnatural colors for highlights, but that these colors will seem subdued onscreen and thus will blend in—and showing the shooting of scenes with actors swinging their swords at dummies and punching bags that will later have CGI imposed to turn them into trolls, all the while a bright green backdrop indicates where landscape footage will be collaged in. Also, the chief conceptual designers Alan Lee and John Howe, highly respected fantasy illustrators, demonstrate how they both draw the same scene, side by side, one in red and the other in blue, to be laid over each other slightly out of synch to show how a scene will look in 3-D with the appropriate glasses. At other places in the video blog series, Jackson introduces costume designers, the caterers that feed the cast and crew daily, and reveals the fleet of trucks (about 140) used to transport the 500-odd crew members and equipment, portable potties, and other materials needed to shoot in any location. All of this matter engages the potential fans who are fascinated by the technical aspects of shooting the film.

All of the above elements of the video blog series also contribute to what Jenkins calls the logic of *immersion,* in which the viewer feels a personal participation in the process of the creation of the film. As literally thousands of viewers on Facebook and elsewhere online had logged in to watch some or all of the ten video blogs in the twenty months before the film's release, this means that those viewers may have derived a sense of vicarious participation in the steps of bringing the concept—as illustrated by Alan Lee and John Howe, for example—to fruition through casting, training (the dwarves are shown riding horses, duelling with large staffs, and in other ways getting in shape to run across country and fight), and filming, both in the studio and on location. The first day of shooting starts with local Maori performing a ceremony to welcome the cast and crew, there are frequent sequences of individual actors and crew members talking directly to us, the viewers, and we feel ourselves to be special guests being shown the secrets behind filming the upcoming movies.

Most of all, Peter Jackson establishes himself as a friendly presence who talks directly to us. Jackson is the chief narrator throughout, although at times others chime in for periods—Elijah Wood, for example, establishes the connection with the *Lord of the Rings* trilogy by describing his feelings at returning to the site of Hobbiton and Bag End a dozen years after the initial film's shooting. However, Jackson first addresses us at the beginning of the first blog from inside Bag End, and starts the second blog similarly situated but in front of a fire in the Bag End fireplace. Just as Steve Jobs was identified as the face of Apple Computers, Peter Jackson is identified as the Hobbit-in-Chief of this continuation of the earlier trilogy. He even "admits" he would like to retire to the now permanently rebuilt Hobbiton, thus reinforcing our

identification of him with the recreation of Middle-earth in New Zealand. In a comment that brings us "into" the action of filming on location, Jackson shows us the rough ground cover in the terrain at one point, both giving us a sense of the difficulty of the actors moving across the brush and scrub, and, perhaps unconsciously, appealing to those lovers of the Tolkien books who treasure the narrator's occasional attention to the specific grasses, tussocks, brambles, and other cover herbiage aiding or inhibiting cross-country movement on foot. All of this follows Jenkins's logic of *identification*, in which the viewers of the blog know themselves to be part of the "inner circle" of diehard Tolkien/Jackson fans, however many tens of thousands that inner circle may contain.

Works Cited

Clark, Carol Lea. Praxis: *A Brief Rhetoric*. Southlake, TX: Fountainhead Press, 2012.

Jackson, Peter. The Hobbit Video Blogs 1-6. Retrieved from http://www.youtube.com/watch?v=zfX1PYv1FEY

The Hobbit Video Blog 8, "Last Days & Comic Con." Retrieved from http://www.thehobbitblog.com/production-video-8-last-days-comic-con/

The Hobbit Video Blog 10, "The Premiere." Retrieved from http://www.youtube.com/watch?v=zfX1PYv1FEY

Jenkins, Henry. *Convergence Culture: Where Old and New Media Collide*. New York:New York University Press, 2006.

"The cultural logic of media convergence." *International Journal of Cultural Studies*. 7.1 (2004) 33-43.

Roberts, Adam. *The Riddles of the Hobbit*. New York and London: Palgrave Macmillan, 2013.

Sobchack, Vivian. "'Surge and Splendor': A Phenomenology of the Hollywood Historical Epic." *Representations* 29 (Winter 1990), 24-49).

Tolkien, John Ronald Reuel. *The Hobbit: or, There and Back Again (Revised Edition)*. New York: Ballantine, 1965.

The Lord of the Rings. New York: Houghton Mifflin, 1984.

David Seltzer

The Meno Paradox in Augustine and Kierkegaard

In this paper, I will focus on the way in which Augustine and Kierkegaard make use of Meno's paradox in order to explain how humans acquire knowledge of the divine. I'll begin by discussing the original Meno paradox as it appears in Plato's *Meno*, then discuss the theory of illumination in Augustine, and then conclude with a discussion of divine teaching in Kierkegaard. I'll conclude by imagining a dialogue between Augustine and Kierkegaard.

I'll start with the *Meno*. In the *Meno*, Meno sets out a destructive dilemma intended to prove that it is impossible to learn. According to Meno, if we already know something, then we have no need to learn it, and if we don't already know something, then we have no standards to tell us how to begin or when we have reached our goal.[1] Meno's paradox presents us with two options. We can either challenge the first premise and give an account of how we can learn when we already have knowledge, or we can challenge the second premise and give an account of a teaching that furnishes its own standards. Socrates considers both possibilities in the Meno. He begins by taking up the first option. He argues that we already do have knowledge, and what we think of as learning is not really learning at all, but rather recollection. According to Socrates, the soul existed before birth and was in contact with the immaterial forms. Upon the soul's birth into a body, it became distracted with other cares, and no longer attended to its knowledge of the forms, which became scattered. Through a process of questioning, the teacher can serve as an occasion for the learner to reorient himself and turn inward, and attend to the knowledge which is within him. As no learning takes place, it follows that Socrates himself is not a "teacher" in the sense of one who imparts knowledge, but rather a kind of midwife, who helps the learner give birth to the knowledge within him.[2] At the end of the dialogue, however, Socrates leaves open the possibility that the gods might choose to grant us divine knowledge.[3] Socrates himself certainly believes in this sort of knowledge. He receives commands from the gods telling him when he should not engage in a course of action, and he also believes that divine inspiration passes through Ion, although Ion himself doesn't retain any of this knowledge. He also believes it is at least possible that he will receive positive knowledge from the gods after death.[4] Therefore it should at least be possible that we could receive knowledge from the gods in this life.

---

1 Plato, *Meno*, 80d-e.

2 Plato, *Meno* 81b-c, 85b86c; Phaedo 72e-77a; Theaetetus 150a-151d.

3 Plato, *Meno*, 99e-100a.

4 Plato, *Apology*, 40a-41c; *Ion* 535e-536d.

Now let's look at Augustine. Augustine did not read Plato directly, but rather encountered Platonism indirectly from Neoplatonists like Plotinus and Porphyry.[5] This means that Augustine doesn't distinguish between Socrates and Plato, and also that he sees the divine and human worlds as basically continuous with each other. According to Augustine, God is Truth, the source of all particular truths, the standard by which they are known, and the light through which they are seen.[6] God therefore performs a vital epistemic role: the knowledge of God ultimately grounds all other knowledge, even though it is possible for humans to be aware of particular truths without being aware that they are ultimately grounded in God. Humans can approach a knowledge of God through a process that resembles Socratic recollection. One would begin with the material things God has made, but then turn inward to find truths within oneself, and finally ascend to God who is above even the highest part of the self.[7] God plays an active role in this process, in several ways. First, God serves as a necessary precondition for recollection to take place. This is why Augustine prays to God at the beginning of the *Confessions*, and why Augustine says that Evodius will reply to himself with God's help.[8] Second, as Augustine tells Evodius in *On Free Choice of the Will*, God provides us with traces or glimpses of the truth to guide us in the right direction. Without these traces, we would be vulnerable to a version of Meno's second premise: we could not even engage in a search without some sort of standard to point us in the right direction. Evodius, in *On Free Choice of the Will*, cannot see how he could be merely on the way to wisdom if he doesn't have some kind of glimpse of where he is supposed to go.[9] Similarly, Augustine, at the beginning of the *Confessions*, seems completely at a loss how to proceed, until he remembers that God has been preached to him.[10] Humans, in contrast, play no more role in teaching than they do in Socrates. In *The Teacher*, Augustine argues that it is impossible for language to actually transfer information from teacher to learner, because language merely consists of signs, which are meaningless unless we first acquire knowledge of the things they signify. In the case of external objects such as heads and sarabara, this knowledge comes by acquaintance, but there are other types of knowledge that can only be found by turning within.[11] Augustine, in *The Teacher*, applies this logic to himself and allows Adeodatus to insist that Augustine has not taught him anything; rather, Augustine's questioning has merely caused Adeodatus to recollect

---

5 Conversation with Frederick Van Fleteren.

6 Augustine, *The Teacher*, 12.40, 13.46; *On Free Choice of the Will*, 2.9-10.

7 Augustine, *Confessions*, 9.10.24.

8 Augustine, *Confessions*, 1.1; *On Free Choice of the Will*, 2.2.

9 Augustine, *On Free Choice of the Will*, 2.15-16.

10 Augustine, *Confessions*, 1.1.

11 Augustine, *The Teacher*, 13.33-36, 13.40.

what Adeodatus already knew.[12] It is even possible for a teacher to furnish the occasion quite unintentionally and without himself possessing knowledge. Augustine gives the example of an Epicurean who recites proofs of God's existence merely as a rhetorical exercise, causing a listener to look within and convert to Catholicism.[13]

Kierkegaard takes up the Meno paradox in *Philosophical Crumbs*, attributed to the pseudonym Johannes Climacus. Climacus first points out the appealing features of Socratic recollection. By insisting that everyone must look within, Socrates addresses himself to the single individual, and not to the crowd. Climacus also points out the humility of Socrates: Socrates claims, quite rightly, that the learner owes him nothing.[14] Climacus thus points out that we really ought to stop with Socrates, humanly speaking, and not go on to, i.e. Hegel, or perhaps even Kant.[15] For Climacus, however, Socratic recollection ultimately turns out to be a dead end. Climacus, writing after Kant's "Transcendental Dialectic," adopts the position that all human knowledge is confined within the bounds of possible experience.[16] There are no innate ideas that we might recollect by turning within. Moreover, as a failed doctoral student in Copenhagen, Climacus is probably aware of S. Kierkegaard's dissertation *The Concept of Irony*, in which Kierkegaard distinguishes between Socrates and Plato, and argues that Socrates is a purely negative philosopher who creates a space which Christianity might fill. Therefore Climacus turns to the second premise of Meno's paradox: that we cannot learn if we don't already know. By following out the logic of Meno's paradox, Climacus develops an account of divine teaching that looks suspiciously like Christian doctrine. Because Climacus refuses to state whether he himself is a Christian,[17] he has to phrase this possibility hypothetically: if there were some other kind of knowledge then it would have to fit the description he gives of it. In the first place, the god would have to introduce genuinely new knowledge, something from outside the self, which could never be recollected through Socratic questioning. The god would also have to provide the condition for understanding the knowledge. Otherwise we would be vulnerable to Meno's objection that there is no standard by which we can recognize the knowledge as knowledge. This condition, again, would have to come from outside the self. Instead of being an attentiveness to the self, the learning would be a total transformation of the self: instead of giving birth to what is already within us,

---

12 Augustine, *The Teacher*, 13.46.
13 Augustine, *The Teacher*, 13.41.
14 Kierkegaard, *Philosophical Crumbs, trans. M. G. Piety*, (Oxford: Oxford University Press, 2009): 88-91, 99-100.
15 Kierkegaard, *Philosophical Crumbs*, 97-8.
16 See Kant, *Critique of Pure Reason*, A580/B608-A582/B610.
17 Kierkegaard, *Philosophical Crumbs*, 87.

it would be a rebirth.[18] Most importantly, the god would have to come to us. Because the "Transcendental Dialectic" rules out the possibility that a human could ascend to the level of the god, the god must come down to the human level, and even to the level of the lowest of humans. This then creates the paradox that a being can be both God and the lowliest of humans. It also creates offense at the thought that a superior being such as God would decide instead to address us in the lowly guise of a servant.[19] Because the "Transcendental Dialectic" leaves an impassible barrier between the human and divine, faith must be involved to bridge this barrier.[20]

At first glance Augustine and Climacus seem to have very little in common. Most importantly, they seem to have incompatible conceptions of Christianity. Augustine takes up the first fork of Meno's dilemma and Climacus takes up the second fork. It seems to follow that each would think the other took the wrong path and came to the wrong conclusions. To be specific, if Augustine can attain to touch God through a process of recollection, then it would seem to follow that there was no need for Climacus look for a teaching from outside. It also seems to follow that, by looking outside himself, Climacus has not in fact found God, but rather a mere subjective projection of himself which he mistakes for God.[21] Moreover, Augustine could argue that, by dismissing the world of the "merely human," Climacus has gone too fast and failed to notice the signs that God has given, and that by abandoning his reason, Climacus has robbed himself of the tool which God gave to him for the purpose of ascending to God.[22] Conversely, if Climacus derives Christianity by following out the consequences of an external teaching, then it seems to follow that anyone who does not rely on an external teaching, including Augustine, does not really go beyond paganism. Climacus could argue that Augustine remains within paganism because he fails to appreciate the paradox and therefore offense and faith, and also because he sees the human relationship with God in primarily intellectual terms.

---

18 Kierkegaard, *Philosophical Crumbs*, 92-6.

19 Kierkegaard, *Philosophical Crumbs*, 106-7.

20 Kierkegaard, *Philosophical Crumbs*, 128-9.

21 Of course, Climacus always admits the possibility that we can never verify that his version of faith corresponds to anything, but Augustine would say this is positively the case.

22 Augustine wouldn't bother to argue with someone such as Climacus who will not take a position on Christianity, especially because he is a pseudonym and doesn't actually exist, and he wouldn't bother to argue with any theology that Kierkegaard didn't sign his name to. He would see the need to argue against some parts of Kierkegaard's direct authorship, but I can't see Augustine bothering to defend the Danish People's Church against Kierkegaard's attack.

Augustine and Climacus also, it seems, have very different conceptions of God. Augustine mostly emphasizes God's perfections. To make a more general point, Augustine talks a great deal about God, but he doesn't talk much at all about Christ, and even less about Jesus. Furthermore, even when Augustine does talk about Christ, Christ appears as superhuman. Christ has one thing in common with man, his mortality, and one thing distinct, his justice and goodness.[23] Augustine's Christ only partially descends from the divine to the human level, and even his mortality barely counts because, after all, there is another and more important sense in which He and all of us are immortal. Christ assumes just enough humanity to give humans a hint; nothing more. Augustine also emphasizes Christ's role as intercessor, and as the coeternal wisdom and word of God.[24] Climacus, in contrast, isn't all that interested in enumerating God's perfections. In fact, except for the ends of the chapters, he preserves the pretense that he's talking about the god (small g) and not God (capital G). He's interested in God actually becoming the lowliest of humans, God suffering, God bound, as it were, to follow out His commitment to remain in earthly form.[25] Of course, one could object that Augustine and Climacus are both talking about Christianity, and so they must ultimately have the same conception of God, but even so, the aspects of God they choose to emphasize are radically different.

Along with this, the epistemic problems Augustine and Climacus seek to overcome are entirely opposite. For Augustine, the epistemic problem is how a human being, mere sinful dust and ashes, could ever rise to God's level.[26] Even if God could come to him, as God does in Climacus, that would be no help to Augustine, because such a God could never provide an epistemic ground for our knowledge. In order to ground his epistemology, Augustine needs God *qua* God, not God *qua* human. For Climacus, in contrast, the epistemic problem is offense, the unwillingness to accept that God could ever assume the status of the lowliest servant.

Even the language they use makes this point. Augustine uses soaring rhetoric, both when he talks to God, and also when he merely writes about God. His elevated language emphasizes the majesty of God, and his aspiration to rise to God's level. Climacus, as an unbeliever, doesn't speak to God, but when he writes about Christianity he self-consciously describes his writing as a shabby piece of plagiarism and a bad joke.[27] Climacus's language is offensive, in the same way that his description of God's journey to us, seen in the wrong

---

23 Augustine, *Confessions*, 10.43.
24 Augustine, *Confessions*, 10.43.
25 Kierkegaard, *Philosophical Crumbs*, 106-7, 125-6.
26 Augustine, *Confessions*, 1.6.
27 Kierkegaard, *Philosophical Crumbs*, 109.

light, would appear as a rather tasteless joke God played on us. Presumably, if Climacus did speak to God, he would use the same kind of everyday language. The problem for Climacus is having the courage to converse with God as an equal.[28] To put it in even more basic terms, Climacus assumes that one *can* have a conversation with God, in human language. When Augustine does have his taste of eternity in Book 9 of the *Confessions*, he describes the experience as super-linguistic. Even Augustine's elevated language is still insufficient to describe God, because it is limited, in the sense that is has a beginning and an end.[29]

Thus far I've described the differences between Augustine and Climacus, but there is another way of looking at their views. Both Augustine and Climacus seem to see learning about God as a two-step process. In the first step, God comes to us from outside; in the second step, we recollect the knowledge we acquired in the first step. Climacus talks mostly about the first step, and Augustine talks mostly about the second step. My suggestion is that Augustine and Climacus might not disagree so much as talk past each other. To see that they agree, we would need to compare Augustine on divine teaching to Climacus on divine teaching, and Augustine on recollection to Climacus on recollection. When we do this, we can see that Augustine and Climacus are actually very close.

To being with divine teaching: Augustine, like Climacus, thinks the divine is ultimately something outside the human. God is not found in Augustine's memory in the same way that the forms are, but rather resides above the topmost part of his soul. For Augustine, Platonic recollection can get us most of the way to God, but it cannot, as in Plato, get us all the way to the highest truth and wisdom. Augustine, like Climacus, thinks the content ultimately comes from outside, in the form of the preaching and the glimpses that God gives to guide him. Augustine, like Climacus, thinks that God provides the condition. And Augustine, like Climacus, thinks that this condition is not accepted because of sin. All of these positions differentiate Augustine from a pagan such as Plato. Climacus, for his part, sometimes sounds like Augustine.

---

28 I'm reminded of Nietzsche's comment that Luther talked to God as a peasant, and did not use the refined expressions that one uses in the presence of the nobility as a sign of respect. *Genealogy of Morals*, 3.22. But for Climacus this is precisely the point. God wants to speak with us, even the peasants, as an equal. But see also the next footnote.

29 Augustine, *Confessions*, 9.10.24. Marianne Djuth, "Augustine, Monica, and the Love of Wisdom," *Augustinian Studies* 40, no. 2 (2009): 225-6, calls attention to two early dialogues, *De beata vita* and *De ordine*, in which Augustine acknowledges Monica as a true philosopher because her wisdom is a gift of God whereas Augustine still tries to acquire wisdom by reading books. Thus Augustine's language is not necessary. Monica manages to get farther than Augustine without any of the rhetorical or even philosophical fireworks.

For Climacus, the first step in the process of coming to God involves Socratic self-understanding: the god makes the human look within and realize he is untruth.[30] Climacus also admits that one can see traces of God: to one who already believes, his own existence is a sign of God's existence.[31]

Similarly, when we compare Climacus on human teaching with Augustine on human teaching, they seem relatively the same. The one who informs Climacus' follower at second hand really has no active role but is just an occasion. The believer, turned to God by the follower, owes the god everything, but he owes the teacher who made him reflect on the god nothing.[32] Climacus may even be like Augustine's Epicurean. He personally isn't willing to become a Christian, but he provides an account of what Christianity is, which could potentially stir someone else to become a believer.

---

30 Kierkegaard, *Philosophical Crumbs*, 92.
31 Kierkegaard, *Philosophical Crumbs*, 97.
32 Kierkegaard, *Philosophical Crumbs*, 167-8.

Fred Siegel

Magic Class

As a teacher of first-year writing since 1987, I have learned to share my passions with students. Sharing what really matters to you can lead to deep learning, but it can also involve emotional risk.

In a class that focuses on using research, writing, and re-writing to think about the connections between literary texts and our lives, I have chosen a theme I think about a lot: Deception. We read short stories in which characters deceive or are deceived. How many of these stories do you recognize?

- A young woman who is very smart in some ways but less smart in others has her artificial leg stolen by a con man.

- A wealthy woman pretends to be a governess for a day, and "teaches" using extremely unorthodox methods.

- A woman has an affair during a Louisiana storm and yet it doesn't hurt her relationship with her husband.

So far, nothing unusual. The emotionally risky part comes from the final assignment: They have to find, learn, practice, and perform a magic trick.

Now, Teaching Police, don't get excited. We aren't playing with whoopee cushions and joy buzzers. Magic is a serious pursuit with a long history. Students have to do a research log, with citations, in which they explain how they found the tricks they perform. Students have to do a practice/performance log, in which they discuss the process of learning the trick, document the process of figuring out how they're going to present it, and think deeply about how they're going to make people enjoy it. And, yes, students have to get up and do the trick in front of their classmates, and then write evaluations of their own performances. (My colleagues in the university writing game will note that this performance composition process mirrors the writing composition process that we have been working on all year.)

My magic assignment inspires emotions ranging from joy to terror. Adventurous students welcome the whimsical assignment, look forward to learning how to fool their friends, and embrace a chance to do something a little less "school-y" than the usual. Other students are freaked out. What if I drop the cards? What if the trick doesn't work? What if I look like an idiot?

I appreciate the vulnerability of my students, so I assure them that if they drop the cards they can pick them up and there are many magic tricks that do not require difficult sleight of hand and the class will be supportive in the event of a mishap. Also, it's a writing class, not a magic class. Most of the grade is based on the written assignments. You can mess up the trick and still get an A.

I try to alleviate students' fears and help them to take the risks necessary to succeed. But what about the risks I take in giving this assignment?

You see, I love magic. I have loved it all my life.

When I was a boy, I loved when my uncle Phil pulled quarters out of my ear. I loved watching a girl turn into a gorilla at a grind show in Atlantic City. I loved performing at an all-girl birthday party thrown by a seventh grade classmate who kissed me in the powder room. I loved that I could avoid physical confrontations with tough kids by apparently swallowing objects and then pulling them out of my behind.

During graduate school, I loved performing alongside a sword swallower and human blockhead in The Coney Island Sideshow, I loved befuddling professors with my blindfold act at school functions, and I loved writing my doctoral dissertation on vaudeville magicians.

These days, I love attending magic shows and conventions, performing the "Fred's Magic World" theater show with my wife, sister-in-law, and brother-in-law, reading *Genii, The International Conjurer's Magazine* every month, developing and performing my autobiographical show, *Man of Mystery*, and doing card tricks with other magic freaks for hours and hours and hours.

But because magic is absolutely essential to me, there are challenges as well as triumphs with my magic assignment.

The enormity of the Internet makes finding tricks to perform easy in one way and difficult in another. Google "easy magic tricks" and you get 4,610,000 results. But how does a student with no magic background choose? Just as they sometimes do in a more conventional research assignment, some use the first source they find and attempt to make it work, rather than spend a little more time and find a better one. In a magical world with many great tricks for beginners, it pains me when my students choose tricks that aren't fun to perform or watch.

It also pains me to see genuinely interested students attempt to do tricks that are way too difficult for a beginner to master. At the risk of sounding like a cane-wagging old man, this, again, is an effect of that new-fangled Internet where all ideas have an equal chance at getting "clicks." In the digital wild, students can't always tell if they're picking a doable first trick or a knuckle-busting sleight of hander. I don't want to discourage anyone from doing difficult things, but it's hard for me to watch someone concentrate so hard on their "triple lift" that they are unable to make it clear what the trick is supposed to be.

Also, in a digital world without gatekeepers to decide what is worthwhile and what isn't, anyone with digital video capabilities can make an instructional video, expose any trick they know, and put it out there for anybody to see. To my disgust, youngsters who know very little about magic teach tricks on their webcams to show how smart they are, not to show others how to mystify artfully. In my classes, some perform tricks poorly, even though they are doing it the way the kid in the video demonstrated. (To be fair, some students come in with really good tricks—much better ones than I knew when I was starting out. This, too, is an effect of a free market of ideas.)

All of these research problems are surmountable, of course. I can meet with students, if they have the time, and help them pick appropriate tricks from the digital wilds. I can loan them a book, or I can send them to the public library and look for 793.8—the most thrilling number in the building. Or, I can just teach them a trick. After all, consulting with an expert is a legitimate form of research. Students who do that get a dedicated mentor. I can show how to replace a strip-out riffle shuffle with a much easier haymow shuffle and still get the same effect. I can explain that slow and clear is better than fast and crazy. I can explain the tremendous power of looking at the audience and smiling.

So, I should be happy....

Well, mostly, I am. But here's the problem: If students use inferior sources to write an uninteresting essay about the short stories of Flannery O'Connor, Saki, or Kate Chopin, it doesn't bother me, at least not in a personal way. If they roll their eyes at the prospect of writing a paper comparing food trucks to the school cafeteria, I carry on. If they can't fix their comma splices no matter how many times I point them out, I can slough it off. Hell, I can even sympathize.

But what if they roll their eyes at my magic assignment? What if they put as little effort as possible into the most enthralling pursuit of my life? What if they just don't like magic?

On the last day of class, everyone performs a trick. They get an introduction from me, the master of ceremonies, and they get applause upon their entrance. At the end of the trick, students get more applause, ranging in enthusiasm from respectful to genuinely impressed. Students are excited and terrified and supportive and, in more than a few cases, a little triumphant. And even if not all of the magic goes perfectly, the final logs are always fun to read. They reflect learning, even though it might not be the kind of learning that people usually expect in a writing class.

How will they remember magic class? How will they remember me?

Sharing passions is risky. For now, I think it's worth the risk.

Kathleen Volk Miller

Let's Not Stay Inside

Thirteen summers ago, my family and I went to the fireworks show in our small New Jersey town. We were so close to where they were shooting them off that we had to lie on our backs to see. The lights rained down upon us, bits of paper falling onto our faces. I started to panic. What about the kids' hearing? What chemicals were we breathing in? I looked at my husband. His face told me he had the same concerns, but we were in it now, so we might as well go with it. The kids squealed when the ash landed on their little bodies, and our middle child reached out her chubby hand and yelled, "I so happy, Mommy!" And I knew she was, and I was, too.

Four months later, my husband was diagnosed with a carcinoid cancer, a rare form we were told was "manageable." Nine months later, he died. In his final weeks the doctors kept saying he'd pull through, so I told my children the same thing. In May, while he lay in the hospital in a medicated coma, I assured them we'd be fishing in the Poconos by August.

The morning their father died, I called the kids to the couch and made sure I was touching each one. When I gave them the news, my oldest screamed, "You're lying!" The other two, sobbing, said, "You said we were going fishing! You said we were going to the Poconos!"

Relatives and friends took over the house, bringing food and flowers, wanting to do the impossible, which was make us feel better. Then, finally, it was just us, sitting at the table in our new configuration. We left Dad's seat empty. It was mid-June, and summer loomed ahead.

"You guys," I said. "The most horrible thing that can happen to a family has happened to us. There's nothing I can say or do to make that less true. But we have a choice. We can pull down the blinds and stay here and just be. Or we can be thankful for our friends and family and each other. We can go to the beach. We can still have a summer. We have to decide how we want to live."

Hayley, 11 years old, said, "I choose the second thing. Let's have fun. But can we still think about Dad, too?"

Allison, 13 years old, said, "Of course we can think about Dad. But he wouldn't mind if we had a summer."

Christopher, our baby, was 5. He said, "Let's not stay inside with the windows shut, except when we have to."

We agreed. Let's stay inside only on days we have to.

It turned out that sadness didn't last whole days, just parts of days. Allison watched videos of her dad late at night and cried body-wracking sobs. Hayley stormed around, making demands: "What are we going to do now? What's for dinner? Can we go to the mall?" Chris lay in bed with the 8 x 10 of his dad carrying him on his shoulders. He would weep, not wanting me to remove the photo, but also not wanting to look at it.

We didn't bother with blind optimism or denial—we were all keenly aware of what we had lost. Instead, we approached every hour with the aim to take from it the best we could. One day we were in the car when "Hey Ya!" by Outkast came on the radio. It seemed to be everywhere that summer and was impossible not to dance to. So we did: Windows down, radio up, we sang loud and bounced hard. A few blocks from home, a neighbor on the corner watched us pass with a look of abject horror. Here we were, so publicly happy, though my husband, their father, was only six weeks gone.

The neighbor didn't understand how joy could exist in the midst of tragedy. To be honest, neither do I. But it can. It did. And we were grateful.

Scott Warnock

Writing, Technology, and Class Mannequin Challenges

Recently, I gave a talk at a high school about how college students today are learning online and with ed tech in general. The audience was parents, and it was interesting to hear how they perceived the learning their children were doing in front of/with a computer and how they felt about it.

I started off by asking them this, workshop style: "How did you learn when you were in school?" Not surprisingly, many of them recalled learning environments that were full of lectures and memorization.

From there, I focused especially on teaching *writing* in interactive e-environments. In the back of my mind was a recent *Huffington Post* advising "What To Do When Your Child Announces Writing as a Major." The author, Frank Wu, a law professor, said he has "every confidence" in his niece's recent decision to declare writing as a major: "I am convinced that her decision to be a writing major will give her a rare skill."

In fact, at Drexel, we're right now hoping to launch a writing major because that rare "skill" of writing is indeed a package of creativity, thinking, communicating, and problem solving -- oh, do we need to cultivate these things across the board right now.

But writing is not just useful as a focus of study: Writing helps students actively engage and learn any content. To me, here's where the technology has been fascinating. Learning technologies could certainly be used to dump content on students (hold that thought for a second), but they also offer new ways to have students *do stuff* in their classes, to engage one another.

Those of you out there with kids on their way to college, think about it: What do you want your kids to *do* in their college classrooms? We don't put nearly enough thought into that question. College seems like a generalized *experience*, and we don't consider what it will look like in its specifics.

Go out there on the wild Web and Google [lecture hall] and think about the images you see. While there's nothing inherently wrong with a lecture hall and a good teacher can deliver stimulating content to hundreds, too many educational experiences take place in settings like that. (There was a surge of interest in scaling this massiveness online via MOOCs, massive open online courses. After initial over exuberance, MOOCs have cooled down.)

In a writing course, the students involved – soon, my own children, by the way – are often actively doing something: writing. In an online writing course, they really write a lot as they move through the course: Tens of thousands of words beyond course papers.

Mannequin challenges are everywhere. (I love some of the wrestling ones.) You can find online examples of classroom mannequin challenges, but the ones I saw were whimsical. I thought about what a real mannequin challenge might look like in college classes. Think of those lecture hall images: In many cases, the class might look like it's filled with a bunch of mannequins *even when the students weren't trying.*

So, it's not just that writing as a subject of study is valuable, but writing in a class can help students learn better and be more connected to and engaged with what they're learning. I want my students *active* in my courses. I want them learning not just specific content but how to act and write about problems of all kinds.

If you see my students, in a room or at a computer, I hope they're working. Learning should be like that. Whether onsite or online, I wouldn't want you to see a bunch of them and think, "Oh, that must be one of those mannequin challenges" because they are just sitting there -- like a bunch of dummies.

Robert Watts

Breaking Baccalaureate: Why non-academic skills are as important as the traditional academic stuff

This past spring, I attended a championship story slam with a student I have advised and whom I know well. This student is a gifted writer and a funny, self-deprecating storyteller. I could easily claim that I thought attending the slam might give her insight about a research project I was advising her on. But the truth is that I simply thought she would enjoy the slam and might find an outlet for her own storytelling. The issue of engaging with a student outside of formal class time is, of course, a tricky one these days, especially if the professor is a male and the student a female.

So there we were the other night — my student and I — sitting in a small club with about 75 people in the audience, at another story slam. This time I had challenged her to sign up to speak, and she agreed as long as I did the same. About an hour into the story slam, my student's name was called. She smiled and made her way to the front of the stage. I looked on nervously as she told a funny story about her confusion regarding the men she likes. Her voice was strong and confident, and the audience laughed at the right moments.

When she made her way back to her seat, I stood and clapped and congratulated her. "You were great," I said. She sat down and seemed pleased, still riding the tail end of a performer's high. Then came the judges' ratings: They were far lower than I thought she deserved, lower than the ratings of many of the speakers who preceded her. I was worried. My student can be harshly critical of her writing until it is fully polished. Having encouraged her to speak in front of the crowd in the first place, I didn't want her to turn overly self-critical or feel dejected by the ratings. And so for the rest of that night, I was clear about my teacher mission: I wanted to celebrate her courage for stepping up to the microphone.

In his recent book, *Helping Children Succeed*, Paul Tough writes about the startling conclusion of a massive study of teacher effectiveness. According to Northwestern University economist C. Kirabo Jackson, who tracked the performance of 500,000 students in North Carolina over seven years from ninth grade on, there emerged from the data set two categories of highly effective teachers. In the first category were the teachers who consistently raised student test scores. These are the teachers who win awards and receive high evaluations and sometimes bonuses.

But it is the second category of excellent teachers that fascinates me. I'll call this second group of teachers "nurturers," though you might also see

them as inspirers or motivators. These teachers don't raise standardized test scores. Rather, their achievements show up as better student attendance, fewer suspensions, higher on-time grade progression, and higher GPAs.

Lest you think that the nurturers are the easy teachers who artificially cheer on students and hand out inflated grades, consider this: The GPAs of students improved not simply while in a nurturer's class, but also in subsequent classes and in subsequent years as well.

Indeed, when Jackson added up four measures the nurturers excelled at — school attendance, on time grade progression, suspensions and discipline, and overall GPA — he found these measures to be, in Tough's words "a better predictor than a student's test scores of whether a student would attend college, a better predictor of adult wages and a better predictor of future arrests."

Of course, many inspiring, motivating, nurturing teachers (and the students they influenced) have long intuited that their good work produced results beyond what was seen on standardized test scores. Ironically, it has taken the arrival of big data to highlight the magnitude of what they accomplish. The term frequently used to describe what students develop working with these nurturing teachers is "non-cognitive skills." These are skills or traits such as persistence, ability to get along with others, ability to finish a task, ability to show up on time, and ability to manage and recover from failure.

Long before I heard of Jackson's study, I had become convinced that cultivating non-cognitive skills was one of the best steps I could take to help my students with their academic (cognitive) work and help them long-term in their lives. The first-year students I mostly teach, around ages 18 and 19, often don't know how to work through a bad day or a bad week or how to talk to a professor when they blow a deadline or miss an assignment. I have long noticed that if a student misses a class, there's a good chance they will miss another class. The student then feels guilty and too embarrassed to contact me. In short order, the student falls so far behind on assignments that catching up seems overwhelming and impossible. And so they skip class again.

The irony of course is that if a student simply comes to class and pulls me aside to explain what is going on in their life, I can help them prioritize what to catch up on and provide words of support. To minimize this problem — the missed class, leading to more missed classes, leading to failure — I now insist that students come to class even if they are unprepared, no penalty attached. But when you're not prepared, I tell my students, you must approach me before the start of class and tell me so.

Knowing at the start of class that a particular student hasn't completed a reading allows me to avoid embarrassing that student by calling on them to answer a question related to the assignment. Sometimes I can even take a few seconds to fill in background information so that the student can participate in the class discussion.

I insist that my students come to class when they are not prepared because they can still gain a lot from the class. They will feel connected to the course and to me, and they won't feel so paralyzed by guilt. They are also much more likely, in my experience, to catch up. Since I've started this policy, I would say my attendance has increased, but to be fair, I've improved in other ways as a teacher, so I can't chalk up the improved attendance solely to this no-guilt policy about being unprepared. There's been no decline in the number of students who come to class fully prepared. The requirement that they tell me in person when they are behind is apparently enough to discourage people from abusing that option.

I've made other changes that are designed to lure my students out of the binary, good/bad, perfectionist framework that a number of them seem to bring to college from high school. I used to yell at students who were sleeping in my class. These days if I see a student sleeping, I will calmly ask them to take a walk to get some fresh air or I might suggest they get some coffee. The first time I responded to a sleeping student by suggesting coffee and a walk, the student bolted upright. "No, I'm good," he said. He no doubt sensed a trap. Why would I suggest he get coffee unless it was part of some devious scheme? I told the student there was no penalty for stepping out for a few minutes, but he wouldn't move.

Finally, I pulled out my wallet, handed the student a few bills, and told him to get *me* a cup of coffee and to get one for himself if he wanted. It was only after I specified two creams and one sugar that the student relaxed and realized I was not plotting a scheme. Invariably, the times I've sent sleepy students out for a walk or for coffee, they have returned within minutes, awake, in a better mood, and able to participate in the class.

My goal in taking this less harsh approach to students is not to be nice. Being "nice" without clear boundaries and limits is a recipe for chaos and student dissatisfaction. My goal is to model for young people how to think maturely, precisely, and creatively about problems they face inside and outside of class. How can I expect them to engage in imaginative thinking on an assignment if I don't cultivate imaginative thinking on the practical problems they face in class? Yelling at sleeping students, as I did in the old days, didn't show students how to handle sleepiness. Yelling only made them

feel bad, and the result at best was a student who fought to keep their eyes open. Spending all your energy to keep your eyes open leaves little energy for listening, learning, and engaging in the class.

My student was seated by the time the story slam host called on the judges to give their ratings, which were much lower than I had hoped for. I asked her how she was doing and showed her my rating, which was the top possible rating with a bit of extra credit. She was proud of herself, she said, and felt great about speaking at a slam for the first time. She didn't care what the judges said. Her confident words didn't prevent me from checking in with her for the rest of the night and the next day as well.

I offered no critique of her performance and no tips on how she might possibly get higher ratings. I focused on her emotional well being because as long as she felt good about her performance and proud of taking the risk, she would come back and speak at another slam and perhaps another, and without the slightest bit of coaching from me, she would invariably get higher ratings. After the event, we found a grille and munched on some French fries. I'm betting it won't be long before I get a note from her about attending the next slam.

Contributors

Lloyd Ackert is a historian of science who specializes in Russian contributions to biology, ecology, microbiology, and soil science, He is currently an Associate Teaching Professor in the Department of History at Drexel University and directs the Emerging Scholars Program for undeclared majors in the College of Arts and Sciences. He has found a second home in the Pennoni Honors College as a lecturer, mentor, and interim-director of The Symposium. His interest in Russia takes him to College Fairs in St. Petersburg and Moscow each year for Enrollment Management. His current projects build on his work, Sergei Winogradsky and the Cycle of Life and include a broad history of the concept of the "cycle of life" and a scientific biography of the ecologist Ruth Patrick.

Stacey E. Ake is an Associate Teaching Professor in Philosophy at Drexel University in Philadelphia, PA. She has a Doctorate in Biology and a Master's and a Doctorate in Philosophy. She was the editor of Metanexus: The Online Forum for Science and Religion from 2001 to 2003. Her interest include semiotics, biosemiotics, evolution of consciousness, and existentialism.

Jesse Antonoff writes, draws, makes music, dances, anything to relax his often chaotic brain. He is studying English until the fall, and then he's done with school (possibly forever) and then probably off to the mountains or fulfilling his, according to his boss, Quaker destiny.

andré carrington, Ph.D., is Assistant Professor of English at Drexel University. He is the author of *Speculative Blackness: The Future in Science Fiction* (University of Minnesota Press, 2016). His writing on race, gender, and genre in Black and American literature and culture has also appeared in *Present Tense: A Journal of Rhetoric in Society*, *Lateral: Journal of Cultural Studies Association*, and numerous anthologies. He blogs at andrecarringtonphd.com.

Eunhye Grace Cho is a rising sophomore studying nursing at Drexel University. She enjoys playing tennis and going to the gym in her free time. Cho has enjoyed writing since middle school specifically through journaling about her life. She hopes to continue writing throughout college.

Dr. Ted Daeschler is a paleontologist at the Academy of Natural Sciences and an Associate Professor in the Department of Biodiversity, Earth and Environmental Sciences at Drexel. He has an active fossil research program working on Devonian-age fossil vertebrates from Pennsylvania, Arctic Canada, and most-recently Antarctica.

Pauline "Daisy" Good wrote "Feed Him Once a Day" as an assignment for her English 101 class with professor Robert Finegan. Every word of the story is true. Daisy is a biology major and a member of the Drexel Dance Ensemble. She has previously been honored in the Scholastic Art and Writing Awards and the Hershey Story Writing Contest.

Sharee DeVose is a junior honors student majoring in International Area Studies: Literature, Culture, and the Arts, minoring in Spanish, and pursuing a Certificate in Writing and Publishing. DeVose has written as a reporter for Voice of America international news, 5027mac.org, and Drexel University's College of Arts and Sciences. Besides writing, she enjoys singing, cooking, baking, her enormous family, and anything that respectfully pays homage to Jane Austen.

Sarah DrePaul is a freshman English and Global Studies (in Human Rights) major. She loves all mediums of storytelling, which she explores on and off stage in theatre and poetry cafés. She is also actively demystifying Slytherin's bad rep.

Timothy Fitts is the author of two short story collections, *Hypothermia* (MadHat Press 2017) and *Go Home and Cry for Yourselves* (Xavier University Press 2017). His novel, *The Soju Club*, is forthcoming with MadHat Press in 2018. Fitts teaches First-Year Writing at Drexel University and serves on the editorial staff of *Painted Bride Quarterly*.

Benjamin Folk is a Finance major in the LeBow College of Business. His passion for writing blossomed in his sophomore year of high school when he was cycled into a creative writing class by chance. He makes an effort to write daily whether on independent projects or on his blog, "Prosaic Illustrations from a Wayward Mind." He has also recently taken up the guitar.

Valerie Fox is the author of several books, including *The Rorschach Factory* (Straw Gate Books), *The Glass Book* (Texture Press), and *Poems for the Writing: Prompts for Poets, co-written with Lynn Levin* (Texture Press). *Insomniatic [poems]* is forthcoming from PS Books. Fox has published work in *Painted Bride Quarterly*, *Philadelphia Stories*, *Ping Pong*, *Hanging Loose*, *Apiary*, *Juked*, *Cordite Poetry Review*, *qarrtsiluni*, *Mockingheart Review*, *Sentence*, and other journals.

Tamyka George was born and raised on the twin islands of Trinidad and Tobago, and in her professional pursuit of accountancy decided to attend Drexel as she is also interested in traveling and becoming globally minded. She intends to travel to at least three countries during her studies.

Angelina Gomez is a first-year Biological Sciences major. Her hobbies include cooking, photography, collecting vintage clothing, reading, and writing. She has always enjoyed writing, and she wrote articles for school newspapers and various organizations during her high school years.

James P. Haes is a Communications major by day and aspiring author by night. He spends his free time exploring his creativity through the written word. Currently finishing his first novel, he has hopes of being published in the near future and plans on pursuing a career as a novelist and screenwriter. When he can find the time, he enjoys a good cup of coffee, rewatching episodes of Friends, and spending time with his family.

Hunter Heidenreich is an Electrical Engineering major with an interest in robotics and artificial intelligence. Originally from Charleston, South Carolina, he prefers Philadelphia and living in the city, although he continues to think about how he can improve things back home.

Heather Heim is an English major and French minor at Drexel University. She loves baseball and traveling. She works as a peer reader at the Drexel Writing Center.

Stephanie Heim is pursuing a BS in Environmental Science and is passionate about environmental education. She has completed internships at the Philadelphia Zoo and Silver Lake Nature Center, where she taught visitors about native and exotic plants and animals, environmental issues, and conservation. She likes to inspire people of all ages to learn more about the environment and what steps they can take to help with conservation efforts.

Henry Israeli is the author of the poetry collections *god's breath hovering across the waters* (Four Way Books: 2016), *Praying to the Black Cat* (Del Sol: 2010), and *New Messiahs* (Four Way Books: 2002). He is also the translator of three books by Albanian poet Luljeta Lleshanaku.

Joshua Jager is Animation and Visual Effects major and hopes to eventually work in the film industry. He has always loved drawing, and although writing was an acquired taste, he thinks he's getting the hang of it. His previous writing experience includes many, many assigned essays as well as the occasional clever note in a birthday card.

Shelby Jain is a Biology major in the BS/MS program at Drexel. She is from Freehold, New Jersey. Her hobbies include playing the guitar, singing, reading, and wandering the city. She has not had much writing experience other than assignments for classes and the occasional journaling. Aside from that, she hopes to pursue a career in medicine.

Neida Mbuia Joao is a freshman English major. She loves reading, writing, and gardening. In the 9th grade, she was voted "most likely to write a best-selling novel" and hopes to soon fulfill that dream.

Sarah Julius is BS/MS student in Biomedical Engineering, with a certificate in Medical Humanities. She has been writing since she was young, enjoys reading, and love movies. She has been previously published in scientific journals, but this is her first time being published in the humanities.

Miriam Kotzin writes fiction and poetry. *Debris Field* is her most recent collection of poetry, and *Country Music* is her most recent collection of short fiction. She is also author of a novel, *The Real Deal*. She is a Professor of English in the Department of English and Philosophy, where she teaches literature and creative writing. She is a contributing editor of *Boulevard* and founding editor of *Per Contra*.

Yih-Chia Lam is a sophomore studying Criminology and Neuroscience. This is her second year participating in the DPG Essay Contest; her first entry was on the ethical implications regarding CRISPR-Cas9 gene-editing biotechnology/ She likes to read Wikipedia articles when she knows she should be sleeping instead.

Davina Lee is a giant ground pangolin who believes in the power of friendship. Hold on, let's try that again. Davina Lee is a poet who also happens to be a third-year Biomedical Engineering student. She loves rocky beaches, Louise Gluck, reading the Old Testament, and vacuuming her apartment.

Lynn Levin, a poet, writer, and translator, is Adjunct Professor of English at Drexel. She is the recipient of thirteen Pushcart Prize nominations for poetry. Her most recent book is *Birds on the Kiswar Tree* (2Leaf Press, 2014), a translation from the Spanish of a collection of poems by the Peruvian Andean poet Odi Gonzales. Her poetry collection *Miss Plastique* (Ragged Sky Press) was named a finalist in poetry in the 2014 Next Generation Indie Book Awards, and *Poems for the Writing: Prompts for Poets* (Texture Press), the craft-of-poetry textbook she co-authored Valerie Fox, was a finalist in education/academic books in the 2014 Next Generation Indie Book Awards. Lynn Levin's poems, stories, essays, and translations have appeared in *Ploughshares, Boulevard, The Hopkins Review, Michigan Quarterly Review, Green Hills Literary Lantern, Per Contra, Painted Bride Quarterly, Verse Daily,* and Garrison Keillor has read her work on his radio show The Writer's Almanac. Her website is www.lynnlevinpoet.com.

Chandni Lotwala is a Chemistry major with a minor in Biology. She will be matriculating at Drexel University College of Medicine as a member of the class of 2021. In her free time, she enjoys cooking and reading.

Richard McCourt's research is on the biodiversity, evolution, ecology, and systematics of green algae, specifically a group known as charophyte algae. These green algae are among the closest living algal relatives of land plants and include some well-known algae such as stoneworts and Spirogyra. McCourt has also conducted research on the ecology of intertidal algae in the Gulf of California, Sonora, Mexico. He has also published on the Lewis and Clark plant collection at the Academy, and he worked as a freelance science reporter for National Public Radio.

Caitlin McLaughlin is a pre-junior in the BA/MA dual degree program in English and Publishing. This is her second publication in *The 33rd*. Her writing interests include mental health advocacy, LGBT issues, and feminism.

Kate Medrano is a Biomedical Engineering major on a pre-medicine track. She lives in Danbury, Connecticut, but was born in Australia and has lived all over the world. In her life, Medrano has had to overcome countless personal trials, but she is a better person for it today. These days, she prides herself on her academic success and strives for a bright future.

Michaela Michener recently graduated from Drexel University with a degree in photography. She enjoys photographing people and capturing the relationships between them. She is from New Jersey but is currently based in Philadelphia.

Sean O'Donnell is a Professor of BEES and Biology at Drexel. He is a tropical biologist, visiting Central and South America annually for field research and teaching since 1987. He is currently researching thermal physiology and climate, brain development and evolution in social insects, and interactions in bird mixed-species flocks. O'Donnell has appeared in three TV documentaries about army ants.

Hannah Pepper is a Chemistry major pursuing a career in the medical or research field. In her free time, she loves to bake and hike.

Cindy Phan is a multi-media communications professional living and working in Philadelphia. She loves food and plants. If anyone asks, she is trying her best.

Kimtee Dahari Ramsagur is a Biomedical Engineering major, and she is currently a freshman. She is passionate about dancing and has been performing for a national dance group in Mauritius Island, her home country. Social work has been an important aspect of her life, and she has been advocating for animal rights, teaching underprivileged kids around her island, participating in mangroves and endemic plants, and leading a beekeeping project.

Don Riggs discovered *The Hobbit* when he was in the 4th grade and has been reading the novel and teaching it repeatedly. He was very excited to see the videoblog leading up to the film's production, but was less enthusiastic about the film itself.

David Seltzer is an adjunct professor of Philosophy at Drexel University. His main research interest is in existentialism, particularly Kierkegaard, Sartre, Beauvoir, and Levinas. He has published articles in *International Studies in Philosophy* and *Philosophy Today*, and guest-edited an issue of *Listening: Journal of Communication Ethics, Religion, and Culture*.

Fred Siegel teaches in the English and Philosophy Department at Drexel University. His writings have appeared in *The Drama Review*, *Journal of Modern Literature*, Kugelmass, *When Falls the Coliseum*, and *Painted Bride Quarterly*. He also performs magic shows in a variety of venues, and plays the role of "Fred" in the autobiographical performance, *Man of Mystery*. He has lied for money in the Coney Island Sideshow (1989-90), and has been logging his dreams since 1993. He also does improvised performances with Comedysportz Philadelphia and Tongue & Groove.

Samantha Stein is a freshman transitioning into the Custom-Designed major with an emphasis on interdisciplinary solutions to medical inequality. Stein enjoys researching (she is currently conducting a project on the value of the medical narrative within evidence-based medicine), spending time with her three lizards and boyfriend, and writing on taboo topics. She strives to promote universal eudaimonia.

Zachary Stott is an English major. His previous writing experience includes all manner of writing-intensive courses at Drexel. This is the first essay he has submitted to a writing contest.

Kathleen Volk Miller is an essayist, a professor, and Director of the Graduate Program in Publishing at Drexel University. She has written for *O, the Oprah magazine*, *Salon*, *The New York Times*, *Family Circle*, *Philadelphia Magazine* and other venues. "How We Want to Live," an essay, was chosen as the penultimate piece in *Oprah's Book of Starting Over* (Flat Iron Books, Hearst Publications, 2016). She is co-editor of the anthology, *Humor: A Reader for Writers* (Oxford University Press, 2014). She is co-editor of *Painted Bride Quarterly* and co-host of PBQ's podcast, Slush Pile. She has also published in literary magazines, such as *Drunken Boat*, *Opium*, and other venues. She consults on literary magazine start up, working with college students, and getting published in literary magazines.

Scott Warnock is an associate professor of English at Drexel and Director of the University Writing Program. He writes the bi-weekly blog/column "Virtual Children" for the website *When Falls the Coliseum.*

Robert A. Watts is a former newspaper reporter, who wrote about education and race for *The Atlanta Journal-Constitution* and the Atlanta bureau of *The Associated Press.* He has taught writing at Drexel since 1997. In recent years, he has taken an increasing interest in the role of motivation and resilience in determining student success.

Nicholas Yurcaba is a Drexel student who dislikes writing biographies.

Julian Zemach-Lawler is a General Business major at Drexel. In his free time, he enjoys listening to music, going to the gym, and exploring Philly with his camera to take photographs. Writing has always been one of his hidden passions, and often he feels that he expresses himself best on paper, where he can deliver his experiences in life in the most impactful way.

Want to appear in the 2018 edition of *The 33rd?*

Drexel Publishing Group
Creative Writing
CONTEST
Open **Fall Term** for

- Poetry
- Fiction
- Creative Non-Fiction
- Opinion/Editorial
- Humor

Drexel Publishing Group
Essay
CONTEST
Open **Winter & Spring Term** for

- Social Sciences
- Humanities
- STEM
- Graduate Student Essays

ALL Drexel Students are eligible
See *5027mac.org* for more information.

The 33rd